Here's Where It *Ends*

MONICA JONES

authorHOUSE®

AuthorHouse™
1663 Liberty Drive
Bloomington, IN 47403
www.authorhouse.com
Phone: 1 (800) 839-8640

Published by AuthorHouse 08/31/2016

ISBN: 978-1-5246-0517-9 (sc)
ISBN: 978-1-5246-0516-2 (e)

Library of Congress Control Number: 2016906709

Print information available on the last page.

CONTENTS

A TYPICAL INDEPENDENT WOMAN

Just getting in from a long day of work, I checked the caller ID to see who called and like almost always, it was sure *`No damn body worth calling back.'* First of all I am frustrated as hell, and trying to figure out a plan to leave Miami. I am just so tired of this same old bullshit, and my home girls, let me tell you about them. By the way my name is Mona, but everybody calls me Chocolate. The one who analyzes all the problems, who doesn't goes for any old thing and a single parent to a beautiful daughter named Shanice. I am mainly straightforward and don't mind voicing my opinion to my girls which is why our friendship is so genuine and boss. Over the years, we grew as adults, and our parents grew closer as well. Jasi mom, whom name was Ms. Pumpkin which was the only one missing from the grownups talk every afternoon and that was because she was deceased. I could remember her when we were juniors in High school; Ms. Pumpkin was a hard workingwoman who bought Jasi anything that her two jobs could have afford. Ms. Pumpkin was rapped and brutally killed one afternoon; we found her by the door as we returned from school. Jasi went through counseling, and all but was never able to overcome the horror she endured. Although my mom and Ms. Cure whom had no kids were neighbors they accompanied one another on their porch every afternoon. Ms. Minnie would come every afternoon also, bringing her daughter Becky along while staying the longest out of the three ladies daily. I loved that so much because it gave Becky & I more play time. I must tell you I use to get so upset every time they had to leave, until I became old enough to know that Ms. Minnie had a life of her own also. Ms. Minnie calls her daughter Boosie for short; now that's my girl. Becky is single, pretty with big hips, big tits, and a tap of ass with a sassy mouth. She also has three beautiful kids Lil Corey who is now 6, we call him Poppy because of his complexion. Then there's Julian he's the baby boy who looks just like his no good ass daddy Corey. Last but not least brilliant Brianna who's personality and attitude introduces her everywhere she goes. All Becky kids were from the same stupid ass, money-getting nigga named Corey who they call Black for his street name. Which is "SOMETIMES" her man and doesn't do shit for the kids! Maybe a happy meal here or there and a shit load of problems with his side chicks. Hear me out when I tell you this, he act like he has all the money in the world and aint got a dime to his name! Always depended on women, and his ass would make you believe he could build the biggest mountain out of a molehill, just by his fast talk and thuggish expressions he presents. Especially When we come up in the neighborhood where it was known to be popping, without a doubt he was always there standing on the corner. Just as soon as he spotted Becky Lexus jeep he would run his wanna be caring, oh so loving ass over and post up in the window. I mean really as if he read today's paper, while they all sat around eating breakfast at the same table. I just get so mad sometimes, and just stare at him. The worst part about this shit Christmas and a Birthday just left, and he didn't even make a phone call, give a toy truck nor doll. Must I tell you he only rolls and dresses to whatever is in style at that time in moment! He's rolling on 22-inch rims, with TV's imbedded on his headrest of his black Chevy Convertible. The interior was beautiful black leather, with a stitching of charcoal grey thread in the middle of the seat which read "1978". He also wears a platinum chain, a kick ass pinky diamond ring, and you best to believe its all carbon free. Don't get Becky wrong, she got taste but just for the wrong accommodations. Well let me answer this ringing phone; trust me you will have a time with these here sisters.

"Hello."

"Hey Chocolate, what you doing?" Becky asked.

"Nothing just got home from work." I responded.

"Where Shanice?"

"She went to see Lionel today; she should be over Pricilla house by now."

"Oh, well come ride with me?"

"Where!"

"I don't know, lets ride somewhere with the kids."

"I don't really feel like it, but if you take me by Pricilla house later to get my car & Shanice I'll ride with you." I added.

"Come on man, damn I aint gone be gone long." Becky said.

"I said alright but you have to take me to pick up Shanice from Pricilla house later! I yelled into the phone.

"Yeah!" Becky yelled back and we both started to laugh.

"Well let me get out of these work clothes." I said going through my closet.

"Hurry up, because I'm in your parking lot already!" Becky said, like always rushing, and on the go.

I hurried and got dressed. Nothing spectacular, because where we might be going aint shit around there. The younger generation behind us, are now dealing with the boys on the block that we use to think was the shit once upon a time. As the years went by, it's a known fact that they weren't shit from day one.

I slid into a little dress, pulled my plats unto a ponytail, and hurried downstairs.

"Hey Poppy." I said, as he got out of the front to sit in the back for me.

"Please don't call him Poppy, he claims that's a baby name." Becky said as Julian started laughing.

"I'm sorry Lil Corey."

"I guess he going through that stage but I still be calling him Poppy sometimes, and so do my mama. You know how it is, when you hate them nick names, because I sure as hell hate my shit."

"Chocolate, where is Shanice?" Brianna asked from the back seat.

"We gonna pick her up a little later." I said, as Brianna sat back and finished watching the installed TV behind the driver seat.

"Ma, I'm hungry." Julian announced.

"Boy you better wait! As a matter of fact let me see if yall Daddy out here." Becky responded as she veered off into our old neighborhood. Everything was just how I saw it twenty odd years ago, just younger boys and more houchies on the street all time of day and night. The only thing was missing was the real money getting boys who would be having big parties on the street corners, barbecues, and car washes. There would also be Convertible candy painted Chevy's sitting everywhere if not racing up and down the street, with the music banging so hard that the windows in your house shuck. Their white walls around their 22 inch tires were white as white... while the black of the tire shinned out with armor. Those were the days that were truly missed. Hell what can I say? Their only missing cause the Feds done snatched half of them up off the street and dam near forgot about them in prison. And the street DJ's there aint even no more on any corner, and if it were you better believe the police made sure they came with about six or seven cars ready to haul the first bad motherfucker to jail. Then if that don't happen you can almost predict that before the party would be over there was going to be some young buck who was ready to fire his artillery, or take whatever he needed from anyone he could. O my gosh and the summer on my block which was down the street from the community park that was known for the best splash downs ever, but hell just about all of the crowd either in prison, dead, or scared of a stray bullet. I tell you these girls don't know what fun really was living in HUD neighborhoods because it was more besides the ghetto it was a Prestigious Street University.

The kids began to scream `Daddy' as Corey approached the car; Becky turns her ass facing the rear of the truck smiling from ear to ear, as if he asked her hand in marriage.

"Why you didn't call my baby for her birthday, and what happened to Christmas?" Becky asked Corey, as I turned my head wondering why the hell she put up with this looser. She could have had more things to ask him about why and what happened, but of course like an average man he put on that serious face and let out a strong voice.

"Man, you know I was out of town!" Corey said.

"Child please, whatever!" Becky replied, as she turned back around in her seat, while I'm on the passenger side, just burning up with disbelief. He was out of town!

"Now aint that's some bullshit!" I mistakenly thought out loud to myself, but quickly silencing my thoughts as I continued ranting in my head. Then he had the dam nerve to throw twenty dollars in the car. I was hoping her intentions were to throw it back.

"Man, just go ahead and get my kids something to eat." Corey said and begins to walk away.

"I'll call you later." She replied, as if she was leaving on a good note.

"Bet that up, about 1:00am." He instructed, as she pulled off yapping like always.

"His black ass tripping, he thinks we should be back together."

"Uhh-ahh." I mumbled sarcastically and loud.

"Child please, I don't won't Corey ass even if he was dipped in gold."

"Becky who the hell, you think you talking to? We both know anything Corey says goes." I said as she pulled into the nearby McDonalds, and the kids leaped from the truck.

"Julian yall stop running!" Becky said, as she and I got out of the truck.

"Chocolate I am dead ass serious! Just like I was through with Andy, I'm through with Corey. Becky said, as she stepped up to place her order.

"Whatever, could you order me a caramel sundae with nuts, a small fry, and we will talk about how much you love Corey when you get through ordering." I said with a look that said fuck Corey because you been leaving him since Julian was a month old and now he's 11

"Lil Corey don't jump on my baby!" Becky yelled, as she came outside with a tray full of food.

"Chocolate girl, I'm serious I'm not studying Corey. He has the nerve to want me to come around there when Shawn goes to work." Becky continued, as she barely sat down and started to sort the food.

"How in the hell you have anything to say to him, after all he did miss Christmas without a toy nor did he call your baby on her birthday. He doesn't give you anything for the kids' not even time. What part of father does he play? You really need to ask yourself that girl."

"Fuck you Chocolate! It aint like your baby daddy at every PTA meeting, play Santa every year, blows balloons and boils hotdogs at every damn party either! Now let's face reality here. Let me rephrase that, the reality we live in "Heather". Becky said, which was a name she would only call me when she thought I was acting like a finicky white chick.

"No I am serious Becky."

"Whatever Chocolate, see I can't talk to you on some issues cause you want to tell me advise that we aint even introduced to... better yet shit you seen on lifetime that you know dam well aint gone happen in our cases! Shit I still rather have a piece of man than having none at all." As Becky continued, Brianna came running and crying, apparently Corey had kicked her in the nose. Becky jumped up from the conversation with the same tone.

"Let's go! We are going to mama house right fucking now! I can't take yall nowhere without acting out!" I gathered their food up and we all got in the truck without Becky giving them a second chance.

Riding in silence, the kids had fallen asleep. Becky was quiet and paying extra attention to the road as if she was mad at the facts of my advice. What can I say, if you don't want an honest opinion keep it to yourself. That's the way I've always felt.

"Chocolate lets go and get Jasi. Maybe have a few long islands at wet willies."

"Girl I have to take a bath along with a short nap, this sun has really drained me today, and I'm fixin to pick up Shanice." I said avoiding the ride.

"Where you say she was again?" Becky asked.

"They flew Tuesday to see Lionel in P.A."

"Why didn't you go?' She asked with a big smirk.

"Funny Huh?" I said because she knew that wasn't possible; Lionel is my daughters, father. He went to prison on some type of shit, he never told me why. However word on the street, was counterfeit machines and a shit load of money. He did his father part while he lasted on the street. Even before he left, we really didn't get along. We talked when we had to, but otherwise the hell with him. I could remember, when I was pregnant all I wanted was him there and we raising our child together, meaning the same home I was raised in but as you see that aint even happen for the first two years.

Becky dropped me to Pricilla house, which was Shanice godmother.

"Chocolate call me, and let me know what you are going to do later." Becky said.

"I will, after I get Shanice and get settled. I'll call." I said, as Becky drove off, and Shanice came running out.

"How'd you get here lil missy?" I asked Shanice as she came outside on the walkway.

"Grandma took me to here." She responded, in her kiddy voice.

She was dressed in all red looking cute, had the red bows and ribbon going on in her thick black hair. Not like me or any young girl would've dressed her, but the look sure gave her that split image of Lionel.

"Mama I seen my Daddy, he say he gone sleep to my house with me." Shanice said smiling and giving me a hug.

"Oh did he really." I responded, and not tackling what sounded like a dream. Cause Lord knows, over my dam dead body if he would sleep under my roof. I never did show my dislike of him, if anything Shanice will always know I love her father and her father loves me for eternity.

"Where's Pricilla Shanice?"

"She's changing the baby pamper." Shanice replied. She was only five years old and had since like a fifty year old women.

"I'm back here!" Pricilla shouted from the back room. Shanice came behind as I left her at the front door.

"Mama can I stay?" Shanice asked.

"No, Shanice grandmamma want to see you."

"I already see her."

"No Shanice." I said, as she turned and started to play with the baby.

Oh Mona, Robert bought your car back. He said he finished it and that you didn't need a new radiator cap.

"So will it not run hot again?"

"I guess. He said he was finish and gave me your keys." Pricilla added.

"I hope so, that dam car get on my nerves."

"It aint nothing worse than car problems besides moving."

"Tell me about it." I replied.

"Where are you going?" Pricilla asked.

"I'm going over my mom house. How about you later?"

"I don't know, I suppose to be going to my friend girl Regina engagement party." Pricilla said.

"Oh I thought maybe you might would want to join us at wet willies."

"Nah, there's a variety of drinks at this party and they are free baby." Pricilla said laughing.

"Ok then don't say I never invite you out with the girls."

"Maybe next time."

"When did they bring Shanice?' I asked.

"Ms. Crawford bought her about twenty minutes ago."

"Alright then let me get over here by mama house." I said walking to the front door.

"Ok then Chocolate call me tomorrow." Pricilla said as she walked us to the car.

"Come on lets go.' I said as, Shanice ran in front of me and to the car.

"Bye Pricilla!' Shanice shouted as we proceeded on.

"Shanice did you have fun?" I asked.

"Yes, my daddy bought me some M&Ms and me and auntie ride that big slide." Shanice said, with a great big smile, she had a heart for that family that was real. She loved those people to death, after all that is her family.

Before we could unsnap the seat belts, Shanice jumped out like she hasn't seen my mama in ages. My sister Peggy and my mother were out on the porch talking, while you could hear kid voices trailing from around the backyard where Shanice was headed.

"Come Shanice and give granny a hug." Shanice turned around, braced herself against mama and took off again.

"Chocolate who did your hair?" Peggy asked. I wore these real skinny pin plats all over my hair half way to my back.

"This girl named Anita from pine crest."

"I don't want to know how much she charged, but she did a great job." Peggy said.

"Them children love that trampoline, I keep a yard full of children." Mama mentioned as the yelling grew louder.

"I see." Peggy added

Chocolate where have you been? Mama questioned.

"I went to work, and then when I came home I rode with Becky and the kids to McDonalds."

"Becky had the kids today?" Mama asked, which was shocking to everybody because they knew Becky never had to worry with those kids.

"Yeah Ms. Minnie needed to do a little shopping, so she told Becky to mind them." I said, as my cell phone began to ring.

"Hello" I answered.

"What's up baby?" The husky voice asked.

"Nothing chilling." I responded.

"What you doing?'

"Over my mama house talking."

"Well call me when you are finish."

"Ok." I responded to my boo Chuck, whom I often called MY nookie caresser. I sat for another second, but couldn't resist another moment as I wanted to sex Chuck like right now.

"Mama I got to go home for a minute, I will be right back." I said, quickly thinking about that massive good tongue of chucks.

"You know that girl is not going to want to go home, and there's no one there to play with her."

"Well what you want me to do Mama, come back and get her?" I asked hoping she would say yeah, because I sure had a little steam to blow off.

"You're her mama." She said, rocking back and forth in the rocking chair.

"And you are mines so, do you want me to take her or not?" I questioned in a joking way because if not, by now I might be swallowing a couple of my teeth.

"Mona care your loafing ass on down the road." She said as Peggy started to laugh and so did I.

"Shanice!" I called.

"Go ahead on and leave the girl." Mama insisted on just what I was looking for her to say. So I picked up my pace and made it to the car.

Riding home who do I see? Mr. Chuck, I glanced at my rear view mirror, watched him made a U-turn at the light and started after me. So I pulled over.

"I told you to call me. Where are you going?" He asked as if we were really on that level.

"Home." I answered.

"Can I come along?'

"No Chuck I have to clean up and bathe." I said trying to play hard, cause it turned me on to hear him beg for me.

"Well damn cook me something to eat!" He said, as I took this queue to beg for money.

"I don't have nothing in my fridge to cook!" I said in such a sassy tone, as he reached in his pocket and handed me 150 dollars.

"Go buy some groceries and put down in the kitchen I'll be there about 8:00. Then we maybe can do a movie?" He said as I thought of how, he might be able to have made my day, if he didn't come with that MAYBE shit, as if I'm not worthy of it or he has to think hard if I deserved it.

"Just call me. I'm not sure about a movie, I have something to do later." I said, trying to sound busy. Knowing god dam well, I wasn't going to be doing nothing but sleeping.

"Alright." He said, pulling off in his GS400.

That was his way of making up when I would tell him I'm tired of all his bullshit. His lady, lies, games, and not to mention his specialty `beat me mad' when he is the one dead ass wrong. I wonder did he do something, and one of my girls saw him, cause this 150 was not like chuck. Especially when we could have went to some restaurant and he pay forty or fifty dollars without leaving a tip now that was more like him. Hell I don't get this much if I needed a pair pants and a shirt. So I assume he wants to make me feel good before the news make it back. I guess I'll call my girl Jasi the party animal. Oh, I'm sorry I forgot to finish telling yall about my two girls that makes this clique so real. Jasi is the luminary of the group the one with a home in Weston, Gucci and Prada bags, VS clarity Diamond on her finger just for promises, credit cards feeling up each slot in the wallet, and not to leave out the car which is known only by numbers. That's right a 745LI BMW and she is only 22 years old. On top of that she has her own money as well. Her mom house was willed to her and two insurance policies that became hers when she turned 18 which she haven't even touched. Her college tuition at Florida State University was fully paid through her Dads lawsuit. He was an exterminator and was poisoned through the cheap mask the company provided. The lawsuit was over a half million dollars. Jasi is unlike Becky with the material things; she has it all but never let it get to her. Then came along Bruce, now that's how she caught a meal ticket and she deserves it too. Bruce is a 42-year-old married man but yet an entrepreneur with mega bucks, who was a very heavy gambler, which didn't mine loosing 20 or 30 thousand a night. It would be times he would invite Becky and I to come along on some of their gambling dates. Just to make us comfortable he would give us five hundred in cash to play the slots. Jasi would get at least a grand just to cash in his chips, while she was working as a bar tender on the casino boat where she met him. From my understanding, Jasi put that snapper on him, and that's what added the icing to the cake. Then he asked her to quit, so she did. One thing about Jasi she never settled for less, although she had somebody else's man, he respected her and she respected him and neither paid the unconcerned marriage any attention.

She has a brain that's designed for success, and knows what she wants out of life. Now let me get back to the story.

Walking into the grocery store talking to Jasi on the cell. She said she had a nice time in the club and that she will fill me in. According to the hesitations and boring tones in her voice, I instantly knew Bruce was home so she couldn't go into detail. So I decided to quickly end the conversation, and agreed to meet up with them later.

I finally made it home around 6:00pm, to only begin putting up the groceries, when the phone loudly rings. Glancing at the caller ID by the sink it read Minnie Pearl Jackson that was Becky phone registering in her mom name.

"What's up Becky?"

"You tell me, is it still on for the beach?" She asked with a bit of attitude, as if I said *no* already.

"Yeah I just talked to Jasi, Bruce was home so she said she would call us a little later."

"She makes me damn sick! Bruce always got his old ass there, tryna hold shit down! God dam give the girl a fuckin break." Becky said, sounding so bossy.

"Oh Becky now nobody tell you what they think of Corey black ass, and besides you know that's her bread and butter." I quickly said, before Becky cut me off.

"Child please Becky got her own dam money! Anyway what time are we going?"

"I think around 11:00 or midnight, that's when shit normally get started right? Wait let me call you back this chuck on the other end." I said, and clicked over.

"Hello."

"What's up?" Chuck asked.

"Nothing boo, just here putting on dinner." I said trying to sound as if we are happy as one.

"Yeah what are you cooking?" Chuck asked.

"Cabbage, rice, steak and cornbread." I replied.

"Are you almost finished?" He asked

"No! You told me at 8:00. It's only 6 something with your impatient ass!"

"Whatever, impatient for you baby. But I am on my way." Chuck said.

"Bye!" I replied as I started preparing myself for a smell good session, because I knew for sure I was about to be licked like a lollipop.

After taking a shower, I sprayed a bit of Vera Wang perfume and greased my body with baby oil. I put my favorite Tupac CD on #9 unconditional love, while I searched for something to throw on just when the phone began to ring again and again. The caller Id registering `the security desk'

"Hello." I answered.

"Hello Mona, you have a guest by the name of Chuck. Is it OK for me to let him up?' The heavy accented Spanish guard questioned.

"Yes thank you." I replied.

"No problem you welcome." He said as I threw the cordless to the bed, slipped on my big Snoopy shorts, no panties, a T-shirt, no bra, and pulled my exotic braids to the back into a ponytail. I washed the apricot facial scrub from my face, brushed my teeth, and traced my eyebrows with water just when Chucks knock came over the door.

"I'm coming!" I yelled in a sexy tone as I walked over fidgeting with my shorts as I opened the door.

"Hey you!" I greeted him as I walked away in a hurry towards the kitchen.

"Dam all that ass!" He replied just when he somehow manages to slap me on my butt.

Chuck is a nice cool 6ft 4, dark skinned guy. Who knows his skills in bed. He's a very hardworking man, who works construction at night and drive county trucks through the day. He has no kids, but a dingy ass girlfriend who I don't care two fucks about, and a string of groupies that love to be silly for him. Now what actually destroys this picture? He's a very cheap nigga, who wants ALL for a little of nothing! We have been seeing each other for the past 3 years. I could consider him mines but there are things I don't vouch for in a man. #1 a cheap man which is Chuck #2 A Lazy man and #3 A man with no rhythm in bed.

I left chuck in the kitchen and walked back into my bedroom to remove the CD which had started skipping. I replaced it with Teddy P, what a combination I thought, as I came back walking down the hall. Chuck was sitting patiently on the couch, so I plopped next to him. He grabbed me up in his arms, the way I always loved him to without a prompt.

"Why are you always talking shit Mona? You're never satisfied. What's up with that?" He asked, rattling three questions under one sentence, without giving me a chance to answer one.

"Go ahead on Chuck, need not me to get into that." I quickly replied as he played around my face, I got a little technical.

"Chuck will you please stop playing, I don't know where your hands been. Suddenly his lips sacked against mines. I couldn't do anything but smile.

"Boy you got a problem." I said, trying to get up from the chair, as he pulled my shirt and I fell on top of him. Without rejection I positioned myself as sexy as one could be. I wanted him and I wanted him bad, I really needed those lips of his against these furry ones of mines below.

Chuck started squeezing up my ass and rubbing down my back with his strong hands. It felt so right, I was waiting for every touch as they came one after another. A quiet moment came along, and our eyes met each other and in that instant I cupped his face in my hands and we began to kiss. Our eyes were closed and heads were slowly turning in motion. He then put his hands up my thighs, and of course I spread them even further, without any cause of interruptions. I began to suck on his neck, immediately followed by licking and blowing in his ears as he rested his head back on the couch. His moaning and grunting sounds were turning me on as his muscular voice raised and fell to such seductive tunes.

By the time I reached for the soft flesh; it had formed into a hard heavy stick, just the way I needed it. He gently and quickly switched the position by laying me on the couch. Without hesitation he carefully pulled my loose shorts to the side, where he found nothing but a bare hairless pussy. Oh my god what a cool feeling I thought to myself. He stroked his tongue up and down as if it was a piece of candy, but of course that was what he classified it as from day one. The flowing juices began straining from my body as his tongue wiggled side to side and finger positioned in and out simultaneously. Instantly my legs flew to the air as he continued to smack and suck on me. It felt so dam good inside until my emotions completely took over me and the hormones no longer could hide. I was indeed horney as hell... Before I could say slow down I was coming out of my shorts as if they had gasoline on them and someone was going to throw a match. He handled my large body by positioning me in the corner of my love seat. By that time the beat of the music was just right, and I was left with no choice but to throw it back. He was livelier than I was, and just as ready as I was also. Chuck didn't stop while he was playing in me, he didn't slow down while he was grinding in me, or utter a word while two fingers was deep in me, he just did his work and I let the trembling take control.

"Oh Chuck. Chuck. Chuck please! OH OH Chuck. Chuckie oh Chuckie stop baby oh stop it baby!" I said screaming, squinting and so turned on by the love sounds we were making. He reached to the floor and grabbed protection, without fondling with the wrapper. Less than two seconds Chuck slid the head of his penis in the rubber and massaged it down as if he was practicing a fire drill climbing down a rope. I laid there undisturbed, as I needed him to take no pity and give me what he came here for. When he turned me around, I put one knee in the couch and one of my feet on the ground for balance. He slid his tongue across my pussy for one last time, I smiled as my clitoris began to throb more and more. He did it again, and this time I arched my back as deep as I could get it for more. With so much affection he opened my two bald lips and slid his dick in like a perfect pair of fitted gloves. He slid it back out, and without force it was wet enough to do a number one job, but instead he went back to licking it. Believe me this hot pussy of mines was throbbing loud enough for him to hear it if he'd just listen.

"Auhhh." I moaned, as he came up and kissed me down my neck and around my breast. He hitched one leg up and slowly slid his dick back into me.

"Dam baby this pussy tight." He whispered as he continued to dace in me.

"You so good." I added.

"Who pussy this is huh!" Chuck asked finding a corner where he humped up, down, in, out, and side to side.

"Yours baby yours!" I said as my voice escalated.

"Kiss me baby kiss me?" He said, as he gripped my shoulders and I was for sure throwing this pussy to him. He held on my hips with one hand which he guided them perfect, as I shifted my body with my back in motion.

"Oh you so mannish....Oh Chocolate this pussy better than good." He said breathing in long segments, while moving extremely fast. The more he panted for breath, I continued to throw this pussy harder than I thought he could handle.

He suddenly stretched over my back loosening up his grip on my shoulders, and fell to my side. Moments later he was out and breathing like he had just ran a relay.

"God damn baby, this pussy gets better every time I get it!" Chuck added while trying to catch his breath as if he lasted for thirty minutes when it was a well four-minute fuck.

"That pussy was wet like you poured something in it." He said as I rubbed his breast and he just about jumped out the chair.

"What's wrong?" I asked. "Nothing baby, that just was a crucial nut I had and every touch tickle right now." He replied. Without another word Chuck laid between my legs as we listened to Al Green voice echoing thru my apartment, whilst the air conditioning was cooling our wet sweaty bodies off. A few minutes later before the next song started Chuck added to the noise by snoring away. I squeezed from under him, and he didn't attempt to wake up.

My Knees is shaking and my nookie (*pussy*) felt as if it was torn or fell off a bike from those rough four minutes. I walked in the kitchen to turn off the stove, and I immediately returned to lay on the sofa adjacent from him. The phone began ringing away about 10:00 I knew it was nobody but Becky. I ignored the phone and finally fell asleep too.

By the time I awake the clock-registered 2:45am and Chuck was still asleep. I got up to use the bathroom, being I got up on a growling stomach; I went in the kitchen to get a bite also. Fixing my food pots were clashing and utensils was rattling. After what Chuck gave me tonight, riding and clubbing was sure far from my mind.

"Baby did you fix mine." Chuck asked startling me as I left him sleep. However he was standing right before me naked rubbing his fat dick, and leaving it standing as if it wanted more. I acted as if I didn't see by quickly pulling out another blue dish to prepare his food as well. We both sat at the table as if we were a married couple without a single child insight.

"WHAT A FRIEND IS REALY FOR?"

Jasi and I were walking through the mall, and of course having our girl talk. Although we speak about one another to each other, it's never nothing too serious we can't talk it over, and it's never a hush hush thing that most stupid ass girls do.

"Jasi how does this shirt fit?" I asked buttoning the shirt up to me.

"It fits you nice, but I don't like it." She replied frowning her face as if she wanted to smell her top lip.

"When I put a tight pair of jeans and belt it will look better." I explained trying to convince her about the eccentric shapes and sleeves that detailed the shirt.

"You and Becky with that hippie ass look. I'll just continue to stay classy." She said smiling at a little skirt that hung outside the dressing room door.

"Oh Chocolate girl, Becky called me all night! I didn't even answer my phone because Bruce was still there, and I told her earlier that I would call her when he leave. I know she's mad with me, but shit she knows how the routine goes. Just as long as my man is there I am as well. Becky wants to ride or club every night. I'm not able to roll like that; there is school in the mornings and Bruce sometimes throughout the night. Becky needs to have a seat, deal with those kids, and give the street a rest." As Jasi complained as if she was upset with Becky's going obsessions.

"Girl I don't know why you worry yourself about that crazy ass girl, that's just Becky. She's out there in that big lonely house, doesn't work, and no man for now. Of course she needs some type of entertainment in her life. I tried to get her a job with me but she didn't want to work? She loves her fast times either getting money or popping pussy. That's the home girl we've known over the past years, and you know if it works for her well it works for us."

"Shit, we all have flaws about each other, but we just have to stick it out." Jasi said, as she tried to butter the situation up about "partying ass Becky".

"Now I'm the one she's really going to mad at. Last night I turned off my ringer, after agreeing with her that I was going to the beach. I ended up staying home with Chuck, but I was truly going it's just that I fell asleep and woke up about two in the morning.'

"She may kill you." Jasi replies through a loud burst of laughter while swinging her bags from Sacs Fifth.

"Jasi did you know that Maya Angelo foundation is having a big poem recite for HIV awareness, at the convention center. I added trying to change the negative conversation around in which we were just having.

"Did you join?" Jasi quickly asked.

"The grand prize is just 5000 though." I replied with a frown on my face.

"Well Chocolate it's not all about the money, look at it as a breaking point to be recognized!"

"You're right; it is a time I could be recognized. Becky and you both better come, even though she's always mad with you and me. Being she's the sweetheart of the group I know she will forgive us regardless!" I said as we proceed to exit the mall.

After leaving the mal I swear I could not go another day of not knowing. Luckily Jasi & I went in two different cars. Because ALMOST IMMEDIATELY I must ride through Coconut Grove. Which supposedly is Chuck's new area and I heard about some little girl who he's always with. But of course you know Becky said it. She's the only one who's in the way of something, and she sees everything especially the late night moves. I'll give her a call to see what's up? She may not answer the phone, as I didn't answer mines last night.

"Hello." answered Becky.

"Hey boo, what's up?" I asked?

"What do you want, Mona Dashawn Anderson!" Becky voice escalated in a serious tone.

"Don't be calling me out, by my government name. Becky Lee Jackson!" In the same tone I responded.

"Girl Chuck came over, and you know what took place." I explained.

"Whatever! You at least could have answered the phone and let me know something, but fuck you and Jasi confused ass!" Replies Becky.

"Now shit, nobody owes you any damn excuses! When you leave and skip, State to State with your sorry ass baby daddy! Do we fuss? Hell Nah, anyway what you doing?" I asked.

"Just coming home from the Beach. Fake friend." Becky added.

"Becky stop that fake friend shit. What you doing just coming from South Beach it's almost nine at night. Besides who your stankin ass stayed out with all day and night?" I asked.

"None of your damn business, and what do you want?' Becky still was a little upset, but she wasn't a person to hold grudges.

"Let's meet at Shorty's and get some ribs?" I asked in a calm decent manner

"Jasi with you?' Becky questioned.

"Why? Don't be like that, but no she's not with me." I said, knowing all she wanted Jasi to tell her she was sorry, she just felt as if she was the baby of the group.

"I'm in Dadeland where you are?" Becky asked.

"I'm just leaving the Grove, so you can meet me at the barbeque pit."

"Alright." Becky said ending the call.

I got out of my Honda which was smelling like burnt oil, and the water in my radiator was boiling like it was popping popcorn. I was looking plain and ordinary, tight jeans push up bra, which helped the tits fill the tiny shirt I wore. Becky steeped out of her Lexus jeep, wearing Gucci pants and a blouse looking so classy. I knew it wasn't her taste, yet it was a very hot Vogue look.

"Oh Ms. New look today huh." I said smiling as she twists and turned in a circle. She looked nice, the pants and blouse matched and fitted well.

"Girl let me tell you about the beach last night, even though it wasn't that crowded. Nikki and I. You remember Nikki don't it?' Becky asked, barely walking away from the jeep as if she couldn't wait to tell me the story.

"Yes." I responded, and thought to myself how I could forget someone that sleazy.

"We went to some Spanish joint, it was tight. You and Jasi gots to go. I met some Colombian named Marco. He was all over me in the club."

"What you had on Becky." I asked, just to here because I know it was always a fashion statement.

"I wore this little dress, and it chased this shape! That man was buying crisp and lobster all night while Nikki and I danced our ass off. Kurt had came and you know what happened next. Nikki had to care her behind home. I stayed with Marco and we left about 530am and went to eat at Big Pink. He left the waitress a 100-dollar tip girl!" Becky said sounding unbelievable. "He just loves this fat ass of mine, girl he was rubbing me up and asking when I will be able to fly to Britain. I told him maybe, but anyway to make a long story short. We went to his penthouse in Brickell; it was oh so nice. The man had every tie, shoe, and cologne in a raw ass house with a good personality to match. There was a his and hers matching Mercedes parked down in the garage. Chocolate girl I am not fooling you, but this just seems to have been the picture perfect man for me. We chilled pooped crisp, but he was a cigar smoker that was the only problem I had with him." As Becky went on, I didn't say anything, I sat and was saving my response for last while nodding my head and surfing through her materialistic mind.

"Earlier today he had mentioned that he was going to England to see some friends, but he had to go shopping first and asked me to come along. We drove down to Bal. Harbor, he knows his shit too girl. He bought himself about four ties and that was around 800 dollars. Buddy pulled out the platinum card baby and swiped it without a problem or second identification, then he bought a 4000-dollar suit and to the Gucci store for me he spent 8000 on panties, matching bras, two pair of sandals and this pant set. Later on we went to watch the horse's race, and then we went back to his place to pack his things. He got dressed, Chocolate the man was Prada down with matching hat, shoes, and belt along with the simple shirt and pants. Looking sharper than a preacher and smelling good like a Cuban. Then he asked me for a ride to the airport, you know your girl said *'sure'*. How about Mr. Marco grabbed his Prada brief case put his two cell phones in his pocket, two way on his side, and a wad of money with the matching Prada upside down triangle symbol money clip. Patted me on the ass and said: "Baby lets go" with his sexy accent." Becky continued on and on telling her story as if it was never going to end. I couldn't hold out any longer I had to interrupt this bogus ass situation she thought was so romantic

"Where are your kids, or did you call them?" I asked.

"Yeah, but child on our way to the airport he was jotting down my numbers and writing his as well, soon as we made it he jumped out and through me a bundle of money with a rubber band wrapped around it." Becky continued as if I didn't interrupt.

"How much was it?' I asked.

"It was 7 grand." She said whispering and smiling.

"Damn Becky what you did, swallow the nuts or licked his ass. Nah tell me you didn't go pass the girls tradition, not the girl's tradition.' I asked laughing.

"Just there bitch, I didn't fuck him neither." She said with a serious face.

"Whatever Becky!"

"Chocolate all he wanted to do was eat me with all types of freaky shit. Bananas, whip cream, and strawberries, now don't get me wrong, he was so good. I wanted him bad too, only because his finger and tongue was using me."

"You off the chain Becky."

"You know me doing my thang."

"So Miss Lady. Are you going to Britain with him?' I asked as Becky eyes got bucked.

"Shit from the looks, Chocolate I'll go to Mars!"

"Girl you crazy."

"Nah you crazy." Becky responded as the waitress walked up.

"May I take your order ladies?' She asked standing in her red and white 60's dress.

"Yes can I have a slab of ribs, 4 corn on the cobs and 2 butter rolls?

"Anything to drink?' the waitress asked.

"I'll have a sweet tea." Becky said ordering the normal which we would split amongst the three of us.

"I'll have a root beer and a baked potato." I added.

"Will that be all ladies? She asked.

"Yes" Becky responded.

"I'll have this out to you ladies in 10 minutes." The waitress said, packing her notepad into her pocket and quickly picking up the menus.

"Thank you." I replied as she walked away saying you welcome.

"Well Miss Becky how does this Marco look?"

"Chocolate you know I'm not like you, my man has to be on top. He's dark tan about 5'9 long black silky hair, thick chest, and arms. He's just handsome." Becky said throwing her hands in the air as if she was helpless with finding words to describe him.

"Becky that man is going to cut your neck off. You know some men from other countries are really crazy." I said laughing.

"Bitch shut up you watch too much lifetime." Becky said laughing along with me.

"Just tripping girl, do your thang. Make that money, but Britain." I responded as I recapped the whole conversation.

"Did you tell him you have three kids, a sick mom, and two girls who loves and need you home?"

"Child please" Becky said, always when she wanted me to shut up, but I refused.

"For real though Becky think about that."

"Think my ass, girl I know I'm going and there will be NO, IF, ANDS, or BUTS, about it!" Becky said, as her head started to roll in motion, lips pocked out, eyes dancing around and around which let me know she was ready for a debate.

"You know Becky anytime you and I get into a deep conversation, there's an argument between selfishness, and things you should already know. You always think bullshit Becky! Maybe if sucking dick was a job. I know you would have top performance. Unfortunately it's not safe anymore! You already get by with no job, no kids to be bothered with, your house and your cars are paid for. Boo you got it good you need to be thankful for your mother and you really need to slow down." I rattled off with frustration in my voice.

"Chocolate fuck it!" she said in a loud careless voice.

"Becky, just don't be weak for no man, especially one you know very little of and that's all. Fuck picture perfect Becky!" I said, as I grabbed control of my voice and slightly whispered. "Whatever happen with painting your own picture how you want it?"

"Nothing's perfect." Says Becky, without giving my suggestion a thought.

"Damn, Becky everything can't be perfect right off hand, that's why you have to build it." I explained.

"Chocolate why you always so hard on me?" A question I couldn't believe, Becky asked.

"I'm not, I love you. I'm trying to show you experiences aren't always the best teacher. Instead of hitting rock bottom, take the learned lesson of someone else, cause some experiences come too late." I expressed.

"Chocolate can I ask you something, why didn't you discuss this with Jasi, when she met Bruce or did you forget he was married? Now tell me adultery aint worse than having fun with a rich ass Columbian. Or is it because she's in school, no kids, and the Ms. Missy." Becky said, as she rolled her eyes, and motioned her neck along with the tone of her voice a bit harder.

"Nah Becky that ain't hardly it. None of us is ugly, nor bad shaped besides looks mean shit. One thing about Jasi, she will work. She knows when to stop, and she knows when there's no end to a situation. But you, you act as if you don't care about anything and you sure think you live in this world alone. You don't! By the way don't you ever think comparisons between you and Jasi makes any situation ok or the same." I said, going on and on regardless how it sounded, we always told one another the truth and not a lie for comfort.

"See Becky with you there's a new man, more promises and a different Becky. I just ask that you live for you, forget about shopping sprees, and traveling right now. Your mom needs you most, Becky she's in and out the hospital. You don't have any need to be even considering Britain. Ms. Minnie has no one but you Becky, and those kids. She keeps them so they don't be a problem to you. Besides it's too many killings, and diseases to be playing hooky anyway!" I said.

"Come on now, St. Mary. We all have weaknesses now you sold a lil pussy RECENTLY." Becky said, raising her eyes as if she was waiting on an answer.

"Yeah you right, but like I said don't let your weaknesses over power your mind. You have to let some things pass you by. Even the greatest ball player doesn't catch every ball, to afraid; it's going to sprang his finger or injures his hand before the playoffs. You feel me?" I said, expressing my friendship manner. She said nothing, just looking. Seems to me I've brought her back to earth, she sat and listened without a word. So I continued while I had the opportunity. "You can't just think with today, and leave latter, tomorrow, next week or next year behind. These are the keys to your future baby." I said as if I was searching for answers or even a reason why she'd think the way she does. "Becky you know I don't mean no harm. I'm just being a friend. Work for what you want, and then you won't have to settle for what he'll give you." I said.

"Chocolate you're right, I'm going to find my own man. Believe it or not we are both going to have career jobs, plan my pregnancies, and read your poetry! Huh, what do you think?" Becky answered so sarcastically, while totting her lips to a fake smile.

"You know Becky from this day forward, I'll promise you before WE end OUR friendship. I'll leave the advice shit alone. Being you make no mistakes and need no opinions. Of course not to mention if you don't care. I wouldn't care, and become that fake friend with no advice."

"Whatever Chocolate, call it how you see it!" Becky said as she smiled and pulled the lemon from the glass of ice tea.

"Anyway did Jasi tell you about the trip?" Becky asked switching subjects, so easily.

"What trip?" I asked trying to calm my nerves, which didn't seem to bother Becky.

"A trip that we can take the kids, I think on that Disney Breeze ship. Bruce has a time-share; Jasi says he gave her free passes. Two adults and two children. We would just need to pay for two extras, and that wouldn't be a problem. Becky said.

"When yall planning this?" I asked.

"If I'm not mistaken I think she said Labor Day weekend."

"That's cool, at least it will buy us some time to recuperate from the Essence Festival on the fourth." I said remembering that big event in Louisiana from the pictures Becky bought home last year.

"Oh yes, I can't wait!" Becky said, as she crossed her legs, and clapped her hands together in excitement.

"Chocolate have you been shopping already?"

"No not really."

"I really need my Gucci visor, which SOMEONE left in Chicago." Becky said smiling at me. "I have some tight Daisies with some sexy BCBG pumps, I'm going to wear on the park that Sunday." She said sounding like she was defiantly geared up.

"How many outfits should I carry?" I asked, as the conversation grew friendly.

"Well me, I'm going to wear one there, because I know we will be sightseeing and going to malls upon arrival. Then that night on the town, there is always a lot of parties, and then a big concert. Saturday everybody goes to this strip, where there is just an opened field. Girl it be so crowded. Music, food, and the brothers! Honey you talking about 6 packs, bowlegs, and dark chocolate kind of men riding Harley's or big nice cars now that's the best day to me. Then there is Sunday which is the big park day. They throws a nice party, but nothing like the one on Saturday. So actually that's like two dressy outfits, two casuals, and of course "that catch me if you can outfit" ha ha ha Becky laughed out loud and so did I. "Yes chocolate that's what I'm going to bring. Oh yeah last but not least don't forget those comfortable shoes, leave those stilettos and killer scrap ups here in Miami, cause your ass would be left behind trying to find Dr. Scholes."

"Only you Becky would have calluses, and corns on them claws. How could you think of some crazy shit like that? Girl I told you Ms. Minnie dropped you on your head." We both just laughed, as if we didn't get through arguing. However this is one thing that defines our friendship to be rich. We can argue and bless each other out this second, and smiling the very next without a spec of bitterness.

"Becky I guess I'm going to have to go shopping, because I'm not wearing nothing from my closet. I may come back with a husband."

"Yeah you need something in your ass every now and then, you're so bitchy like nobody ever gave you anything!" Becky said; raising her eyebrows to what she thought was a solution.

"Child please dick don't mean nothing because I had some real good dick last night. The kind that keeps you trembling, squeezing your toes, and fucking real fast and good like you twelve years old. So I know it's not a dick I need! Besides I have a big one that stays in my dresser drawer, which doesn't cheat, it keeps a hard on, and wont nut in the nookie." I said, laughing at the obscene look on her face.

"Your nasty freaky ass, you better stop playing with that plastic, because it got your ass fool."

"But for real Becky I need a man. My OWN man. Perhaps a father figure just like my daddy, a devoted man to his wife and children."

"Why you can't just keep screwing Chuck `the good dick man'!" Becky mentioned.

"You think I'm happy with Chuck like that?" I questioned

"I really can't tell." Becky replied.

"Hell No I'm not! It's like an emotional roller coaster ride. I'm Happy today, sad tomorrow, then he answers the phone when he feels like it, or come to visit me when he gets ready and leave when he's tired. Then he has to be at every party, hell I need me a responsible man. I told you one somewhat like daddy a hard worker, who's devoted to his wife and kids, take long vacations; relocate between summer and winter. You know explore the real world. Sky diving, mountain climbing, hunting and baby you know what else comes along. We will be constantly working on those two kids.' I said starring at the ceiling tiles.

"Yeah Heather you and Billy shall I say... You guys should also buy a ranch and raised the little motherfuckers!" Becky said, laughing so loud and sarcastic bringing so much attention to our table.

"Becky for real, you think we're not going to grow old. We're not always going to want the latest, on every scene, and willing to leave our man for any reason to start back over? Maybe you will when you're about 40, but me I just love that family type shit. Father, Mother and Kids you know staying home cooking and fucking wouldn't be so hard if you think about it." I said looking her dead in the eyes, hoping she would relate.

"Shit you even crazier, when you mentioned more kids. I wish I had just one." Becky said as the waitress walked up.

"Ladies" the waitress called, interrupting the conversation, and bringing the big dishes loaded with vegetables and meats.

"I'm sorry can I please have a little more butter." Becky asked, slicing the bread open.

OUR NIGHT OUT!

"Hey Chocolate you have my powder blue belt?" Without a hello Becky asked.

"Did you leave it here?" I questioned.

"I think, look in your closet, while I call Jasi and see if it's there."

"Yeah." I said ending the call; to think of it Shanice had that belt yesterday playing dress up with Michelle. I might can't even find that belt, just like I can't find my diamond studs. I need them tonight too; I kind of hate them cause they are the clip on ones. I guess I have to call over mama house and ask Shanice, aint no need for Becky to look and I know it was over here.

"Hello." Mama answered the phone.

"Ma, is Shanice asleep?"

"Yes Mona, what is it you want from her anyway. It's something to 10 at night.' Mama said.

"She had Becky belt, her and Michelle playing dress up, and Becky needs it tonight." I said trying not to add me as a part of the group.

"Mona do yall have to go every night?" Mama asked, including me in without a doubt.

"Ma, I went home and fell asleep yesterday."

"Hell you act like that was something you didn't wanna do. Think of the ones in their graves, their eyes shut and mouth glued tight every day, and night." Mama said raising her voice as she went on.

"Come on Ma, not tonight. Is Michelle awake?"

"Yes Mona. All right now busy people always wished they had the time to listen to the word, but because they're busy, they will always learn too late. But you just hold on, let me get Michelle on this here phone."

"Michelle! Michelle!" Mamma called out, as I pulled the phone a bit from my ear cause of the way she screamed into the phone, I just waited patiently without another word because I knew from the start she never wanted me to go anywhere. She is so protective, but I know she loves her baby; I love her too she just got to let me be a woman. I do appreciate her awareness and carefulness; some people don't even have a care in the world, my dad he's the same way, now that's my boy.

"Hello." Michelle answered.

"Michelle did you see that blue belt Shanice was playing with?" I asked.

"Oh it's in the toy box."

"Have you seen my earrings, the diamond clip ones?"

"It's on the yellow bunny rabbit ears." Michelle said, knowing where each item was as if she put them away.

"Bye, and tell mama to go to bed." I said as Michelle started to laugh, cause she knew mama was going to get to cursing.

I walked into Shanice room and started pulling toys from the box, just when her little picture album fell out and opened up to one of Lionel's picture. A feeling of lust, and a variety of memories just rushed me as I thought of how much I missed him. You ladies understand me. I'm talking about those feelings that resurface anytime but will fade away by one simple thought instantly, that's what I was feeling. But he was doing his own shit he didn't give a dam if I see him or not. As a matter of fact I better had not part my lips to say *'I seen him'* or even *'I heard he was cheating.'* That was grounds for an ass cut out of this world. I'm glad in the way were not together. I do miss him, but will never want him back. Even if he had platinum around his balls.

"Yeah!" Becky answered the phone loud and frustrating.

"I found the belt, and what the hell you wearing this color?" I asked.

"Good, my shinny iceberg pants. What about you?" Becky asked.

"This peach pants set. Did you call Jasi?"

"Yeah I was calling her for my belt but that girl done transferred her house phone to the cell, and on her way to my house."

"Damn Jasi wants to hang out for real."

"I'm glad she does, because otherwise leave it up to you, we won't be going nowhere. Lord knows if you get a piece of dick we sure aint gone get you to even answer the dam phone!" Becky said, laughing out loud.

"Alright Becky let me finish getting ready, with your silly ass."

"Make sure you bring the belt down with you."

"Alright." I said ending the call, as I started to search harder for my peach handbag, which was nowhere to be found. I must have thrown almost everything from my closet trying on different outfits, figuring which one fits better and which one I have all my accessories to match. I slid on a tight black dress that tied like shoelaces from my waist to the tip of my breast which sat like they were ready to pour out. I sprayed a little romance, did up my makeup and modeled in the mirror about five minutes just when I heard a continuous horn blow. I knew it was them because the security never called me whenever they arrived. Francisco would be so hot after Becky finished showing her tits or dancing like she was some exotic stripper so therefore the rules NEVER applied when he saw her.

"Hey ladies!" I said standing to the front door pulling and twisting it lock.

"Ow who's the big luminary starring for tonight?" I questioned, as Jasi went to the trunk to put her huge purse away. I then took full notice to her mini dress draped with silver shingles which bounced to her every movement, and my gosh the kick ass pair of silver stilettos she wore which barred a single strap around her ankle that hung the same shingles as her dress which was undoubtedly sexy.

"This is so hot! These shingles doesn't scratch you?" I asked as I made it to the rear end of the car.

"Nah, that's how I love it. Touchy!" Jasi said, as we took our seats and she pulled off in the Beamer. Perfume scented through the air, due to a car full of smelly fine ass woman, which was sure going to rock the club tonight.

"You both look nice." I said to them as Becky packed her purse from one to the other.

"You look nice too child, I thought you were wearing pants?" Becky turned around in the seat making eye contact.

"Nah, I thought about those long vacations, so being sexy might just catch his eye." I said laughing.

"Which club are we going to?" Jasi asked.

"It's been so long I don't even know which club jumping?" I added.

"Well, being it is Friday night we can go to Bermuda's, Level, Crystal or Crave pick one." Becky said.

"Not Crystal!" I added.

"Well Bermuda's is a nice club that carries a very important crowd. No kids allowed and they don't play about that dress code or your ID." Becky said, trying to convince us.

"I guess it will be Bermuda's then." Jasi said as we veered on to 95.

"Hey yall I heard next week Levels having a big Memorial Day party. The guest is Trick, Eve, Mystical, the Baddest bitch, and the Eastside boys. I know we all going right?" I said, as the expressions on Becky face became surprise.

"I don't know about that one ladies. Bruce wants me to go with him to the Bahamas to a tennis tournament that week." Jasi said in doubt.

"Well guess what? Your ass lucked out, cause Chocolate and I going. And you better know that baby girl! Whenever the Prince from the south comes to the MIA, I'll be there." Becky said, staring at Jasi with a serious look on her face.

"Well Bermuda's it is." As Jasi repeated herself looking over at Becky, ignoring her comment.

"Yes it is. Is this your first time going Chocolate." Jasi asked, overseeing Becky funny behavior dancing in the seat.

"Yeah." I answered.

"I've been once." Jasi added.

"You will like it. There's all type of men, red ones, black ones, Asians, Africans, Columbians, Cubans, entrepreneurs, thugs, ballers, and them big truck boys. You name it and they are there." Becky expressed as we approached the night club.

"VIP it is ladies?" Jasi asked.

"You better know it." Becky replied, as we observed the club which had a line so long, and the parking lot was packed with cars rolling slow on Spree wheels, 24' rims, or Lamborghini doors turned up for style. VIP was even crowded; every car was 50 grand or more. Parked out front close to the club sat two Rolls Royce and a Mayback that spelled fascination when you looked at it.

"Oh this my type of shit here yall, the club is pumping tonight!" Becky said swelling her chest up clapping her hands in the air for excitement.

"It sure is packed." I added, as we departed from the car and went through the VIP line in a swift minute.

Walking in the club, of course the first thing we had to do was head to the ladies room and fix up nice again. Before we could get there so many guys stopped us, but we continued towards the ladies room.

"You ladies look nice, can I get you all a drink?" This corny ass rayon shirt wearing, yellow jewelry, out of shape ass Afro nigga asked us. As we veered off to the right and entered the VIP which was even crowded with more attention at our side.

"Excuse me ladies, would you all like to have a drink?" A light skinned husky guy asked.

"Yes I would like a Hennessey, cutie" Of course that was big mouth Becky.

"A Remmie and coke." Jasi added, as I still stood quiet, and quite surprised Jasi was going to accept a drink.

"And you sexy." As he came direct, I didn't want to be rude by myself.

"A sex on the beach will be fine for me." I replied as always sticking to the fruity drinks, because I knew I couldn't handle anything else. The guy was handsome though, but the brother was a bit too light for me.

Becky suddenly spotted her friend Nikki, and the both of them walked away bobbing through the club, while Jasi and I stood around.

"Chocolate do you like it?" Jasi asked screaming over the music.

"Yeah this is nice!" I responded.

"Let's go in the Champagne room, and play a little pool." Jasi said, as we headed in the opposite direction. As soon as we entered the room, there was a very black handsome thick guy standing by the bar. As I walked it seemed like every man was either pulling my dress or calling me *'sexy'* I just kept walking. It wasn't no need for me to stop when I had already knew upon entrance what I wanted, which was that black man over by the bar. He wore a Kango hat, with a neatly trimmed goatee mustache that aligned his perfectly round shaped face and sparkling white teeth. He was dressed in pinstripe trousers with a white and Grey stripped shirt, sparkling from his wrist he wore a Diamond Corum watch and a Bvalgari pinky diamond ring on his finger. I definitely could have written a short story about him here in the club. The way I peeped over everyone shoulder to acknowledge his presence, was just ridiculous but I didn't even care. He looked so good at the moment, I could have crowned this king instantly. I stepped a little to the side to get one good look, and when I did look in his eyes he finally noticed me. I then tried to play hard as if I was looking for someone. Jasi was no help; she was already talking to her friend Edgar. I was so glad that a friend of mine walked and started talking to me in the mist of this attraction. His name was Todd he owned a catering business, but graduated from Howard University majoring in the medical law field. He was madly in love with me after high school, but he was one of those too damn smart niggas. When Todd walked away, I notice the guy from the bar was looking directly at me again but walking towards my direction. I was so nervous I couldn't say a word, my heart was racing like a horse and I aint even know the man name yet. Before I could put Jasi up on what was going on he squeezed beside me and whispered. `*You know you are sexy.*' My tough ass couldn't do anything but smile, my nerves were so uptight I didn't know rather to respond or leave. Unthinkably I just walked over to the wall and got one of the sticks as I could feel my hips just shifting and my ass jumping to what seemed like a long walk.

Jasi and I started playing pool, and he was not clearly visible anymore. Before I knew it Jasi called eight ball. Not like I knew how to play anyway.

I stood against the table totally and I mean totally seeking for that black ass cute man, and there he was this time standing in a perfect view of me. A clear walkway seeing him from head to toe. He caught me again by the time I looked away; he just came walking as if I had given him a signal. It was all happening to fast, and boy I liked his appearance alone.

"Would you like to play another game?" He asked.

"I'm really not a good player." I said.

"That's ok, I just admire your company." He said, as I'd assume he knew I was watching him all the while.

"Ok well, let me go and get a drink I will be back." I felt myself sounding as goofy and scared as Jasi turned back to someone else talking again.

"How about I'll go and get the drinks you just set the game up for us?" He asked.

"Ok that sounds alright." I said trying to lighten up.

"What kind of drink, would you like?" He asked.

"A coke will be fine." I said not even interrupting Jasi; I didn't want to cause anymore attention than I already was. As he walked away Jasi ended that conversation as if she was timing us.

"Jasi did you see that man, I was watching home boy since we entered this room." I said.

"Yes he is handsome. I heard your soft ass ordering a coke." Jasi said laughing.

"Why you just didn't order your fruit drink?" Jasi asked fixing the game back up again.

"Whatever Jasi, you know Becky is not riding home with us and if so, she will already be drunk as a skunk and you are tipsy. Who the hell else is going to drive us home safe?"

"Please mama may I!"

"There is your lil friend, I'm going to go over here with Becky and dance a little." Jasi quickly said as she walked off and disappeared into the crowd.

"What is your name?" He asked.

"Mona, but you can call me Chocolate." I said in a routine.

"I'm Dale."

"Nice to meet you." I said as he stood holding the drinks.

"Are you sure you wanted a coke?" He asked.

"Yes, thank you." He then placed his tin pale on the edge of the table, and asked me to start first. I shoot the first ball and it rolled in so smoothly. The second ball just went wild.

"Chocolate relax, you got the ball jumping instead of rolling." He said, as he started to show me how to hold the stick. He straddled over my back, placing his thick hands around my waist, positioning my hips and arch. My I must tell you, I was getting hot all at once, and my heart was racing 100 MPH. He was so in control, like a captain would on his ship taking a wave.

"Chocolate, you smell so good." He said very close to my ears, that the very thin hair stood up. I was only wearing romance no drop-dead shit, but he smelled it.

"Thank you."

"What is it you are wearing?" He asked.

"Its romance." I said and continued to act so focused on the game I was apparently loosing.

"You smell like candy, are you as sweet?" He asked, sounding like he was trying to be fresh with that lame ass quote. However what he don't know this chick loves and plays every smart talk game even if it's not to satisfaction.

"Isn't candy you suppose to always taste and find out?" I said looking so charming and sexy at the same time.

"Wow, and answers with a sexy reply too." He said as if he was surprised I had something to go along with that little slick, sexy phrase.

"You have to position the stick so it can hit in the middle, therefore you can stay in control of the ball at all times. Now if it hits at the bottom of the ball it will jump all over the table making it impossible to score." He said, as my mind wondered in all the wrong places. I continued to shoot missing every ball, he felt sorry so he went ahead and let me win.

"You're good!" He said.

"No, because you let me win." I said smiling as he was laughing.

"Would you like to play another game?"

"No thank you, Mr. Dale."

"Well is it possible that I can see you after the club, maybe breakfast, a phone # or even a talk outside?" He asked.

"How about you give me your number?" I responded.

"I have no problem with that. Will there be a problem with you giving me your number." He asked.

"No it's..." I started as he interrupted me.

"I do apologize Chocolate. First off are you single?"

"Yes Dale I am, and how about you?" I asked.

"I'm a single lonely man. I have no kids, no wife, no girlfriends, all I have is a yorkie her name is Sasha and about 8 big fishes." He said as I laughed, at this nice looking brother who had a little since of humor.

"Well Dale I have a daughter that's five years old, unfortunately I have no pets, and never been married." I said as he nodded his head for approval.

"If you don't mind me asking where is her father?" He asked with a different expression.

"I don't mean to be rude, but that's another story." I replied.

"Oh that's ok. Can I take you out to breakfast after the club?"

"I'm sorry Dale I won't be able, I'm here with two of my girlfriends and they PARTY when we club. There is never a next designated driver." I said, as he laughed it off.

"No problem you can bring them along, I'll feed all of you. I just want to see you a lil while longer." He said sounding as if he wouldn't mind begging.

"Nah, they may want to just go home and rest." I said.

"I tried." He said as he shrugged his shoulders and continued. "I can't have breakfast, or a phone number. Are you always this mean and hard?" He asked with a serious look upon his face.

"I'm not mean!" I replied, knowing I was going to call him I just was playing that hard game, I can't always make it easy for them. After he saved his number in my phone, we both walked down the stairs together but acting, as if we didn't even meet. Three AM had rolled around so fast, standing by the picture booth was Becky, Nikki and Jasi. They were posing away; stomachs was sucked in, with their unit on their faces like gangster bitches, and one of the boys from field mob had Becky ass palmed in his hand. I walked up closer for a better view as the other chicks stumbling over each other, waiting, and watching so they can get a picture with the celebrity also.

"Come on Chocolate take a picture with us!" Becky screamed, so I got in knowing I wasn't to fund of Ms. Nikki. She was all over my back smiling, like we once played marbles together. Shortly the photographer man gave us the photo, we all looked like a raw click just handling shit.

"Alright ladies it's time to go." I said, becoming bored with the crowd that was constantly coming in. As we headed out, Becky walked and pinched every guy ass she walked by or stopped beside them.

"Damn Becky you stepped on my toe!" I yelled in pain as her stilettos poked my bare feet wrapped in leather scraps.

"I'm sorry Bookie." Becky said grabbing my jaws, as we stood by the bathrooms.

"Don't start any of that drunk bookie shit tonight Becky nor throwing up!" I said as Jasi started laughing when I was serious. I think we are too cute for the embarrassment shit tonight.

"It's always a don't start shit, well where the fuck does it ends! It's always a beginning and an end ain't it Nikki?" Becky asked with a slurring speech which indicated she was drunk once again. Nikki, Becky, and I walked outside the club, leaving Jasi talking to some guy who's a good friend of Jada kiss about a video shoot tomorrow. She was taking too long, and Becky began to talk yet all out of direction. We stood on the sidewalk waiting on the valet guys. A wet cherry color antique Cadillac with cat shaped eyes on spreewells pulled up. It was Kurt, Nikki's baby daddy.

"Girl I'm gone I will call yall tomorrow!" Nikki said sounding so loud and ghetto. I wasn't sure if she was expecting a see ya later back because Becky was too drunk to respond, and she already knew I didn't fuck with her period so I kept my mouth shut and eyes in a different direction. Shortly there was a burgundy BMW truck pulled up with dark tinted windows. The window came down, and instantly my heart started to flutter. It was Dale, yes the black guy from the bar.

"You need a lift to your car?" He asked as I stood and Becky leaned over my shoulder.

"No thank you, the car just pulled up behind you belongs to my home girl." I explained, as the chaffer stepped out and stood in the door waiting on its driver. I saw Dale quickly looked in the rear mirror observing the car behind him.

"Nice." Dale said.

"Thank you." I replied

"Chocolate is everything a no answer?" He asked giving me a very handsome look, I already see he was up on the game, and had sweet unthinkable things to say.

"No, just at the time." I said, as Jasi walked up, and we walked towards her car.

"Oh Chocolate was that the guy you were playing pool with all night?" Jasi asked as I watched him turn left towards the beaches and we went right towards the city.

"Yes girl that's him!" I very excitedly said.

"Man I'm hungry let's eat?" Becky added with her eyes shut and scratching every part of her body except her ass.

"Becky what is it you want to eat?" Jasi asked, turning to her direction.

"Let's go to the IHOP down the street." Becky said not realizing that we were already on 95, just that fast.

"Becky please, I have to get home. Bruce is coming by before they go on the keys fishing and it's already 4:45am. Why don't you just eat McDonalds?" Jasi asked.

"No I want some pancakes, steak and eggs." Becky stressed.

"Becky come on now we past all the IHOPs." Jasi continued pleading.

"And I am not turning around!" I added making my point very clear.

"Alright, I'll eat McDonalds! Next time I know to drive my own shit, so I can eat when I leave. Cause see I be dancing my energy away, while yall be standing looking pretty and shit." Becky said as we both burst out in laughter.

"Whatever Becky all that absolute, Hennessey, Hypnotic, and don't forget Nikki was there, we you know you had some trees. Now that's what trades you for your energy to the munchies. "I said, as we laughed and in an instant she was fast asleep before we could get to the next McDonalds. She was just like a rotten grown ass baby. We just left her sleeping and drove on home.

"Chocolate I like that club." Jasi said as the radio was blasting and I was speeding down the road trying to stay awake.

"Girl its cool, I met that one man from the bar."

"He was cute!" Jasi said.

"Yeah he was."

"When I tell you I am so sleepy." Jasi said, as she yarned.

"You! Girl me, and I only downed one watery ass sex on the beach and about three cokes." I said. (Yarning)

"This shit contagious."

"What?" I asked.

"I just yarned and so did you." She said as I yarned again and so did she and we both laughed just before getting to the house and exchanging seats.

"I had hypnotic, and that shit there don't play." Jasi said, changing CD from the steering wheel and adjusting the seat.

"Girl I got to stay up." She said as she blared Trick Daddy CD, and Becky still laid sleeping with her panties showing and one breast practically hanging out her top.

"Becky sweetie, wake up we are at home." I said shaking her shoulders.

"All her ass out!" Jasi said with laughter.

"Girl she don't care." I added laughing, shaking and even pulling her ears a bit, but Becky was out like she was a wino on a store porch.

"Becky come on!" I yelled in her ear as she jumped up like she was heading out the window.

"Why you didn't stop to McDonalds!" Becky said looking around.

"I did, but you didn't want to wake up." I said trying to allow her a minute to get out the car on her own.

"Girl get your ass out and go in the house and sleep somewhere!" Jasi said pushing Becky in her back while she sat up in the back seat half way out.

"Are you staying over here Chocolate?" Jasi asked handing me Becky purse.

"Yeah, go ahead home. I'll take Becky truck in the morning, call me later." I said, as Jasi drove off into the wee hours of the night.

"I'm sleepy." Becky said as she staggered everywhere.

"Give me the keys!" Snatching them out of her hand, quickly I used the correct key and gained access to the house.

"Go in you nut!" I said to Becky as she landed on the couch and no further. I then landed on her king size canopy pillow top bed, and thought about calling Dale until I somehow fell asleep.

10:20am, rolling over to pots clashing, music blazing, and pine sol scented all through the air. I stumbled out of bed, pulled down my mini dress, and headed towards the kitchen.

"No breakfast!" I said as I walked in the kitchen, Becky was slumped over the mop scrubbing the floor, and there was an empty stove.

"Ms. Becky!" I screamed over the blazing music of Stephanie Mills. "Where's the breakfast?" I asked.

"I drove my fast ass to McDonalds, while you were sleeping, and I did not bring you NOTHING!" She said smiling.

"That's nice."

"Hell it was very nice to by-pass all those McDonalds and didn't even try waking me up." She said stating back at last night.

"It's too early for all that girl, anyway who coming around here today, why you up scrubbing and shit?" I asked, moving back towards the dining area as she came closer.

"My kids and my mom you know she had a treatment Thursday to prepare her for that major treatment next week, and it makes her feel down for the first couple of days. I'll be so glad when this is over." Becky said pausing and taking a deep breath.

"No you better appreciate every moment of her speaking, fussing, even sick. Cause you never know how things may end." I said.

"I know; I just hope she gets better. I'm the only one she has." Becky responded in a sad voice. "That's why you should consider having more kids Chocolate? I'm telling you its misery without a sister or brother." Becky said looking at me shaking her head.

"I am, as soon as I meet Mr. Anderson." I said, as Becky shaped her lips up.

"Girl you keep looking, your daddy is a man of the past, trust me the future produces no such thing in our years or years to come. Wake up sister and deal with what you got!" With a loud laughter, Becky dipped the mop back in the bucket and started in the dining room. I grabbed a chair and placed my feet into another while she continued to mop.

"Who was that man you were talking to last night?" She asked.

"Oh did you get a look at him?"

"Yeah! I saw you playing pool when I went to the back to talk with Corey. He was handsome." She said.

"His name is Dale." I responded.

"Chocolate did you give him your phone number, or did you act like you were a newlywed with about 6 children." Becky asked, digging my style right out in place.

"You know I did, but I got his phone number."

"You kills me with that lil funny acting shit! Knowing your ass have lonely fuckin nights, horny days, and boring ass evenings." Becky said laughing.

"Fuck off Becky, you have to play hard, don't let the men think you are an opportunity hell make him know you are a privilege." I added.

"And what does an opportunity or privilege have to do with a relationship?"

"Simple Becky an opportunity is based on many chances and choices that's given to you. Meaning I am a privilege something they have to work hard for, and keep up the work to earn me baby in an honoring way! Are you feeling me? You better take notes on your girl style." I said as we both started laughing.

"But trust me I am going to call him later."

"You better." Becky added as she dipped the mop back in the water.

"Becky are you going anywhere?" I asked.

"Yes, I have to go and get mama and the kids after I finish."

"Oh you going to pick them up." I asked.

"Yeah, I dropped her back home last night because she said she was gone pack her things and stay with me for a few weeks." Becky explained.

"Well let me borrow one of the trucks to go home and pick Shanice up from mama house." I asked, as Becky walked back over to the kitchen drawer and pulled out a set of keys.

"Here drive the jeep, it hasn't been on the road for about a month."

"Oh I almost forgot to tell you Jasi called just morning. She said Bruce paid for the other tickets, so don't worry about it. All you would need to bring is spending money, the ship is ready for us tourist." Becky said smiling, placing her neon green channel glasses over her head from the junky kitchen drawer that kept just about any and everything in it.

"Becky, are you going with us to that poetry contest at the convention center hosted by Maya Angelo?" I asked as we walked towards the front door.

"When is it?"

"It's Friday."

"Which poem are you doing Chocolate?" Becky asked.

"I don't know yet, I have to write up something." I responded with a smile.

"Well if the topic is about friends or you happen to need a character, use me." Becky said just as excited as she would when I'd make up short poems when we were teenagers using her and Corey names. She loved it.

"Girl you still haven't forgot about that lil girl shit. The topic is about AIDS." I said.

"I'll be there." Becky said changing her voice from excitement to exhaustion.

"Well let me go now and pick up Shanice, after all its going to be a bored long ass day." I said getting in the heat filled truck.

"Don't feel bad. I'll have three of them, but they are our kids and this is what we make out of our lives **"BORING SITUATIONS!"**

"Oh girl please! What you getting your baby Daddy for Father's day." I asked just for a laugh on the road.

"Bitch that is not an existing day on my calendar even if we is together! Now what the fuck you getting that bird for Father's day?" I could barely catch my breath from laughing at her so hard.

"I'm buying my Daddy a Bulova watch and Lionel a card from Shanice."

"That's cute. They said you always loved Lionel." Becky added standing in her doorway grinning.

"Girl let me go you full of shit." I said shutting the door, and turning up the music. Eight ball was playing '*like that*.'

"Chocolate!" Becky screamed, "Let's ride a little later."

"Today is family day, let's just stay home with these babies and see the fellows tomorrow." I said and speed off down the road.

6:00PM in the evening, the sun was beaming through the verticals which woke me up. Shanice and her friend Ashley were watching TV, but it wasn't long before she knew I was awake and came messing with me.

"Ma Ma!" Shanice yelled, running down the hall.

"Yes Shanice." I answered.

"Fix me and Ashley some ice cream." She asked standing at the foot of the bed.

"Did you eat yet, while you talking about some ice cream?" I asked as Ashley came entering the room.

"Yes, my mama gave us some spaghetti. Now can we have some ice cream Ms. Mona?" Ashley asked.

"Come get it." I said as I rolled out of bed slipping my slippers on.

"Mommy!" Shanice said standing in the kitchen screaming as if I were downstairs.

`Shanice do you have to call my name like that?"

"No, one more thing mommy." Shanice said. "Can Ashley stay to our house?"

"I don't know Shanice." I said, giving her the eye. She could never play with someone without inviting him or her all night.

"Ashley mommy said she could come." Shanice blurted out, and held her mouth at the same time. She knew, ***NO*** means ***NO*** and ***I don't know*** means the same as ***NO,*** as well as my evil look means ***NO***. Ashley is Trina's six-year-old daughter, from down stairs. Shanice loves to play with her, she is a sweet little girl and so are her parents.

"Ok Mommy?

"Let me think about it Shanice." I said looking the other way.

"It's gone take a long time mommy?" Shanice asked as she started to beg, something I always hated no matter where it came from good or bad, it was just a sound of a pest.

"If you worry me Shanice I'll say no!"

"Leave her alone Shanice, cause she gone say no!" Ashley said, convincing Shanice as well to be quiet.

"Here yall stand right here and eat this." I said handing them both the ice cream on the tiled kitchen floor.

Observing my fridge I noticed there were three boiled eggs from Friday. I took them out diced them and added some mayo, onions, tuna and a slice of pita bread. I left the girls in the kitchen and camped on my bed in front of the television, watching lifetime. There was a good movie on about a young girl in love with a married man. Shall I say so in love that she killed the wife? I sat on the bed, my mind rested on Ms. Minnie for a minute so I decided to call, and see if Becky crazy behind went to pick her mom and kids up yet.

"Hello." A scratchy voice on the other end of the phone answered as if they were so tired.

"Becky!" I yelled into the phone.

"Huh." She answered very low.

"Girl, wake your tired ass up!"

"Call me back!"

"Well let me talk to your mama." I asked.

"Brianna, Brianna!" Becky screamed in attitude "Come take granny this phone."

"Hello." Ms. Minnie answered in her sweet little voice.

"Hey Ms. Minnie what you feeling like over there today?" I asked, and smiling as if she could have seen me.

"Oh baby alright, I can be doing worst, but with the lords mercy I'm doing fine. Where did you girls go last night why Boosie so tired?" Ms. Minnie asked calling Becky out her nickname.

"We rode around and went to the club." I said, without a touch of fun in my voice.

"Oh like usual." She responded.

"Ms. Minnie can you make me some Banana pudding, when you feel up to it?" I asked, leading her to another subject.

"Yes baby, I reckon I'll make you some, where's that lady of yours?"

"She's in the kitchen enjoying Ice cream with her friend Ashley."

"These kids are too much." She said laughing.

"Yes they are."

"Chocolate where is rabbit I haven't seen or heard from her in a couple of days?" Ms. Minnie asked.

"Oh she's doing well, she went with us last night too. She's maybe home sleep." I said. When she called 'Rabbit' she was talking about Jasi, Ms. Minnie gave her that name from a child also; they always said Jasi was a fast baby. You know these country folks have a nickname for everyone they meet.

"But I will tell her to call you." I said, as she ended the conversation.

Ms. Minnie is a very sweet old lady. She treats Jasi and I no different from Becky, you would think she had three girls instead of that one loony girl of hers, but they are both sweet. I hope and pray all the time, that Ms. Minnie doesn't leave this world any time soon. Becky would be a pitiful woman. She's a big baby and a mama's girl with the same token. I remember when her father left. Becky used to be crazy about her Daddy; everything was wait until my daddy comes, or my Daddy going to buy me this and that. Eventually Becky realized her Daddy had rested on the store porches and stayed on dope more than she could call his name. So the love she had in her heart soon built anger. He comes around sometimes offering her kids candy and cookies, he got from the back of some store because they were stale and no longer good to make a profit. Becky was never embarrassed and would never disrespect him no matter how dirty he or the goodies were. The children were trained to call him Granddaddy and accept the candy but yet to always throw it out when she reached the end of the street. Jasi always told Becky & me that we are blessed to have both parents around regardless of any situation. '*Thank you lord'* I say to myself all the time when we got on that conversation. Jasi always said there's nobody like Mama or Daddy, not even us girls. The thoughts of Jasi, made me give her a call.

"Shanice, Shanice!" I screamed, as she came bursting through my door the next second.

"Mommy, you call me." Shanice said panting for breath, as if she ran a mile before getting through the hallway."

"Yes go take this bowl in the kitchen for mommy, and please turn that radio down." I said as you heard Bow wow coming from the opposite side of the house.

"Ok Mommy." Shanice said, shutting my room door. I dialed Jasi number up as the phone rang and rang. I wondered where she was, more than likely she might just be sleeping. I was the only early bird; let me find somebody to talk to. I started dialing chucks number, but immediately one of my good since kicked in, and the attitude was No. I'm not going to do that. He's going to want some of this nookie, and not tonight.

After looking through my cell phone several times Dale named seemed to have been typed in bold capital letters, so I pressed *67 to block my number. Just when I thought to myself this is since less. I know I want the man to have my number. I hung the phone up and dialed him from my home phone, so he wouldn't have to ask for the number because the voicemail would read my cell number back also if I weren't here.

"Hi how are you." I said nerves as hell, trying to sound friendly and sexy at the same time.

"I'm doing fine, and who am I speaking with?" He asked, not being so friendly.

"Should I make you guess?" I said changing my voice.

"Only if I can have a hint." He said agreeing to play along.

"Sure. What's sweet and keeps you popping?" I said, grinning.

"That's not a helpful hint. Can I have one more please as that one does not count?" He demanded.

"Well you cheater." I laughed, "What's sweet and stick to your hand?"

"Um, I give up." He said taking a breath without another guess.

"Who is this?" He asked.

"It's me Chocolate, don't be so feisty." I said with a sassy voice.

"Oh sexy. I have been waiting on your call?" He said, as I giggled into the phone. "I was telling my boys about this Chocolate sexy broad, I meet last night. What's up?" He asked.

"Nothing, just home watching TV." I responded.

"What you watching." He asked.

"I was watching lifetime."

"Yeah, I watch lifetime too, can I join you?" He asked sounding so desperate, damn why I called him from my house, he must be one of those `begging to get the nookie and after wards pay your ass no attention niggas'. That's what Becky call this type.

"No, I'm chilling with my daughter and her friend." I responded, turning my lips up.

"Is it always going to be ladies day and nights out?" He asked.

"You are crazy." I started up a fake laugh instead of telling his ass what ***NO*** means.

"Just kidding baby, I'm with my girl also. She had her nails clipped and her hair trimmed a little while ago." He said, as I registered every word in my mind and gave it that final thought one like *`I will not be fucking with your ass'* I thought he told me he was single.

"She looks real nice, maybe we will go for a walk in the park where she can find Mr. Lucky instead of bones." As Dale went on, I remembered that he did tell me, he had a dog.

"I'm very happy you called me though." He said, as I sat speechless for some odd reason. "So Chocolate now that we are out of the club, tell me a little about yourself?"

"Dale what is it you want to know?" I said, hoping to avoid that question.

"Anything, about Ms. Mona." He called me by my first name, I guess he really was not only paying attention, but he remembered what I was saying."

"Well Dale, I'm not a talkative person, but if you will ask what you want to know, I'll answer with the best of my ability."

"Ok that will work, don't feel offended by my curiosity Ms. Chocolate." Here he goes again with that sharp talk.

"That's not a problem, don't feel offended by my precluded notions." I said in a very sexy tone, meaning half of his curiosity would be prohibited anyway.

"Chocolate, why a sexy lady like yourself doesn't have a husband?" Although I hated that question he gave me the benefit of having a husband and not a boyfriend.

"I haven't yet found that right man." I said in full truth.

"A woman like yourself, I wouldn't mind being Mr. Right." Dale said as I started blushing my ass off, while the phone continued to beep indicating someone was trying to get through.

"Dale are you able to hold on, while I answer the other line.

"Yes go ahead." He said, as I clicked over to Becky, which would keep calling. I had no choice but to answer.

"Hello, Chocolate." She said wide-awake.

"What! I'm on the other line!" I said very loud and mean.

"Wait wait, please Chocolate can you come and sit with Mama and the kids while I go and meet Marco."

"No Becky, I'm doing something. Bye." I said and clicked back over to the other line.

I'm sorry about that." I said.

"No, no problem, now where were we?" He asked.

"On Mr. Right." I responded eager to know what he thought about Mr. Right again.

"You think you can give me a little cheat sheet to become Mr. Right?" He said, slicing my mind in pieces trying to answer his questions.

"There is no cheat sheet necessary. It's just communication, time, respect and most of all being you. These are the answers, there's no need for questions baby." I responded, trying to say everything that was too hot for his mind, so he wouldn't keep coming back with sharp questions. He seemed to be a little more my type a mind challenger and far from a fool.

"Oh, you're even more sexier when it comes to explanation."

"I'm sorry Dale, can you hold once again?" I asked as the beeping either interrupted me or took away my focus.

"Sure." He said, as I clicked over to Becky again.

"Becky, stop calling me I told you I'm on the phone talking to someone!"

"Mona Mona, listen please." As she begged I listened "Can you come and watch the kids with Mama, I'll be gone only 3 hrs."

"Why didn't you call Jasi?" I asked.

"Come on Mona please! I said please. I don't want to leave Mama and the kids alone." Becky said with no other choice.

"Becky bye!"

"You gone come?" Becky asked.

"When I finish." I said clicking back to Dale.

"Before I was rudely interrupted, I just would like you to know, I like to keep it real." I said finishing what else I had to say.

"Baby that's good, because I'm a real good man who keeps it real, no time for the games, or the lies. What I speak is what I mean." He said, and I liked the sound of that, which means he's a man if he stands his word. Don't let me do all the talking, hammering, and decision-making.

"Alright Mr. Dale I hear you. Can I call you back in about 30min?" I said, hating to hang the phone up just then.

"Ok sexy I'll be waiting on your call."

"Ok talk to you later." I said, as I laid in the bed thinking about this damn Becky how she gets on my last nerve, she hardly ever has these kids. You would think she would try to spend as much time with them and her mom, knowing her mom is undergoing a new treatment next week. Neither, the doctor or Ms. Minnie knows the outcome. It seems the more I talk with Becky the more she seems to do, but she needs to show appreciation in some way. She never has time for them and they love her so much, I guess she will never adjust to motherhood.

"Shanice put your slippers on?" I yelled down the hall.

"Are we going to see Nanny Minnie and Brianna?" Shanice asked as Ashley looked up at me, and said she was going home. She waited until we got ready so we could walk her outside.

By the time I arrived Becky Acura jeep was gone and Nikki's Maxima was backed in. I just don't know about my friend, if we don't go she'll find someone to party with regardless what she's doing or have to do. I tell you she got her priorities fucked all up. Becky just pissed me off, she acts like she has to chase behind these mans. Fuck them, she doesn't need them. I know if Ms. Minnie had the strength she had when we were teenagers. She would knock

Becky out regardless who was sitting there, and Ms. Nikki I just don't like her, Becky says it's because of chuck, but I see through all of that. She's just nasty, has no morals, low self-esteem, greedy, and a big liar. Trust me Nikki couldn't be called nothing no better than a gutbucket, and that was practically to clean for her. Nikki slept with whatever, whenever, whoever or however and Becky trails right behind as if she's a queen to be. This shit gets even bigger. I'm not going to give myself a headache with that crazy girl.

"Get out Shanice."

"Mommy Becky home?" Shanice asked, crossing over the seat.

"She went to work.".I responded in a lie, if not Shanice would have asked me a thousand more questions before I got to the door.

I opened the door; with the spare key she gave me in case she lost hers.

"Is anybody home?" I yelled.

"Hello" Shanice said behind me, as a trail of voices came running from the back of the house. All three of them were running screaming Mona, so happy to see me.

"Where's Nanny Lil Corey?" I asked.

"She in the kitchen cooking." He said and gave me a hug.

"Get down Brianna." I said as she climbed up on Becky yellow leather chair.

When I walked to the kitchen, what I saw bought tears to my eyes. Ms. Minnie was too weak to stand over the stove, so she sat in her wheelchair with flour sprinkled all over her legs that had fallen from the counter. The kitchen was hot and had appeared back messy; she was sweating but still had that nice smile on her face when I walked in like nothing was wrong.

"Hey Baby." Ms., Minnie said.

"Hello, how are you doing?" I asked, didn't want to sound like I was surprised, or angry.

"I feel really bad." She said, and if she didn't say it, you couldn't tell by her appearance.

"What's wrong?" I asked.

"I feel weak; Becky left and know her kids haven't ate, and I'm not able to be taking care of these kids. Did she call and tell you where she was going?" She said looking greasy and upset.

"No Mam, I haven't spoken with Becky from morning." I said. hating to lie to Ms. Minnie but

I did not want to tell her the truth; that her daughter cared more about chasing money and men instead of being a daughter and a mother.

"Becky left here, with that thin gal I believe her name is, Nikki. They both had bags, like they were going somewhere or another." Ms. Minnie said.

"I don't think so, she would have at least said something to me."

"I hope not neither, she knows I have to go in the hospital next week. So they can monitor me on this new treatment." She said reaching over in the pot flipping the meat, while dodging the hot grease which was popping from the skillet.

"Ms. Minnie she'll be back, do you want me to finish frying this chicken for you while you rest?"

"Would you please baby." She said so desperate and restless. I pushed her into the living room and turned the central air on. Standing in the kitchen flipping chicken, as I truly couldn't believe Becky didn't cook before she left, if anything she could have put the chicken in the oven. I hope Becky stupid ass didn't fly to Britain with that man. Knowing her and Nikki they might would try some shit like that. Don't get me wrong; I know I ain't Mary but hell I am far away from Jezebel. I have never ever seen such money hungry girls who are willing to try and chance anything with life. Could you believe they still don't get shit worth it?

"Lil Corey take this juice to your Nanny." I said as he stood in the refrigerator getting some grapes.

"Nanna Nanna!" he called.

"Corey don't call her out loud, she don't feel good take it to her." I explained as, he stood listening along with Shanice.

"Mommy, what you cooking, in Becky house?" Shanice asked.

"Some chicken and macaroni." I responded.

"Why she not cook?"

"Shanice cause she's at work. Why don't you go and take a bath with Brianna?" I asked trying to avoid the questionnaire I was given. I called Becky phone to see where she was. The phone just rang rang and rang no answer. I couldn't even leave a message, knowing it might just will have ended this twenty something year friendship. I have nothing nice that's going to come from my mouth, just the thought of her carrying luggage provoked me to have a paragraph of cursing to do...

The kids had eaten and were put to bed, and still there was no Becky. Ms. Minnie had fallen asleep watching the TV. I got a blanket and wrapped it around her. I didn't even have a chance to call Dale back. I don't know what time Jasi will be back home from the keys because she was not answering her phone neither. Maybe somebody can understand Becky, because right now I'm all out of it for her. I continued calling Jasi but still there was no answer. Couldn't believe Becky didn't even bother to call to even see if I came like she had asked me. Not even to check on her mother or the kids. I just don't understand, there's no need of me trying to wait up until she returns. She's not going to lose any sleep thinking of home so why should I.

Two mornings had come and gone, I was working on the third one preparing breakfast for the kids; Becky has not yet come. Maybe I'll give her another day, if she don't call or come I'll just call the police. I had to take my vacation early; I'm assuming not all 14 days. Jasi came by to help out with the kids. She was in the room her and Julian sleeping.

"Mona the phone ringing!" Lil Corey yelled out, as I was so deep in my thoughts until I didn't hear it ring. Brianna reached over and answered it. I didn't want any mix-ups, or slight hang ups, so I took the phone from Brianna's hand before she could say hello. Looked at the caller id it registered *`unavailable'* it had to be Becky or Nikki, talking about what they came up with. Nikki a usual, *`Don't know a damn thing'* like an average bump on a log. I went into the room and shut the door.

"Hello, Hello!" Becky voice said.

"Don't hello me. Where the fuck you at!" I yelled into the phone.

"Child, this damn Nikki got us on a cruise to London." Becky responded.

"London!"

"Girl Nikki got us way over here." Becky said, as if I was ok with it.

"Fuck what Nikki got you doing. You are an adult now; there's no blame to count for. Not only did you leave three kids, but also you left a very sick mama and you knew that. If it means anything to you, I have a job and a life of my own, to not make those kind of decisions, and here you go with the ***'I don't give a fuck attitude."***

"But Chocolate you're not letting me tell you."

"Becky would you hear me now! There's not a damn thing you can tell me right this moment or any other that you're not here! How the hell you gone up and leave supposedly for 3hrs on Saturday and today's Tuesday. How the fuck can you possibly ask me to listen!"

"Chocolate I'm sorry if you." She said as, I interrupted her; being her answers wasn't as good as her presents.

"There's no `if'! You never think of no one but yourself. It's always sorry! This is what sorry is for; baby you better know there's a heavier load to be carried. Don't you know your Mama goes to that treatment Thursday?" I said in an apologetic manner.

"Damn! I really forgot."

"Well nothing surprises me, you forget any and everything, that doesn't revolves around you." I said, trying to laugh this whole matter off.

"Hell I can't keep up with all her damn appointments!" Becky said in a frustrated tone, as if I really had given a fuck.

"But of course you can keep up with what's in the club next week."

"Chocolate I know you are mad, but I thought we were going on a 1hr cruise." She said stumbling across her words.

"Don't lie to me, your mama said you left with bags. Becky I can't believe you have the nerve to even try to lie!" I said taking a deep breath and going back at it. "Fuck it I don't have time to prove your lies, rights or wrongs. The bottom line is I just don't like this stupid shit you pulled off." I said trying to finalize this scenario.

"I promise when I come back, I'll pay you for your days off, and we will go shopping."

"That's your damn problem Becky. You think money is the solution to all problems; not acknowledging the fact it's the root of all-evil. I don't know why the hell I am stressing all this shit to an empty brain. When the hell you coming back?" I had become so frustrated, in my own way I felt as if I could go through this phone and slap the piss out of her.

"Sunday morning 5 Am." she said so easily, like she had already known her return date upon arrival.

"Sunday!" I said thinking, about her mom, my job, these kids and the frustration.

"I didn't know, it was an eight-day cruise." She said, forgetting about the 1hr lie. I couldn't even fuss anymore. Things that sounded dumb from her mouth just registered since less to talk about, let alone more than a headache.

"Well you have 5 more days, to think about Marco, his money, and your drug using ass friend. Ask yourself is this worth your love and is that where & who you can turn to when you are in need."

"Chocolate we just having fun." She said. *`Having fun'* when she doesn't know in the next five days will her mother live or die.

"None of them means you no good, and you know it, as long as Marco can get that ass he's satisfied and Nikki. Something as simple *`can she be down with your friend'* and then smoke and snot them away. Jasi and I the only girls you really have, but you meet a stranger and go astray with some silly shit, leaving the country. Becky shit has to get better; rather if `change is for you or adjusting would be the best." I said mad all over again.

"Umm huh." She mumbled.

"Anyway `parent of the month' do you have a contact number, I can call you on if anything goes wrong."

"No, my phone doesn't work over here."

"Oh jackass you thought it would?"

Come on now Chocolate." Becky said, as she chuckled.

"How about him? Does he have a hotel number, pager or some type of communication, a fax is even good." I asked, not entertaining her foolishness.

"Damn chocolate, you know all that shit is for business." She said, as I tried to restrain my anger.

"Business my ass, what about your family! That's your business, correct me if I'm wrong."

"Nah but."

"You know Becky, you're just as silly as these daily motherfuckers come. Call me tomorrow, when you finish drinking your crisp, having strawberry massages and maybe even getting a Moe hulk for your pussy. Whichever pampers you best? Actually you can call Thursday if that's not asking too much or interrupting your vacation. Meanwhile Becky, I do not have the patience to hear myself repeat the same shit, which you can't seem to make any since out of. I'll talk with you later."

"Alright you damn grouch!" She said, as I hung the phone up without a good bye or anything.

As soon as I opened the door, Ms. Minnie was right there. I immediately said I was sorry for the language.

"Don't worry about it, I know Boosie will have you say things out of your mouth until it's unbelievable, but she means no harm. She's just young, experiencing life. I hope she'll be all right, and not only experience life but understand the gift it brings. As for her kids they need her the most, I'm not able anymore to play games, go out to movies. I just can't! I just can't give those innocent babies the excitement that I brought forth to her. The kids are getting older, and able to relate to their surroundings on what Nanny did for us not what Mommy did for us? When you become a mother Chocolate, there is going to be a lot of things you use to do but you just can't do it anymore. Once you were blessed to bring another life in the world, there's so much that's not going to even matter like the jewels, fancy cars, and mob men. You know these simple things are at risk not only to you but your child. Boosie is too smart to let her life pass her up, to sell her soul to satin for what? MONEY or FAME. If you didn't know Boosie, you would think I mashed her in a box, and left her until she bloomed without any love in her heart, attention at her side, morals or respect for herself or others. Robert shattered her life and the kids father almost in the same path, she knew how she felt. You would think she would better herself in their hearts by molding herself as a good mother, giving all the love she possibly can instead of sharing amongst others that mean her no good. Oh Jesus I pray for this all the time. Where is she anyway Mona?" Ms. Minnie asked, after pouring reality out.

"Ms. Minnie she went on a cruise to London."

"Oh Lord! Who did she go so far off with?" Ms. Minnie asked in tears.

"With that girl you seen her with and Marco." I said trying to sound as if I had knew him when I didn't.

"Why does she always put her trust in her so called friends' hand, before knowing about her friends?" Ms. Minnie said as if she knew all of them. I know Ms. Minnie was mad, she had all the strength in the world to speak about Becky. She was talking on things I didn't think she even knew.

"Mona when Becky comes home I'm letting my hands go free, just like hers. I did my job of raising my child. I have no business hollering, making sure they ate, bathe, and neat, that's a mother's job. Maybe if she wags with her own kids she will see life with more wisdom, and take it more serious." Ms. Minnie continued on, she was talking so much until my legs were going asleep propped under my butt. I could hear Jasi fixing the kids food, hoping she would walk by and Ms. Minnie will shut up. But she continued rattling out of the mouth. She really was upset and my ear was where the anger lingered.

Later that evening we all put on clothes took a ride down to the mall for a day out the house. The kids loved to hang out especially the mall they knew it was time for new things. Ms. Minnie sat in her wheelchair eating pretzels and roasted corn on the cob the whole way through. The kids played the video games and ate, just about every candy and mixed popcorns there was to eat.

By the time we made it half way home, everybody was asleep. I was so tired believe me when

I say *these kids had ran me crazy enough, I don't think I need any more if this is the way you feel at the end of a day.* However I enjoyed the day, they were funny little people, I just know they gone run poor Jasi AWOL while I take Ms. Minnie to the hospital 7am until when??? That I don't know.

THE LONG WAIT

Ms. Minnie looked real pretty. For some reason, her face had that stress-free look and wonderful glow like she's more than healthy. In her lap was a little basket of fruit she bought along to say thank you in a thoughtful way.

"Good morning, Ms. Minnie looks like you are in high spirits." I said with a generous smile gathering my purse and keys.

"I am baby every time the lord awakes me and my kids. The spirit is there." She replied smiling.

"Ms. Minnie you're not scared?" I asked.

"Let me tell you something. Once Jesus is there for you, the devil can do no harm. Now before I was born again, when I first was diagnosed with cancer; I admit I was so scared. But baby my god has no such word as fear. Believe him Mona; anything in this world if you just ask he shall give, and he will never put nothing on you that you can't bear. Try him I know and believe; if he did it for me he'll do it for you." She said sounding like my grandmother. Granny had a lot of belief in the Lord and could have your attention at her side with the conversations of the bible. It just was something about Ms. Minnie when she preached the word, it was something that stayed with you all day. You would practically think someone scribbled it over your mind. Although my grandfather always said *'Jesus is around everyday, you never know how he will come to you, to deliver his word.'* I've always known from Sunday school, he is a good god and all it takes it faith.

I watched the oncologist head nurse roll Ms. Minnie to the outpatient center, for the new treatment. Although she seemed not to have a worry in this world, I know she at least would have felt a little better if her one and only child was here to hold her hand. I sat patiently in the waiting room, just as my phone ring.

"Hello." I answered.

"Hi sexy." The deep voice on the other end said.

"Who dis?"

"Dale." He said, as I felt the embarrassment from my ghetto slang.

"Hi, how are you?" I asked.

"I'm doing fine, and yourself?"

"Just here maintaining." I said as I smiled and pushed my body low in the recliner.

"Did I scare you that bad?" He said, as I thought back to Saturday. Lucky he listened to my voice mail and didn't feel afraid to call the number that I didn't offer.

"No you didn't scare me at all, I just was a tad bit busy then the usual."

"If you don't mind me asking, Can I lend you a hand?" He asked, I kind of started liking that, he was ambitious and it showed across his chest, and most of all he didn't seem to have that shit that fucks up everything. 'PRIDE' I can certainly tell you I sure as hell had enough of it for a family of ten!

"No Dale, not so much busy physically but mentally busy." As I said summing it up.

"Do you go to school Chocolate?"

"Not exactly, but I take writing classes here and there at a vocational school."

"I see you have great interest for your spare time. That's good, maybe one day I'll be able to read your books or poetry." He said.

"Dale if you're that interested, there's a big contest on Aids awareness hosted by Maya Angelo, that I've been entered in." I said, just trying to test his perspectives.

"That's great, Chocolate when is it?" He quickly asked. I swallowed and smiled, not thinking he would go on.

"I am sorry for such a short notice but its tomorrow at 7pm." I said, thinking the more that comes to see me, the more I'll show off.

"Time is not an excuse for me, I'll be there." Shortly after Dale ended the call, the doctor along with a nurse came and walked up to me.

"Ms. Jackson." The nurse asked as if she weren't sure.

"Yes." I nervously answered the name that should have been Becky Jackson.

"I am afraid the treatment that was being administered into your moms' portal didn't go so good."

"I am sorry." The doctor said, as I began to get weak as if I was going to go through the chair, and my nerves wouldn't let me detect was she dead or alive.

"She has slipped into a comma, her diabetes count was 880. It did not agree with the treatment." As he stood without a care on his face but yet a sorry from his mouth. My world had caved in, by the shiny tiled floors, thick plastic brown molding that edged these scary white walls which felt and surrounded me like death.

"Would you like me to show you the way to the room?" The nurse asked, as the doctor excused himself by the loud speakers that were calling *code blue*.

The nurse and I walked down quietly, while the coughing, sneezing, beeps, and complaining became so loud to my ears, as I tried to block out my surroundings and think of home. I walked through the double doors known as the Intensive critical care unit. The tears leaked beyond my chin, they were tears I couldn't hold back, tears that fell as if she was my mother. She laid there peaceful with tubes through her nose and countless beeps from the machine.

"Would you be alright alone?" The nurse asked.

"Yes" sniffing and wiping the tears with my pull over Armani sweat shirt.

"Buzz if you need any assistance, the phone is at the front desk if you need to contact any other family members." She said as if it was a chorus part of a song, rehearsed and routine.

"Thank you." I said as the nurse headed out the door. I thought about it in silence. She has no family only Becky. She hasn't yet called either; I hope she doesn't call too late.

"Jasi" I called, as I snuck and held the phone to my ear, I could barely speak from the tears.

"What's wrong? Chocolate is she alright!" Jasi asked.

"No." I couldn't finish what I wanted to say, the tears seemed to continue, and no matter how I tried the words couldn't come.

"What happened?" Jasi started to get frustrated, and told me to calm down repeatedly.

"She's in a comma!" I burst out in more tears than that had already fallen.

"Oh god, Chocolate I'll be there." She said without another word. I tried to call Becky over and over again from my cell, but I was only receiving the voicemail.

"Becky this Chocolate, call my phone." I said trying to sound as happy as possible, I didn't want to scare her nor did I want to be the one to tell her. However feelings is not something easy to hide. I hope she calls today. I walked down to the nurse's station for Ms., Minnie a pair of socks for her feet, so she wouldn't be cold. Jasi came walking down the hall.

"Are you alright?" Jasi asked, with a comfort hug.

"Yes, where are the kids?" I asked.

"I dropped them to your mom house."

"Becky call you?"

"No" Jasi responded.

"Mona why you sounding so sad. It's going to be alright." Jasi said as we entered the room.

"I hope she be alright." I said.

"She will, don't worry." Jasi said, as she rubbed Ms. Minnie hands.

"Damn, I don't know what to say about Becky." I said in frustration.

"Things happen Mona, you think if she would have known this; she would have went out of town?" Jasi asked.

"Whatever Jasi, She knew I had a job, and a life of my own now didn't she?" I asked, placing my head in my hands.

"What are you going to do about tomorrow?" Jasi asked.

"I really don't know right now." I said. "I don't know about anything but, she came here so calm and easy, and now she lay silently with all these tubes, nobody next to kin, not even her daughter!"

"Your mama coming in the morning." Jasi said, as I just stood praying that Ms. Minnie eyes would look up at us or even a toe would wiggle. Maybe that would relieve this stress, which stared me in the face.

The next morning everything remained the same, except for Ms. Cure and my mom came to visit.

"Hi Ms. Cure, how are you?" I asked.

"I'm doing fine and yourself?" She answered.

"I'm ok."

"Mona where are her charts?" Mama asked as she was well aware of hospital procedures and messy doctors' notes; she works down at the pharmacy. She wants to know about the medication, nurse, doctor and her friend...

"I think the nurse has them." I answered.

"How's school going?" Ms. Cure asked, as she always would try to change and take my mind off what was impossible to show me possible and what was sad she'd express the happiness about the sadness."

"It's ok."

"Are you still using that special talent?" Ms., Cure asked pulling up a chair.

"Yeah, I write when I have a chance."

"Did you hear about that contest down at the center?"

"Yes, I was selected through my writing teacher." I mentioned.

"It is today!" Ms. Cure questioned, yet wondering her eyes around.

"Yes, at 7:00." I said.

"So you're not going?" Without a chance to give an excuse, something she never invited to her ears.

"Wait. I know you wrote something or maybe you can even dig back in your notes and recite something." Ms. Cure said as I smiled because she always had great confidence, and belief in me. She was a very smart woman who seemed to know her goals perused them, and didn't bother to procrastinate.

"Yes, I wrote one. It's about HIV."

"Is that what the topics about?" She asked raising a brow up.

"Yes."

"Girl go ahead and use your talent, do you remember it off head." Ms. Cure asked, as I rehearsed the first line in my head.

"Yes, I think so."

"Go on let me hear what you got to tell them today." I stood looking in her dead serious eyes, as she got comfortable in the chair. Standing in the middle of the floor; mom turned the TV off and towards me. I just went and gave it a try rather I knew it or not.

Lying in a bed, with silk white sheets.
Moonlight shinning towards my feet...

"I couldn't really remember all the parts, but I know once I get there it will hit home with expressions and all." I said.

"Go, ahead girl, I'll sit all evening. You got it just read it again and be ready for 6:oo." Ms. Cure said.

"No it's at seven."

"I know baby I heard you said it the first time, but I want you to stand in that mirror and recite your poem to your audience at six cause at seven you done already won. You just gone be celebrating and reciting it in front of folks you aint never seen before, and when I say reciting it you gone already have in your head you won. So therefore scary aint gone turn down the volume in your voice, and those nerves aint gone tie your guts together when the judges listening. So hear me when I say at seven you done already won, and at six pick your own audience in the mirror which everybody in that mirror is gone be you." Ms. Cure said as mama looked at me.

"Present yourself, you never know how many eyes you may open tonight with that message." Mama said in a caring voice. Ms. Cure waived her hand for me to get out and get downtown.

"Show them what you got baby, he gave you that for a reason." Ms. Cure said, as I gathered my bags and purse before dashing out the door.

Dale had been calling this evening; he wanted to go out for dinner before. However the nervousness on both ends were pulling, in the hospital and on the stage which was enough to full me up on the spot. I called Jasi up and we went by my abandoned house finally. Finding the house extra cold, and pillows were thrown where I left them.

"Chocolate let me hear what you got to say." Jasi asked.

"No, Please Jasi wait till you see me on stage."

"Come on."

"Please Jasi no not till I'm on stage."

"Alright, baby girl. You better be first runner up. Or else you will be walking home." Jasi said teasing me.

"Jasi, girl I am really scared."

"Why chocolate? You know you can do it." She said, sitting on the edge of the bed. "Mommy always told me, if you believe in your heart and know with your mind. Its right, go for what you know." Jasi said, as I dug in the closet almost teary eyed. That was the best advice Jasi ever told me in her whole 24 yr. of knowing the old girl. We got dressed and headed downtown.

As we reached the convention center, my heart fluttered, and the heat came over me. I just prayed that everything would be alright.

Maya met and spoke with each contestant, wishing us luck along with a prayer that sounded as if she took a scripture from the preachers Bible.

The first contestant was a girl, whose voice was so loud & strong until you couldn't help but to know she was trying. I hoped that I sounded just as loud but realistic. Each time applauds grew louder, I knew I was one step closer. Sooner than I realized it was my turn. The audience was so crowded; I couldn't recognize no one, but the judges and Maya. My hands were shaking and sweating, just when my nose felt as if the blood was ready to pour, until my eyes stretched to find the destination of Jasi, but it was not found. I caught up with my heartbeat as the words began to flow.

"Lying in a bed, with silk white sheets.
Moonlight shinning towards our feet.
Kissing my lips, with a sexual taste,
Stroking my hips, and slowly rubbing my face,
While making my soul feel it's amazing grace.
As he caresses my body up and down,
Without a doubt true love is what I found.
Departing ourselves slowly from one another,
Wishing I could be your 1st and only lover.
Lying in a bed with soft beige sheets.
Sunlight Shinning, towards my feet.'

The words flowed as If I had just wrote them, my steps were as if I was on a runway and my voice sprayed as if I was at the inauguration addressing the world without a mic.

Before I could realize I was talking. The audience let out such a grand relief of tears, smiles, head nodding, and loud applauding. I smiled and bowed. *`**Thank you Jesus!'***

Maya greeted me with a hug and tears, hold your head up high and believe in the lord. Your road can only go steady. Soon they escorted all the contestants out, the audience applauded as Maya unwrapped the gold ribbon from the envelope. I placed my head down; it didn't matter at that moment if I won. What mattered to me was, did the audience understand my message?

"Third runner up is Talia Davis reciting *a care in the world*." Maya announced as my heart raced faster.

"Second runner up is Toya Adderley reciting '*You gave me what you gave me*'.

"And the first place winner tonight is" Maya paused for a long second.

"Mona Anderson!" Spluttered from her mouth, as my knees jerked before they moved, I had never felt more contented and yet alleviated than I did that fleeting moment than I have done in my entire life. It seemed as if I couldn't even hold the weight from my own head.

She had a speech that couldn't be derivative not even with the same words or tone. It was a speech from her heart.

As I walked pass, I had tears of joy but hugs of comfort from anyone whom stood near or backstage. Before I could place a face to the near strangers, only Jasi, Bruce and Dales face became visible. Not only was I shocked by Dale appearance but abandoned by my friend Becky.

"You did it!" Jasi screamed, jumping all over me.

"I knew you had it in you." Jasi said, releasing me with a kiss.

"Congratulations, young lady." Dale said, pulling a bouquet of sunflowers from behind his back, which actually brightened my day. I blushed and as I reached not only for the flowers but his hug in which I was so willing to accept by grasping on to him like he was mines.

We later went for the car, after meeting several publishers, and very important people offering me their business card, phone numbers, waived membership fees, etc... I took them with a smile along with a confidence look. Jasi and I stood around talking to friends whom was there; Bruce stood talking with Dale. Engaging themselves in our conversation.

"Let's go out for dinner." Expecting to hear this comment from Bruce, but Dale seemed to have been more interested and polite.

"Ok, Rhode house." I respond and everyone agreed.

"Since you guys came separately, how about you two follow us." I asked. And they did.

I had about 10min to recap the whole evening. The first question was: How did Dale have enough care in his heart not only to attend but to show up backstage with a bouquet of flowers like we knew each other for years. Just to think the woman who presented me this award, inspired me throughout my years regardless of my turnabouts. I was always felt empowered after reading any of her novels, poems, articles, or quotes.

Before we knew it threw all the laughing, drinking, and eating not to mention the personal conversations, it was time to return to the hospital. Jasi said she would pick up the kids, and take them home with her, while I stay with Ms. Minnie. Dale had offered me a ride back to the hospital, being I didn't have my car. I was going to say yes, but Ms. Jasi replied so quickly, hell I thought he'd ask her. I assume she might have thought I was going to pretend to be that newlywed with about 6 kids. He's scored quite a few good points tonight I highly doubt if I act like that tonight.

We all started at the door, I watched Dale talk to Bruce. They had so much interest in their conversations, they exchanged numbers, and that was something I never seen Bruce do, let alone hold a conversation other than sports. He wasn't interested in conversations that weren't affiliated with stocks, trading, and investments. Although Bruce does love gambling I'm sure he didn't need a partner for gambling and he certainly didn't need a friend to show him how to spend it especially with Jasi on his team. Jasi and I stood whispering, and wondering what was so special about their conversation. I couldn't compare careers, or any similarities. I didn't have enough information, thanks for the interruptions from Becky.

"Are you ready?" He asked.

"Yes, I am." I said, walking towards him twisting as hard as I can while his eyes was pinned to me. I thought to myself this one brother I would take around the world for show & tale, and wouldn't wink or twist for nothing else.

We joined hands and walked to an aqua Jaguar. He opened the door, I arched my back to sit in the coupe, and he gently shut the door and proceeded to the driver side. Tonight has really taken me by surprise, I thought to myself riding the long stretch road at ease. I started to think `what kind of man is this and what was he doing in the club? But baby wait until I really get to know him. My nosey ass may know all about the ex-mother in law and all.

"What's on your mind beautiful?" He asked.

"Nothing much." I said, with a smile. Knowing I had enough on my mind for a nervous breakdown but replied nothing.

"Why are you so quiet, something's there?" I couldn't even prepare a word for him, being the Aries that he was he just couldn't sit in silence.

"Bruce is a very nice guy. Is that Jasi's husband or friend?" He asked, and I was unbelievably shocked he wanted to know. I certainly couldn't let him know Bruce was someone else's husband.

"Actually they have been friends far too long, I would say he's her significant other." I said, trying to make her and him be as closer than friends as possible.

"She seems to be a pretty cool person. Where is the other busy buddy of yours?"

"Becky, she's out of town." I said, crossing my legs, hoping he wouldn't ask me another question about her, because I might just retaliate on him. However we continued to get to know each other. He is a Bounty hunter, and originally from Houston TX.

We had finally made it to the hospital, although we talked all the way here, he still had more to talk about. We walked through the double sliding doors, of the main entrance to the hospital. I asked him could he go by the vending machines and buy me a Twix on the way to the room because I had a sweet tooth thinking this would at least give me enough time to relieve mama and Ms. Cure. I most definitely didn't want them to spill the beans or opening the door for questions.

Mama and Ms. Cure were ready to go upon my arrival. They were planning on going to play bingo on their way home. Mama and Ms. Cure hugged and congratulated me, after learning the news.

"Chocolate, watch Ms. Minnie, she received a higher dosage of her insolence."

"Alright mama." I said, as they left, perhaps passing Dale in the hall without a clue that was my mom and he was my new friend. I quickly called to see if Jasi had made it home safe with the kids. She answered the phone as if she was sleeping forever, and mentioned everyone was sleep. Moments later Dale tapped on the door.

"Hey you?" He said, which I thought was cute.

"Hey..." I replied with a juicy smile, as he began opening my goodies.

"Thank you."

We sat in silence watching the late night show, just when Nurse Karen interrupted.

"Ms. Jackson you have a phone call." The nurse claimed as I could see half her face peeking through the door.

"I'll be right back Dale."

"No problem" He replied as I exited the room.

"Hello." I said knowingly this was mama, but the voice on the other end was Becky.

"What's wrong with my mama?" I couldn't even be as rude as she tried to sound concern. However my respect wouldn't let me roar the way I wanted to.

"Boochie I need you here, your aunt medicine didn't work as plan." I said, calling her by her nickname, and claiming her mom was her aunt. I could hear the break in her voice; she immediately caught on and started crying.

"Would mama be alright though?" The tears begin to whelm in my eyes as I searched for the right words.

"She's in a comma." I heard the phone drop, and outburst crying. Sympathy played its part for me, although I was the comfort for her mother, my girl needed her girls. There was no need for me to ask for Nikki or Marco. It wasn't a time to make her stumble about her mistakes; it was a time for comforting.

"Hello." another voice answered.

"Who is this?" I asked.

"Nikki. Why Becky crying?" She asked sounding dumb founded as usual.

"Her mom is in the ICU." I said, and didn't want to.

"For real what had happened to her?" Nikki asked, who knows nothing about Becky or her family? I rudely asked Nikki to put Becky back on the phone.

"Becky, Becky, Becky!" Before I could realize I was calling her the name I was not supposed to be.

"Be strong Boochie. I need you to see if you can come home." I said.

"I can't until Sunday." Becky announced.

"Why you can't just fly from the location you at now?"

"Mona, I can't." Becky said in a more serious tone. I wanted to ask her why, but I didn't want to work her up any more than she already was.

"Be strong Becky." I said ending the call, as I walked away leaving the nurse in doubt of who I really was.

Dale was sitting in the dark by the time I had made it back to the room. I flicked the light on; he sat steady in the rocking chair as if he was waiting on me to return from a late dance.

"Is everything all right?" Being I was a bag of water, the trace of tears wouldn't let me deny this conversation. He walked over and put his arms around me. I snuggled in just right, bracing my head against his muscular chest as all the tears that were built in the past few days had finally burst. He gripped me in his arms, like he had knew my situation. From the warmth of his body and the strength of his muscles leaded me in a comfort field, where I just let those feelings ran free, as I watched Ms. Minnie lay helpless.

I jumped as I heard a loud noise, there stood the nurse standing with the menus.

"Good morning, I'm sorry to have frighten you." She said, as I looked around the room for Dale.

"Looking for someone?" She asked. "He left shortly before I came in."

"What time is it?"

"15 until 7." The nurse replied. I looked towards Ms. Minnie she laid the same way the night before.

"I'll leave this here for you to complete, you'll need to complete it for lunch and dinner." The nurse explained before exiting the room. Hours later I got bored watching the same shows that played; hearing the beeps from the machine, and nurses every fifteen minutes peeking in and driving me crazy. I got a little break from it a lil earlier when I walked to the gift shop and purchased Ms. Minnie a gown that read *`Somebunny loves Me.'* which was the truth. I damped a rag, washed her with baby soap, and shinned her with baby oil, which looked much better than that dry wrinkly skin from this germ prevented air. Soon after bathing Ms. Minnie, a knock came about the door and the nurse pepped in.

"Ms. Jackson is your name Mona?" I was instantly frozen I didn't know rather to answer yes or no.

"Yes I'm sorry." I said, starting to apologize, for what I didn't know.

"Because, there's a gentlemen who's calling to the front desk for a Mona, and mention she was not a patient. So I figure it maybe you." The nurse explained, as I thought to myself who could that be, but somehow I couldn't register a clue.

"Can you sit here for a minute while I take that call?"

"Sure." She said, as I went out, and down the hall. The phone was sitting at the nurse's station alone.

"Hello." I said.

"Hello, how did you sleep my doll?" The heavy voice on the other end of the phone asked.

"Dale I really needed that."

"I know; you fell asleep in my arms while I was talking to you, so I knew you were tired." He said, as I felt a since of embarrassment but yet a bit comfortable.

"What time did you leave?"

"About 630am." He responded.

"Oh."

"Well can I come back, and be your company today." He asked.

"Today I'm going home and Jasi's going to stay."

"Would it be ok, if I could take you and your daughter out to dinner and a movie?" He asked.

"No thanks." I said.

"Would you ever give up?"

"What." I said playing dumb.

"Why you can't give me a chance?"

"It's not the point of giving you a chance, I've just got so much going on. Now next week I'll be more than glad to accept your invitations." I said as I felt myself getting upset, because that's where I wanted to be, but so much was in my way that I couldn't say anything but no or later.

"Chocolate I know you have to go back to the room with your aunt, but I really would like to spend a little time with you." He said.

"Ok, I'll call you a little later, when Jasi comes to relieve me." I said, placing the receiver on the hook and left the nurse's station with a smile. Walking back into the room.

"Ms. Jackson, we don't need your mom catching pneumonia. You want to make sure she stays warm." The nurse said while putting Ms. Minnie socks back on her feet.

"Yes." I answered with a smile, getting use to the name Ms. Jackson.

Jasi finally made it to the hospital. She couldn't come up, because she bought Brianna, and there were no kids under fourteen allowed. I met Jasi, down at the elevator, and couldn't tell her much about last night. Especially while Brianna in our present, she might start asking me questions or telling my business as well.

"Chocolate, I left the other kids over Peggy house" Jasi said.

"Good that gives me enough time to go by my house, enjoy a bath and get more clothes for Shanice and I. Now give me the keys." I said reaching my hands out and so ready to walk out into the fresh air.

"Oh Chocolate, I didn't drive your car, the back tire is flat." She said jerking her shoulders up.

"Damn man, this just isn't my week."

"I just was telling you that tire was low. You know you can use my car, it's parked down by the emergency entrance." Jasi said, as Brianna continued grabbing her dress.

"What's up Brianna baby?" I asked stepping up closer engrossed by her attention.

"Jasi, won't buy me no balloon." Brianna said, twirling her thumbs.

"Why she won't buy that baby no balloon?"

"Her say I was bad!"

"Were you bad Brianna?"

"Yeah." Brianna said, gazing her big eyes at Jasi.

"I thought you were going to be good for Nanny?" I asked her.

"Julian made me mad!"

"Ok Brianna we will talk about getting the balloon." I said, knowing I was going to get that balloon for her. As Jasi handed over the keys and a Chico-stick that she supposed to have bought me yesterday.

"Ok Jasi. There are no cell phones, and no phone in the room, so consider the nurses at the desk your friend. Oh and be sure to call the nurse before leaving anywhere, they'll be glad to assist you, by the way her name is Karen." I explained.

"Chocolate who do you think you're talking to." Jasi asked, smiling.

"Just refreshing you're nursing skills baby." I responded.

"Bye Chocolate, and good luck with those hyper ass kids!" Jasi said entering the elevator, while Brianna and I exited the hospital.

Brianna buckled up in the back seat. I turned the music up and stopped at the first store I saw.

"Brianna, you can't have ice cream in the car. Get some chips." I said.

Brianna, ran to the back of the store, and came back with a bag of 25cent chips and a tray of cookies.

"Brianna you can't eat all that; you are going to get sick." I said.

"Uh-uh!" she responded.

"How about you put the cookies back."

"No, these Nanny cookies." She said, as tears filled my eyes. These kids really loved their grandmother; I just couldn't resist buying all her junk. Riding down the road I found myself praying to god that Ms. Minnie would make a full recovery. Not only would she be missed, but also she would destroy three precious little hearts that's too young to try and understand. Which death to us adults is something we can't even get used to, let alone understand?

"Who make you cry?" Brianna asked, rising up pepping in the front.

"Nobody Brianna."

"Uh Ah! Why that's on your face?" Brianna asked, pointing at a tear almost smeared away.

"Something blew in my eye Brianna." I said trying to change her mind.

"Oh!" Brianna said, as she sat back in the seat.

"Turn the radio up Chocolate?" Brianna asked.

"What is it you want to hear?" I asked, looking in the compartment seeing Jay-Z, Trina, and Juvenile CD`s.

"Turn it up." She asked again. I turned the music up a touch and Bow-Wow was already playing. I guess Jasi must had her listening to this on the way to the hospital, because she certainly can't listen to these in the compartment.

"Brianna, can you please give me my purse?" I asked.

"Where your purse?" She asked, shoving chips in her mouth.

"Look on the floor."

"Thank you baby, now sit back for me." I asked in a baby sounding voice.

I tried to phone Dale, after ringing a couple of times I ended the call without a message. Soon after; my phone went to ringing back.

"Hello."

"How are you?" Dale asked.

"I'm ok, and you." I responded.

"I'm doing pretty good, just was taking a swim this nice Spring day." Dale said.

"It is hot, and yes we are only in Spring." I responded.

"Would you and the kids care to join me?" He asked. I almost forgot about last night, being I was so emotional obviously I told him I was babysitting my friends kids until she come back out of town.

"I can't swim, neither the kids."

"That's fine, I'll teach them. We can have Barbeque chicken, and ribs. Let the kids enjoy themselves and you relieve some of that stress." Dale said, without giving me a chance to think.

"Dale!" I called.

"Come on beautiful, please at least let me spend some time with you."

"Ok Dale."

"When are you coming?" He eagerly asked.

"I have to get our clothes together." I said, trying to buy me enough time to pamper myself.

"Maybe an hour?" Dale asked.

"Have you forgot, its four kids and me alone. About 3:30." I said adjusting the time by two hours.

"3:30 will be fine, I'll just run down to the grocery store, and pick up a few packages." He said quickly mapping out his plans.

"Ok Dale I'll see you soon."

"Later." He responded, ending the call.

I really would like to know what's up with this Dale dude. He dresses really elegant, has no kids, and no woman. You know I need not to question my faith; maybe he's the one for me.

"Hello." A voice answered.

"Peggy, what's up?" I said catching the voice.

"Nothing."

"Where's the kids?" I asked.

"Out back on the trampoline. How's Ms. Minnie."

"She's still in a coma." I ungratefully said.

"How's Becky?"

"She's holding up ok."

"I can imagine how she feels, out in the middle of nowhere, can't get home, and then have to depend on someone getting you there in time. Shit I'll take a raft or a life jacket back if it was my mama."

"Peggy you crazy. Have your kids came back yet?"

"Girl let me tell you about that bastard! Can you believe he didn't let the kids call or he won't answer his phone?"

"Why Clive do stupid shit like that?"

"Girl don't worry about it, I'm taking that bitch back to court cause this just aint going to work." She said, as she had already won the divorce and child support case with results which totally ripped through his bank account and gave her possession of his million dollar home back out in the Redlands.

Brianna had fallen asleep by the time I reached home. Looking in the rear view mirror, Brianna's look had favored Becky so much until it looked like she had no other partner involved. Good thing she was asleep, I could just leave her in the car with the air on, and go get Shanice and I clothing. Looking on the caller ID, noticing Chuck had called at least ten times. But baby boy just don't know, he's about to get his pussy took. Why he thinking it's cool playing with me, and telling me his capabilities that he just can't seem to follow up on. He was on my voicemail Tuesday when his tired ass left my damn house Saturday, with hugs, kisses and sincere words. Now he just wants to call with that threatening shit. You ladies know what I mean that `*beat you mad*' attitude. Chucks good at it, lay up all night then come calling three days later like he mad with the world, cause I'm living and haven't seen or called him and it's not like he was looking or calling neither. That's just some of the slick junk he try to do, I can't take a smart ass dumb nigga. Yeah, that's what you call them so smart until they dumb.

I hurried and packed a few things, stopped and picked the kids up from Peggy and followed the directions as Dale instructed me, without missing a single turn nor a sign.

GETTING TO KNOW HIM

There were beautiful Crystal chandeliers, and elegant drapes that hung from the tall circular ceilings to the shiny waxed marble floors. He stood his dull handsome body before me with a look of compassion and mutual admiration.

"Hey sweetie, where's the kids?" Dale asked.

"Hey there! They are waiting in the car." I said.

"Excuse me." He said and through the door he went. I observed his strong legs as he slightly jogged wearing the same colors I wore, except for his Miami Dolphin visor. Dale wore beige and brown swim polo shorts, I could tell how the pants creased in his ass that he didn't have on any under wear. It appeared through my x-ray vision he had a decent bubbled ass, thick muscular legs that matched his broad back and shoulders. This brother was definitely nothing to play with; he is to be dealt with for sure. He opened the driver side, making wrestling noises while the kids laughed out. The car was jumping, from the kids juggling around from him. Half his body was through the window and his arms were invisible from him tickling the ones in reach. I went out and started taking the bags from the trunk; he immediately stopped, and diverted his attention on carrying the big gym bag into the house. Dale ran ahead of me and the kids ran behind him, as if they been knew him when in fact they just met him less than five minutes ago. He placed the bag upon the eight-seated aquarium dining table, where the kids were amazed at the huge fishes, corals and ships that decorated the salt water aquarium. Which looked as if only kings and queens sat here for lunch only. It didn't take long before the loud noise ringed from corner to corner, the kids chased him and he chased them.

I funneled my way to the bathroom in his big lavish home. As I walked through the beautiful white and gold french doors. There was a sea shell shaped Jacuzzi and sink, his and hers toilet, looked to be made from glass not white porcelain, which is a very sexy elegant look just to sit your ass on it. Decorated towels were centered neatly and potpourri filled the air.

As I began to undress on the sand felt tiles I could hear the kids making so much noise, if I didn't hear Dales I would have been embarrassed at the lack of home training they were showing. Just by the noise alone I could tell that Dale is a family man, I guess he has scored a few points for that without even knowing.

My bikini shorts hugged around my 25-inch waist, and 38 inch hips while the skinny bikini top was filled with dark luscious skin that flowed to the rimming of my 34b cups. I hung my Capri's and shirt on the wooden hangers that were in an empty closet for guest. Pulled on my gym shorts over the bikini bottom, and headed down the hallway in silence.

Dale stood at the bar, filling a pale with ice.

"Where are the kids?" I asked. Being it was so quiet all of a sudden.

"In my favorite place." He responded.

"Dale, and where is that?" I was hoping he didn't say the pool, and we both were standing here.

"In the movie room." I paused for a minute adjusting to the size of his house to have a movie room.

"Can you take me there please?" I asked, as he placed the pale on the bar. Jokingly he grabbed my hand spinning me in the opposite direction, before coming to a complete stop.

"I think I have a winner!" Dale said looking me in my eyes, I didn't bother to answer, because I had the same thoughts for myself. I was yet wishing that my question could be answered. Knowing how my feelings be getting caught up, and that seems to be the road its taking.

His eyes were between my breast, and hands were placed around my waist.

"You are so beautiful, let alone sexy." He said standing so manly before me.

"Thank you."

"You don't have to thank me. I just want you to know." I became instantly shy; I couldn't say another word. He stood starring into my eyes as I stared into his while wanting to kiss him so bad.

"What do I have to do to be yours?" Dale suddenly stumbled over a question, I was never able to answer all my dating years, and I didn't want to feel foolish or sound like I wanted the world.

"Just be yourself." I responded, finding that answer dumb founded.

"Baby trust me, believe in me, and that should not be hard. You in my corner and I'm in yours, that's an undefeated team." Dale said, as he walked behind me and we walked stair to stair, as I felt his warmth breath around my neck.

The view of his house from the circular mahogany stairwell was very gorgeous. From this view you could see the whole setting in sight, from the matching marble floors, to the crystal chandeliers. He led me to a curved hallway.

"I'm sorry, I hadn't showed you around or let you meet my lady Sasha." He said, as we went around another hall that connected to another part of the house. There was a pool table that sat in the center of the room, colorful deco and chaise loungers, surrounded by colorful deco painted walls. Adjacent was the movie room where the kids were knocked out sleeping. He turned the volume down low on what seemed to be some sort of Disney movie.

"I keep my Disney movies on deck." He added as I thought that was rather charming.

"That's cool my favorite is Little Mermaid."

"Got that one too, but my favorite is Beauty and the beast." He replied with a grin.

"I never saw that one before."

"Looks like a movie date next." He added just before shutting the door and opening the next.

"This is my pad. I spend all of my nights here alone; in this great California king size bed. Maybe soon I wouldn't be alone? What do you think Chocolate?" Dale asked looking at me mysteriously, as I laughed that question away, and continued to expect MY house to be. Where what would have been walls in any other house, were only windows surrounded in Dales room, which made the back yard basically in his room...

His bathroom was a big opened space, with black marble everywhere. I could go on but I'm sure you can imagine his exquisite stylish taste.

After walking through all eight of the bedrooms, we went down to the patio. The water was so sparkling and clean, I wanted to just jump in but instead we walked to the back to meet Sasha.

"Dale I really don't like dogs, but if she's little it might be ok."

"Baby, I'll be your shinning knight, and will be sure to protect you from anything that comes your way." He said in a joking goofy tone.

"Sasha!" Dale yelled and she came running on the first call. Jumping all over Dale and me. We didn't stay long, the sun was beaming and the wind didn't seem to blow, so he insisted we went back in.

I sat on one of the lounge chairs, blowing floats and balls when all at once a sad feeling came over me. I knew I was missing Becky.

"Dale can I use your phone?" I asked.

"Yes, it's on the sofa table, by the stairs." He pointed.

"Excuse me." I said as I walked over to the phone wanting to call Becky but I knew she wouldn't answer her phone so I called Jasi instead.

"General hospital, how may I direct your call?" The operator asked.

"Yes, may I have room 321b?"

"One moment please." She responded, placing me on hold for at least a minute. Dale walked through the sliding glass doors, making faces as I just smiled hoping he wouldn't come over and sit by me. Knowing I was up to a little of gossiping and maybe even crying, but he just passed right by carrying a bottle of Mojo sauce towards the other kitchen outside by the pool. I sat silently waiting on Jasi to interrupt the annoying elevator music.

"Hello." Jasi answered.

"Hey what's going on?" I asked.

"She's still asleep." Jasi answered.

"Did Becky call?"

"I thought you were her, she called at least 6 times already."

"That's good at least she's showing concern. Was she still upset?"

"She sounded sad, and she asked about the kids, and where were you. Oh Dr. Boer came by today. He said he would be back by tomorrow to run more test between the hours of 11am till 1pm." Jasi explained.

"I don't know about that busy ass doctor. If he's not trying something new he's limiting his time, she needs a caring doctor."

"That's true, but there's nothing you can do, it's all in Becky hands." Jasi said.

"That's true too but." I said, trying to think of more to say.

"Mona, why are you worrying yourself so much? Everything is going to be alright."

"The way you say that, you act like it's for certain."

"Mona, just pray that everything will be alright. Cause nothing is for certain not a healthy life itself."

"You are right, well let me go and I'll talk with you later." I said with a dragging voice as if there was still more questions I might would have.

"Mona what time is it?" Jasi asked in a different tone lightening me up a little especially using my real name and she knew I didn't like it not one bit.

"No, the question is when the fuck you started calling me Mona like that?"

"All girl please that's your damn name! Hell I want to see you being called Chocolate when you on a cane, ass shriveled up, tits hanging and no damn teeth." Jasi said laughing.

"That's how you gone look, girl! Its 4:36 though." I said, as it registered on the oven clock.

"What time should I be back?" I asked.

"Child please, just know I have school in the morning."

"I'll be there about 8 tonight."

"No go ahead and relax, just pick me up in the morning, get some rest. You better not forget when Becky come home you do have a job to go back to. You may not be tired but your body is." Jasi said, starting to sound like my mama.

"Ok mama, I'll see you in the morning." I said joking, as she sucked her teeth which made a smack noise.

"Ok, what the kids doing, because I sure don't hear them." Jasi asked, trying to keep me on the phone.

"They are in the movie room." I responded.

"What! A movie room!"

"We over Dale house."

"OH OH I know we have to talk tonight, call me." Jasi said sounding hilarious, and sarcastic as she whispered into the phone.

"Ok, bye Jasi."

"Bye." She said, as a smile arched over my face.

"What did you do to those kids? Dale asked walking down the stairwell."

"Nothing, why?"

"Because they up there snoring away." He said, reaching the last step as I couldn't keep my eyes off of him. Everything I mean everything was in place. His chest from the glance shinned and appeared swollen as if he was just lifting a few weights, and his muscles jumped while he walked in my direction. I promise you I was stunned, couldn't move think or say a word because handsome had done caught my undivided attention and just slung me on the floor.

"Would you like to take a swim?" He asked.

"Yes, in a minute." As I got up and walked back towards the bathroom.

"How's Ms. Minnie?" He asked as I smiled because he not only just listened to my problems last night but he cared and remembered to ask about something that was troubled in my life, which really plays a big part in my heart. You know most men wouldn't care if cancer was eating your Mama whole body and it was tearing you apart, they'd still tend to forget to just ask you how she doing or what you feeling like.

"She's not any better." I responded, as the smile erased off my face I turned the knob and entered the bathroom.

"I hope she gets better." He said, yelling loud enough so I could hear him in the bathroom. "Chocolate, you don't have to bring any towels, I have towels out by the pool." He added.

"I'll be there soon."

Standing in the mirror, sucking in the little belly I did have, as I pulled off those gym shorts and turned to look at my phatt ass, making sure everything would at least be in place or look as firm as possible. Good thing I don't have any cellulites, and the few stretch marks Shanice left me wasn't bad at all. I turned to the left, which looked very slim and just right, but when I turned to the front my thighs had looked bigger than usual for some reason. Any hoots thanks to this tiny waist, this itty bitty thigh gap that drew itself between my legs, and my flat stomach which gave me all the curves like a true coke classic bottle in high definition. I pulled my cheese that was cuffed in my right cheek, traced my sideburns with water to take away those kinky curls that had rolled up, and lastly I tightened my braids unto a ponytail ensuring I had every new growth pulled as tight as possible. I looked back at myself once again before exiting, and this time everything looked just how I needed it. Hair pulled so tight I was looking like a Japanese by the eyes, skin was nice and rejuvenated, tits sitting right and bikini top tied tight enough to make them look like they were in one of those fifty dollar IPEX bras from Victoria Secret. I walked out of the bathroom in a normal pace, but before I knew it my hips were prancing as if I instantly hit an automatic buttoned. By the time I made it to the end of what should've been a runway there was no judges or crowds and Dale was not their neither. I took off my slippers and seated myself on the wall of the pool, waving my feet through the cold water which looked like it should've been hot from the beaming sun.

Unexpectedly the television that was installed in the ceiling came on. I looked to see if I saw anyone, but there was no one. The previews began to play; it didn't take long before I could recognize the movie. I smiled from ear to ear; it was my favorite movie *Pretty Woman*. I knew he was somewhere doing this. I turned to look, and there he was with a vase of beautiful yellow roses, two champagne glasses and a bowl of strawberries. My heart was beating twice as fast, my insides were hot as fire, my hands started to shake, and my nerves rattled like a wino. He just really had what it takes to keep me going, and the thing about it is I love flowers yellow ones at that and I don't think I told him, maybe it was his intuition or intriguing ways that lead him right all this time.

"Oh Dale how sweet."

"All for a sweet woman." He said placing the tray on the leopard-decorated bar. My intentions were to pour me a drink, however these reflects of mines did another. I hugged him so tight, unaware back down memory lane. He did things I wished Shanice father would have done, but in a thoughtful way and not because I asked, or because I was mad.

"Ah, that's what I'm talking about, stop being so tight up with me. Put your guards down baby." He said kissing me on my forehead. Dam I thought to myself he racking up some points today, and I am about to lose count.

"Would you like to have some Moet?" He asked, grabbing a strawberry from the bowl placing it to my mouth and I sucked on it as if I was on a porn flick, as his eyes went into a dream site. I pulled away rubbing my tongue across my lips, allowing him the chance to pour the champagne.

We sat back on a single lounge chair, me in between his legs sipping on Moet and eating strawberries, while enjoying conversations about our past.

"We were lovers since our freshman year of high school, but things really became serious after we both left for college." Dale said, as the cool air was breezing and the sun was setting.

"Did you both go to the same college?" I asked taking another sip.

"No, but we had planned on going to the same college, just when she won a scholarship for Georgia state university in journalism and I went to More house. I still have that poem she wrote which changed a lot for her and I." Dale said, as he got quiet for a second or two.

"What was your major?"

"I was majoring in science, and couldn't adjust to all the math, so then I left her and went to the Army where I was stationed in Jacksonville. I was about twenty."

"How long were you in the army?" I asked as I arched my eyebrows mentally noting happy faces to my inside 'checklist' of a *good man.*

"For ten years." He said, taking another drink.

"Wow, over those ten years did you get to go see her." I asked, as he got comfortable in the chair, and I prepared to be nosey as usual.

"The first year I was in the Army, she failed badly in health. She couldn't handle the stages of her sickness alone anymore, so she was forced to leave school. I went to see her every chance I could. After a while I couldn't bare myself to see her suffer any longer. I've always stayed in contact, sent letters, cards, and flowers sealed with real love, hurting love, and pain, cause there was nothing I could do." He said sounding a bit pitiful, as I wanted to learn more.

"Was she mad, about you stop seeing her? I asked and mad at myself, what the hell I was trying to do make the man feel guilty.

"No Patty was a real respectable person. Who understood rather than questioned or blamed? Everyone knew I loved her deeply. I could only stand back and watch." The conversation began to get real sad and so did Dales voice. I never experience a close death so I really couldn't relate or make the best out of the conversation.

"I had to learn, there are something's that you would face in life alone. Where there are no spectators, or crowds allowed, and that time had come for Patty. That's when she learned to put matters aside and build a relationship with God. He is the only one that could make matters right." He said as I could feel my body rise from him taking a deep breath and a swallow before he continued. "During the desert storm, which then had made it my fourth year, I was getting ready to be discharged for reserves. Just then she had died. I then stayed for additional six years, I didn't want to go home knowing she wouldn't be there anymore." You could tell by the tone of Dale's voice that he cared for her and the hurt remains in his heart, as he took another breath and a big swallow this time. "I was crushed. It was a terrible let down, knowing this was the one woman who I wanted to spend my life with for eternity and then through all my suffering, and pain, sympathy easily snatched that love away from me forever. I felt as though she shared her life with me and that she left me all alone. I found myself at times, acting as if everything's cool, you know just like a clown putting on a show. But nobody really did know but I, how I ached for her love and cried for her disappearance just by the very thought of it." He continued as his voice escalated in sad whispers and hurting words he didn't sound like he wanted to say as he continued. "Then as the time went by, I was put into all kind of camps for different training's receiving stripes and tassels, including a purple heart I then came out of the army and here I am as a bounty hunter searching from country to country." Dale said, completing his story which gave him all the points in the world to be with me tonight and days to come.

"Do you like your job Dale?" I asked glad to overcome the sad conversation.

"Yes, it's good in the way, I travel a lot, but love my job when I'm in Bahamas." Dale said, reaching down for the bottle of Moet.

"Is it really nice there?" I asked.

"I take it as if you never been?" Dale said, turning me around by my shoulders, looking me in my face as if this was somewhere I needed to go or should have already went.

"No." I said, with a shameful murky look.

"It's beautiful, the people are so friendly, and it's just really a nice island for vacationing." Dale said, as he swallowed the end of his third glass of Moet. I reached over and got a float from the pool and hit him over the head. He couldn't do anything but laugh.

"Alright I'll get you." He said as his voice dragged the words out.

Moments later when I was obviously not paying attention he bear hugged me and we both fell right over into the water. When I came to shore, he took his gentle hands and wiped the water from my face, pulled my hair from my eyes, and landed a soft quick kiss on my lips like we both were afraid. He looked at me and I looked at him, then we kissed again, but this time it was so romantic. You couldn't hear anything but the burner on the grill, and the beautiful canary birds chirping with the wind. I started kissing Dale as if I learned a new game; that I didn't want to stop. However we both were influenced with Moet, not drunk or anything just feeling a bit loose as a quick thought came over me. *Mona you don't want to do anything you're going to regret*. I suddenly came over that thought and our tongues released.

"I want you to be my girl." He asked as we floated around the pool. I hated myself sometimes from being so bashful. I couldn't and didn't say anything. I only rest my head on his shoulders as he continued to ask who and what questions that I really couldn't answer.

"What's wrong baby?" I ignored him and kept my head pinned to his chest as we floated about.

"Look at me?" Dale asked. I slowly lifted my head up, and he had quickly stolen a kiss.

"Would you like to race?"

"Dale, you know I don't know how to swim!"

"Ok, I'll teach you." He said, waving his arms for me to float to him.

"Wait let me go up and check on the kids." I said, starting to float my way to the edge of the pool.

"No I'll go, just pour me another drink." Dale suggested, as he swims his way out. He bounced out of the pool as the water was dripping from his muscular body. His shorts was stuck in his ass and my gosh he had a hard on that told me he was bigger than any man I ever had. Dale got a towel from the shelf and wrapped it around his waist and went inside. I took a few breaths and floated around the water before getting out.

The marble stairwell caused a noise of two sets of bare feet instead of one, I knew one of the kids were up. I hurried and poured his drink this time Remmy and coke, but of course pouring more coke than anything. I didn't want him to be real drunk although tipsy was ok. Looking through the glass doors, Corey came dragging his hands around the handle of the stairwell, and Dale was now partially dry.

"We have a guest, Corey Cold!" Dale yelled as he entered the patio. He came over to the bar and rested his hand on my shoulders with a gentle kiss. Just the littlest touch from him, made my pussy jump and I most certainly don't want to accommodate him with this just yet. Perhaps my company is well enough.

"Good Morning Corey!" I said sarcastically.

"Chocolate, I'm hungry." Corey responded without a smile.

"Corey do you want all the ribs or just two?" Dale asked. Corey started to laugh knowing it was a joke by the size Dale held with the huge fork.

"After Dale seated Corey to the table along with his plate, he walked around to the bar drinking his coke filled Remmy which didn't seem to bother him. Soon as he placed his glass on the bar I jumped on his back and we both fell in the water. I couldn't see Corey when we fell in, but when I came up you could hear him laughing so loud. Minutes later Dale came charging at me.

"Stop Dale, please stop!" I yelled as he picked me up out of the water, attempting to slam me. Corey was cheering on the side, that Dale should slam me back in the water.

"Cannonball!" Corey screamed as he held one knee just before landing in the water which splashed everywhere. Dale instantly stopped as we watched Corey swim to us like a fish and started jumping all over Dale, which he quickly joined the game and began throwing Corey all around the pool? The two of them was having so much fun that I left Dale and Corey in the pool and started for the bathroom, finding Shanice and the rest walking downstairs. There was no need for me to change, being these three were up, I minus well float along the pool while they enjoy.

"Hey yall!" Dale yelled from the pool.

"Oh I want to swim with Corey!" Julian said with much excitement.

"You have to eat first."

"I'm not hungry." Julian answered.

"I know because you see all that water over there."

"Shanice you ready to eat?" I asked.

"No mommy I want to get in the pool."

"Me two." Brianna added.

"And me three!" Julian said, as he started to pull his shorts off revealing his swim trunks. So I gave in and the girls quickly pulled off their clothes almost pulling their bikini bottom down in such a hurry. Julian leaped in the pool and so did the girls, but me I had to ease back in cause the water to me was freezing. Everyone begin to enjoy themselves, especially Brianna and Shanice trying to see who could hold their breathe the longest. Then we started playing games such as Frisbee, tag, race, and even chicken fight. It was a good thing we were in the inside because day had quickly turned into night.

The kids started getting out one by one and getting dress. Shanice and Brianna were the last ones to get out; their little hands were all wrinkled. I took Brianna's shorts and finished dressing her, and Dale did the same for Shanice. Before leaving, Dale must have asked me a thousand times can he join me at the hospital.

"Chocolate, can I come along, or are you all going to leave me here by myself." Dale asked, looking lavish yet lonely.

It was not nothing wrong with him, I just felt I didn't need to be getting use to someone I know little about.

"Dale I am very tired, and I don't feel it would be fair for you to come and watch me sleep." I said, hoping this was a good excuse.

"I watched you sleep last night, and that was so pleasant."

"And I am so sorry, for acting out too." I said, as he placed his hands over my mouth.

"No there is nothing to be sorry about, I really appreciated last night, and I must say again I loved your poem, your stylish ways, your tears, and definitely I loved your time today." Dale said, standing as meaningful and priceless while the kids ran up the stairs for their shoes.

"So can I come and watch you sleep?" Dale asked again, more determined than he was black. "I truly considered that as a privilege." He added.

"Dale I just wouldn't feel comfortable." I said, trying to sound hard yet sweet.

"Ok Chocolate I'll take your word, if you could return a favor." Dale said, as the kids stood to the door, twigging their toes in the flappers they wore.

"Replace a favor?" I said wondering.

"Would you promise to spend the whole day with me tomorrow?" He asked folding his arms across his chest.

"Dale I don't know I will try." I said, as we started walking towards the car and the kids were ahead of us.

If you were a driver by passing the street, you would have no idea that we weren't a family of six. He scrapped the girls in the back with Julian, and placed his Dolphin visor over Corey head for keeps. Dale walked over to the driver side before I could get in.

"I really enjoyed your company." He said, as I gazed in his eyes, quickly over his nose, shyly at his milk white teeth, and smile, knowingly this was all just so perfect for me.

"I enjoyed myself too." I said, as he took my hands in his.

"You are very special and I can tell already." He added, as the kids begin to make noise.

"Hey yall folks in here what's wrong?" Dale asked.

"Julian messing with me!" Brianna shouted in the mix of tears.

"Alright Dale I'll see you." I said quickly before the kids got all loud and embarrassing.

"Julian man I thought big brothers supposed to love their little sisters." Dale said as Julian looked with a respectable smile. I stood with my arms folded across my chest observing Dale through the tinted back window.

"They alright." Dale added as he threw his arms around me.

"Well I have to go now." I eagerly said as I couldn't take it anymore looking at the two of us in the window which was a beautiful combination already.

"Behave yourself and take care of the kids, and don't forget to tuck them tight and pass this kiss to all of them." He said, kissing me on my forehead.

"Good night Dale."

"Goodnight beautiful." He said as he watched me pull out of the driveway, and the kids screamed and waved good-bye.

I drove to mama house happier than a pig in shit. I really enjoyed being around him, he is so sweet, and I can tell it wouldn't be hard to get use to him neither. I can't wait until Becky comes home I have so much to tell her. Although Jasi is waiting for the story, I can't express the real feelings. She thinks liking someone takes months and to kiss or fuck them is years. So instead I rather tell Becky because I know she's going to relate and trip off this type of shit and really crack jokes about me acting like some white chick named 'Heather'.

"Shanice go tell grandma to come to the door." I asked Shanice, as she leaped from the beamer and the kids followed. Shanice stood banging and kicking the door, as if this was some type of emergency. I know my mama was going to slap her face because Shanice knows better than that, I sat and said not a word. Within seconds the porch light came on and the door opened.

"Mama is not here!" Peggy yelled, and not letting the kids through.

"Peggy, can you please watch them till I drop Jasi her car off at the hospital and she will be back to get them."

"Hell nah I'm going somewhere!" She yelled still standing with her foot propped in the door.

"Please it will only take about thirty minutes." I begged.

"Don't play with me Chocolate. I'm dead ass serious, we going out tonight." She added, as she moved her leg and the kids went pushing through the door.

"You and who going out?" I questioned.

"Me and Rachel, but she just left and went to the store to get me some thread. So yall better have your ass back less than thirty minutes if not you better believe they ass will be here by their selves!"

"Alright man!" I said. Pulling off, and observing the blinking phone, that I had left on vibrate.

"Hello." I said, without noticing the caller id.

"What's up Miss Lady?" I paused trying to recognize this familiar voice.

"Why haven't you been calling me?" he asked, and that was the tip that revealed his excuse filled ass.

"Please Chuck! Is that the excuse why you haven't been calling me?" I asked.

"Come on woman don't start that arguing, why I have to always here that silly shit!" He said in a serious yet aggressive tone which provoked me to act bark like a dog.

"You know my god damn name, and don't woman me nigga! Besides I care motherfuckin less about arguing with your punk ass! You called me, I aint call you!"

"Hold up hold up!" He tried to interrupt, but I was full of fuel and ready to burn through his ass.

"Hold up my ass, you listen here partner! Don't be calling my damn phone like you mad with the damn world! Knowing good damn well you pretending to be mad cause I aint call you in a couple of days, or let the truth be told is it because you think I know about your little bitch in the grove!" I said, leaving him in silence about two seconds before saying another word.

"What's up Mona, what's wrong?" He asked. I wanted to say I just had so much fuckin fun, and your want to be mad ass getting on my last damn nerves.

"Nothing Chuck." I said, not even trying to make the situation no better. To be honest it really didn't even matter if he had called today, I could deal with him not ever calling at all, and he hasn't been on my mind.

"Well where are you headed?" He asked.

"To the hospital."

"Are you sick?" Chuck asked.

"No, I'm going to see Becky mama."

"What's wrong with Ms., Minnie?" Chuck asked.

"She has problems with her diabetes." I was answering each question with an attitude and not a care in the world.

"Oh will she be alright."

"Yes she'll be ok."

"What time is visiting hours over?" He asked, trying to ease his way in cause he knew the way I was cursing I was hot as a fire cracker.

"At 9:00"

"Hell it's almost 9 now."

"I know, I'm just taking Becky something to eat."

"You cooked today." Chuck immediately asked as I quickly tried to think of the next lie in order to keep him from Becky business, but at the same time I was fucking myself up.

"No mama cooked something for Becky, which she promised she would bake."

"What time are you going home?" He asked as I knew from here forward I didn't want nothing else to do with him.

"A little later." Another quick lie rolled from my tongue.

"Well can I wait up for you?" Chuck asked, and I wasn't too thrilled about him not now anyway. Actually he picked the wrong time to have wanted some of this pussy and he was most certainly going about it the wrong way.

"No chuck, I don't know what I'm going to be doing later." I switched, with a nonchalant attitude that was lashing and didn't care what part of his feelings I was about to fuck up.

"So you just don't have any time for me right?" In such an inconsequent voice, as if he were going to get his way by pretending to be mad. Before I knew it, I couldn't bear to hold my filthy tongue anymore.

"It's not that I don't have time for you! When you come when you want to, leave when you tired, and all that beat me mad shit. Hell nah I have no time for yo ass!" I said, as my body became overheated with anger, and my mind registered that nothing good came from his mouth, not even how are you doing. I just hated everything he said, I instantly hated him for every single thing even the way he ate my pussy which use to feel so good to me.

"Mona, why are you acting up like this?" He asked seriously as if I had not had a reason.

"Fuck you Chuck, and leave me the hell alone!" I screamed into the phone with frustration, powering my phone off and sliding it into my huge purse, as I pulled into a vacant parking spot. I took a deep breath, smiled about earlier today, before getting out of the car.

"Nice car." Someone said, as I hit the alarm switch walking to the entrance of the hospital.

"Thank you." I responded to a young difficult looking guy who was walking behind me carrying a basket of colorful ripe fruit.

"Would you like one?" He asked staring at me.

"No thanks, but thank you anyway." I responded.

"Are you visiting someone tonight?" he asked.

"Yes, my friends' mother." I answered, wondering what this corny motherfucker wanted.

"I'm here visiting my friend, they were supposed to release us yesterday, but the doctor didn't approve." He explained as we both walked up to the elevators while he continued running his mouth, luckily I was going to the third floor and he pushed the fifth for him.

"I'm sorry, I was just running out the mouth. What is your name girlfriend?" He asked in a girlie manner.

"Mona, but you can call me Chocolate." I said, slightly exiting the elevator.

"Well I'm Tyrone, they call me T." He said, with a big smile.

"I hope to see you around!" T yelled out as the elevator door shut.

I entered the room across from the elevator, Jasi was kicked back in the chair, watching American Idol as Fantasia was just about to take the stage. Bobbing out with a green dress and a smile that spelled FRIENDLY.

"What's up chic?"

"Sh sh" Jasi said, putting her index finger over her lips. It appeared that I was distracting her especially while Fantasia was on stage. I tipped on around the bed, Ms. Minnie laid there; her face was so clean with such a pleasant glow from the grease that shinned her two corn roll braids which Jasi neatly braided. She wore a gown that fitted as if she dressed and laid herself down. I sat at the foot of the bed, waiting patiently to tell Jasi a bit about Dale. Unfortunately right here and now Fantasia had the country's attention the way she sat on the floor singing '*summertime*' so sassy, easy, and perfect.

"You go girl!" Jasi yelled as Fantasia let out a note which led goose bumps up and down my spine.

"Damn Fantasia aint no joke!" I added.

"I know that's a bad sister right there." Jasi said grabbing her cell phone to vote, just when I felt a sudden movement that came from behind me. I jumped and so did Jasi. When I turned to look at what I thought touched me; it was Ms. Minnie lying there with her eyes wide-awake.

"Thank you Jesus!" I screamed as her eyes rolled around in space, as if this was her first day in the world. I was so happy, I ran down to get the nurse and called my mama immediately, I even called Dale. Although Becky was the most important person to contact, unfortunately I only received a full voice mail; I didn't bother about getting upset again.

I was just too happy that I could see the white of her eyes. The nurses and doctor came along with a phlebotomist in their footsteps. They took many tubes of blood and an instant sugar test.

"Hello Ms. Jackson." I nearly answered, but he was talking to the real Ms. Jackson and not Ms. Anderson, she didn't respond but she coughed.

"How are you Ms. Jackson?" The doctor asked.

"I'm tired." Ms. Minnie answered, we all looked at each other with puzzled faces, sleeping for five days is enough to have someone scared to sleep I thought to myself, as the doctor prepared to take her blood pressure.

"Ms. Jackson your pressure is just as good as an eighteen-year-old woman." He said laughing which prompt Ms. Minnie to return a pleasant smiled.

"Yes it most certainly is 104/69 and that's great." Nurse Karen said, reading the pressure gage as the Doctor gathered and scribbled on the paper work and they all headed out.

"How are you feeling Ms. Minnie?" I asked standing on the side of her bed.

"Where's Becky, Chocolate?" She asked, looking up in my eyes. Although Ms. Minnie was abandoned, she was still concerned about her daughter. That's one thing; I can truly say there is no one like mama. No matter how harsh we may be at times, they still continue to love you without a doubt. Now that's a mama.

"She will be home tomorrow morning." I responded.

"What is today? Ms. Minnie asked as she squeezed her eyes for a deep thought.

"Today's Saturday." Jasi responded, rocking in the chair.

"So where is my babies, if the two of you are here?" Ms. Minnie asked as she lifted herself straight up in the bed and began talking, like the old Ms. Minnie I used to know years ago.

"Mama has the kids."

"Call her up on that phone Chocolate, let me speak to my good friend." Ms. Minnie said.

"She was up here all day yesterday." I added.

"She was? Isn't that something I just was sleeping huh?" Ms. Minnie asked and started grinning and clapping her hands together.

"Ms. Minnie I can't call from this room. They don't have a phone in here."

"Well you or rabbit ain't got no cellular phone?"

"You can't use them in here, something about their monitors."

"Oh, well then I guess I'll see at her tomorrow." Ms. Minnie said, just when Dr. Bower and the nurse came back into the room.

"Ok Ms. Minnie I'm going to stop by and see you tomorrow, you have any questions for me?"

"No, but I sure is ready to get home." Ms. Minnie replied in her southern accent.

"I know you are, but you will be getting home. I mean sooner than I thought you would." The Dr. said laughing, as he scribbled some orders and passed them to the nurse.

"Well Dr. Bower all these test you ordering for me I appreciate it, but when I going home?"

"As soon as I get your results I would let you know." The Dr. responded, as Ms. Minnie positioned her legs to come out of bed.

"No No No!" Dr. Bower nervously, putting his hands to block her, and slamming the clip board on the pullout table.

"Ms. Jackson Ms. Jackson, are you aware, you were in a coma for the past five days. Meaning no food, liquids, just feeding through your IV. You may feel 16, but you're as weak as a newborn baby. Allow yourself sometime, maybe dinner tonight and a good breakfast in the morning, then you'll find your strength gradually coming along. Until then Ms. Jackson, let your daughter do your walking, she's been great these past days. Had you looking and smelling lovely, each time I stopped by." Dr. Bower said, smiling looking over at the both of us.

"Yes Dr. but I have to be able to go to the bathroom." Ms. Minnie added, without realizing the doctor's comment.

"Alright Ms. Jackson, I'll get you a portable stool, where you don't have to walk a distance." The doctor said, while ignoring the fact that there was a catheter already inserted in her just before he exited the room.

Ms. Minnie went on and on about our childhood days, she was well rested and happy by the tone of her voice. The conversations she voiced about bought on the attention that she is missing Becky. We sat for hours laughing and talking. Jasi gathered her items and searched around for her keys as Ms. Minnie continued on talking.

"Where's the keys Chocolate? Peggy is going to kill you."

"Girl please, Mama done made it there already" I responded back, and pointing to the shelf where the keys sat. She stood in the middle of the floor pushing her sheet, charger and bowl into her designer hand bag,

"Rabbit baby." Ms. Minnie called.

"Yes Mam?" Jasi answered.

"Are you expecting?" Ms. Minnie surprisingly asked.

"Nah! Ms. Minnie this got to be the dress." Jasi said running her hands up and down her belly. "Not me!" She added.

"Ok now." Ms. Minnie said, and turned towards the TV.

By the looks of the letter F's that decorated the Fendi dress not only made Jasi look pregnant but she also appeared to have gotten a bit wide overnight. Jasi kissed Ms. Minnie good night, as she walked towards the door.

"Excuse me, I'm going to walk Jasi down to her car, please don't get out of bed." I politely said.

"Ok Baby take your time, I aint going nowhere." Ms. Minnie said, as Jasi pulled the door open.

"I'm sorry!" Jasi said as the nurse was walking in at the same time.

"No that's ok." The nurse looked in my direction "There's a phone call for you.

"Thank you." I responded as Karen took a seat and Jasi and I proceeded to leave the room.

"Hello."

"Hey what's up?" The voice of my dear friend asked.

"Hey Becky baby what's up!" I happily asked, as I felt a load of stress free released from me.

"Hey freak!" Jasi screamed realizing it was Becky.

"Who's that?" Becky asked.

"Bitch, Jasi!" I said, to her as if she had forgotten the voice.

"Tell my sugar I said what's going on?" Becky said. "How sweet the two of you are there with my mama. You guys make me feel terrible." Becky added.

"No don't feel sorry, let this be a lesson learned, and always help your mama first."

"How she doing today?" Becky asked taking a deep breath.

"Girl her pressure reads like a sixteen year old, and she talking just as much as a two year old. Now you tell me how's she doing?" I asked.

"Really! I called all day and Jasi was telling me she still was asleep."

"She was but about one hour ago she woke up. The Dr. ordered a couple of test before he releases her, so I'm not sure of what's next." I explained.

"There's nothing physically wrong with her is it?"

"Why? Would you be ashamed of her?" I asked in questionable.

"Cause Chocolate I want to know, she is in fact my mama." Becky said, as if she just had realized it.

"Oh she is, damn I thought you forgot her." I bluntly said, as Jasi shoved my shoulders and shook her head saying no don't tell Becky that. "No Becky her diabetes escalated while being under treatment. She did not have a stroke doe doe." I said laughing and so was Jasi.

"Shut up I'm just asking! Can she talk on the phone?" Becky asked.

"No, but I think tomorrow she will be in a room, with a phone." I said.

"She misses your raggedy ass too!" Jasi added as she rudely grabbed the phone, which was something we were used to being rude towards each other at times.

"Becky child all she talked about was when we were little girls, she even went way back when you fell from Ms. Cure mango tree and broke both of your legs." Becky explained with laughter.

"Hey are both of you staying there tonight?" Becky asked. Jasi nearly hitting me in the eye with the phone while passing it back to me.

"Hello." I answered.

"Why she had to pass you the phone! I was asking Jasi was the both of you staying the night with mama?" Becky asked.

"No, I just was walking Jasi downstairs, so she can go and pick the kids up then go home."

"Oh ok, well let me speak with her again." Becky asked as I handed Jasi the phone.

"What's up baby!" Jasi said, immediately as she put the receiver to her ear, and laughed as they talked on. Jasi and Becky couldn't even shop together without a fight, but that still didn't damage their friendship. "Alright I'll meet you at the Port 530 in the morning." Jasi said, handing me back the phone.

"Are you staying there tonight Chocolate?" Becky asked.

"Yes Mam I am!"

"I thank you Chocolate, I really do. If I never find a real friend again, I can honestly say I had one in you." Becky said sounding serious.

"Well what is wrong with you being that friend to me? Just do what I ask you to, nah actually do what's expected of you."

"What's that chocolate?"

"Being a daughter to your mother and a mother to your children."

"What the hell you talking about Chocolate, I am just that."

"Yeah we all know you are, but being a daughter and a mother, takes good quality time, and that need to be your first priority. I'm telling you, once she leaves this world there will never be another like mama ***"They don't have second chances"*** Becky.

"Yeah Mona your right, I'm not going out of town anymore, now is the time she really needs me the most."

"You are most certainly right about that Becky, trust me if you need her you know she'll be there for you. And you know that, it wouldn't be a place she wants to go, or a person she would care to see, if it takes her away from you." I said, as Jasi paced the floor looking at the pictures that hung aside the walls.

"Ok Chocolate I'll be there in the morning." She said.

"Alright Becky."

"Tell Jasi to bring my kids."

"No! It would be damp from the morning air, you'll been done give them children pneumonia."

"Damn I don't think they walking." Becky added.

"No they aint, but they not coming out that early either." I said in demand.

"Chocolate, alright just kiss my mama for me."

"Yes I will. Bye!" I said ending the call as I noticed Jasi face; she had water in her eyes. Jasi had always felt sad any time it had something to do with motherly love. I guess the little lecture I gave Becky was a reminder to Jasi, especially when I stressed there's not another one like Mama.

"Jasi are you alright?" I asked.

"I'm ok, just thinking of mama." Jasi said, as I thought I had advice for every situation, but when it dealt with Mom and Dad there was nothing I could say. Death is something we all have to deal with, just that we can't get comfortable with the unexpected loss of someone we dearly love. Even if they had a thousand years on this earth we still wouldn't be ready for someone we love to die. Just the thought of my Dad or Mama dying brings tears to my eyes. I placed my hand around her back as she cried all the way to her car.

"Will you be alright Jasi?"

"Yeah, I just feel good when I cry about her. I'll be alright though."

"Are you sure? I can call Bruce if you want me to."

"No, that's ok I'll make it." She said wiping the tears from her eyes, as they refused and continued to fall.

"Go ahead, I'm alright!" Jasi said getting into her car with a smile that didn't match her eyes right now. I really didn't want to leave her but she insist that I did.

A NEW BEGINNING

The sun shined bright Sunday morning, through the room window. Ms. Minnie was awake, with the blinds pulled back eating plain corn flakes and a spotted ripe banana.

"Good morning." I said squinting my face from the sun raves.

"Good Morning, have some breakfast?" Ms. Minnie asked.

"No thank you."

"Well I ordered you some breakfast anyway while you were sleeping."

"I'll eat a little later Ms. Minnie."

"Ok. I sure hope these doctors let me go home today. I sure would to join Pearl at some yard sales."

I knew sooner or later she would be asking about Becky, but I sure didn't want to tell her she called last night and I didn't let her talk. Being the phone was down the hall, and the doctor already said he didn't want her out of bed. If I would have told her she might thought she could have ran to the nurse's station. She had already been up using the bathroom and noticeably opened the blinds.

"You sure you aint hungry gal?" Ms. Minnie asked as I stood up folding the sheet that I used to keep me warm last night.

"Um fixin to eat, soon as I finish folding this." I replied due to her insistency.

"I wonder how come Becky hasn't called me yet?" Ms. Minnie asked as the thought just popped out of my head.

"She called yesterday, but you were still asleep."

"Even though that fool run the streets like her head cut off, I sure miss my baby, when she don't call or stop by. She really needs to put them streets down now, the world aint like it used to be. It's so easy to get into trouble and hard as the devil getting out, but Becky just doesn't see that. I'm more than sure she doesn't go out of town like that all the time with no job for nothing. Lord Jesus I leave her in your hands, only you know best." Ms. Minnie said, getting so emotional as if she knew more than I did.

"I just pray that Becky is around to watch her kids grow." Ms. Minnie said continuing on with my undivided attention. "I never raised Becky to run the streets, and I know I didn't raise her in a Baptist church, but I did taught her the bible, and consequences that life can bring. I know I can't change her personality, but life itself will bring changes you have to accept. We all got to stand before the lord someday and that is something each one of us has to face." Ms. Minnie said wiping the tears from her eyes. "You know back when I was a young girl, my Mama told me this story one day, and I wasn't able to understand until I've gotten older. She once said, "Why settle for only two corners of a triangle when you can have it all?" Which was the man, his love, the lord, and I can assure you the notes in heaven will sing in harmony instead of your soul burning in the pits of hell." Ms. Minnie said, as I thought to myself maybe she knew all the while the things we do, yet we still flock around with these little girl smiles on, while acting as precious dolls. "It's not like I'm trying to drag her through the church! I'm trying to show her the best way to go. Once the gate is open every man and woman is accountable for their own sins. It's not like I can say `Lord Jesus, Becky is my daughter. By me having faith in him, believing in him, knowing he died for our sins, and I paid my offerings every Sunday, will not be enough for her to pass through his gates." Ms. Minnie had started a little church in here; she said things that made me reach for the bible.

"You grabbing that book is a start, you need to get into someone's church and pray as well."

"Yes Mam." I said, ashamed cause I couldn't admit that I was a member already, but I know and believe in the lord just the same. Soon the nurse walked in.

"Excuse me ladies, the phone is for you Mona." Good thing the nurse didn't call me Ms. Jackson, because I know Ms. Minnie would've corrected her this morning. I quickly headed to the nurses station soon as she pulled up a chair and started conversation with Ms. Minnie.

"Hello." I said.

"Hey baby, how are you?" Dale asked.

"I'm ok and yourself."

"I somehow got a cold, I guess in and out the air yesterday. I'm on my way to the pharmacy now to pick up something for it." Dale said.

"Yeah, that sure will give you a cold, you should try Sudafed. It works well for me."

"Yeah, Chocolate I think I'll pick some up. What are you going to be doing later?" He asked.

"Just resting up from this long week unfortunately, I have to return back to work tomorrow."

"Oh oo, are you ready?"

"No not at all." I said.

"Well I was wondering if you aren't too tired, will you like to go on a bike ride or maybe catch the sunset?" Dale asked, as I began to clearly blush.

"Let me get a little rest, then according on how I feel I'll let you know."

"That will work." Dale agreed.

One thing I realized about Dale, he always had something for us to do. That's my kind of ideal man, never bored, adventurous, and always determined. Loves to spend time, knows the lord, dresses nice, smells good, perfect job, and to top it all off he's single with no kids I just can't express that to myself enough. I can't beat this with a steal bat.

"Yesterday, when you all left, I thought about you a lot." Dale claimed.

"Do you mind sharing your thoughts?" I sarcastically asked.

"Yes, I thought about what good challenge I'm up against, physically and mentally. A strong black, smart, beautiful, intelligent, independent, ambitious young lady you are." He said, describing me better than I could do for myself.

"Well, that's nice to know. I'll tell you what, if I'm that good, I've always been told working together we can conquer and challenge almost anything." I boldly said.

"Yeah, you are absolutely right, but the thing is. Are you ready to put me on your team?" As Dale asked, I wanted to scream "*YEAH*", with a little boy to hold the house down when you're not there.

"Dale, you sure know what it takes to butter me up huh."

"No, it just seems as if I've known you for years. You're more than that sexy woman I met the other day, you have a personality that shines and a mentality to set and change a person." Dale said things that weakened my knees, and left me in silence often not only today.

"You don't have to sit puzzled baby, I want to be yours and all yours?" Knowing I wanted to be the same all of his, but this pride of mine never engaged or agreed to the right scenario.

"Dale you are too sweet." I said and meaning every word, letter and vowel.

"Only the inside, can reveal the outside. Can I see you later?" He asked.

"Once I get a little rest I'm going to call you." I said.

"Ok baby."

"Bye Dale." I said and began to walk away as I had everyone's attention as if it was just a love scene even the sissy from last night, with the fruit basket.

"Hello gorgeous?" He said.

"Hi how are you." I said, putting on a friendly smile.

"I'm ok, just came here to get some ice chips from the vender."

"Oh ok." I said, trying to walk away, he turned into my direction and started rattling from his mouth.

"How is your friend's mother doing?" He questioned.

"She's doing well, how about your friend?"

"He's finally in the process of getting discharged now."

"Oh that's great." I said sounding so phony, and wondering why the hell he's getting ice if their going home. Maybe that was his excuse to hold a conversation. The icemaker was right down from Ms. Minnie room, as he stopped to put ice, I didn't want to be rude so I stopped as if we were together.

"Chocolate do you live around here?" Tyrone asked.

"Yes, I live in the Cutler Ridge area, and you."

"I live in Weston." He responded. I took another look at this stringy little s-curl wearing; tan skinned guy who was dressed in Gucci sandals, tight fitted jeans and a simple T-shirt. He sure didn't look like he was from that area. He just wasn't attractive at all, although he was very friendly, but that's in every queer and that's what I think he is.

He placed the bucket under the vendor, which didn't exchange any ice.

"Do you mind walking with me to the cafeteria?" He asked.

"Sure." I said, knowing I didn't want to go but I was determined to see if he was a queer or what.

We got on the elevator, as he continued to talk.

"I am so tired of this hospital, my guy friend was on a motorcycle accident about two weeks ago on his birthday and shall I mention on his brand new Ducati which landed us here ever since! I'm so glad we finally get to go home. I've been from work to here, not even a decent bath, only a wash off and then go." T said.

"Tell me about it, I hope neither one of us has to return." I responded, as we steeped in the doorway of the cafeteria.

"Excuse me Mama, may I have a taste of ice." Tyrone asked positioning his lips in a way that made his veins arch up in his neck as the cashier looked at him in a strange way.

"How do you think, I will look with long braids?" Tyrone asked and was serious.

I couldn't picture corn rolls or long plats on him because I really thought he was already ugly but he somehow had class in which I liked.

"What kind of braids are you talking about Tyrone?"

"T is the name queen!" He said in such a ladies tone, which signified and let you know he was indeed gay.

"You know those plats Janet Jackson wore on Poetic Justice.

"Oh ok." I said, but still puzzled of how he would look changing from this wet shit to exotic braids.

"Those are nice." I said, but most definitely not on him.

"What you think? But picture it plum." T said, as I was really about to scream "*HELL FUCKING NO!"*

"Chocolate you didn't answer me." He said, as I thought oh my god, he was dead serious. I wonder what he would look like with plum synthetic hair.

"I think black would be better, they sure last longer." I said as the lady brought the bucket filled with ice, and handed it to him.

"Thank you love!" T said with a very quick smile, then grabbed a banana from a near fruit basket and walked over to the first available cashier.

"That will be 35 cents sir." The cashier said, as he dug into his little Louis Vuitton pouch and pulled out a crispy dollar bill and walked away. I walked along in silence observing everything that I had apparently missed when I first met him. He had the sexiest walk for a bad ass chick to sport. Now I really didn't know how to address this boy/girl.

"Where do you work Chocolate?" T asked.

"I work at Motorola." I responded.

"Oh isn't that a coincidence. I'm a marketing manager for AT&T, what position you hold."

"I started first as a clarity programmer and now I'm an executive secretary."

"Wow Ms. Thing, that's a very important position."

"It's ok, and easy but stressful at times!" I said.

"Ditto about my job too child!" T defiantly had feminine ways about him, but it wasn't so bad. He wasn't loud, but very professional when it came to his conversations. I was so anxious to ask him do he have a lover, but was afraid to get that personal. When I really didn't know him like that. He slid his thin self into the elevator as it partially began to close.

"Do you have a pen, so we can exchange numbers before I leave today?" He asked.

"No, I don't but I'll get one from the nurse's station." I replied, as we exited the elevator.

"May I borrow your pen please?" I asked a nurse that was passing by.

"Yes you may." The nurse replied removing the pen from her jacket, as I quickly jotted my numbers down and T's also.

"Thank you." I said to the nurse, as she continued on her duty.

"This is my home, and this is my cell. Stay in touch now, maybe we can do lunch or shopping."

"Ok that's cool." I added.

"Alright, I'll call you. I'm going to head back to the room before a warrant is issued for my arrest." T said amongst a hideous laugh which made me laugh as well. "Chow girlfriend!" T then added in Portuguese just before stepping back into the elevator.

"Bye." I said walking away. He had a super personality and a style of his own. He now seemed to be someone I could eat out and most definitely shop with. But clubbing and inquiring on my personal business, I don't think we have nothing in common.

I was gone quite a while, but by the time I reached the room you could hear laughter loud in the hall. Mama, Ms. Minnie, Pearl and Ms. Cure was going on and on with their conversation.

"Hello Chocolate." Ms. Minnie said sitting up in a chair with the bed made up, as if no one ever slept in it.

"Hello everyone." I responded as Mama and Ms. Cure spoke back.

"Chocolate, I have good news for you." Ms. Minnie said.

"Whats that." I asked.

"I go home on Monday." Ms. Minnie announced.

"That's good! Becky will be here in the morning." I said, as they ignored me as if I was speaking about someone they didn't know.

Monday morning had finally made it here. I must have awakened at least three times last night, so anxious to see my girl who supposed to have been here yesterday. Ms. Minnie was still asleep, but of course all through the night she was awake each time I opened my eyes. 7:00am had come and gone, I went to the nurse's station to see if I had a phone call from one of my girls. While I was resting on the counter, just before I was going to make a call, a visitor was apparently coming through the elevator. Reflections of balloons and scented flowers covered the person's identity. Shortly the vent blew the balloons and there was Becky and Jasi coming through the doors. I was so happy to have seen Becky, until I never really knew how much I loved her until that instant. She's never left us more than three days; we always had been like three peas in a pod.

"What's up burger?" Becky said, placing the waving balloons, roses, teddy bear, and fruit basket down on the nurse's counter. We hugged each other so tight until the strength of our arms explained how much we missed each other.

"Damn Becky why you so dark?" I asked standing back observing her pecan skin that was slightly darker than usual.

"Bitch out in the ocean for 7 days, I wouldn't think tan would be my complexion, besides I still aint black as you." Becky said, as Jasi and she went to laughing.

"Baby Black is Beautiful, Unique, Essence, and Modern."

"Whatever!" The both looked at each other and said at the same time.

We had to spark up a little debate, which was the main founder of our friendship, while the nurses stood there laughing.

"Where's my mom room?" Becky asked picking up the fruit basket, and Jasi with the balloons and flowers. Being that we had the nurse's attention, they just stared, and I pinched Becky big mouth ass.

"What the hell you pinched me for?" Becky asked as we walked down the hall.

"Have you forgotten I was you for the past six days, and all of them call me Ms. Jackson don't make me face these people knowing I was lying? Cause they do know she only had one daughter."

"Hell I didn't know. Fuck it I'm here now!" Becky said, grabbing the strings that dangled in Jasi hand as I pushed the room door open.

"I miss you, I miss you, I love you, I love you" Becky said singing, as Ms. Minnie stretched her arms out for a welcoming hug.

"I miss you too baby!" Ms. Minnie said in tears. Jasi picked the basket up from the edge of the bed and placed it in the window, I gave Jasi the eye and we both headed out the door, leaving our disappearance unexplained. I know Ms. Minnie wouldn't mind, she has far too much to tell Becky.

"What!" Jasi said, as we stood outside the room door.

"Let's go, and let them talk. You know Ms. Minnie and Becky has enough to talk about and with us present it wouldn't be a family matter." I said, as we walked along the hall. "You know Ms. Minnie didn't like the fact, Becky left on something this important."

"Oh well, I didn't mind it one bit." Jasi replied as we walked on.

"Well it wasn't an experience I enjoyed." I said as the elevator doors slid open and there was T and this handsome light skinned guy in a wheelchair. T was carrying the bags on his shoulder, and the guy had a radio on his lap with the balloons scrapped around his chair, as if they were coming from the maternity ward.

"Hello again!" T said with a smile, as the guy in the chair didn't part his lips nor did he move a muscle.

"Hey, how are you?" I said.

"I'm doing ok."

"And how are you?" T asked looking at Jasi.

"I'm ok!" Jasi replied, without another word.

I thought you were going home yesterday." I said striking up a conversation, embarrassed by Jasi nonchalant attitude.

"Oh my gosh, yesterday was just pure chaos with his so busy doctor!" He replied.

"So are you ladies heading out to breakfast?" T asked.

"No, we finally going home too." I added, as the elevator came to a stop. Jasi struck out as if she was in a walkathon.

"I'm sorry we haven't quite met, but my name is Safari." The man in the chair said, finally coming to life.

"And I'm Chocolate, nice to meet you." I said, giving him a handshake. His hands were as soft as mines, his hair was full of silky black curls, and his complexion was compatible with a Georgia peach without a bruise or bump. I took it, as if he wanted to bring himself to my attention because I wasn't studying his jealous ass, T must be his man. He continued to stare as T ran his mouth to us. I tried to get away, but he still was in my path. I didn't know which way to go, but the alarm signaled me in the right direction as Jasi pressed it.

"Ok T and Sofairo." I said to break off in my direction.

"It is SA-FEAR!" He pronounced it in a way that made his lips spread almost wider than his face.

"Anyways!" I said especially to this sophisticated ass punk "I'll see you gentlemen, maybe another day." Calling them the last name on earth they may ever want to be.

"Ok take it easy, and keep up that body girl! You just showing it all today." I laughed and pranced on to the car.

"You mean to tell me you know those dick in the booty ass men?" Jasi said, immediately to me as soon as I arched to sit in the car and we both went to laughing.

"No actually, I met T Saturday, on my way to the room. Now that other cutie I don't know him, but I think that's his lover." I said.

"Yuck now that's disgusting, I might would have gave cutie a lil chance. He's too handsome for that, but the other one he has no choice."

"I don't know about that Jasi!" I said laughing, and Jasi hit her horn as we drove pass. T was putting the wheelchair in a cute silver big body Audi A8L bent all over, like he was ready for someone to pump him.

"Now it don't take all that." Jasi said, giving me a hellish look.

"Girl leave them ladies alone." I said laughing.

"Anyway's, what's up for today?" Jasi asked.

"I'm going to go see Dale a little later."

"Well what's up with this Dale guy?" Jasi asked.

"What's up with him?" I repeated and took a big deep breath. "I really don't know myself. I know one thing from the browse of it, I think we may work at something, he seems to be what I'm looking for."

"Oh, your mean ass know what you want from a man now?"

"You damn right! I always knew." I said looking at Jasi. "Saturday when we went to his house. We talked for the longest, cooked, played, and swam, I really enjoyed myself."

"Ms. Dreamer, is that when you told me the kids were in the movie room?"

"Yes child, his house is just that big he has an inside theatre!"

"I know you wasn't doing the nasty already bitch!" Jasi said looking at me cocked eyed and lips perched like Tweety bird.

"Trust me Jasi I aint gone lie, I wanted it so bad girl. To tell you the truth out of temptation and Moet it was a real HARD ass challenge to accomplish."

"So do you like him?"

"I think so Jasi, he's pretty cool, body made to be loved, skin so dark. Our arms, tummy's, waist, weight, feet, fingers, curves, all fit like we were pieces of the same puzzle." I said closing my eyes and licking my lips.

"That's one thing about an Aquarius, you can steal their love." Jasi said.

"Shut the hell up, what the fuck being an Aquarius has to do with anything you zodiac bitch!"

"Nothing nothing, end it end it here" Jasi said laughing so hard.

"I guess I'll go home to my mind-numbing ass Bruce."

"Well, let's go and get a bite to eat, I'm hungry." I mentioned.

"Yeah, we can do that. IHOP it is." Jasi said.

"Yeah."

We stopped at IHOP and it seemed like we talked forever, until Dale called the phone.

"Sh Sh," I said with my index finger over my lip.

"Hello." I answered.

"Hello baby." Dale said.

"Hey how are you!" I asked; excitedly as if I didn't know it was him.

"I'm just fine, leaving the gym"

"Oh Ok, Jasi and I having breakfast over at IHOP."

"Which one?"

"Near the hospital."

"Is it too late for me to join you all?"

"Actually I'm on the last pancake baby."

"How about dinner?" He asked skipping lunch, but I didn't question.

"Sure what time?"

"Is 700pm. Ok?"

"Sure that will be fine."

"So see you then."

"Ok later." I said ending the call, smiling and dancing in my chair at the same time.

"Damn, if he make you blush and kick your feet like that, what's gone happen if he lick the putty cat? You might just kill the man!"

"Jasi it's not just the conversation. He just seems like that man I once knew, but all my dislikes about that one man is a dream come true! You feel me?"

"No I don't feel you gangsta!" Jasi said with a weird face.

"One thing about Dale, He likes to spend time and you know that's a shell for a relationship"

"You right, but chocolate don't sit there and let trust takes place, you most definitely gone be gone for real."

"I know but he seems so perfect."

"Come on Chocolate don't overdo Dale now, you acting like that hoe named Heather again."

"I'm serious." I said.

"Even if he do have a main lady and you find out later down the line will you still be with him?"

"Now where that came from Jasi, I told you he aint got nobody."

"Honey Child, that's what they all say! Until that one day you get that phone call talking about they found your number in their husband cell or he slack up on coming around."

"Well guess what, I aint gone settle for two. I think I can be a hell of a wife, in or out of bed, and I cover all my bases so he wouldn't need a team of women."

"Answer your phone or press end crazy?" Jasi asked.

"That's Chuck wasted ass calling." I said, looking down at the phone.

"Oh wee, I know you aint ignoring Mr. Pussy caresser?" Jasi asked, as we went walking towards the car.

"That's the only damn thing he's good at." I said tapping the window.

"Wait now! The doors were already open, pay attention get your mind off Chuck." Jasi said joking.

"Are you going to your mama house and, pick the kids up?"

"No, drop me off home please, so I can find someone to fix my tire." I said, as Jasi drove on.

"I was just playing the other day; it aint anything wrong with your tire." Jasi said as she drove me on home.

I felt so relieved; there was finally a blank space on my agenda. I jumped in my non-air conditioned Honda and drove down to the Garden store and bought a few Arizona Sun flowers for my patio, and next I visited the grocery store for a few cleaning products. I had felt the need to do a little spring-cleaning, although "summer" is in and I mean SUMMER. I just had to do something constructive besides chuck smacking on my pussy or Shanice running me crazy until 7:00pm. By the time I made it home Chuck continued to call not only my cell but my house phone as well until I was forced to turn my ringer off. I truly believe he was going nuts right now. I continued cleaning, and definitely leaving Shanice room for last. If I wouldn't have known better I would have thought I was in *toys r us* on Christmas Eve, but of course by the time I was finished it looked like one of the kids room on the cover of a *Jcpenny home* catalog and so did her bathroom.

I was exhausted from all the cleaning, I just stretched myself across the circular zebra couch in the living area, and pine sol was in the mist of the air. Before I knew it I had fell asleep on the big cushy pillows that decorated the sofa.

I had awakened about 8:30, the caller ID green light was blinking and my cell phone had 10 missed calls. Five belonged to Chuck whom I thought should have forgot my number, one from mama, two from Dale, and two from Becky at the hospital.

I called the hospital first and checked the condition of Ms. Minnie they said she was in stable condition. I didn't ask them for Becky because I really didn't have time to catch up on the day's gossip we missed, I'll just wait until the morning. I called my mama back, but the phone just rang and rang. So I decided to check my voicemail in the event mama left a message. Of course the first person I heard on the voicemail was Chuck. I didn't even let the entire message play before erasing it. Next it was Dale which said for me to give him a call when I received his message. Must I tell you I listened to everything even the dead air before saving his message? I ended the voicemail call, and dialed Dale number with a huge smile scattered across my face without a bit of effort.

"Hey boo?" He answered.

"Hey what's up?"

"You tell me."

"I'm so sorry I fell asleep, and just waking up a few minutes ago." I explained.

"That's ok, you needed that. Are you ready for dinner?"

"Yes."

"Anything in particular?" He asked.

"Not really."

"Ok I'll think of something. Are you going to tell me where do you live, or are you going to meet me somewhere?" Dale asked, as it registered to me this wasn't my man yet and he has never once been to my house.

"No Dale I don't care to drive. I live off the express way on 216th St. in San Reno Towers."

"Is that Cutler Ridge Chocolate."

"Yes, right behind the clinic."

"O yes I know exactly where you are talking about."

"But just give me an hour before leaving your house." I asked, giving myself time to get ready.

"Ok, my black Nubian Queen?" He called.

I jumped in the shower and lavender my body with Sweet Pea shower gel. After showering I lotion down with Christian Dior Jadore and squirted a bit on my wrist, behind the ear, and of course around my neck. My wonder bra was a perfect supporter for these little tits. They sat as if they were paying close attention; I slid on the sheer aqua shirt that was beaded with silver rhinestones that read BEBE along with a pair of stretchy tight snack skin slacks. The colors Royal blue, Dark blue and Aqua that fitted like glue to me, my hips, butt and thighs all stood in place which sent the pants in a dimension look. Along with my rhinestone belt that obvious matched the logo on the shirt, and my glass slippers which the heal was filled with silver beads. I had my little handbag that looked so sexy around my wrist, which only held my lipstick, eyeliner, powders sponge and keys.

I sprayed my hair with oil sheen, wrapped it in a bun, and stuck a sharp rhinestone chopstick to hold it in place. I walked by the mirror, and I had to stop. I looked from the side which looked nice, I turned to the back and the front they all fell in the same category. I looked very classy and not a bit scampi, I paced the floor a while loosening the corners of my shoes, until the security called the house phone.

"Hello" I answered.

"Hello Mona, you have a visitor named Dale." He said.

"Ok, you can let him in." I replied as I was completely ready. I grabbed my little handbag from the table and re-sprayed myself for a fresher smell of Jadore.

I walked outside and down the stairs, Dale was standing outside a silver box porch. I was delighted by his hot car, but of course didn't want to look surprised, as I turned in the opposite direction and locked my house door. I walked down the stairs inspecting his dress code, with a glimpse. He wore dark brown leather paints, a Cleveland jersey with orange and brown pony tennis shoes.

"You look nice Chocolate." Dale said, as he stepped back to take a better look.

"Thank you." Walking to the car as a gentlemen would do he opened the door; and waited until I sat down gently before shutting it. Leather interior had fumed the car; I positioned myself comfortably as he walked around and took his seat. Now that I had a better view I truly exercised it, he had one hand on the gear stick as I observed his nails which were clean and neatly trimmed. His pinky finger wore a ring full of dazzling diamonds and the base was designed with crackling baguettes. His goatee was trimmed neatly as if it was drawn and shaded in, along with his sharp Philly haircut.

"Mona I'm going to be leaving town next week." Dale said placing his hands on my thigh.

"Oh really! Where are you going?" I asked with a smile.

"I have to finish a case in the Bahamas." He said, looking through the rear view mirror switching gears and lanes.

"So when are you coming back?"

"Actually it's a trial, so it will not be until a verdict is reached, which can take two days or even weeks." He said, as I thought maybe this isn't the one for me, especially if he leaves and don't know when he comes back.

"Would you and your daughter like to come along?" He asked, as I paused to recruit a way to respond to this thoughtful lovely idea.

"No, I'll be going back to work tomorrow." I answered, knowing I was trying to come up with an excuse to extend my vacation instead splitting it for the New Orleans trip.

"What days are you off?" Dale questioned.

"The weekends."

"What time do you go to work?"

"I work Monday through Friday from nine to five." I boringly replied.

"Well if I'm there for the weekend, will you come?" Dale asked.

"I'll have to see." I said.

"Because I can just purchase your tickets before I leave, so that you can catch a flight Friday night and return late Sunday evening."

"Can I get back to you with that, tomorrow." I asked.

"Yes, but I sure would love if you can come and stay over a couple of days." He said smiling as I sat trying to figure, if I had any extra PTO time, sick time, or anything. I was thinking hard about calling in saying I had death in the family for three bereavement days; but the devil so busy I better let that excuse float on. We pulled into this beautiful restaurant decorated with lights, palm trees, big windows and chandeliers as if I had seen this on the cover of a magazine once before.

The valet guys were dress to perfect, and trimmed neatly, clean cuts, all suits creased and shoes shined.

"Good evening Mam." One of the guys said, as he opened the door, and politely handed me his hand. In an elegant manner he presented me to Dale and we proceeded into this immaculate restaurant. The waitress was neatly dressed with hosiery, and the waiters wore slacks, ties, and stylish tuxedo jackets. Behind the mahogany podium, there was a beautiful Thai woman.

"Good evening madam and sir, thank you for choosing Houston's for your selection this evening." She was not only beautiful, but she was professional and kind.

"Would there be any more joining." She asked.

"No Mam." Dale responded in a respectful manner.

"This way please." She said, walking ahead. I observed every inch of this place, there were no booth seats, rugs, or boosters in the isle, not even light bulbs or ceiling tiles. The inside was just as gorgeous as the outside. The chandeliers glistened, the tables wore white silk linen, and crystal bowls which were filed with water and a lighted floated candle for romantic dinners throughout the restaurant. We were directed to a table where we had our own privacy, and a view of a beautiful mini bridge over a large body of water, which was lined with lights and palm trees, alongside pathways there were beautiful tikki huts. I was mesmerized, but now could relate to the pictures in the magazines of how beautiful the magic city really is. He held my hands while we sat down; I was too shy to look him in his face or even to grip his hand back. Instead I wrapped my feet around the legs of the chair so they wouldn't cause any more distraction that would involve me to look or talk any more than I already was. Luckily the waitress walked up, she wasn't like the one from the door, she was dressed a little different, but still appeared to look nice.

"Good evening my name is Tammy, and I'm your waitress this evening."

"Good evening." We responded just when the waitress placed two thick pamphlets with tassels hanging from them on the table which were menus.

"Would you like a drink, or appetizers while you look over the menu?" The waitress asked.

"Yes Mam, I would like to have a bottle of champagne." Dale responded.

"Anything different Madam?" the waitress turned and looked at me with a smile. She had the whitest teeth and a wide smile.

"I'll have a hot tea." I responded.

"Ok, how about an appetizer? Our favorite is the stuffed crabs dipped in our house sautéed sauce, and homemade cheader bay buns, along with our specialty finest honey butter."

"I'll have cheddar buns." I immediately said, while I could feel him start to stare.

"Whole wheat or white?"

"Wheat please." I said, trying not to look nervous or shy.

"Thank you." As the waitress turned away, I purposely licked my lips in slow motion, and turned towards him. His eyes landed flat on my breast, I took up the menu, and so did he. The menu had every casserole, pasta & seafood you could possibly think of. He gently locked his legs around mines and finally eye-to-eye contact took place. I sat there looking at him and him looking at me; I smiled and placed one leg in his lap. He rubbed under the legs of my pants back and forth, as we both continued to look through the menu.

"Do you like oysters Chocolate?"

"No I really don't care for seafood, with the only exception of crabs and conch."

"I'm sorry baby would you like to eat somewhere else?" He asked grabbing my hands, and giving them a kiss.

"No Dale, there is more on this outrageous menu besides seafood." I said just when the waitress, came up with this beautiful platter a lined with bread and dip in the middle, and another waitress walked up with two champagne glasses, a pale which buried the bottle champagne under ice, a few strawberries and a small hot tea for me. I guess she bought two glasses, meaning I will look better holding this one instead of this.

"Would you care to place your order now?" The waitress asked as she placed the buns on the table.

"Yes indeed." Dale said, rubbing his tummy.

"And what may be your order today sir?"

"I'd like a baked sea bass with garnish rice.

"And for the soup?" she asked.

"I'll have clam chowder, along with an order of clams." Yuck, I hope he's not expecting a conversation or a kiss on the way home, I thought to myself.

"Any salads or vegetables sir?" The waitress asked, I wonder was she trying to feed a horse or a human. But I guess in these big to do restaurants you got to go home full for the prices I'm seeing.

"No thank you, that will be all for me." Dale said as she turned to me.

"I think I'll have the Chicken breast wrapped with turkey, p-low rice and for my vegetables I'd also like Broccoli and for the soup I'll have mushroom and onion." I was astonished by his actions; he got real sexy, and started to rub his finger around each of my toes and along the side. I paused and just looked as he continued to read the menu, as if this wasn't his intention. Maybe it was just the romance in him. I am and always were so insecure about my feet that I never let a man play with them not even Lionel. Lord knows we did everything from skinny-dipping to sixty-nine, I mean I never let him touch my feet not even when Twee gives me a fresh pedicure.

"Would that complete your order?" Tammy asked.

"Yes Mam." I responded, as Dale finally looked up and let go of my pinky toe.

"Ok enjoy, your champagne and I'll be back shortly." The waitress said, and pulled two long candles wrapped in a fancy wrapping, with the most gorgeous holders. They were Angels which you stick the candle through their hands. She even had a nice silver flicker to start the flame.

"Excuse me baby." Dale asked, removing my feet off his lap unto the floor as I slid my feet back into my heels.

"I have to use the restroom." Dale said, taking my hands into his with another delighted kiss, and tonight Remy Martin plays no part. I'd rather have the tongue I wanted to say, but instead I smiled and he walked to the bathroom. I looked around, and everyone was casually dressed and coupled off. I sipped my tea and read the fancy writings along the walls.

"Excuse me madam." Dale asked. By the time I placed the glass down Dale was in my face, with a single yellow rose. I smiled and wondered why is he so sweet, and I hope not for a piece of pussy, cause he was trying too hard. Dale then leaned over and gave me a kiss before sitting down.

"Mona can you share a little champagne with me?"

"Yes just a little." I said, taking a deep breath. Dale popped the bottle and poured him and me champagne.

"To the most gratifying, immaculate, wonderful, charming, black woman."

I was blushing, so hard that I knew you could see I was smiling on the outside. He truly surprises me in everything he does, without a doubt he keeps me smiling.

"You are more than beautiful and amazing to me." Dale claimed, as a young black guy walked up, bowed on his knees, taking my hand, and started to sing *"you are more than beautiful" By* Brian McKnight. About six waitresses with candles came along also, which all looked to have been perfectly planned without me noticing at a thing. I was so overwhelmed with happiness, I gave Dale a hug and kiss my while sitting on his lap watching the guy sing his heart out, even the other couples had turned to watch. The longer the guy held the last note the crowd began to clap, as he bowed and vanished behind a little door. It all had happened just that fast. Not only did he stole the show, but he dam sight stole my heart tonight. I liked him and I could feel it coming on.

"You are more than beautiful to me Mona." Dale said in a secured voice, as I took my seat.

"C'mon Mona...Lets go; come go with me to the Bahamas."

"I wish Dale, but I can't afford to take off another week, I already have another week off for the 4th"

"I wish I could have had you there with me. I'm feeling the since of a strong relationship again. I look forward to hearing your voice, and seeing you every day, I really do. Your personality, is a shining star, you have a great sense of humor, well kept, independent, just as beautiful than America, and fine ass all out doors. Now wouldn't you think that's enough to be missing for the next couple of days when I'm gone and can't see you?" Dale asked, not knowing all these compliments tonight was just clamping unto my heart; he said things that sent butterflies to my stomach, that drove the desire for me to scream, but it was too many quests.

"Oh Dale!" I replied with very little to say, because my mind was scrambled and my tongue was tied.

"You are, you are truly an inspiration to me. I don't care if it's only been a month, you can tell when it's real. I know right here and know I can learn to love again, which was something I never wanted to invite back into my heart." Dale said with eyes that held the true gleam of passion in them as I just looked with a smile that practically spelled DITO.

The champagne had me drowsy so I laid down in the car on my way home. I could have felt Dale hands several times rubbing my forehead to the mid of my hair.

"Baby are you alright?"

"I'm alright just a little sleepy." I said, as he continued to comb his hand across my head as he drove me home. I loved the way he talked to me, I loved the way he touched me, I truly think this could be the one for me, I've searched for years. Even if he isn't the one for me, I don't want to believe it. I'm just going to enjoy each day he brings happiness to me.

He opened my door as he did on any other occasion, handed me his hand as I got out. Placed my head on his shoulders, and his husky left arm around the small of my back. The warmth of his body, the beat of his heart, and the smell of his cologne I admired every bit of it. To tell you the truth, there was nothing I disliked about this man at this moment. Not only tonight but on every occasion in which I met up with him, I get that gushy feeling and a hundred reasons why I tell myself to act right and not HARD.

"Goodnight sweetie." Dale said, as he grasps me in his arms tighter. He hugged me again this time so tight like he wasn't sure if I would walk through the door and never come back.

"Can I have some of those luscious lips?" He asked, as I perched my lips together, he pried his tongue in between them and we kissed. At least a second, a kiss that made me think my pussy had a heart of its own, it was beating as fast as the one that kept life flowing in me.

"Goodnight boo." Dale said.

"Goodnight." I responded releasing the hug we shared.

"I wish I can have a uh-huh hug." Dale asked. I had no idea what was an uh-huh hug; I just knew it was coming from him.

"Your wish is granted, can I have a uh-huh hug." I asked, as he grabbed me up in his arms and place his two big hands, one on each cheek, and slightly squeezed. It felt so nice I arched my back so he could get a better grip, while tiptoeing for another kiss. To his advantage he palmed my entire phatt ass as we stood in the door kissing. I started rubbing my hands up behind his neck, through his Philly cut; while he rubbed my ass, as if this was the moment he was waiting for.

"Woe..." He replied just when our lips released.

"Ok..." I added while taking a step back closer into my house.

"Goodnight baby, sweet dreams." I said.

"Mona." He said pausing. Staring eye to eye in a daze licking his lips. "I really enjoyed tonight."

"I did also." I responded.

"Will I be able to see you tomorrow?"

"Yes I get off at 500pm., maybe a lil later."

"Sounds better than no to me." He said with a GQ smile. "Will you call me when you think of me?" Dale asked.

"Yes indeed."

"Goodnight baby." He said again smacking me on the forehead with his soft lips, and down the stairs he started.

"Good night Dale, hold me in your dreams tight." I announced with a smile, as he took steps to lower ground. He held his head up, and turned towards me.

"Can I get an uh-huh hug in my dream too, if you are really there?" He asked with this sexy smile upon his face.

"Dale, if it was anything like tonight, I will be there." I said, as Dale opened the car door, he turned and couldn't do anything but blush with me.

"I'll never let you go, if I ever touch bases with your heart!" He said as he got into his car leaving me with such a good feeling, let alone with no choice, but to want him even if I was wrong in any way. I sat on the couch, listening to *"Cater to you"* by Beyoncé and just charmed by my night. I thought of everything from his looks, to his sweet kisses, I loved his gentle touch, his amazing thoughts were sincere and very heart filling to me. I was touched, I sure was touched by a whole new dimension of dating which almost felt like love at first sight.

The night just went by, I slept like a baby until my phone sounded off.

"Hello." I answered, as the ringing phone had awakened me.

"Hey where you was all yesterday?"

"What time is it Becky?"

"6:02 in the morning."

"Becky, why you up calling this time of the morning, folks still sleeping."

"Nobody told you to hang out all night and know there is work today."

"I know damn well you aint talking." I seriously said as I sat up in bed. "What Becky! What is it you want to know?" I asked taking a deep breath.

"Why you left, and stayed gone all yesterday?"

"How's Ms. Minnie?" I asked ignoring her question.

"She laying here sleeping, and you need to answer me slut I asked you a question! Where were you?"

"Girl, don't start fucking with me this early Becky!"

"There you go." Becky said.

"Anyways I went on a date yesterday."

"With who?"

"Dang nosey, touch your nose!" I said laughing, as I was sure fully awake and ready to gossip.

"I know you aint calling no damn body nosey."

"Now Becky I missed your ass when you were gone, now don't be fucking with me this early in the AM."

"Damn it's like that!" Becky said sounding rough.

"Girl, I went to dinner with Dale, you want to know what I ate too? Nah let me stop tripping." I said knowing my girl Becky wasn't gone stop until she caught up with the weeks news, so I sat up in the bed and reviewed the week she vanished.

"Who's Dale?" Becky asked.

"Doe-Doe the guy from the club!"

"Which club Chocolate?"

"What's the last club your ass went to in MIA with us?" I asked, just as she played forgetful.

"Oh the black boy from Bermuda's in that Beamer truck?"

"Yeah! The kids and I went to his house for a swim."

"Really! Where do he live?"

"He lives out there towards Weston, I think that sign said Williams Mark Island."

"Fuck... What he do living out there, I almost certain there is nothing under a million!" Becky said, sounding quite familiar with the area.

"He's a bounty hunter."

"And what's that?"

"Damn, Becky you should have paid more attention in school. In your terms, a motherfucker looking for fugitives from state to state and making mega bucks."

"What the hell he was doing in Bermuda's?"

"Becky I'm more than sure, PEOPLE with a job has a life after work too."

"Oh damn you, I don't need a job!" Becky said so quick and defensive. "Anyways how this man house look?" Becky asked like always, wanting to know every single detail.

"Becky it looks like it should have a wife like myself, three kids, two maids, homemade cake filling the air, my Bentley and his Rolls Royce parked outside the garage." I said, fabricating a thought.

"Bitch you crazy!" Becky said as we both laughed.

"No serious the closet bigger than my room, the bathroom is my living room, and the things I could do on his California bed. Umm umm I can see me sliding down them big post or using them to balance myself on the big dick."

"Oh I know you didn't fuck that man already!" Becky yelled into the phone.

"No I didn't Becky and his name is Dale and not that man."

"Whatever child!"

"Becky I don't have to explain it to you, however all we did was talk, kiss and watched pretty woman while sipping on some Remy."

"What the hell you got that man watching that old ass girly movie for!"

"Becky he didn't mine, he turned it on. Then the kids got up; we barbecued and played games in the pool."

"Well Chocolate, it sounds like you met a family man." Becky said, as I always thought she knew me better than Jasi. She knows what to expect out of me and what I'll accept from them, unlike Jasi she has to search for the principle, locate a solution and discover a cause, after analyzing a reason but she still my girl.

"You like him huh?" Becky asked.

"Becky, he is another Lionel."

"Hell no, you don't need another one of those!" Becky quickly interrupted me.

"Would you listen? He somewhat like Lionel but he doesn't have those busy, untruthful thuggish ways like Lionel has well at least not so far."

"Well you only live once, so go for what you know and continue to do what makes you happy." Becky somehow had her priorities all fucked up, but she just seemed just like me. She sometimes thought the way I thought, seen things in my perspectives, our style, and sensitivity, all works the same. She always made me happy and spoke the truth, when I asked for an opinion, although she had to joke about everything first, but she always had the right words to say.

"Girl no listen. Last night we went to this restaurant called Houston's. I was so happy, I believe if I had the nerve I might would have asked him his hand for marriage."

"Houston's... what's that?" Becky asked.

"It's a restaurant off Biscayne on the marina." I responded.

"Oh, you talking about the one with all those lights out by the water."

"Yes! Then to top it off he bought me one single rose and had a guy to sing "***You are more than beautiful!***""

"Aha... That's so sweet!"

"And girl everybody was looking."

"Did your scary ass run out of the restaurant?" Becky asked joking.

"No, I sat on my man lap honey!"

"Oh shit! You was Chocolate, not Heather huh." Becky said laughing.

"Girl please, damn yall with that Heather shit."

"What did you wear?"

"I wore that aqua outfit from BEBE, and he looked damn good too. You couldn't tell me that wasn't my husband, he held my hands as we walked the Pier, gave a toast, feed me some of his food, and I fed him some of mines"

"Oh oh, doesn't sound like you gone give him up easy."

"Not even for all the tea in China." I said gazing at the clock that registered 7:30am.

"Becky. I'll call you later, cause I have to get ready for work its already 730!"

"Where is your cordless Chocolate!" Becky said, as she always thought she owned me, as you can see. She loved to play and aggravate me.

"When your mama going home?" I asked, picking up the cordless.

"I guess when the doctors come." Becky replied.

"Oh the kids are over mama house."

"I know I talked with her last night and the kids, while cupid was out shooting her arrow." Becky said laughing out loud which caused the same reaction for me.

"Whatever and he asked me to go with him to Bahamas next week."

"Girlfriend pack your gear tight! Oh hell nah the Essence is in two weeks! You can't go no dam where."

"I already took a week off thanks to you."

"I'm sorry sweetie just go for the weekend. The weekend is better anyway, the club be bumping, and the men in the Bahamas. Black as you ever seen black before. I mean black brothers, look like they would keep you hollering, and they love American woman." Becky just rattled on missing the whole point, which I had finally found someone I liked. But being she had been all around the world, she just about knew what to expect from each state, country and island. What she was not understanding that I didn't care about the clubs, let alone the men. Now that I have Dale there wasn't a thought, not even a glance at another man. Being alone with him and far from home, would be the biggest deal and the deepest dart thrown at my heart.

"Corey came by my house?" Becky asked as she just didn't know that question had only added salt to a wound.

"Nah girl and I really have to get dress before I'm late! And I'm not putting my phone in the shower to talk to you. So I'm gone call you later, because I need to hear about this voyage, and I must tell you about this queer I met at the hospital while I was there." I said, trying to hurry off the phone.

"Oh you didn't tell me how the contest went either."

"And I won't! You should have had your ass there, anyways I won 1st place. They gave me a laptop, five grand, a few other incentives and I met a couple of publishers."

"Congratulations." She responded.

"I'm gone call you on my way to work."

"Alright chocolate, if I'm not in this room, you know we went home."

"Alright Becky." I said ending the call, searching in my closet for something to wear. I forgot everything was in the cleaners, except for this ugly brown skirt set which I hated, but I had no other choice.

"Hello." I answered the phone.

"Mommy!" Shanice called.

"Yes baby."

"Can you go to the gas station and buy me some Kokomo, grandma don't have no more."

"Ok Shanice." I said ending the call, gathering all my things and placing them by the door.

"O heavenly father that...' After my morning prayer, I grabbed my bags and blazer and headed out.

(Beep Beep!) As I got closer to mama house I begin to blow the horn, Steve who is one of my brothers came to the door and Shanice was right in behind him.

"Would you get out and knock on the door, there is people still sleeping around here!" Steve shouted, even though he didn't live there. He and his homeboy had their own little hoe house two buildings from mines, but he was of course a titi sucker which was something we called him since he was a little boy.

"Shut up boy, and go home! Here Shanice." I said reaching a bag of Kokomo for Shanice and Becky kids that were still there.

"Shanice aint even got on no shoes, stay in here." Steve said, as he walked over to my car and got the bag. Pushing me in the head like we would do when we were kids.

"Now you shut up!" He said.

"Boy you better be lucky I am late for work."

"Or what!" Steve said, grabbing a few of my braids wrapped around his hands.

"Mama!" I said screaming to the top of my lungs, and so did Shanice in the doorway. He still didn't stop, but started chopping me around my neck gently, as he pulled my hair.

"Tell me you gone stop blowing that horn huh huh! Say yes sir! Say it..."

"Boy what you doing!" Mama asked with her hands on her hips, and hair full of big orange rollers.

"Tell her to stop pulling up here blowing that horn like she crazy!" He released my hair and laughed as if he was joking.

"Yall still act like damn children! Leave that damn girl alone boy." Mama said, as Shanice stood in the door laughing.

"Ah ha. Uncle Steve in trouble!"

"Bye Shanice." I said, as she blew me a kiss and I pretend to catch it.

"Bye Mama, and you big punk!" I said pulling off and intentionally holding down the horn.

*****

The same old Mon-Fri 9-5 bagel and cream cheese, with a cold Hawaiian fruit punch drink for breakfast. Aggravating security guard, schizophrenia ass boss, complaining customers, meetings and memo changes every hour, was enough to get on my nerves for one minute. Just to think eight hours of pure torture at this bull shit ass Company. They never knew what to keep or what to throw away, anything just to make the day a little smother.

"Good Morning Ms. Anderson how was your vacation?" Ms. Horowitz the CEO of the company asked. I started to say, looking at IV, meeting new nurses, and taking turns babysitting, was just fine I thought to myself.

"Oh it was nice!" I responded instead, sounding so phony just like the rest of the big to do employees.

"How are you today Ms. Horowitz?" I asked just to be courteous. However in actuality I didn't really give a fuck how she felt.

"Well I'm delighted after seeing you; I missed you this past week."

I bet she is delighted to see me, no one to get her fat ass coffee, keep her organized, or neat. Shit I guess I took her only mind, which I was. I think I'd miss my mind too; after all it is a terrible thing to loose. Ms. Horowitz is the CEO of our phone company, whom I couldn't no longer stand to look at anymore. I am her Executive Secretary, whom she claimed to love so dearly, which I know was phony too. Must I tell you one day we were attending a Halloween party, she had at her big luxury home in Deerwood Estate. I dressed as a maid with the fishnet stalking, pumps, apron, duster, and all, which I thought was appropriate for the theme. She politely asked me to hold her drink? Being she had 4-5 treats stuffing her fat ass face, so I agreed and held her drink as we walked and talked. Shortly within walking she bumped into one of her important friends from another firm named Mr. Grasso, who often visited our office for luncheons and meetings. She sparked up a tone I never heard over the five years of working with her, and that laugh was enough for me to just knock her ass down in public where she pretended. Mrs. Horowitz turned to him; as if I never met him, and said meet my little black servant Mona. He handed his hand out and said glad to meet you as if I was really a little black servant, and her stomach was jumping up and down in her cow costume as she laughed the not so funny joke off. I couldn't believe her, I was so in shock that I left his and her ass right there. I grabbed my jacket, and out the door I was gone in a flash. I had never in my life felt so little and disrespected, until I didn't even care if I had a job that following Monday or not. Later that night she had the nerve to call and leave a message that I embarrassed her. Although I was born many years after slavery, I took black servant as a racist phrase especially coming from a white American woman. I just couldn't figure how she could have joked, about something that has pierced history in such a terrible way. A day or two later I called her back and told her exactly how I felt with nothing more or less.

"Listen here Ms. Horowitz being called a black servant is more embarrassing to me, than shaking another billionaire's hand! I'm not sure if you would have appreciated if I replied *Thanks for the introduction the slave owner's daughter!"* She said nothing but I'm sorry, however what she didn't know IM proud to be a black woman, we have such great history about ourselves that they try to bald down and hide. Never will I lower my standards or laugh at her jokes about my history or color to remain on salary or to wear this plastic badge. That's when I wrote a nice little poem she would see and understand what kind of beauty, gratitude, and knowledge this Black Woman has, each time she entered my office. Sometimes I'd even let her knock longer, just to be sure she read the entire poem upon entrance.

There she was!
Before my eyes she stood with a pretty dark face,
Yet the most smallest waist.
Her hair draped below her shoulders, and
Her teeth glistened one after another.
There she was
She had a walk that went from side to side,
And a talk that blurted dignity, and swallowed the pride.
There she was
She positioned herself in such a strong stand,
Just to let you know her dreams were already placed in high demand.
She had breast that sat so firm, and hips that engaged
the body as if they were only concerned!
"There she was!"
A woman!
A sexy woman!

An independent woman!
Now you ask yourself; are you a woman with her own
Mind, Intelligence. Dreams, and set Goals?
A woman with a ready-made mind!
Which is what we need these days and time.

"Ms. Horowitz, would you like a doughnut?" I asked, trying to get rid of the stale doughnuts from the lobby"

"Sure."

"Oh they are delicious." She said, as her big mouth clamped on it like it was bait.

"Are there any memos you need to go out today?" I asked, as she didn't bother to wipe the jelly from her chin.

"Yes." She said, sliding the chair everywhere around the office; she hardly ever got up only for lunch or if I didn't answer my phone.

"Mona, here is a folder; enclosed are memos I suggest need revision. It's a horrible mess as I tried to do it myself." Ms. Horowitz said. In that case I knew I had to make new memos ONLY as revision could never right her mistakes. I don't know how she's come so close to her retirement, which is in about a year.

I went into my office, and closed my door. I had tons of emails to read, and work to correct. I turned the radio on, and ignored the ringing phone, which was everyone in the office welcoming me back. I may not even be able to eat lunch, because I have so much to complete by then.

"Mona." Ms. Horowitz called over the speaker.

"Yes." I answered.

"Can I please have the spread sheet from the month of June?"

"Yes, I'll be there soon." I said, stopping everything and start surfing my files for it.

Lunch had come and gone almost three hours ago. I had so many spreadsheets, copies, and faxes overflowing, that there was no time to speak with Lisa, or Karla which were our two account managers who I often spent lunch with. I realized I wasn't going to get much work done as I begin to feel overwhelmed.

"Hello." My phone rang as I sat on the crowded expressway.

"Hey Cupcake!" A loud voice said.

"Hello!" I said again, sounding puzzled.

"Hey girlfriend, aint nobody gone cut ya! It's only me T."

"O!" I added with a slight smile over my face.

"How are you?" T asked.

"I'm ok and yourself?" I responded.

"I'm alright, making my way home. I was actually calling to invite you and your friends to Safaris Birthday bash, given from his woman who is the magnificent I." T said, addressing my thoughts very clearly. Him as the woman, and Safari as the man.

"So when is it?"

"It will be this Saturday at the Biltmore." T voiced bragged, as I quickly referenced his crowd of friends must have been some sort of lavish company he kept close.

"Yes, I will be there."

"Cupcake it's going to be a night of fun, starting with dinner ending with strip teasers." T commented, sounding so ugly, but he didn't seem to care what I thought.

"You better be dressed nice, because when I tell you there will be body builders, strippers, Politics, Governors, CEOs, Policemen, Entrepreneur, Spokesman, Doctors, and Lawyers. Cupcake girl, you name the profession and I'll find them." Damn. Now, where the hell he knows all these type of people from, but of course he is a punk and they are non to be the friendliest shit starters ever.

"It's Chocolate." I said correcting him.

"I know its Chocolate girl, but Cupcakes are always sweeter."

"Yes Ms. T, you don't have to worry because the Chocolate that I know will be dressed to impress." I said giving him the opportunity to wear a handle on his name that wasn't fit for him.

"That's right, Chocolate Strut those hips and move those lips, cause honey child you deserve a house on stilts." T said, as I laughed along with him.

"Alright T I'll give you a call a little later.

"Yeah, but Chocolate if you got anymore friends you can also bring them along too, act as if this is pick your career slash man day!" T Said, in such a devious unladylike laugh.

"Ok, T Bye!" I said, trying to rush off the phone so I can revert the news to Becky whom I knew would be *all in for this*.

"CHOO-TA-LOO's!" He said ending the call.

I hadn't spoken with Dale all day, now that my mind rested on him I really wanted to see him.

"Hello." I answered as my phone began to ring, just when I was attempting to make a call.

"What's up Chocolate?" Said Becky.

"Nothing much just sitting here in traffic."

"Why you aint call me, like you said you were?" Becky asked.

"Girl I was really going to, but I had so much work to do that it wasn't a break in a minute. Then my fat lazy ass boss had me fixing this and fixing that. You know how that dumb bitch act. She wouldn't have gave a care in the world if I was out sick for five days, she would still have those same expectations as to what she urgently needs! You ought to know how this fat bitch is by now."

"Auh-huu Ms. Lover." Becky, said, debating for an argument or discussion, as if I was making up my story.

"Becky, do you want to go to a party Saturday?" I quickly ignored her sarcasm.

"Who party, Chocolate?"

"This really cool queer, I have been intended to tell you about."

"If Mama alright to stay alone, I don't mind going." Becky said, with a response that didn't sound like her. I thought maybe I would hear her say *hell yeah, pick me up last*, or *I have a flight in the morning*...but instead she thought of her Mama first.

"You asked Jasi?"

"No, I called but she aint picking up and her cell phone sounds like she turned it off."

"It was like that since noon, because I was calling her, maybe Bruce there. Any who Shanice is over my house." Becky explained.

"Alright, I'm gone stop by there. First, I have to go and get Lionel a card being Sunday is father's day, and pick my Daddy up one of those propane gas grills. Are you sure you don't need me to pick Corey up something?" I asked knowing she was going to explode.

"Hell nah, and fuck you!" Becky added just as I thought she would.

"You are so silly. Now I bet you next week yall gone be back in love." I said laughing.

"Whatever! You made it to the mall yet."

"No, I'm by your house now."

"Oh I thought you were coming when you leave the mall?" Becky asked.

"I was, but the mall is closer to my house. So while I am by here I minus well get Shanice."

"Alrighty then." Becky added in her Jim Carey voice.

Shanice and I walked through the crowded mall; there were many nice shirts and sales hanging in almost every store window. I was Confused like hell, I really didn't know what to get. My daddy hardy ever wears the clothes you buy him, and if he decides to, he wears them in the wrong places like plowing the fields, or doing his mechanic work. There were so many new hi tech DVD players, but then again my Dad is use to the one I bought him for his birthday 3 mos. ago, and he loves it. After 4:00, he's glued to the chair and eyes pinned to the TV. So instead I may come out better by just buying him the grill. Lionel, hell the best thing would be a card. That's all Shanice can give right now; and my grandfather, and Brother whom I loved and missed so much a bundle of flowers for their grave, would complete Father's day shopping for me.

My feet started to hurt and Shanice was running through the racks, practically driving me crazy if not up the walls. We walked along the mall and I mistakenly let Shanice pull me into the toy store, spending more than I definitely planned for on three *Bratz* dolls that cost me damn near seventy dollars. Across was this new store that had a lot of cute dresses in the window, I just had to go in and peep this store out.

There was an aqua bustier dress that looked to stick to your body, from the very top to bottom. I went into the dressing room and tried on a small instead of a medium to draw a direct figure.

"Shanice you like Mommy dress?" I asked, as she played in the mirror.

"Yes. That's pretty Mommy, you gone buy me one like you?" She asked, as I laughed and so did she. The mirror presented the dress, as if it had a voice of its own shouting '*I would bring that husband home if you wear me!*" The color matched my complexion so well, and the material looked to be painted, but the only problem would be is buying shoes.

"Mommy!"

"Yes Shanice."

"I want to eat."

"Ok, just a minute." I said, twisting and turning in the mirror.

"I want chicken nuggets." Shanice said as if she was demanding me.

"Wait, let Mommy put back on her clothes?"

"Why you don't wear your pretty dress?" Shanice asked as I slid it over my head.

"I have to pay for it first." I said, as I hurried my clothes on and paid for the dress. I knew Shanice like a book, all she wanted was a toy from McDonalds, and I am more than sure Becky feed her already. The mall was so crowded for a Tuesday; well Father's day is coming and everything on sale down to the cookies in the food court.

"Hello, may I take your order?"

"Shanice what do you want?" I asked, as she stared at the picture menu on the counter.

"I want chicken nuggets, soda and French fries."

"Yes may I have a chicken nugget happy meal, without the toy and an orange drink?"

"No! Mommy." Shanice interrupted as the tender took the order.

"What's wrong?" I asked.

"No Mommy, I want a hello kitty like this!" She said pointing at the picture. Shanice was like any other kid, loved their McDonald's figurines more than they loved the meal. After eating we walked over to hallmark, to find Lionel a card, Shanice was picking up all the cartoon animations she wanted him to have. She ended up picking two with blue's clues, which I couldn't resist buying. It had blue's clues painting happy Father's day, leaving footprints of paint behind.

I know IM always in the way
But this is a card just to say
Happy Father Day!

It was rather cute, she was always into something, and this card really describes her best. So I bought this one and another one she liked. We hurried pass every store, and shopper that got into our way.

By the time I reached the car, my shoes were killing me, and my panty hose looked as if I had worn them a thousand times. When I sat down it was a relief; I had to take a moment before letting Shanice in, as she paid no attention, playing with the toy. I unlocked the door and Shanice got in.

I drove on and entered the highway, as I dug in my bag for my ringing phone.

"Hello" I answered.

"Hey girl what's up?" Jasi asked.

"Nothing, Shanice and I coming from the mall."

"Why did yall leave me I needed to get Bruce something?"

"Well I didn't know you needed to go, besides folks been calling you all day."

"Well just stay, till I come please!"

"Uh-ah Jasi, my feet hurt so badly, and I'm almost by your house anyway."

"Alright Chocolate how about tomorrow?" She asked.

"Alright that's cool. Anyways, let me ask you this before I forget. Do you want to go to this party with Becky and me Saturday at the Biltmore?"

"Who party is at the Biltmore!"

"T."

"T! Who's T?"

"T, the queer guy from the hospital Jasi!"

"Oh ok. No I do not want to go, I'll pass this one." Jasi said sounding confused. More than likely she wanted to go, but she may was gone hang out with Bruce.

"Alright then we might use your car; and tell your dead ass about our evening!"

"Whatever, I don't have time to figure out who play with who. Anyway are yall ready for Labor Day!"

"Damn Jasi you just forgot about the fourth, and Father's Day which aint even come yet."

"Whatever! This for the kids, I don't want no shit."

"Well Jasi I'm ready for that, I mean I have me and my child beach attire already."

"Ok, well next week girl I might be sick getting all these shots." Jasi said, jumping from conversation to conversation.

"What shots!"

"Our Marine Biology class supposed to go to Africa for the winter."

"I hope you don't get to sick, the fourth is around the corner."

"I know right, and I really don't even want to go but it is 40% of my grade that semester."

"Well Jasi you better do what you gotta do."

"I know. Hey Chocolate, come by my house before you go home."

"Jasi I'll be by later."

"Why and you fixin to by-pass me soon to get to your house." Jasi said making much sense.

"I know but I don't feel like stopping."

"Girl bring your ass around here."

"Child you aint got shit to show me that can't wait till later." I said as Jasi exit was coming near.

"No later I have class, come on now I want to show you my new furniture."

"Alright Jasi, I'll be there." I said exiting off her exit.

Driving through the magnificent neighborhood, decorated with tress, nurtured grass, sprinklers were sprigged from the ground, roofs were covered with red tiles and big fancy windows were the eyes of these beautiful homes, which is where Jasi resided. There wasn't a ball in the street, garbage can on the corner, not even a child in the road, or dogs without their leash or owner; it was a comfortable clean nice area.

Jasi BMW was parked outside the garage, as if she didn't plan to stay long. I left Shanice in the car while she was a sleep, and rang the doorbell which sounded off *Twinkle Twinkle little star.*

Gazing through the verticals, Jasi was trotting down the stairs.

"Who is it?"

"Hello Jasi!" I said.

"What's up?" Jasi said opening the door. "How, you made it here so fast?"

"I told you I was right by your exit." I responded.

"Oh, where is Shanice?"

"She in the car."

"Let me go get my baby from this hot car!" Jasi said.

"No Jasi, I ain't planning on keeping you company, as I pulled her along to the front room."

The new sofas were very huge; they were white as cotton, with big plushy pillows. Behind the chair there was of course Bruce famous aquarium which was the wall reconstructed, it really gave the living room its look. There was a sofa table made of concrete palm trees, holding a thick glass table on top of the leaves. Above was a huge mirror, which covered another wall and framed with palm leaves. The dining table matched, it even had four classy chairs made as if you were sitting on leaves. Decoration sure claimed this house.

"Do you like it Chocolate?" She asked while I stood awestruck.

"I love it! It is beautiful, creative and elegant. Who did this Jasi, cause I know you didn't."

"Can you believe this was Bruce whole idea?"

"Jasi, girl that's bad the man got better taste than you."

"Whatever! How is Ms. Minnie doing Chocolate?"

"She was asleep, when I went around there to pick up Shanice."

"How about black boy Dale."

"Everything's going good so far, but he has to go to the Bahamas for trial in two weeks."

"You going?"

"If I could miss work I will, but baby I need my job."

"Chocolate, you gone work your life away."

"Child please, that's life you got to do something with it." I said going towards the door.

"Damn, why you rushing?"

"Jasi, I don't feel like playing with you today honey, I got to get some rest." I said joking with a big smile that went up and back to normal.

"Alright now, you just don't forget about the mall tomorrow." Jasi said.

"Ok I will not forget, call me after class." I said, as Jasi started behind me reciting Shanice cheers in which she had learned in last year's summer camp.

"Stop Jasi, she is tired." I said pushing Jasi by the shoulders.

"*Sha Walla Walla umm sha bang*!" Jasi said clapping and yelling.

"Alright wake her up, I bet she will be right at UM with you!" I said, in a serious tone before getting in the car. Jasi kneeled across the passenger seat and gave Shanice a kiss, while I picked my phone up from the floor which registered 1 miss call from Dale, and boy was I happy.

"Move Jasi! Would you please let me go?"

"Alright Chocolate see you tomorrow, drive safe, and put that damn phone down!" Jasi yelled, as I pulled out her driveway with my hand on the send button.

"Whatever! Later girl!" I said, placing the phone to my ear.

"Hello sweet heart!" Dale said, as if he were waiting on my call.

"Hey, how are you?" I asked in a sexy relaxed tone.

"It's been pretty good so far, running around all morning trying to pull a couple of permits. But how has your day at work?"

"Busy all day, but I'm headed home for some much needed rest. Maybe that will equal it out."

"Well would you happen to need a massage?" Dale asked, in such a sexy tone.

"Well! Would this masseuse care to bathe me if I am just that tired."

"Baby I'll do just about anything, I'm just a ring away." Dale said, as the butterflies flirted through my stomach.

"Chocolate where is Shanice?" He sounded funny to me, because I was always particular about Shanice knowing another man was in my life, other than my Daddy and Lionel. For some reason Dale personality made me feel more comfortable than I've ever felt with any man.

"She's in the back seat asleep."

"Poor baby, she must be tired. Listen if you have any time; can Shanice and you join me for a movie or dinner."

"Dale, although school is out for Shanice I do have work in the morning."

"Well how about dinner, we can see Scooby doo at the movies this weekend." He said including us in his plans.

"Ok dinner will be fine."

"Does Shanice eat seafood?"

"No, and as you know I am not too thrilled about it either."

"Ok baby. Red Lobsters is out, how about Flannigan's."

"Sure that's much better."

"Will 8: oo be enough time?" Dale asked just insisting that we were going.

"Yes Dale."

"Alright baby, I'll call you a little later." He said, ending the call, but not wiping the smile from my face. I wish there was some way I could look inside to see if he really enjoyed me the way he claimed too.

By the time I made it home, Shanice was still asleep. I didn't want to wake her; neither did I want to walk up three flights of stairs holding her. I saw my oldest niece, which supposedly be my brothers' daughter. Whom he didn't claim nor did she have that Anderson resemblance. She had looked more like that big greasy ass man, who fathered the other four.

"Hey auntie!" Maya said, as she came riding up on the raggedy ten-speed bike, using her feet for the brakes.

"Where you get that bike from, I haven't seen one of those since I was about 12yrs old."

"Mr. James gave me this." She said referring to this fresh ole man that lives across the street from the condos. "You bought me something."

"No Maya, but can you please take Shanice in the house for me; while I take these bags upstairs."

"Ok!" Maya said. Hoping off the bike and leaning it against the wall being it had no kick stand. She was a big girl for her age, very smart, intelligent, and to mention she's an honor student every semester. She grabbed Shanice up and headed up the stairs, as I started up behind them. I noticed there was red juice all over the stair's, and chips that had apparently fallen from a small child bag.

"Maya, who was up here today?" I asked.

"Bri-bri and Bae-Bae was playing on the steps." She responded. Bri and Bae-bae was two out of the six kids Tracey birthed. One was in her mom's custody, two was with their grandma and she couldn't control the three she had living with her.

"Oh my..." I said covering my mouth, and holding in the anger, while Maya just stared.

"Now enough is enough!" I yelled from the smell of the black marker that they used to scribble on my door and a continuous line, which left a mark on every door after.

"Where was Tracey all day, why these kids messed up around here like that?"

"She was home." Maya replied, as we entered my house.

"Lay her in her room Maya, and have a snack, while I go and talk to your mama." I said mad enough to run down the stairs without caring that I have to walk back up.

"Who is it?"

"Me, Tracey!" I said, as she opened the door wearing a big T-shirt that reached below her knees. It had every grease stain, dirt stain and holes that could be. Peas rolled from under the dingy headscarf, as she stood stepping on trash that should have been swept in a dust-pan for garbage.

"What's up?" Tracey asked with her hand on her hip, and pinky finger in her teeth.

"Look Tracey it's got to be a better way, you really need to do something with them bad ass kids!" I said, as she started yawning without having the manners to cover her mouth. The flies foamed over her porch, which looked like someone poured syrup over it.

"What they did Chocolate?"

"Not what they did! You should know what the fuck they did! Damn you don't miss your 2 and 3 yr. old when they out your sight?"

"No hold up now Chocolate, I was in there sleep. And I told them to stay on the porch." She said, sounding as dumb as she looked.

"Tracey, you and that poor ass excuse, don't worry about it. You will not watch your kids or you won't work. I'll be damn if yall sit home and fuck up my shit! They made scribbles all on my door and on the building, and broke my plant that sat outside! Then when I come down here to tell you about them, you want to come tell me what they were supposed to be doing! I don't want to hear that shit!"

"Alright do you have to go on like that?" She asked.

"You damn right, your ass said alright last time when Bae-Bae bust my window, you said alright when Bri cut Shanice ponytail. I'm tired of this!" I said.

"Well damn Chocolate, just do what you got to do!" She said in a sassy way like she had every right to be upset or rude.

"Oh no, you don't want me to do what I got to do!"

"And what's that!" Tracey said smiling, but I was dead serious she had really pissed me off.

"#1 have HRS deal with your responsibilities, because it seems you just can't handle it."

"Girl Chocolate I'm coming up there to clean it and paint your door."

"If not, I will paint my door, and leave the rest for the land lord in the morning, and I don't think you want him to deal with it. Cause the 1000 dollars to move somewhere is not included on your voucher, nor is it easy to get with no income. So I strongly advise you to watch your kids or keep them in the house." I said, walking away as she slammed her door shut.

It looked ridiculous; a dirty stairwell, and flies everywhere without a garbage near. Then to top it off, there is an association fee around this motherfucker, and it look almost just as worse as them projects up the street.

Maya had turned on the TV. to cartoons, sitting at the dinner table eating cereal and milk, by the time I walked back inside. I didn't say anything, knowing Tracey she might didn't have anything to feed them. I made up some hot mop water; added some degreaser and bleach for the juicy stairwell, and headed back to the steps. I scrubbed until the water itself was red.

My My My, I thought to myself as this plum S600 pulled through the gates, and parked by my car. I wanted to through this mop down and run upstairs to at least put on a pair matching shorts, or wipe the sweat from my face, but at the same time I didn't want to be nosey or flirty. Maya came running by me and down the stairs.

"What's wrong Maya?" I asked.

"Nothing, I am fixing to go to my friend house." Maya said as she got on her bike. I wiped across the stairs one final time, as the driver took their time to get out. I went and stood on the side of the wall, peeking from a clear clean view so I could see them, but they couldn't see me. The car door had finally opened; and it was Dale.

"Oh my god!" I thought what I am going to do; he looked so good with a canary yellow Cubavera button down shirt and a white NY baseball cap. I wanted to run upstairs, not only were the clothes bad but this greasy face of mines was a problem. I think maybe if I get a bottle of lotion without him seeing would be great and put on some damn shoes. Especially now that the mop water which splashed on my legs had dried, until it left nothing but ash, which is very revealing on this black skin of mines. He placed a beige decorated box, with a gold bow wrapped around it. I didn't want to seem rude by being scared and embarrassed, so therefore I came and stood against the railing, with the mop in one hand. At least he would know this is the reason why I am barefoot and ashy.

"Hello baby!" Dale said, looking up toward the second floor.

"Well hello Mr. Dale, surprised to see you." I said, as it had dawned on me that he came to my house without any warning; and the only thing I was thinking about was lotion and shoes. I know it's got to be something special about him.

"I couldn't bear the thought of thinking of you, so I had to stop by to see your face." He said, as he made it to the top of the stairs and I stood waiting like a true Diva, yet looking like a dirty wrinkled bomb.

He wrapped one of his chocolaty arms around my waist, which had felt so tiny in those gigantic arms. He bowed his head and kissed me on my forehead, and sent chills down my spine. All of a sudden I heard a rumble and a sigh as if it was a kitten moving around.

"Did you here that?" Dale asked with a smile.

"Yes what is it!"

"I bought Shanice a little gift; if it's ok with you." Dale said, as I tried to not only prepare a look, but hope at the same time this wasn't a damn furry kitten.

"Can I see?" I asked, as he removed the lid from the box, and a little furry big eye puppy peeped out at me. "Oh he is so tiny and cute!"

"I thought the smaller the better you girls could maintain him." Dale said.

"Do you think she will like it Mona?"

"I think so, if it doesn't grow." I said, as I rubbed the pup's head instantly falling in love with it myself.

"Oh no she's not going to grow much. It is a full breed *Maltese*."

"Yeah she will like him then."

"I hope he doesn't crawl out." He said, as he placed the box on the ground.

"No Dale I'm finish we can go inside now."

"Oh O.K. are you sure, you are finish?"

"Yes Dale." I said, as he picked the box up with one hand and the mop bucket in the other.

"Well, Dale make yourself at home; I'm going to have a shower if you don't mind." I said.

"Where is Shanice?" Dale asked while placing the box on the table.

"She's in her room sleeping, she will be up soon." I said, walking in the utility closet for soap. Dale laid himself upon the leather couch watching BET, looking good as always. Tank video '*I deserve*' was playing; I went to place the phone on the charger before showering. I was being rather messy as my intentions were very sexual. I pranced in front of the man with only my towel wrapped tight. He pulled my hands, and baby I didn't hesitate, nor did I resist. I sat upon his lap and this time it was not `No or Wait!' I kissed him, and kissed him, and kissed him until his special uh-huh-hands crept up the towel and palmed each bear cheek, in slow motion. I started running my hands down his neck, and gazing him in his eyes, they weren't as beautiful as aqua blue but they were dark brown and sparkling like jewels freshly cleaned.

"Damn Chocolate I want you." He said without a doubt. "I really want you in my life." He said looking so serious. I didn't know if I want to believe him.

"I'll be back, after I shower." I said, smacking him on the lips and ignoring the question. I walked down the hall leaving Dale on the sofa, stiff hard. Shanice appeared to be sleep when I walked pass her room. I grabbed a T-shirt, leotards and the famous G's along with matching bra. I began to bathe, with thoughts that left me puzzled. I never allowed anyone to come unannounced but Lionel, which was not a bother. I think I am falling, well should I say I know I am falling. Only if my feelings were as tough as my mind I would be something else. Feeling a cold air, from the sudden break in the door; I peeked around the curtain, there was the little guy with a small jewelry box barely clamped in his mouth. I couldn't do anything but smile; it might sound like some movie shit, but this man was really romantic. I loved the way he does things, the hugs and surprises beats problems and attitudes any day. I bent over to retrieve the box, and there was a beautiful chain with a platinum heart pendant. I didn't say a word I hurried and dried off. Tying the towel around my breast, this time leaving a space showing hips and thighs. I opened the door; the little pup stumbled and tripped over his own feet trying to get out of the bathroom. Dale sat on the sofa the way I had left him as if nothing went on.

"You are so sweet!" I said, sitting on his lap.

"And you are so special." He said, rubbing his hands up and down the rib area and resting them upon my thighs. I couldn't get as comfortable as I wanted being Shanice was in the other room, so I got off his lap, and my towel fell to the floor leaving me butt naked. His eyes bucked open as I hurried and reached down for the towel, just when he said.

"No. It's alright, please." He whispered, sounding like Percy Pledge or Isaac Hayes with that charming voice and just enough breaks at the right time. So I took two steps back and positioned my body. He stared and I smiled.

"I know I have something to enjoy." Dale said as he got up and slowly wrapped the towel around me, just as neat as I would. "I can't take this no longer." Dale admitted, as I turned away and headed back towards the bathroom to get dress. There was where I leaned against the wall and covered my pussy, which was carrying on as if it wanted to jump away. I know whenever it's time to give it to him, it's going to be worth it. Believe me I have plans for this brother, I slid my panties and bra on, stood for a minute wishing he would enter this bathroom.

Meanwhile Dale had, went out on the patio to watch the sunset over the beautiful canal view.

"Beautiful sunset huh?" I said, pulling up a lounge chair.

"Yes it is very beautiful and bright this evening." He said, as he slid over to my lounger and laid in between my thighs. I rubbed his head as he massaged my leg.

"You ever wonder how the colors dance in the sky just about every day at the same time."

"It's remarkable."

"The blue hides like its shy, while the purple dances so boldly, and the yellows just somehow fade their selves away." Dale said, as the colors did just what he was stating.

"It's beautiful."

"Just like you and me." Dale said, as I felt a bit of shy tearing through me.

"Excuse me baby." He said as I got so quiet. "I have to go and take a leak." He said getting up bare feet going back into the house, leaving the pup and me on the patio. He was most definitely my kind of man, he's intelligent, romantic, and love to kiss. Boy what am I going to do, this shit is getting deep I thought to myself as Dale came through the sliding glass door holding Shanice in his muscular arms. If Lionel was not written all over her face, I would consider what a perfect dad for a beautiful little girl.

"Mommy who dog?" Shanice excitedly asked.

"This is your puppy." I said, as I stood up putting the dog near her. Shanice climbed up, almost over Dale's shoulder because she was so afraid.

"Oh she is scared of him." Dale said, as he backed up. "He will not bite, let me see him Chocolate?" Dale asked, opening his huge hands, where the puppy laid as if it was just enough room.

"Look Shanice; he can't bite you he is too little. He scared of you." Dale said, trying to win Shanice heart over to love the puppy. Before I could look again Shanice hand was on top of Dales rubbing the puppy and smiling. Dale reached to the ground and put the puppy down and Shanice got down also, she followed the puppy from corner to corner.

"What's your puppy name Shanice?" Dale asked.

"It's a boy or girl Mommy?" Shanice asked with a smile.

"It is a girl." I said.

"Ok, umm. BABY!"

"You want to call her Baby, Shanice?" I asked.

"Yeah Mommy Baby."

"Ok Shanice your puppy name is Baby." Dale agreed.

Shanice went for the box, and tried to make the puppy go in but it didn't bother to pay Shanice any attention.

"Chocolate, have you figured where are we eating?" Dale asked, still sounding concerned.

"I guess like you say Flannigan's." I responded.

"How about you Shanice? You want chicken and go see Scooby-doo?" Dale asked.

"Yeah yeah!" She screamed, as she started asking questions.

"My Mommy going to see Scooby-doo too?" Shanice asked.

"Yes sweetie." Dale answered, as I stepped back into the house, to make a temporary home for the puppy until we return. I could just hear Shanice out there babbling away. She had asked the man do he have a girl she can play with, I couldn't do nothing but smile. Knowing Shanice she might just ask what he ate today. I promise you would think she was about 95 years old. I headed back to my room, to change into something casual. Looking through the closet there were jeans and shoes everywhere, there was this green Roca wear jumper I hadn't worn in quite some time. It fitted me rather nice, it was one of those army green jumpers, trimmed with beige thread, and I put on the hot timberland boots with the heel and twirled my hair into a neat bun. I then called Shanice in and dressed her in a long sleeve pink blouse with blue jeans and pink roses trimmed down the legs, along with a matching rose belt and pink rebook classics. Dale put the pup away and was waiting patiently, as Shanice and I both walked out together, greeting Dale in the living area.

"Would you two ladies care to join me?" Dale asked in a joking voice.

"No!" Shanice shouted without meaning, as Dale and I started laughing.

"Yes Mr. Man." I said, as Dale took Shanice hand and the two walked out. I locked up the house, and prayed that no one would see me, who knew Lionel. Shanice holding another man's hand, let alone new friend maybe lover. Lionel ass would have a fit. By the time I made it down to the car, Shanice was strapped in and my door was open and he was waiting.

THE NIGHT OF THE BALL!

Becky, had looked more than beautiful tonight, she wore her hair in pigtail braids that I begged her to get. They were pinned into a nice bun with two beautiful decorated pins to hold it. She wore a halter dress made by Vera Wang. It had aqua yellow, pink stripes and circles along with the matching heels by Stewart Weitzman which were very sexy. One scrap around the ankle, which was pink, and the soles were aqua and the straps between the toes were a mixture. Becky always did look nice, but this particular night she was gorgeous.

"Girl do you like this dress?" Becky asked.

"Its beautiful Becky, and the shoes wow!"

"I got it from this island we stopped on while cruising to London." Becky said as she flipped the mirror down to fix her eye shadow, that she wore very well.

"Alright cruising to London! Your fuck ass is why I can't go with Dale to Bahamas, but it's all right. New Orleans in a couple of weeks. But anyways girl the dress looks nice very hot and expensive!" I said.

"Marco paid thirty two hundred for my dress and sixteen hundred for these heels."

"Must be nice sweetie." I said, as we drove up to the Biltmore. Where there were every Benz down to a Mayback, Bentley, BMW, and Rolls Royce in the lot; luckily we drove Jasi 745LI. Looking just as important as anyone else.

"Good evening Madam?" The sharp valet dude announced.

"Hello how are you?" Becky responded in a flirting tone.

"I'm fine and you Madam?" He asked, guiding Becky to the red carpet.

"Quite contrary." Becky said, and switched off joining me.

"Becky stop, lets act like ladies and not snobs trying to get in."

"Damn Chocolate you just have to spoil the fun." Becky said, as we walked into the hotel, which had ceilings as tall as a castle, and floors just as shinier than dishes. There were guys everywhere, but the problem was so many had looked to be queers. T had finally recognized me, and he came running for a hug. Boy was he dressed, he wore this pinstripe navy blue and beige golfer hat with the pants to match, a red vest and red blue and beige Versace clogs.

"Girl you are stunning!" T said, as moments later Safair came walking over, also with hugs and kisses.

"Well thank you." I said. "By the way T you haven't met my friend Becky yet."

"No I have not, but sister can I have those shoes!" Becky just smiled with her cute and different attitude tonight.

"T this is Becky and Becky..."

"This is the Misses!" Safari rudely interrupted, letting us know T belongs to him. Safair was unlike T he was very rude and bitchy, perhaps he just wants to be seen, but fooling with Becky she will let it be seen. T and I continued to talk, while somehow Safair and Becky had walked over to the bar.

"Chocolate doesn't Safair looks nice?" T asked, as we stood watching him and Becky talking.

"I love those Gucci loafers he is wearing and the suspenders goes right on time with his vintage look."

"Honey I know he looks nice right." T said, gliding his tongue across his lips as if he watched a super model take the runway, but obviously that wasn't his deal. We walked around and I met a lot of T's friends and business partners, which kind of made him a little smarter than just that simple ass punk I met the other day.

The night grew older as we danced, talked, and ate away. Becky and Safair were still missing; by the time we all made it back together it was time for a birthday toast according to the agenda we received at the door. Safair, Becky and I were standing in the audience while Mr. T had made it on stage for the toast.

"Ladies and gentlemen... Queeeeens and Kings! May I please have all the attention?" T said, as the audience laughed at his entrance.

"To my special significant other on a day no other than his birthday I would like to say I love you!" Safair had vanished and appeared on stage next to T. T had hugged him and kissed him disgustingly in front of the crowd, which it didn't seem to bother.

"Kings and Queens can you please escort us to the lobby." T asked, over the loud singing and cheers. In the lobby was parked a 2005 BMW 645c candy apple red wrapped with a big pink bow on the roof of the car, and thick white frost reading *Happy Birthday* in the window.

"Happy Birthday!" The crowd shouted as Safair stepped in it and started observing his gift. Safair had received many other gifts from vacationing to jewelry, all the rich queer doctors and half of everyone else was bringing envelopes and beautiful pink wrapped gifts of crystals and freak toys.

After all the excitement was over me and Becky decided to take a ride on the beach where we later met Dale at *Planet Hollywood*.

"Ladies are you having something to eat or drink?" Dale asked, as we sat quiet.

"No baby, I am still full of cake." I said.

"No thank you on the food, but I guess I can handle a little drink." Becky said. "I'll have a belvedere." She added.

"Chocolate one drink wouldn't hurt, let's try a margarita and a Hennessey for me." Dale said, as the waiter jotted on her notepad.

As we waited patiently for our drinks Becky busted out with laughter after seeing a group of girls that were rolling along the sidewalk with g -string Bikinis and roller blade skates at 2am in the morning. I looked at Dale who didn't attempt to turn his head in their direction either.

"What's up?" Becky answered her cell with a big smile.

Dale placed his hand under the table as he rubbed my thighs; the waiter walked back up with three big drinks. The glasses were so big they looked like you can wash your hands in them. Becky immediately started drinking the belvedere, as I tried to sip on the salty margarita, without hesitation Dale just took a quick shot of the Hennessey and left no trace. After Becky ended the call, she started gulping down the drink while mines remained full.

"What's the rush for Becky?" I asked.

"O nothing, I'm just fixin to leave and go to club *Levels* on the other side of Collins." Becky said.

"How are you going?" I asked.

"That was Marco on the phone, he should be here in a minute. I believe he had said they were down by *Clevelanders* which is just two blocks away."

"Are you sure you are going to Levels and not across the border?" I asked, as Becky laughed.

"Child please find someone to play with. I'm gone." She said as a green Range Rover pulled up along the sidewalk. Dale and I continued sipping on our drinks as time pressed forward.

"Chocolate do you want to go to a club?"

"No not really, I don't feel up for it tonight."

"Well what is it you actually want to do?" Dale asked palming my hands.

"Honestly, I am tired from the party earlier."

"So you want to rest?"

"Not really rest, but just be relaxed." I said sounding so confused.

"Do you want to join me tonight?" Dale asked, as I took a deep breath, lord knows this was what I wanted, but at the same time I didn't want to be the one to ask.

We finally came to an agreement that I would follow him home. I drove behind the BMW truck as if we were husband and wife heading home, but in reality I was just another lonely woman trying to get somewhere. As we approached to the big beautiful house, he pulled in and I pulled behind him. I gathered my purse from the car but at the same time I pepped for protection, because I could feel my hormones racing. We walked towards the door, as he opened it and directed me in first. Clicking the switch that lit the whole front area, he placed the keys on the sofa table and walked towards me lifting me off my feet and carried me up the stairs.

"Baby I want to make sure you relax." He said pushing the French doors with my legs and laying me upon the huge pillow top bed, which felt like a bail of cotton. He kissed my forehead as I moved my lips to say thank you.

"Baby don't say a word, relax your mind, and let me do the thinking and talking for you." He said placing his index finger over my lips. He then raised up and went to the drawer for matches and lit each candle that was carved and decorated in his Jungle that was known for one of his rooms. He then returned back to bed wearing only his slacks. He took off my shoes, my hosiery, and my dress as I laid with only my matching bra and panty set. He placed his fist in the palm of my feet and he massaged. It felt so good, he then placed my ankles in his hand tightly and rotated my feet and massaged me all up my leg. As the CD player played a variety of oldie goldie songs, he kissed my right shoulder followed by the left, then he chased his tongue down my back to the tip of my butt. I really had wanted him but too afraid to start, and I know he wanted me just as bad. I could feel it, according to the pressure of his hands, and by the bulge in his pants. This was all happening so very fast... I booted up on my knees when he began massaging my butt cheeks and my inner thighs as Lionel Ritchie *I'm going Crazy for love* was now playing. He slowly and easily pulled my panties to the side just as the piano was sounding, he was on beat as Lionel began to sing. *I want you to want me... I'm going crazy knowing he will be your lover tonight...* I felt Dales slithery tongue come from the back of my pussy to my clit, then back down and pausing at the anal and back up again. As Lionel now sang the next verse *I need you to need me...I want to hold you but...* as the music blared so loud my feelings ran in the same direction. Dale wasn't rough nor was he sloppy but he definitely knew what he was doing, as I pretended to act rather GULIBLE.

He laid himself under my legs and gently pulled my doggy poised body on top of his face and started licking and sucking to my very movement. It felt so good until I shouted everything in my mind but right. He would be called something like a beast all because the way he yammed on this pussy like it was truly his last super. My gosh I tell ya he was fucking with me so hard I would have thought I was a virgin yesterday, as I promise you I have never been loved this tenderly before. My heart was racing, my stomach was tied in knots, and my pussy muscles was pulsating faster and faster. Lord I like this, and so did he. I was now laying on my back as he licked my inner thighs, and traced my abdominal area very seductively. I felt goose bumps arouse all down my arm which felt as if they were as big as pubic bumps. He moved on and, spread my pussy with his fingers and dove for a wetter taste of me. I rubbed his head, down his neck, around his ears and down his back. Before I knew it I was shaking as if I was having a seizure, I was gritting my teeth, and for a mere three seconds I was totally out of control. Felt like he was sucking the strength out of me. Shortly after He pulled me up from the bed, and to the Jacuzzi we went, which was filled with warm water and silver relaxation beads that glistened from below. He lowered me in and came behind me. I laid in his arms, while he bathe me, rubbed me, hugged me, and kissed me. Gosh I just was in heaven and I didn't even seem to care if he would call me tomorrow; this was a night of a lifetime to remember and I was ok with that.

Morning had come without me even knowing it; I slipped on my panties and got a T-shirt from his chess. I stood over the stairwell gazing at the dinner table where there were golden pancakes, scrambled eggs, sausage, grits, biscuits, and a sexy black hulk in the kitchen with boxer's and an apron. I tipped down the stairs without a crack, and kissed him in the center of his back, as he turned around slowly kissing my lips, as I held my lips tight not inviting on one of those sexual kisses we have been sharing throughout the night.

"Good morning baby, nice shirt."

"Good morning." I said as I placed my arms around his strong neck.

"What would you like to have for breakfast?"

"It looks to me you have made the standards, I might have some pancakes and sausage." I said as I took a seat and he served me.

"Chocolate can I say the prayers just morning?" Dale asked, as I looked shocked but was ready for his intelligence. As he did the prayers he prayed for many more mornings to come the same. I smiled as I was hoping he was talking about us being together.

"Amen."

"Amen."

We began to eat, the pancakes which were delicious so was the sausage, eggs and to mention he made the orange juice freshly squeezed just how I liked it, without any pulp.

"Chocolate did you taste any egg shells or unstirred dough?" Dale asked jokingly.

"No Dale it's really good."

"Well I must say it come naturally cooking for yourself every day. How about you, can you cook?"

"Yes." I said.

"Well how about dinner at your place next time?" Dale asked, as it just dawned on me that I have a home to return to, a daughter to pick up and a car to return.

"Sure I'll make dinner just before you leave for the Bahamas." I said.

"Well that's pretty soon, you know I leave Monday coming." He said.

"Yeah you do leave Monday, and we leave Thursday to New Orleans."

"Oh, the Essence festival right?" Dale asked as I cleaned the table off.

"Yes."

"Who all is going with you?"

"Becky and Jasi."

"O you and your girls stick together, no other friends huh?"

"No, that's all it has ever really been, but we do associate with others but not often. It really keeps down a lot of confusion and side thoughts."

"Haha, you know that's part of being a woman."

"Come on now Dale, we not going to go there, some of these men are truly worse than women!"

"Alright, let's leave that alone." He said, smacking me on the jaw with a soft kiss. We both finished the dishes together and raced up stairs, of course he let me win.

"Chocolate, I really wish you could come to Bahamas at least for one day." He asked as we laid in the bed, listening to sad'e.

"Dale I don't know, I'll try but the girls will be very upset if I leave them. Being we have been planning this for a long time."

"Yeah you are right. Where is Shanice going to be for that weekend?"

"She's going to P.A. to visit her Father."

"Oh, did she go for father's day too."

"No, we just sent him a card, because her grandmother couldn't go that weekend..."

"Oh ok, so what did you get your Father?"

"I bought Daddy a propane grill, and he loved it."

"Really! So he does a lot of cooking?"

"Dale, he always cooking or baking something."

"Yeah! You got to take me to meet Daddy, and Mama soon." Dale said, as I swallowed the whole conversation speechless. Maybe this fellow is more interested in me then I really think he is. I never let nobody meet Mama and Daddy. Lionel met her because I was pregnant, and since that I haven't meet anyone who was worth introducing.

"Don't get quiet over there. I want to meet the whole family. I really want to be with you. I don't believe you know just how much happiness in my heart you've fulfilled." Dale said, turning over on top of me, with a kiss as he got up and went into the restroom. I was not only happy but thankful because he wanted me just as I wanted him. Out of my bad habits I reached for his phone from the nightstand, and quickly dissected the garbage for any empty condom wrappers but there were none. I was even looking to see if the ringer was off being I hadn't heard the phone ring once through the night. The ringer indicator pointed on, hell let me stop looking for shit. I placed his phone back on the night stand and reached for mines which was definitely on silent. I called my voicemail; of course Becky was on there inviting Shanice and me to her little bar b Que that was apparently going to happen this afternoon all of a sudden. Jasi also left a message saying that she was down in Key West fishing with

Bruce and his friends until Monday. Shanice had called at least 5 times asking for a candy bar, and Chuck monkey ass still calling as if he think I am playing this time. I'm dead ass serious, I think I found what I was looking for.

Dale came out of the bathroom, with his undershirt and boxers tucked. His long arms began pulling the drapes, dressing the room with sunlight.

"Come on baby, let's do a little work out?" Dale asked, as I sat up in the bed witnessing a mini gym right outside his balcony slide door.

"Dale!"

"At least I'm not asking you to do the treadmill, let's just do a little lifting. Not like you need any work baby, it's just good to stay fit." Dale said, as he put one hundred and fifty on each side of the bar, while all I did was just look cause I know he doesn't think I can pick this up. He laid himself down on the bench and his chest swelled up as he lifted up and down. After 20 reps he was about out of breath and popping sweat like bullets.

"Now you lift?"

"Dale! Now you know I can't even lift a hundred pounds, and you got three on there." I said rolling around in bed.

"Ha ha ha. I'm just playing!" He said as he took the big weights off and left the fifty-pound weight on each side.

"Dale I can't lift that either!" I added finally dragging myself from the bed.

"So what you want to press Chocolate?" He asked as I looked over at the ten pound weights, because I knew the bar itself was heavy, this sure wasn't some cheap equipment.

"Alright, I know what you can lift." Dale said, as he picked up two of the twenty five-pound weights and put one on each side.

"Alright Dale don't let this thing fall on me." I said, as I slid under the bar.

"You not going to drop nothing! What you told me this mean?" Dale asked, pointing to my three Chinese tattoo lettering on my arm.

"Strong. Black. Beautiful!" I said, as definite and charming as he pecked me on the lip, and lifted the weight for me to begin.

"One and two and....come on I know you can make it three and four and."

"Dale no I don't want to do it no more its two heavy!" I said straining to get the sixth one up without his help.

"See you could have did ten, this is just mind over matter." Dale said as I got up from the bench exhausted.

"Ok you want to do a little jogging."

"Jogging!"

"Yeah jogging."

"Dale, I know I might have worn my welcome out, but all you have to do is ask me to go. Don't try to work the hell out of me." I said in a joking manner but was really serious.

"Oh no baby, I don't think I can ever get tired of you. I'm just including you in my everyday life; I just feel comfortable with you. I want you to be a part of me in everything I do, if you don't want to run we can walk." he said with a smile and a hug.

"I don't have any sneakers, and I sure can't fit yours." I said accepting the walk.

"Well I have lots of sandals you can slide your feet in and gym shorts you can fit all that hinny in." He said smiling pulling me over to the closet. I slid on a pair of his gym shorts and my feet seemed to be so tiny in his size ten Polo sandals.

"You look nice." He said, as he slid on his Dolce and Gabbana slides with a pair of gym shorts, and we headed down the stairs. Dale stopped and got two bottled waters, and a loaf of bread.

"Dale what is the bread for?" I asked as he got the keys and we went out the front door.

"There is a pond in the middle of the track, and there are many ducks. I usually feed them in the mornings when I exercise."

"Oh ok."

We walked in a normal pace talking and laughing along the way. We skipped, challenged each other to see who walks the fastest, and we even did cart wheels. For a quick second I realized I could act silly around him, without feeling self -conscious, embarrassed or ashamed anymore. After feeding the ducks he carried me all the way home on his back. Without a single complaint or argument. I hurried up stairs to the restroom, being he used it on our way out, I didn't think he needed it as bad as me. I was amazed by what I had seen and couldn't believe it. Becky always told me from a little girl. A man who puts the toilet seats down after he uses it; means they know how to treat a lady like a princess. I couldn't even pee at that moment, I was so happy just to have thought of this foolish antidote that has stuck with us far so long. I guess I would be his princess, he put the toilet lid down, and I can't wait to tell Becky this. When I walked out of the bathroom he was laid stretch across the bed, I dove on top of him and smacked him on his ear.

"Baby I'm going to go now."

"Already! Lets take a nap first before you go."

"I have to take Shanice to this cookout Becky is having."

"Ok, I guess I'll see you later?" He asked as if he wasn't too sure.

"Yeah I'll see you later." I said, gathering my purse and dress, he had hanging on the door.

"Dale I'm going to wear this home, I'll bring it back."

"Bye sweet heart." Dale said as I climbed on him and gave him a kiss.

"Later."

"Baby lock the door on your way out please." He said, sounding so drowsy.

"Ok." I said, without an attitude or negative thought, cause he leaves me with no reason to. I enjoyed the night and the morning with him.

I swung by mama house, picked up Shanice and headed home.

"Hello." I answered as the house phone ring.

"Hey, where you at?" Becky asked.

"Doe-doe you called the house phone. I am home, what's up?"

"You know you're a busy bee. So what time you coming, I know you got my message. Had your phone turned off, you must was getting dug in your ass."

"Child please Becky."

"No I called you about four something, just morning."

"What the hell you call me that time of morning for?"

"How bout they found Buddy from the grove shot in the head in his Benz on Alton rd."

"Yeah! Damn that's fucked up."

"Shit and they was saying that motherfucker sick."

"I know I heard that once, I hope you ain't mess with him without a rubber." I bluntly asked.

"I never let him ate the pussy, but we always fucked with magnums baby, besides that was before people started saying he was HIV."

"Damn, I can't believe that, he was a good dude too."

"Yeah, well it's true, and the whole damn grove was down there. So what time you coming Chocolate?" She asked changing the subject without a bit of sorrow or remorse in her voice.

"Well did this cookout have a designated time, because I don't believe it was planned?" I said sarcastically.

"Girl stop playing, come on and bring some ketchup when you come too."

"Yeah man!"

"And don't forget your bathing suits, we getting in the pool too."

"Where your Mama at."

"Chocolate, Mama in the damn pool girl with her bathing suit and swim trunks."

"That's good, I guess she feeling better."

"For real I think she feeling better than she ever did."

"Alright now don't wear the lady down."

"No serious Chocolate hurry up."

"Alright I'll be there in an hour."

"Wait! Why Jasi ain't answering her phone?" Becky asked before I could hang up.

"Jasi, left me a message that she was going to Key West with Bruce and his friends until Monday."

"That lady gone sneak in town, catch her thin ass and put something on her. Jasi is going to be mad with me because I left her so many sassy messages."

"You're always disrespecting people!"

"All damn you chocolate, you just bring your ass on with some ketchup. Bye!" She said ending the call, before I could say another word.

"Shanice!" I called as she came running out of the bathroom.

"Yes Mommy."

"Do you want to go to Becky house and get in the pool?"

"Yeah, yes Mommy!" Shanice screamed and jumping all around before she headed down to the room and came back with her bathing suit.

"Can I wear this one Mommy?" Shanice asked, as she held the tiny shorts and bathing top over her head.

"Yes, Shanice."

"Where your bathing suit Mommy?"

"In the drawer."

"Come on Mommy put it on." Shanice said, rushing me as she was quickly putting her top on the wrong side.

"Girl put that top on right." I said, as she looked at herself like she knew it was right.

"O!" Shanice laughed and fixed her top.

"Can baby come, Mommy?"

"Shanice, she can't swim."

"No I don't want her to swim, let Brianna see her mommy."

"Alright Shanice." I said getting up from the bed, to put on some clothes.

I wrapped my hair into a ponytail, put on my short cotton shorts, and my bathing suit under. Shanice had on her sunglasses and a bag pack for Baby including his toy bone and ball. I got my sunglasses, the leash and we headed out of the door.

Baby's head was sticking out of the big beach bag that I carried her in. Shanice hoped in the back as I placed the bag on the floor.

By the time we made it to Becky house, Julian was outside checking the mailbox.

"Hey Chocolate!" Julian said, running towards the car.

"Look Julian, look what I got!" Shanice said, as Julian gave me a hug. They looked over in the back seat and seen the pups head.

"Wow, who dog?" Julian asked.

"That's my puppy, Dale gave him to me." Shanice gladly said, which I didn't think she remembered his name.

"Can I take him out?" Julian questioned.

"No Julian that's a girl, she not a boy." Shanice said, looking from the corner of her eye.

"That's a girl!" Julian screamed, as he ran inside.

"Can I pick her up Chocolate?" lil Corey asked.

"You not scared of her, are you Corey?" I asked.

"No! My lizard bigger than her."

"Ok." I said, as Lil Corey reached in the back picking the pup up, rubbing her along the side. "Shanice climbed out the car, following Lil Corey and the puppy into the house."

"Chocolate where you get this dog from!" Becky asked walking outside holding the puppy in the air.

"Dale bought me that!" Shanice immediately interrupted and answering the question.

"Oh, Ms. Shanice. Dale buy you this pretty little puppy?" Becky unbelievably asked, and looking at me with such a calm and pleasant voice.

"Yeah and we went to see Scooby-doo." Shanice said, standing there blabbing away as if that was for anyone to know.

"Oh ok, I see Mr. Dale has special privileges." Becky said, looking at me with a smirk on her face. Giving the kids the puppy as we walked back in. The house was filled with sweetness and soul food in the air, Ms. Minnie was in the living area on the phone talking to my Mama with her legs thrown over the arm of the chair, and the kids were passing the tiny puppy around.

"Come back here!" Becky shouted from the kitchen, while she was cutting up some collards.

"Who cooking these greens?"

"Mama cooking this, she just asked me to cut it up. Look in the oven." Becky said, when I opened the oven there was macaroni just as orange with fiery melted cheese, three sweet potato pies, and stuffing. My stomach all of a sudden let out a growl for my favorite foods.

"Who cooked all this?"

"Mama!" Becky said, as I left her in the kitchen and went over to Ms. Minnie.

"Now Ms. Minnie, you really made a dinner today! How you feeling."

"Chocolate, I feel so good. The doctor says he thinks this cancer will be going in remission real soon, and my sugar aint been up since."

"That's good." I said, over happy giving her a big hug and kiss on the cheek.

"Did you look in the refrigerator?" Ms. Minnie asked.

"No I didn't look."

"Well I want you to, and the whole dinner is for you. Thanks for being there Chocolate."

"You welcome." I started into the kitchen, just when the kids came running by to get into the pool. I followed them out to the patio. Coreys Chevy convertible was parked out back. I got so upset every time I thought Becky was back involved with him because she knew he meant her no good.

"Yall put them life jackets on!" Becky screamed, from the kitchen window. I scraped the jackets on the kids and placed the pup in a clothes hamper out back so he wouldn't get in the pool. They were splashing and screaming the whole while. I went back in to get a pitcher of Kool-Aid for them, so they wouldn't be tracking up the house.

Corey and Becky were standing in the kitchen, kissing away.

"Oh oh, excuse me." Becky said laughing as Corey grabbed the pan of seasoned ribs and went outside, without a word to me because he knew I really couldn't stand him.

"Chocolate, I see you let Shanice meet that man huh? You must be really feeling him." Becky asked, jumping on a subject quicker than I can question her about this bomb Corey whom she claim to never go back to.

"Yeah he is a good one. Very thoughtful cares about my needs, nice, and sweet." I said just bragging on what I didn't think she found in Corey.

"That's good. Girl this bastard here trying to get back with me, when I say being nice, I mean nice." Becky said, as I thought of how she was number one with the three kids, and now she has to hide so his new main lady wouldn't catch her; although she had him first. Never would

I have been number one, then come back and settle for seconds. I opened the refrigerator trying not to respond or ask what the fuck Corey was doing over here. In a big crystal dish was banana pudding layered with cookies in such a neat design.

"Oh yeah baby, banana pudding!" I said trying to find another conversation, which wouldn't lead to so much debating.

"Chocolate I knew it was something I had to tell you. Girl I found this um Capri pant set, you know the one that drawstrings up the leg.

"Yeah I like those, I got a pair jean ones and they fit real well." I said.

"Girl they had the jackets to go with them too, it also had the drawstring up the arm. Um gone buy it with some sexy heels and accessories, bitch they gone think I belong on MTV. I got just about everything I am going to wear though." Becky said, as she whipped the potato salad.

"Jasi said she got all her stuff too, I just have to do a little running around." I recalled.

"Chocolate why you always be last. You aren't holding us up for the bullshit, like you did for Cancun.

"Oh shut up!"

"What made you let Dale meet Shanice?"

"I don't know..."

"Then he took yall to a movie."

"I know right, that just don't sound like me huh? But I think I found something in this man Becky."

"I think so too, if he makes you happy. What will you have to lose?"

"Not a damn thang."

"You better go for it."

"Marco bought you home last night?"

"Yes!" She said, as she bucked her eyes and shuck her head.

"So how Corey got here?"

"Girl, that motherfucking Corey got off the chain last night."

"But I thought you were with Marco last night?"

"I was, he bought me home and Corey was inside waiting on me." Becky said, taking a scoop of the banana pudding.

"You know you be playing some dangerous games."

"Baby, I don't know about you but I got all my puppies by their leash, except that rude motherfucker out there!" She said pointing to Corey.

"Here put me some in here." I said passing her a bowl, not even commenting about Corey.

"I am going to go out and watch the kids." I said stepping out back.

The kids were enjoying their selves. Corey was over in the grass area grilling, while Becky remained inside feeding her face.

On our way home, I stopped by mama house. Then Shanice and I stopped by the grocery store, being Dale had to leave Monday and we leave Thursday. I wanted to cook up a great meal and do a little shopping for Peggy since she staying to my house some nights. The phone started to ring and registered Becky.

"What's up chick?" Becky said.

"Nothing just here in the grocery store, what you doing?"

"Mama and me sitting on the porch eating some boil p-nuts."

"Where are the kids?"

"Corey, just took them up the street for ice cream."

"Damn he still there, where Shawn?" I asked.

"He said, she went to her family reunion."

"So I guess, he's playing family man this weekend." I added quickly and blunt.

"Girl please, what you fixing to cook and you just left from eating all this food." She asked avoiding my question.

"No I am just buying some groceries, because I am going to cook Dale a dinner. He is leaving Monday, so I figured a lady should prepare her man a dinner. What ya think?"

"Wow Ms. Chocolate is this the husband to be!"

"Damn you Becky, he's my man!"

"No for real, cause my friend really feeling Dale."

"Becky he is sweet and..." Before I could finish Becky interrupts, as she would always do.

"Like I told you before, I can't keep you happy in every way. Go for whatever floats your boat. Yeah I forgot to tell you Mama said she would keep the kids, while we go to Essence."

"Are you sure?"

"Mama tell Chocolate, you said it's alright?" She asked.

"Go ahead, and you better be back here by Sunday." Ms. Minnie said, answering her question as her voice echoed in the background.

"Well that's good!"

"So Chocolate were you playing earlier, or you really not ready for the trip."

"Yeah I'm somewhat ready, I wish I could be with Dale in Bahamas though."

"If you really want to be with him, Chocolate you know what to do."

"Nah, I ain't gone switch out like that."

"Alright now, better you than me. Nikki is gone be out there with some of her cousins from Jacksonville so I know I may run into her."

"Oh so are you trying to push me off?"

"Child please go ahead on with that lil girl shit!"

"Whatever! You know you change when you get with those dick gobbling ass hoes, and Jasi don't even play with them and you know that!"

"Girl whatever I don't know, why you hate that girl so much? She ain't do shit to you!"

"Yeah, well I was told you don't mix trash with treasure. Do you get it?"

"Ok Ms. Chocolate, I'm gone let you handle that, but um the question was are you ready?"

"Bitch you seem to ask me that shit every day! I'm straight, I think I'm ready to take that flight."

"You better be, and leave that crazy ass attitude, opinion book of yours, and that I don't give a fuck look at home please. I really want to enjoy, we all haven't went out of town together since the classics in 2000, and no I mean Cancun." Becky said.

"I know right." I added.

"Yeah it's gone be fun and so many niggas! How about when we come back all of us go to the Bahamas and have fun. Everybody bring their dates."

"Yeah right, you sure your Mama sitting outside, I think you out there smoking." I said being funny, cause Becky changed her plans like changing her clothes.

"Mama went inside, and I can't smoke Corey coming back in a little bit. But I'm serious we need to start back traveling having a good time, instead of sitting around getting old."

"Well that's a good way to butter up the truth. So if you all did agree to join Dale and I in the Bahamas who would you bring?" I questioned.

"Well lets see, umm maybe who fuck me the best that week, or who spends the most money. Nah let me stop tripping. I'm gone take my man!"

"Oh your man huh, well who is that?" I asked as Shanice was throwing almost everything in the cart from each isle.

"Corey Carter B.K.A. Black the one and only my kids father!"

"So you and Corey are back together now."

"You can say that, this nigga ain't never going nowhere. Even if I fucked his daddy and he caught me in action."

"Go ahead on, well I know there will be no such trip. If so where will Shawn be?"

"How about you stop worrying about that dirty McDonalds working hoe. The wifee back in the picture now."

"So he moving back in." I asked in disappointment.

"I might but not just yet. I am trying to get Marco to through me a party in Montego Bay Jamaica."

"Wow, now that will be a gift!"

"I know right, I am working on it hard too. Sucking, fucking, lying, and kissing ass. I want to blow that sticky brown weed with them dreads straight off the stock and party with my friends as if I'm a star with a few guest."

"Anyways Jasi is ready for New Orleans, the tickets has been reserved and the room." I interrupted her dream, and tackled our plans.

"How about the rental." Becky asked.

"We will have to get it when we get there."

"Alright now, I hope they not sold out, and only have compact cars."

"Shut up, you always worrying about the simple things." I said laughing into the phone.

"For real!"

"Let me finish doing my shopping because Shanice got this cart full of sweet shit."

"Alright call me later." Becky said ending the call.

I put every item back that I didn't need and kept a few Shanice really wanted. I hurried through the line and out the grocery store.

The puppy was still in his cage barking very low in the back seat, and Shanice immediately hopped into the back talking to her puppy.

By the time we made it home I was so exhausted. I lugged all the groceries to the second floor, and Shanice gave Baby a bumpy ride in her cage getting it in the house. Soon as she opened the cage Baby went running behind her. I grilled me a turkey cheese sandwich, grabbed a juice just in time for the 9:00 lifetime movie. I didn't here Shanice but I did see *Baby* walk by the room several of times. I went by her room to check on her and Shanice was fast asleep, while jungle book 2 was now watching her. I cut the TV down and covered her well. I went down stairs to get my phone that I left in the car; it registered 2 missed calls Becky and Dale.

"Hello Becky did you call me?" I asked.

"Yeah, girl let me tell you about this motherfucker in here. His bitch got the nerve to call my god damn house, and he answered the phone, explaining why he was here!" Becky said, upset and screaming into the phone about that worthless ass nigga Corey.

"For real, how did she get your phone number, and how did she know he was over there." I asked, not a bit surprised.

"She might have got my number from his cell, and maybe them nosey ass hoes from the projects told her he was with me. Cause I know his fuck ass ain't got that much heart to call that hoe on my phone!" Becky was going on and on I didn't know what to say, but I could hear him in the back ground saying, *man I don't know how she got your number.*

"Girl and then he explaining, how he just over here watching his kids!" Becky was yelling to me, as she continued fussing with him. "You should have told her how you be licking me in my ass too, since you want to tell her what you here for motherfucker!" She continued on as if I was her shield.

"Man you better go ahead on with all that there crazy shit!" Corey said in the back.

"I ain't better do shit, you always trying me! I gave you and that dirty hoe respect from day one! I have never call yall house, and I had three kids from your sorry ass! I tried to keep your home happy, I gave you to that hoe you. But you let her just run things. Who the fucking man! Huh Corey Huh? The bitch may tell you when and how to come, but she ain't fixin to be calling my damn house straighten a goddamn thang over here!" Becky said screaming at Corey, forgetting I was on the phone or even her mom was in the next room.

"This the shit I'm talking about!" Corey said.

"Fuck that Corey and you know I'm telling the truth! I didn't try you like that when I was number one and engage. But you let this dirty foot dragging, broke, mutted out dancer just pull your hoe card, go all through your personal shit."

"Becky! Becky! Let that man alone."

"No I'm just tired of this shit Chocolate. Every time you look around it's my fault why we can't be together! I try to get down like him, and shit just gets worse!"

"Well look yall handle that call me latter, and leave the police out your business." I said ending the call, because I know she would keep going on and will call the police quick. Without a goodbye she hung up the phone on me. I know by morning they will be alright. Hell she been through worse shit than this with his worthless ass. I guess I called her back at a wrong time, let me call Dale and see whats up with him.

"Hey baby!" Dale said upon answering the phone.

"Hey what's up?"

"Nothing much over at the Krispy Crème doughnut shop, would you like a snack?"

"Oh, did you leave already?"

"Yes, I'm buy the gas station near your house?"

"Dale what you doing there?"

"Well I knew you were home, so I figured I should bring you some glazed doughnuts."

"How sweet can you be!"

"Not as sweet as you like! Would you like something to drink?"

"Yes can you please bring me a chug milk, the coldest one in the store please?"

"Ok baby." He said ending the call as I hurried in the bathroom to wash my face and slip on a cute night short set. I let my hair hang down and traced my eyebrows. Without a call from the front desk, but a knock at the door. I pepped through the peephole and there was Dale waiting.

"Hey sugar!" I immediately said answering the door with a kiss. He proceeded to walk and place the bags on the counter and returned to lift me off my feet. I felt so loved, respected and honored by someone whom I think I love respect and honor as well. However I just couldn't seem to figure out how all this was happening so fast.

"How has the day been?" He said looking me in the eyes and landing another kiss on my lips.

"It's been long and, excellent since I get to see you again!" I said.

"Well I see Baby is camping out tonight by the door."

"Yeah she always sit there." I said, as Dale walked over to get a bowl from the dishwasher and begin to fix ice cream.

"Would you like ice cream baby?" He asked, getting out another bowl.

"Nah baby, I like milk with my doughnuts." I said, as he put back the bowl, reached for a saucer to place two doughnuts on, pulled the milk from the bag, shaking it well just before pouring it into a glass, I sat at the table watching his every move. He is so very handsome MY GOSH!

"Thank you." I said as he placed the saucer and drink in front of me and took a seat for his self. We sat and talked eating our doughnuts and drinking milk. I loved this fuzzy warm feeling I get whenever I'm around him.

"Well I think I better go now." Dale said washing the last glass we sipped from. I didn't want him to leave and didn't know how to ask him to stay. When he reached for his keys, I sprouted up from nowhere and kissed him unannounced and definitely out of order. However he played a long griping me around the small of my back while kissing me as if it was a simple mistake being correct just before walking towards the door.

"Will you stay the night?" I asked standing guilty in front of love. He looked up at me with a smile.

"I'd love too." I walked back and sat at the dining table trying to relate to the shame and embarrassment I felt from asking him to stay, but understanding the feeling and courage my heart was surrounded by.

"You want to watch a movie?" I asked, trying to blend out the attention on me.

"Sure." He said, as I got up and put Baby into her cage and cut off the lights. I invited him to my room, where he had found a movie he was interested in which was `Original Sin'. I put it in the DVD player and we started off with a few kisses in the beginning until the movie had our attention at its side.

Looking up at Dale, and observing the clock which registered 3:45am. I got up and checked on Shanice; she was the same way I left her. I slid back into bed; awaking Dale by my movement he gripped me in his arms and snuggled his face into my back. I laid silently, thinking how this man makes me feel every time he comes around, touch or talk to me.

Morning had come, I got out of bed before Shanice woke up and see me sleeping with this man. I discovered his pants and shirt lying on the dresser. He had stripped down to his boxers and T-shirt, I didn't even notice that's just how much respect he kept for me. Staying the night to him didn't mean he had to beg for my pussy and he didn't and, I liked that. I went on in the living area and waited for Shanice to awake, within moments Dale came stepping out of the room fully dressed. I had quickly came to a conclusion that he must have to make it home early enough to give his girl a good excuse, about the sun barley catching him out. I began to have all these delusional thoughts, how things really appeared in my relationship with Lionel.

"Good morning baby." Dale said walking over to the couch. As I mentally brushed him off not by the smell of his breath cause there weren't any, but because of his disappearance real soon and a good lie he might was putting together at the same time for me.

"Good morning." I shyly replied, trying to avoid *the whatever ass attitude* I felt coming alone.

"I think I better get out of Shanice house before she wake up, I see she talks and questions a lot. I don't think we've built up enough positive answers to tell her what I was doing in her mamas' bed." Dale said as he practically chewed my thoughts out, and embarrassed that self-conscious feeling. Not only did he respect my daughter, but also he respected the situation I was going to be put in.

"Ok baby, I understand." I said, without anything else to say.

"I am going to stop by a couple of stores and by a little supplies and pack up for the Bahamas." Dale said, still adding up the disappointment. I walked him to the stairwell and hugged him goodbye.

Shanice and I had cleaned up and changed my furniture around. The music was blaring and I was singing along with *Shirley Murdock*, gosh I was so happy. It had really been along time since a man had apart to do with happiness in my life, but this one really did. He gave me something to think about all day. He gives me motivation. He gives me confidence. Hell I truly think he is just right, I feel so complete when I see or talk to him. I'll say it just as long as it last "*I love this little fuzzy feeling!*" Meanwhile Shanice was constantly aggravating me, shortly after my sister finally arrived and saved the day.

By the time my food simmered down I went for a shower, coated my black skin with Nivea lotion, and slid into my hip hugging DKNY jeans and sexy muscle top. Dale was leaving tomorrow, and I just wanted to be comfortable around him, by just being plain ole' Chocolate that I am. Baby was sitting at the door as usual as if someone were waiting on the other side for her. There was nothing else to do so I slipped on my house slippers, slid the leash around Baby neck; which didn't seem so small anymore. I picked her up in my arms and walked down by the grass so she would be able to use the bathroom. Baby began to cry like a child when I put her in the grass. Perhaps she felt lonely; of course if nobody knew what that felt like it was sure me. I knew the feeling. I hugged her tight in my arms until she stopped.

Shortly the BMW truck came pulling up; I placed Baby on the pavement where she would walk just a little. I walked greeting Dale with a hug along with a kiss. I just felt as if I was so connected to him. Baby had finally reached us, licking the heels of my foot.

"Hey little girl!" Dale said, picking Baby up by her front two legs, as she just sprayed pee out.

"Oh Oh!"

"Ha ha ha Dale I'm so sorry, I was taking her out for a pee, but I guess she was waiting for you."

"All man, well she missed me by an inch." Dale said as he locked up his truck and went in to wash up.

I watched Dale, as he soaped his hands by the reflections from the mirror that covered the bathroom walls. We were in the master bathroom, while I was getting towels from the closet adjacent from the sink. When I turned to join him, he turned as well and patted both of my jaws. This left bubbles of a fake Santa's mustache. The two of us was laughing out loud while we stood side by side looking in the mirror. He pulled me around by the small of my back and kissed me on the nose. I wanted more I positioned my lips and we kissed and kissed until I found myself sitting on the closed toilet seat, gazing into his eyes, as he continued to kiss me all over my face so seductively. I started rubbing his chest and boldly began chasing my fingers down his pants, gripping what I felt was already owed to me. It was as hard as a stick. He didn't bother about moving my hands instead he leaned back on the counter top for comfort. It was almost a given by the look in his eyes he was silently begging for a blow job. I whipped it out, and without hesitation I licked it with one stroke from the bottom to the top. I tightened my lips and massaged his dick round and around. It caused one of his hands to slide down his face and the other one went around my head. I knew right then I was doing something right. Which provoked me to act like a beast while performing.

"Mona. Mona... huh... Huhh... Baby what ya doing?" He called out in his irresistible rasping sexual tones. I had brother calling me by my real name. By this time I could feel his dick pulsating in my mouth. I carried on as if there was a prize awaiting for me. He grabbed my shoulders with such strong force, and pulled me up as he reached for the towel but before he could... cum squirted all over the Roca wear jeans he wore.

"Huh..Huhh..Huhh...huuuuuh damn...." Dale said crashing his exhausted body upon the mirror as he caught up with his breath. Instant embarrassment I felt, of how into sucking this mans dick I was as if he was a husband of mines. I went into the other bathroom and freshened up. While brushing my teeth, he walked in wearing only his boxers and an undershirt.

"Chocolate what you trying to do?" Dale asked, as that particular question played as a routine after sex, but this time I wondered will my answer be believed and took in consideration. Then again, the question was to self-explained, I couldn't say um or what. Luckily I had a mouth full of toothpaste knowing me I might have said the wrong thing anyway. Actually I didn't know what I was trying to do, all I know I was humming, smacking, and slobbering on his dick like I was for sure a porn star but on another thought I guess I just sucked him up according to my feelings and they were certainly something else.

"Where is your pants Sugar?" With such a concerned voice, I asked rubbing my nails threw the hair on his face and on his chest.

"They are hanging to dry you made me cum on them." He said, as I smiled and excused myself around him in such a cold manner, only to ignore that bulge in his boxers and this throbbing in my jeans.

"Dale, are you ready to eat!" I asked hollering back down the hall.

"Yes baby." He responded, as he walked into the kitchen.

"You like smoothies Chocolate?" He asked.

"Oh yeah." I responded.

"So do I."

"You want to make us one?" I asked.

"Sure." Dale said, as he placed his hands on the small of my back and kissed my face delicately. "You have any fruit?"

"Yes there is different fruit at the bottom of the fridge." I said as he went on as if he lived here.

After I prayed over the food, I lit the French vanilla scented candles that outlined the centerpiece of the dining table. I dimmed the lights, he feed me and I feed him. He cleaned the dishes, I cleaned the dining area, he swept and I mopped. Now you tell me sincere didn't claim this man.

Shanice, Jasi and I had been downtown looking for Shanice a nice leather jacket and strong earplugs or muffs. There were people on every corner selling anything in their possessions. One man had nice kiddy luggage, Jasi thought it was cute and worth it so she bought it.

After we found a cute leather jacket, matching ear muffs, and me a cute skirt in Wilson's leather factory, we headed back to the car. Jasi exchanged all Shanice stuff to the newer luggage; while Shanice sitting in the back looking like Lionel, with her new ear muffs on for real.

"Chocolate stop acting like you don't know where you at! You just missed your turn... Turn there!"

"Girl please, I don't care if it has been ten years, I don't never come alone. As a matter of fact, every time I have gone around here the past year it has been you and I, or they drop her off to me. I don't play like that, you know I can't bring Becky no more after that shit went down over there."

"Yeah, now that shit was wild."

"So because of that I don't, come around with my hands in my pockets."

"Right here!" Jasi yelled. As I noticed the house by seeing Lionel brother Butter Bean Escalade, backed in the yard.

"Damn!" Jasi yelled.

"Girl, what's wrong with you." I asked as we pulled into the yard.

"Chocolate, I don't have time for Butter Bean shit today."

"Oh you ain't got to worry about him, do you see who over there rocking that baby." I said, just before we all got out of the car. Everyone was sitting at ease on the porch; Shanice ran over and gave Granny a hug which was Lionel mom.

"Good evening everyone!" I said.

"Good evening." Some responded back.

"Hey Butter Bean!" Jasi said, as she would do when she knew he wanted to mess with her but couldn't. His face had shocked written all over it, as Meka sat next to him rocking their new baby.

"Oh what's up Jasi?" Butter Bean responded as if he really just noticed her.

"Well here is your granddaughters' luggage. Please be sure she keep up with her things."

"Yeah because I sure have a lot of things in my room bagged up for her." Granny said, as she scuffled to get out of her chair.

"No don't worry, you can get it later."

"Ok well, I'll pack it with her stuff this week, when she leaves."

"Ok Ms. Jasper, yall take care of my baby." I said, as I turned to see Jasi holding Meka baby. Knowing that girl didn't like Becky or me, but in actuality Jasi was the one Butter Bean was buying collectible hand bags and Jacob watches. That's one thing about a dumb and jealous woman, they are so quick to not like a hoe, instead of make friends with the bitch like the niggas do. Trust me eventually a woman will tell on their selves, if not get jealous and curse the enemy out. See a silly broad like Meka, just get played all over, Jasi holding her baby and fucking the dog shit out her man.

"Come on Jasi, I have something to do."

"Alright now, yall be safe!" Jasi said, as we reached the car.

"I bet Butter Bean about to shit on his self." I said laughing.

"Ha ha, I know girl! They baby is so pretty, it look just like his flat face ass." Jasi said.

"So where are we going."

"Let's go to *Bloomingdale's*, I might can find some jeans."

"How about we go pick up Becky cause all of us need to get our shit, Thursday is in three days."

"Well, that's a good idea, but you know Becky got all of her shit."

"Wait, Wait." I said, as my phone lit up caller id unavailable.

"Hello!"

"Hey baby." Dale said.

"Hey honey, I miss you."

"I miss you too! How is your day going?"

"So far it's going good Jasi and I doing a little last minute shopping for our trip."

"Yeah, I was in court all yesterday, and this morning I did a little cleaning, and fishing here on the docks." Dale went on as my smile grew deeper and my heart pumped faster.

"Well today seems laid back. Actually the rest of this week will be laid back; now that they are sorting the jury. Maybe Monday I'll be back busy."

"Dale don't you think you could have stayed back until then."

"No not really, they can call me anytime, besides you are going to New Orleans Thursday aren't you?"

"Yeah."

"Well I just called to let you know I miss you and I'm thinking of you."

"And so am I!" I said with a whisper.

"How about you leave New Orleans a day early and fly to the Bahamas for one day I'll pay for it."

"I don't know Dale; ill check with my girls and see."

"Because I don't believe I can go another day without a kiss or an uh-huh-hug." Dale said, as I blushed.

"Baby ill see."

"Ok well, give me a call later." Dale said, ending the call.

"Damn Chocolate! You really like that man huh, calling him baby and shit." Jasi said.

"I can say I really like him, I will tell you a lie if I say my feelings aren't all over the place."

"I see! You be so happy to hear from him. That's what happens, when they be so genuine and do thoughtful things." Jasi added.

"Girl he wants us on the way back, to come to the Bahamas for a day. He will take care of all the expenses."

"That's good! You know Becky is really going to want to go."

"I know, how about you though."

"Well what about your job, how you gone do that."

"The time with Ms. Minnie in the hospital I use my sick time, I had already requested for my vacation that starts tomorrow until Wednesday of next week.

"When do we come back from New Orleans?" Jasi asked.

"Monday at 2pm, so instead of coming back to MIA let's leave Sunday and go to the Bahamas until Tuesday morning."

"That seems to be fine with me." Jasi confirmed.

"Well we will see, because he just mentioned it to me." I said turning off to *lord and Taylor's*.

"I thought you were going to get Becky."

"I was but I thought about it, she did tell me she had to take Corey to court about some tickets."

"Oh! When her and Corey got back friends?" Jasi asked, with a look like she had smelled something sour.

"Oh I thought you knew. I was over there Sunday at the barbecue and baby daddy was there too." I said, sarcastically, because the both of us was tired of this backwards and forwards relationship shit.

"Girl! She knows damn well, Corey aint worth shit. I just told her ass I seen Katie who lives in the heights, with Corey at Cheese cake factory two weeks ago when Bruce and I went for dinner."

"For real! Didn't they say Katie got that shit?" I asked.

"I heard she is the carrier and her two kids were sick, Tyrone already died and that other baby daddy looking like a mangy dog. They were hollering he had sickle cells." Jasi added.

"Child please, all these niggas Becky run into I wonder why she can't make them out of a NON-custodial father cause the biological father full of shit he loves to live in dangerous zones.

"Tell me about it!" Jasi said, as she rambled on through the racks upon entering the store.

"You know, I need to get some accessories but 20th St. doesn't open until Thursday." Jasi said.

"Well I guess that's when we will go." I said, as Jasi walked off to try on a selection of jeans she picked up along the way.

WHAT A TRIP!

Today was so busy; we all did our last minute shopping for the Essence festival and hurried to our flight that we almost missed. We were checked by the security so serious you would have thought we were down with Bin Laden. We finally boarded the plane; Becky and Jasi sat on the ends with me in the middle. They slept the whole two hour flight and the cocktail wagon had come and gone. Of course I didn't want to wake Becky up; because she was determined to start this weekend as soon as she got in the air. Unfortunately my girl laid with her mouth-cocked open, and head pinned on my shoulder with the tiny pillow the attendants provided.

We had finally touched down and the girls were up. Stretching and looking around.

"Umm Umm Umm Chocolate did you get any rest?" Jasi asked clearing her throat.

"That robot don't need any sleep!" Becky said laughing out loud, interrupting with her sarcastic opinions.

"I dosed off a little here and there." I said. Looking at Becky face to face, in these uncomfortable seats, as she popped a kiss dead smack on my lips. Just before the pilot announced it was safe to get up. Jasi laughed and I was upset, but Becky had made it out her seat; so the aim I prepared for her I had missed. We all just gathered our carried on luggage from the overhead compartments and pushed our way towards the exit.

"Taxi!" Becky screamed so loud.

"Why are you calling the taxi, when Chocolate is renting a car?" Jasi asked.

"I just want to know that I'm out of town for real! Let me see your break lights when I holler." Becky said laughing.

"Girl you are so crazy." Jasi laughed also.

"Damn Jasi, look at them brothers over there?" Becky said, putting her four fingers over her forehead as if she was about to salute.

"Oh yes they are some big body men." Jasi said.

"Excuse me." Becky had walked over to a huddle of about five men. I had walked out to the concourse holding my bags and gripping the rental papers waiting at the curb for the car as I watched them from across the way. Becky was just poised up, and Jasi was taking the pictures. I stood cautiously hoping I wouldn't be invited. Becky and Jasi came back laughing, and giving each other high fives.

"Oh you've made it back, where's the car?" Becky asked.

"They'll bring it around. Now who were those guys you all were taking pictures with?" I asked smiling.

"Some guys from TX, weren't them brothers buffed." Jasi asked.

"Yeah. They look like fresh jail bait!" I said, as the black Denali truck pulled on the curve to let us in.

"Wow, I thought we were going to get a big car? This is tight!" Becky said observing as she took a seat.

"They didn't have any full size cars, they only had compact cars. Did you want a compact car sweetie?" I asked in a joking tone, as we all got comfortable.

"Sure, you just would have been rolling small, along with the big trucks and cars looking down at your sexy black ass!" Becky added with a loud laughter.

"Damn Becky, your silly self don't have to holler like that in my ear!" Jasi screamed, as she tried to get instructions to our suite. Becky held her mouth, and giggled about what she thought was so funny. As we exited the highway down town, there were barricades and policemen everywhere. The gas stations, convenient stores and corners leading to the city was crowded also.

"Hey baby, can I get some of those p-nuts?" Becky said, letting her back window down. Receiving the man's attention, who wore a sign *`p-nut $1.00'*. He came running to the truck Becky handed him the dollar and kicked back.

"Damn you elephant! You love p-nuts, that man might was playing with his balls while packing them bags." Jasi said, shaking her head and laughing at Becky.

"Oh well. You and I have licked balls before right, and besides these p-nuts have hubs on it asshole!" Becky responded as Jasi and I burst out into laughter.

We drove down Burden St, and Becky wanted to stop for water. I found the most crowded corner store possible, just what she would like an audience to show off on. As I was pulling in she started chanting, but yet sitting so still.

"Yes look at all these brothers?" Becky said as she jumped out, making her way in the store from the crowd of men who just went crazy for that loose fitted sundress, big floppy hat and Chloe sunglasses. She walked without an arch in her back and every stride in her step. The guys whistled, and the few who didn't run up to her stared as if she was nude. Becky knew she had it and she did flaunt it, hard enough until the girls that stood near had to see what was so spectacular about her.

"Excuse me, baby. Where you from?" As this tall bright skinned guy approached her on the way back to the truck. Becky did what she always did when she weren't interested; ignored the man. All of a sudden a candy red ninja pulled up, and lifted his helmet. His complexion was as good as a Cherokee Indian, and his side burns were aligned like a baby.

"Can I take you for a ride beautiful?" He asked. Becky didn't bother to say yes or no. She threw the water and her hat in the back seat of the truck and hopped onto the unknown fella bike. Holding the center of her dress down with one hand and the other around his waist. As all the other guys watched her rode off on the bike, and her hair into the wind.

We sat there for about 10 min and waited for her, she left her phone so there was no way to call her.

"That damn Becky, I tell you the truth?" Jasi said. I thought if I keep my comments to myself, Jasi wouldn't be so alarmed by the passing minutes. I decided to take a drive down Bourbon Street, there were people dancing and singing all over the street. Soon we seen that ninja bike, but lost it after wards. So we drove back to the convenient store where we departed, and there she was posted by the bike with her hands on her hip.

"Look at her ass, she think she came here for herself." Jasi said, as I quickly distinguished she had a problem."

"Child let her have fun."

"I want to have fun too!"

"Jasi girl you is, whats up with you?" I asked.

"Shit I'm just saying, if she gone be disappearing like that we aint gone have no fun looking for her through all these parades." Jasi said going on and on.

"Alright alright." I said, trying to end the meaningless conversation.

"You going out tonight?" Jasi asked, changing the subject.

"Hell yeah."

"Shit I want a drink maybe an incredible hulk, Hennessey, or something." She said, as Becky came walking back to the truck.

"Did I hear Hennessey?" Becky asked as she plopped down in her seat.

"Yeah you heard Hennessey but Ms. Becky, you aint the only one that's here for fun." Jasi said, as I knew it was grounds for an argument.

"Oh my god, please just enjoy! Don't be stuck up just have fun. Becky added.

"I know that Becky, but hell don't just leave us here with your Selfish ass! All I'm saying is consider that WE on vacation too!" Jasi said as the two of them went to arguing back and forth.

"Come on girls, you both need to stop, there's enough time for the three of us to have fun!" I said just as I thought the truck grew silence.

"Chocolate, when are we going to eat?" Becky asked.

"There she goes again." Jasi mumbled under her breath.

"Shut up Jasi, before I stuff a big dick in your mouth!" Becky yelled, cause she knew what exactly made Jasi upset, so she just went for it so bluntly. Jasi looked at Becky, where you could recognize the wrinkles in her forehead that she had officially became upset. I tried to hold my laugh, but I couldn't.

"Becky you really need to grow up!" Jasi said in anger.

"Well... If a child pussy is as big as mine, I think you should find a news station to cover this story because you know I'll show it!" Becky said, reaching out at Jasi cheeks, for a pinch, smiling." I love you Jasi!" Becky said as Jasi shoved her hand from her face and turned toward the window to catch the view. I laughed the whole while, because I knew Becky had this way of making anyone mad but she would just laugh about it like you were joking with her. Her mouth could be so dirty at times, and she never cared what you thought or felt. As we ended up in the parking lot at the West Gate it also was packed with guest checking in, and hanging around in the parking lot, hoping to catch a celebrity, or lurking for the sophisticated ones who lived here for the weekend of this extravaganza event.

"Chocolate, why are we here already?" Becky asked.

"We are going out to eat, let's just get settled and then go out." I responded, as we parked next to a group full of guys in a RV. Becky got out and her dress went side to side, the guys forgot about they were unloading their camper as they watched Becky put on her show. Then Jasi and I got out.

"Do you Ladies need any help unloading?" One of the gentlemen asked.

"Sure, you guys are such nice gentlemen!" Becky butted in and answered for all.

"My name is Earl I'm from TX and this is my boy Tim from NY." Earl said, as he gave Becky and me a hug, but Jasi reached her hand out for a shake.

"I'm Becky, this is Chocolate and this is Ms. Jasi" Becky explained.

"Well nice to meet you all, our other friends went in the inside to take in some luggage, they also will be glad to meet some fine dark chocolaty sisters like yourself." Earl said, sounding so country. He put two of the gym bags on his shoulder, and the other one on top his head, which never tilted or fell.

Jasi came and sat next to us in the lounge, and said she was waiting on the clerk to enter her information. The two helpful guys placed the bags into the chair and went to continue unloading their things. As soon as they reached the door to exit, Jasi grabbed her bags.

"Come on ladies!" Jasi proceeded towards the elevator. Becky and I grabbed our bags simultaneously looking at each other while following Jasi's instructions.

"Jasi I thought you had to wait for that lady with your information?" Becky asked.

"I didn't, I just did not trust those guys taking our luggage to the room. They might think they can come back later for something." Jasi said.

"Girl please!" Becky had seemed to get a little upset, being friendly is a part of her wild personality and being stuck up was something she hated.

"Look ladies, I hope you two aren't going to go through this the whole weekend." I said as we entered the two-bedroom suite.

"I'll take the room with the bathroom." Jasi said ignoring me and pushed her way through.

"Umm, I'll take the room in the back. How about you Chocolate?" Becky asked.

"It doesn't matter, I plan on having fun not sleep." I shouted back, as a plopped down on the pullout sofa just when my phone began to ring.

"Hello." I answered.

"Hello, baby how are you?"

"Hey honey, what's going on?" I asked with a huge smile, as I was so happy to hear from him.

"I'm ok, just doing a little work to the beach house."

"Ah, I will like to see it one day." I said.

"It's only a ticket away." Dale replied.

"Dale! Have you forgotten, the girls and me are in New Orleans?"

"No Chocolate baby, I haven't forgot." He said as he took a deep breath "I miss you; have you and the girls thought about it?" Dale asked.

"Well our flight leaves out Monday afternoon, and I mentioned it to them but no response yet; and then I have to return back to work Wednesday."

"That's pretty good timing. As I mentioned last week maybe Sunday afternoon you can catch a flight alone over here and fly back home Tuesday evening." Dale quickly reminded me of his coordinated trip for me.

"Dale I really don't know; I have to see if the girls will be alright with me leaving the fun we planned over a year ago." I said.

"No chocolate, no big deal if you can't, but truthfully and selfishly speaking I'll be more than glad if you could accommodate me here in this lonely beach house." Dale teased me in such a pitiful voice.

"I'll see baby."

"So what are you ladies doing?" Dale asked.

"Actually, we just settled in and now we are going to get something to eat."

"Ok Baby I'll call you later. Do you have a pen?" Dale asked.

"Yes I have one." I answered. Grabbing the one lying on the table along with a note pad.

"This is the number to the house where I am, if you need anything give me a call." Dale quickly recited his number and kissed the phone and so did I just when Becky barged in.

"Damn who was that?" She asked.

"Now you in my business!" I said, smiling while busying myself by unpacking.

We all were ready for dinner. Becky wore a beaded top with blue jeans that fitted to each curve with a pair Steve Madden pointed toe leather boots with silver stiletto heels. Jasi wore capris with the matching top with her green pumps, and I wore my hip hugging short jean skirt with a small Bisou Bisou top and my hot pink pumps.

"Ladies you both look nice." Becky said.

"Thank you, and so do you Becky." Jasi said smiling.

"Thanks Becky, you are working those jeans." I said, as the three of us got into the elevators switching hard, laughing loud, and talking shit.

"Ok who's driving?" I asked.

"I'll drive." Jasi claimed.

We drove and drove all around town; we went through Magnolia, and all the wards. There were music playing, and food selling everywhere on one particular corner a huge sign and a line for a plate of seafood rice and Alaskan steamed crabs for six dollars sure got our attention. Each of us bought one and sat in the truck to only devour it as if we didn't eat in days.

"Dam this shit is so good." I added as I washed the spicy Cajun seasoning down with a sweet ice tea.

"I hear yo greedy ass back there smacking!" Becky responded with her mouth full of food

Traffic was so baked up and restaurants were over flowing, New Orleans sure was the spot to be in this weekend.

Night had fallen and we still were out, having drinks and so much fun.

"Oh Becky lets go find us some bikers." Jasi asked. I knew then Jasi was getting tipsy.

"Come on Chicken lets flaunt it!" Becky added. Just when out of nowhere there were about 20 Harley's bikers, some with crocodile leather seats, chromed out wheels and pipes.

"Would you ladies like to ride with us?" One of the gentlemen asked.

"Sure." Jasi came from around the truck and hopped on the back of the bike. Taking the man's helmet right off his head and placing it on hers.

"How about you two ladies?" Another gentlemen asked.

Becky jumped in the truck, and pushed the locked button. Looking at me as if I better get out and get on, so we both hopped on the bikes.

I felt so sexy; I rode the bike in the way I wanted to ride Dale, back arched and ass straight in the air. Jasi was ahead of the both of us, waving her hands in the air, and Becky was to my right with her ass high as she could get it.

We rode for hours, felt like we rode all over Baton Rouge.

By the time we made it back to the truck, Jasi was still ready to drink more. She had become more of the attention than Becky. However; Becky did realize Jasi was drunk, so she let her have her fun, because they knew I couldn't handle the both of them.

"Hey Baby, its JASI the queen is in town!" Jasi shouted, getting into the truck. Becky looked at her and laughed.

"Girl; I tell you if Bruce could see this Hippie back here; he would kill us." Becky said laughing.

"Can I have just one more cup, this stuff is sweet." Jasi said, reaching her cup towards the front seat for some more belvedere, as Becky poured her a shot of tequila straight instead.

"You have to drink this shot straight up if you bad!" Becky said as Jasi took the cup, which was big enough, for at least three shots and turned it up.

"Au au auhhhh! Um um um ummm" Jasi moaned, as she scooted up in the seat and squirmed all around holding her throat while Becky and I laughed.

"God damn that shit strong!" Jasi said, as she looked in the empty cup and tossed it to Becky.

"Why you did that?" I asked to Becky beneath laughter.

"Shit Jasi can handle that!"

"I show can, give me another one." She said, dragging her speech.

"No!" I shouted.

"Girl shut your ass up!" Jasi said, as I continued to laugh.

"Pull over there!" Becky yelled, pointing to a stand that was selling honey roasted Turkey legs.

"You want one Jasi?" Becky asked as she stood with the door open and the smoke was seeping its good grilled scent.

"One of what?"

"A dick!" Becky jokingly said.

"Girl a Turkey leg." I asked turning towards her in the back seat sweating bullets, hair scattered and eyes blood shot red.

"Yeah." She replied.

"Bring me one too." I added, as Becky walked over to the stand.

Before Becky could have made it back Jasi had fallen asleep.

"Chocolate we need to give her that all the time, look back there." Becky said, as Jasi laid with one leg in the seat, and the other rested on the floor. Her mouth was open and her capris were unzipped. Becky took at least four pictures of her; she even took Jasi hand placing one of them in between her legs and the one finger up her nose.

"Jasi, Jasi!" Becky and I called; she didn't attempt to move or say a word upon our arrival back at the hotel. Luckily there was Earl the guy we met earlier.

"Earl." Becky called; he turned towards our direction as she baited him over.

"Well did you ladies find yourself around to have a good time?" Earl asked.

"Yes, but we have one that had too much fun." Becky explained.

"What happen?" Earl asked.

"She just had far too many drinks." Becky added.

"Would you like me to take her to the room?" Earl politely volunteered.

"Would you please?" I agreed.

He reached in and put Jasi over his shoulder, her body hung over his as if she was lifeless.

"Boy if Jasi could dream this, she would kill the both of us Chocolate!" Becky asked.

"Well, I damn sight can't lift her, can you?"

Her hair was dangling, while she was in a partial upside down position. Becky hurried ahead of Earl and opened the room door. Becky held the knob of the door, as Earl laid Jasi on the bed. She still laid quietly this time with her heels dangling from the edge of the bed.

"Thanks Earl!" I immediately said.

"Well you ladies welcome, anytime you need me I'm in the Checca Lodge next door." Earl added.

"I don't think we would be needing you no more tonight. I hope." Becky said, as Earl walked on the other side of the door, and Becky closed it behind him in a respectable manner.

"Girl, what else damn help we gone need tonight?" Becky sarcastically asked with both of her hands upon her hips.

"Aw Becky the man just was being nice. Hell if he weren't out there, how the hell we were going to get (drinking Annie) out of the truck?" I asked, as Becky laughed out loud.

"Shit drinking Annie would have had a very nice leather bed in the truck." Becky said, as the two of us went out on the patio and she lit her joint.

"Girl you crazy."

"So Ms. Chocolate what has been going on with this Dale guy which you claim he better than `Good dick Chuckie?" Becky asked laughing while striking up a conversation she knew could carry us through the night.

"Well there is most defiantly no comparison there honey child! Dale is a man for a man; he's no man of excuses, problems, anger and most of all BULLSHIT."

"Chocolate are you serious; your giving up the good dick?" Becky said blowing the smoke through her nose and directly into my face.

"Becky, baby must I tell you that Dale dick and pussy eating skills is so good that it makes me don't even want to cum. It be just that damn good, and I be greedy as hell too. I don't even think about Chuck and no one else. I'm telling you Dale is a complete package kind of guy, fuck them individually thoughtless ass men cause that sure aint him! Dale can cook, clean, have fun, enjoy kids, he is single, has no kids, and a great job. Goddamn let me stop I'm scaring myself." I claimed, as Becky smiled and passed me a drink.

"I'm dead ass serious. I told you it's just something about him, he's too much like myself."

"Are you sure it's like that Chocolate." Becky asked, as I took a swallow.

"Well I'll tell you what; if it is wrong, baby I'm not trying to make it right. Becky girl I like him and I mean I like him a lot. His personality shines, his thoughts are far beyond belief, his admiration is something I can't explain, oh and most of all his sweet affectionate ways sweeps me off my feet."

"Ok baby, I got you!" Becky said with an approved smile.

"Becky, I do. I really like this guy."

"Chocolate, take a chance. Just remember if you like him that much, put down that wall you have built around that selfish tissue called PRIDE. Play for a husband this time. Let there be exemption for some of the rules." Becky said, dangling her legs up and down, as she coughed off every other pull she withheld from her joint.

"I know right." I said, as Becky yarned very loud and sarcastically long.

"Shit I'm sleepy Chocolate." Becky said.

"Well care your tired ass to sleep." I said, as Becky went in.

Morning had come, by the sound of gagging and spitting had awakened the two of us to find Jasi sitting on the side of the toilet. Teary eyes and gagging.

"What's wrong Jasi?" I asked.

"I don't know." She said, as Becky stood in behind me.

"You know Chocolate! She drank too dam much last night. Go make some coffee and drink it hot and dark, you'll feel better." Becky said, and walked back towards her bed.

"Jasi continued to gag, while I was in the kitchen making coffee. I was not sure how to prepare it dark, with sugar or not. I had to ask the semi drunk Becky whom went back to bed.

"Becky!" I screamed, as Becky head was planted in the pillows.

"What, do you want?"

"Do I put cream and sugar?"

"No! Just leave it black and give it to her!"

"Here Jasi, drink this Becky say you will fell a little better." I said, as Jasi leaned back over the stool.

"I'll never drink again; if I have to feel like this." Jasi said, as she reached for the coffee mug. Her loose hair dangled to her wet lips, and her eyes were still red especially now that she was straining to throw up. She sipped and sipped until it was half gone.

"Chocolate, I am so weak. Will you please help me back in bed?" Jasi begged.

"Now Jasi I know that liquor didn't do that much to you." I replied as she placed one hand on the tub and the other around my waist.

"Jasi, just lay here." I said, throwing the cover over her legs. I walked out to the screened in patio overlooking the parking lot. There were guys and women loading up for breakfast; snapping pictures and laughing with one another. I stood sucking in all the fresh air, and letting the sun shine on my body just when my cell begins to ring. I was unaware who it is this time because the caller ID was reading *unavailable* for every call.

"Hello." I answered.

"Good morning suga, How are you!" Dale sounded so happy.

"I'm doing great, how about yourself baby?"

"I'm doing good, but it could be better if you were here with me. By the ocean under the cool breeze." He said charming me by his surroundings.

"Well sounds like you're relaxing more than work?"

"Tuesday I will be back in court again."

"Oh well that's not so bad at least you have a couple of days to play in the sun." I said, smiling.

"Where's Jasi and Becky?" He asked.

"Becky is sleep and Jasi also she doesn't feel well."

"What's the problem, did you guys party hard on that liquor?" He asked.

"Well you know Becky, she had Jasi taking liquor shots. When she doesn't even drink much. So she was Errling (*vomiting*) all in the toilet this morning."

"Hahaha, Becky is a trip, why she did lil Jasi like that?"

"They just be having fun, with one another and then she took pictures. Jasi is going to be something mad with Becky." I responded.

"So Baby, are you enjoying yourself?" He asked, as I took that question by surprise honestly I really wasn't having fun as of yet. However, I didn't want to chicken out and leave the girls on our trip that we planned to enjoy. I tell ya it seems so funny I supposed to be enjoying this but instead my heart really wanted to be with Dale.

"It's been pretty much different; it's ok." I responded.

"Over here, of course it's like home, but I miss you and I'm not having a bit of fun without you." He explained.

"Awe that was so sweet, you'll see me. Let's see what goes on today and I'll see if I can get away." I added.

"Who has Shanice?" He asked, jumping to another subject.

"Shanice went to see her father in P.A. This weekend."

Oh, ok. So if you need anything you know to call me on the house phone." Dale instructed.

"Ok baby, I will talk with you later."

"Yes, you will talk with me later, and hopefully see me soon." Dale responded.

"Bye baby!" smacking my lips together and making the kissing sound.

"Bye baby!" Dale said as he did the same in return.

I sat on the comfortable lounge chair rocking back and forth with a smile. Thinking how good it will be, if this is the one I have been searching, and praying for. I shut my eyes and tried to retrace every day I seen him, every time he smiled, the way he looked, the way he dressed, the way he smelled, even the way he would admire me when he thought I wasn't looking... I was so deep in my imagination until I was just about to holler thinking he was here with me running his tongue back up my pussy like he did weeks ago. However I was slightly distracted by Jasi's phone which had ranged about ten different times; and she didn't bother about answering it once. I went into the kitchen and fried me two eggs and a toast for myself along with a hot tea as usual. Becky had made her way out of bed, finding me on the patio enjoying the scenery and my breakfast.

"Damn why you didn't cook enough for everybody?" Becky asked, peeking her head through the huge sliding door.

"Well you ladies was resting so good, I didn't feel the need to bother you all about an egg or toast. I'm not your mama or your man." I said munching on my toast with a smile.

"Ha ha ha, you are silly! Did Jasi drink all the coffee?" Becky asked.

"Yeah, but she threw that back up too." I responded.

"Oh no; that aint no empty stomach shit, or no hang over. Jasi ass might be pregnant!" Becky claimed.

"Girl please. Well I don't know your mama said that the other day too."

"Chocolate, I'm going to go jump on her." Becky said.

"Leave that girl alone!" Becky still, headed towards the room Jasi slept in.

"Jasi! Oh Jasi belle. Wake your ass up!" Becky was singing to her own tune.

"Becky would you leave that girl, she doesn't feel good." I said, as Jasi laid in the bed moaning.

"Jasi when the last you seen Ms. Mary!" Becky said in a serious tone, all I could do is laugh. Becky was most defiantly crazy she always called her menstruation Ms. Mary as if it was a real person.

"Stop leave me alone Becky!" Jasi said in a very weak voice.

"Come on now, is there a lil Bruce in here?" Becky said as if she knew this for a fact.

"Jasi I'm talking to you, can you hear me! Do you see me?" Becky put her lips to Jasi ear with the crazy questions. Jasi jumped up from the bed and towards the other room she went.

"Look at her." Becky teased as she went behind her, then there was the loud bang; her slamming the door.

"Chocolate! Chocolate!" Becky called, as I heard her voice trailing back to the patio.

"Yes Becky?" I answered.

"Do you want to ride for a little breakfast, maybe a turn through Bourbon St.?" Becky asked, standing in the doorway one hand on her hip and the other in the corner of the door.

"Maybe?"

"Look now I aint with this shit, yall wanna be sick and missing motherfuckers. I want to have fun and not stay stuck up in this room." Becky said.

"Becky its only 9:45am, who is on Bourbon St. this early?"

"I don't damn know, all I know it's a lot of people and things I haven't seen. Being this is a vacation lets act like tourist, and not grievers." Becky said.

"Alright, then you driving." I said as she ignored me and went on talking.

"I wonder if Nikki came out here or did she go to Brooklyn for the weekend?"

"Are you going to keep on those pajamas?" Becky asked Jasi as she continued digging in her luggage.

"Where are we going Becky this early?"

"Just put on some clothes, you never know who you may see." Becky said, as she threw a towel over her shoulder and headed towards the bathroom.

While Becky was in the shower, I ironed our jeans. Jasi had come from the room and into the kitchen for water. She had looked so drained and eccentric for some reason, and I don't think the liquor is a factor neither.

"Jasi what's up are you feeling a little better?" I asked.

"NO, I just feel like I am on a boat with rough seas girl." She said barley making it to the half bathroom just when she leaned over to the garbage and dashed out a big ball of spit and then some.

After all the commotion was over, I peeked into the bathroom as she was holding the base of the sink while brushing her teeth and gagging all at the same time. Becky stepped through the door with a single towel wrapped around her, meeting Jasi as she bent the corner to the living area.

"Well, I see you got out of bed. What's going on are you feeling better?" Becky asked, as Jasi took a seat at the dining table with a big glass of water.

"Jasi, you know if you have a hang over the worse thing to do is drink water like that. It will make you feel drunk all over again." Becky said.

"I don't feel drunk or anything, I just feel really nauseated." Jasi said, as she shoved the water away.

"Drink some more coffee or orange juice. Actually another shot will put you back on your feet." Becky instructed, and was dead serious.

"Becky look I'm not up for the games just morning; I feel very sick. The coffee made me throw up also."

I gave Becky her jeans and I left the two of them talking, because any minute I knew they would be arguing again.

"Jasi just get up and put on some clothes, maybe you need to eat something." Becky said, as she sat and lotion her bowlegs, on the edge of the sofa chair. Jasi got up and disappeared for a minute or two. When she came back she was wearing a comfortable flair skirt, matching sexy top that cut to hang off her shoulders and some very cute sandals that tied once around her ankles. She didn't have a bit of makeup on, neither a touch of oil sheen on her hair, or any accessory of any kind. She just looked plain and not feeling good. I finished my shower and dressed into my Frankie B jeans a cropped top, and my Channel stiletto heels. Becky was standing in the doorway impatiently wearing her Sergio jeans which look like they were painted on her.

"Well ladies seems to me everyone's ready." Becky said as I stood in the mirror, oil sheening my hair. Jasi just waited in the living room, talking to Bruce on the phone in such a sober voice.

"Alright let's go, I don't know what Becky wants to see early this morning." I said.

"Anything besides the damn bed!" Becky replied, grabbing the keys, and camera from the table while Jasi and I just followed her out.

"I guess this means since I want to go, I have to drive too huh?" Becky added as we approached the truck.

"Well, that would be nice." I said.

"Chocolate your pretty ass never want to drive!"

"Girl shut up and let's go eat." I said sitting in the passenger seat as she stood in the driver door.

"Turn the air on!" Jasi yelled, as she laid in the back seat.

"Well what yall, hoes are going to eat?" Becky said in a joking manner, pulling off in full speed.

"I don't know, just something to take this feeling away." Jasi added.

"Shit we could have walked to one of the restaurants." I said, as I viewed the chain of shops and restaurants minutes away from our hotel.

"Let's eat something from this Pancake house." Becky said at the same time pulling into the parking lot. Jasi jumped out of the truck before it could make a complete stop, throwing her cell in the seat, and begin gagging again.

"All now, Jasi. I don't think liquor do you that bad unless you've gotten liquor poisoned; and there is nothing wrong with me as we were drinking from the same bottle." Becky mentioned as she came around the truck with napkins in her hand and the truck engine was still on.

"Please, yall take me to a hospital." Jasi said in a desperate tone.

"Jasi try eating something first. If that doesn't make you feel better, then we will try the hospital." Becky said.

"I don't want to go in there like this!" Jasi had started to cry; we knew then, that she really wasn't feeling well. Becky suddenly left all the jokes alone.

"Well I'll go and order the food, while you and Chocolate sit here." Becky suggested.

"Alright that's ok, bring me a hot tea and a club sandwich." I requested.

"Jasi I'm going to bring you a soup and some crackers maybe that will soothe your stomach." Becky said, as Jasi stood with both hands on her knees throwing up yellow vomit.

"Yeah that should do it Becky." I said, rubbing Jasi on her back for a little relief.

Becky started walking towards the restaurant, making a call on her cell with her big purse swinging to her every movement.

"Chocolate I want to go back to the room." Jasi said, as she stretched across the back seat.

"We'll drop you off when Becky come back." I said, as she closed her eyes and rubbed her stomach. Pulling up next to us was a cute couple, a guy who favored Chuck, with a very thin young woman. She wore a nice short jean dress decorated by multiple colored stones and a pair matching boots looking cute and classy. Her dude was dressed rather thuggish with his jeans pulled half way down his ass. Becky had then came walking out of the restaurant with the drinks in one hand and a bag in the other hand. I saw her head glance at the guy and apparently Becky thought the same, if not she would have squinted her face or mimic the couple walk. However he was very handsome, stylish, and thuggish while she was pretty and looked to have been about that money. Flossing a style that looked to be quite lavish.

"Nice looking fella! For the record I am not fixing to drive now, but I am going to eat first." Becky profoundly stated before sitting in the truck. She then passed the food around as her phone rang just when she was getting ready to put a spoon full in her mouth. She fastened her tray closed and stepped outside the truck to answer the phone call in private. Overhearing her conversation Ms. Nikki was here in Baton Rouge and Becky was secretly making plans to meet them somewhere.

"Jasi do you got your food?" Becky asked as she returned to the truck, observing Jasi food which remained on the side of her untouched.

"I'm going to eat it." Jasi uttered in a weak tone.

"Jasi you need to get up and make yourself eat. The longer you wait the worse you are going to feel." Becky added while opening Jasi container of soup.

Jasi sat up, squinting her eyes and reaching for the soup. She slowly opened her fork and went for the potatoes while Becky just smacked and talked at the same time. Jasi took a spoonful, but before she could swallow she had to hold her head out the window throwing up the remaining of the orange juice she drunk earlier.

"Becky, please take me back to the airport! I have to go home and find out what's wrong." Jasi said, leaning back in the truck with eyes full of tears and slightly red from all the straining while vomiting.

"Girl you haven't even gave it enough time to see if you are going to feel better yet." Becky said, as Jasi reached for her phone and started dialing numbers. Apparently she didn't get any answer, however she left a message.

"Bruce, it's me please give me a call. I need you to pick me up from the airport today." I knew there was nothing else Becky could say or could do. Jasi really didn't like what she was feeling.

"Alright as, soon as I finish eating Queen, I'll take you to the room to get your things and then I'll take you to the airport." Becky said.

"No, just take me to the airport, yall can bring my stuff back!" Jasi instructed.

"Are you sure you are going to be ok by yourself?" I asked, munching on a slice of toast.

"Yall go ahead and have fun, it's enough people on the flight to help me if I needed it." Jasi said, as she laid back across the back seat helpless.

"Jasi if you feel that bad, I'll just come along." I added inviting myself.

"So what about me, and the vacation!" Becky asked, looking in my direction without a bit of sympathy.

"Well Becky, Jasi sick and I don't think I would let you fly alone feeling bad either." I responded to the selfish question.

"I'm glad Nikki here, cause yall about to fuck up my whole weekend on this liquor shit! When I'm telling Jasi ass, she's fuckin pregnant, all she need to do is munch on some damn crackers, or lick some salt!" Becky said with such a serious face and tough tone. I couldn't believe Becky was acting like this. She immediately got on her phone and called Nikki up, asking what hotel she in, and where she hanging out at today.

She drove unto the interstate following the airport signs. Jasi just laid; she didn't bother to say a word.

"Becky, you know you should have went back to the room so I could get my bag. If not you have two extra bags to check in and one for sure is heavy." I added.

"No, I have to get this Queen to a plane, being she's about to die let's just focus on the airport." Becky said, as she pushes the accelerator harder. While I said nothing else; cause Becky was bound to blow up any minute.

"Chocolate, can you try to call Bruce for me again?" Jasi asked.

"Hello." Bruce answered, I passed the phone to the back.

"Hey baby. As Jasi tried to sound as strong, without a clue she passed me the phone and hung her head in the plastic container gagging.

"Hey Bruce it's me Chocolate."

"Hello Chocolate, what's wrong." Bruce immediately asked.

"Jasi doesn't feel good and we are on our way to the airport to bring her back home."

"Well what's wrong with her?"

"Bruce I really don't know, she just keeps throwing up." I didn't want to tell him I think the liquor made her feel this way, so I kept it the way it appears now.

"Can I speak back with her Chocolate please?" As he sounded concerned, I passed the phone back to Jasi while Becky was cutting her eyes at me.

"Hello." She said with teary eyes.

Arriving to the airport, Jasi told Bruce she'd call him when she gets there, to meet her at the hospital.

"Oh my god Jasi!" Becky said.

"Becky please, stop the bullshit yo!" I said as I became upset; being she only thought about Becky when it came to fun. Fuck what anybody else felt. I hurried out the truck slamming the door and proceeded to open Jasi door. She stepped to ground and we both walked away, as Becky pulled off before we could have made it on the side walk.

"Chocolate, you could have stayed." Jasi said, as we walked through the entrance.

"Nah, I couldn't have let you go back alone feeling like this." I said, as Jasi rested in a near chair, while I went and checked the both of us in.

Luckily the flight was leaving in 45 min. I paid the fee and took a seat next to her. My cell phone begins to ring, as I search through my purse for it.

"Hello" I answered.

"What up baby?" Dale asked.

"Nothing much, just here at the airport." I responded.

"For what!" He asked.

"Jasi still doesn't feel well." I explained.

"From the drinks?" He asked.

"I don't think it's that, she's going to the hospital when we get there."

"Where is Becky?"

"She stayed back with her friend Nikki." I responded.

"Oh, well what time does your flight arrives in MIA?" Dale asked as if he were going to be there.

"At 12:15pm."

"Are you going over to the hospital also?"

"Yes I am."

"Ok, well call me when you get to the hospital, and tell Jasi I hope she feels better."

"Bye baby." I responded.

"Talk with you later baby." Dale said as I powered my phone off with a smile looking over at Jasi who was slouched over in the chair, munching on some salty p-nuts.

"Girl, if drinking makes me feel like this. I will never drink again."

"I hope that's what got you feeling like that and nothing else." I added with a smile.

"Nah, chocolate I can't be pregnant remember I'm on the pill."

"We will see, when you get there what's going on." I said, as she took a deep breath and nodded her head.

"Well when was your last menstrual?"

"Chocolate you know its irregular from them pills, I think about 4 months ago."

"Wow, I don't know, but that will be something." I said as the speakers announced our plane is ready for boarding.

Departing from the plane there stood Bruce in the concourse waiting for us instead at the hospital. Jasi immediately started to cry and in Bruce arms she were.

"What's wrong honey, why are you crying?" Bruce asked, rubbing his hands through her long hair.

"I don't know, I feel real bad." Jasi said making the words out beneath her cry.

"Chocolate, you want to take the car home, or follow us to the hospital." Bruce asked, being we drove Jasi car Thursday to the airport and left it in the garage.

"Yeah, I'll take the car and meet you two at Gen. Hospital." I replied.

By the time I made it to the garage Dale was calling.

"Hello."

"Hey baby, I see you've made it to MIA, is Jasi feeling any better."

"No, but Bruce meet us here at the airport. I'm getting the car now and going to meet them at the Hospital." I said.

"Ok, I just was making sure you made it back safe. Call me when you get a little free time."

"Later baby." I replied. Pulling out from the airport, I think I better go and get something to eat first, no telling how long we will be at that hospital. I stopped by and grabbed some oxtails and rice from Jackson's soul food restaurant in Overtown and got back on 95 following the hospital signs.

Upon my arrival I knew Jasi was being checked in, by one of Bruce close friends as he sat near her bedside clutching her hands. They had the IV running, so I figured it was sort of dehydration going on.

"Jasi how are you feeling?" The tears poured from her eyes before a word came out; I went closer to Jasi and rubbed her head as Bruce kissed her hand.

"Don't cry." I didn't know what was wrong; I just didn't like the fact that she was crying.

"I'm dehydrated. Because I am pregnant." Jasi said as more tears came flowing down. I know she was not ready for a baby; she is too far into school and doing so well but however they can afford it. Bruce hung his head down in shame while I sat and said nothing else.

"I'll be back baby, I'm going to the cafeteria." Bruce mention as he rubbed his hands over her tears.

"Ok." She silently whispered.

"Care for anything Chocolate?"

"No thanks Bruce."

"How about you baby." He asked Jasi.

"No." She replied as more tears ran down her cheeks and he walked from the other room with his hands stuffed in his pockets and head faced down.

"Chocolate, girl what have I got myself into?" Jasi asked as she sniffed in and wiped a few tears away.

"Jasi you are human, not like your life is going to end because you are pregnant. You have Bruce by your side."

"No, it's not that I have Bruce, I have school that's soon to be finish next year. The way I feel I won't be able to do anything." Jasi said as you could now hear her cry, instead of seeing the tears. "Bruce is a married man, I don't want a child from a married man!" Jasi went on, explaining even more positive reasons. I couldn't say anything because she was really hitting some very good points.

"Yeah you are right."

"I know Chocolate, I know I have fucked up my life and career." She said, as we got very quiet. Moments later, Bruce walked back into the room with a bowl of pineapples and a brownie he purchased from the cafeteria.

"Ok, I guess I'll go on home. Bruce and you may have a lot to talk about, so call me Jasi." I said, as I needed to give Bruce this time to calm and talk things over with her.

"Alright." She mumbled looking in one direction.

"Are they going to keep you or what?" I asked.

"No, I just was talking to the Dr. in the hall. He said after the IV goes out he will discharge her." Bruce answered; just as I suspected Dr. Spain was his friend and also their Dr, which he didn't have to wait on anything. Not even a prescription he would call them in, to avoid visiting his office.

Driving along interstate 95, I decided to call Becky to see what's going on up there. Don't know if I shall tell Becky about Jasi or shall I let Jasi tell her. I was surprised; Jasi wasn't a bit happy or ok with the situation. Bruce he would love it, but hell Jasi says she not planning a lifetime with him.

"Hello Becky."

"What's up Ms. Mona?" Becky said, in a calmly matter.

"Nothing much, just leaving the Hospital."

"So what's the problem?" Becky asked, I was stuck for a minute deciding do I want to be the one to tell her, or let Jasi.

"She's pregnant." Without a second thought, I said what I shouldn't have.

"I told yall so." Becky said, without a spick of bliss in her voice.

"Becky please, don't mention nothing until Jasi tell you."

"Girl, I ain't gonna say nothing. I'll let her tell me."

"The reason I say that Becky is because, I know she didn't want you to be right and you was. So don't be teasing the girl, she really going through something right now." As I summed it up a little better, to avoid the curiosity Becky might have had about that little statement '*don't tell*' as if we were hiding secrets from one another.

"Jasi, just got to take it one day at a time. We both know the sickness and felling goes away after a while maybe three or four months."

"Child please that's the least problem Jasi thinking about." I added

"Well hell Bruce aint broke! So what's the problem his age?"

"Nah but she still in school, and you know she committing adultery.

"What the fuck ever bitch we sin every day!"

"So what were you doing?" I asked, quickly changing the subject.

"I am ironing some clothes, getting ready to go out to the jazz parade with Nikki and some friends of hers." Becky replied.

"Oh. Well Becky you be careful out there. Don't act a fool; keep it to a minimum. Meaning take care of you regardless what you accomplish or accomplishing."

"So, are you coming back out here?" Becky asked.

"No Becky. I think I just might go to Bahamas with Dale for the rest of the weekend."

"Oh, that's how you do things. You know what!" Becky started and then paused. "Being you were without so long, I'm going to allow you to try me like this. Yeah leave me out here alone after you done planned it!"

"Oh auh auh Becky, you know you could have came back but you wanted to stay. You know damn well that wouldn't be right to have let Jasi fly back by herself and she was sick."

"Anyways." Becky said, cutting me off.

"Well do you want to meet me in Bahamas, you said you would come anyhow?"

"For what!"

"Just to relax." I added.

"Girl please I know you done already gave that man the pussy, so what I suppose to be doing cock blocking. We too damn old for that shit now." Becky said in a joking manner as I laughed and thought back when we would go to the movies and invite one another, to keep from giving up the Nookie which is what we called our pussy back in the day."

"Girl, go on and have a good time. Bring me some cute accessories the colored ones." She said, sounding as happy as ever.

"Alright Becky. Remember take care of you."

"OK I'll talk to you later." We both ended the conversation, and agreed to speak latter, as I continued down the expressway, while this man in a very raggedy truck began flirting with me. I pushed the accelerator and showed the man what this car could really do even though it wasn't mines. I was Blasting Brian McKnight *`you're more than beautiful'* that had just come on our local radio station 99 jamz. I glanced over at my phone which was blinking Dale. Superstitiously thinking he must be for me since he was thinking about me the same time I was thinking of him.

"Hey my baby." I answered the phone, so happy to hear from him.

"Hello my sugar." He answered back, sounding as if he didn't talk to me all day.

"What's going on?" I asked.

"Nothing baby, just the sun and loneliness won't leave me alone." He said.

"Well is there anything your sugar can do?' I just felt sexy, bold, and sassy at the same time.

"For starts I know if my sugar come; loneliness will leave. Now the sun we both can just play in it all day. What you say about that?" Dale asked.

"Alright baby, I'm going to the airport now. I'm not even going to go by the house." I said.

"I'll be there to pick you up, lonely and I and that's where we will leave it." Dale said laughing and so was I.

"I'll see you soon in Freeport." I said, ending the call. Damn what am I going to do with Jasi car? I'll just leave it at the airport Bruce has spare keys and I know she wouldn't mind. I exited the turnpike and got back on I95 North towards the airport. Chuck kept calling my phone, I don't know what he wanted and most definitely I weren't trying to find out.

Arriving at the airport 5:25pm, the flat screens indicated the next flight to Freeport was 6:30pm. I sat and watched the kids play and got a little upset because Lionel's family hadn't called me or let Shanice call me now in two days. The travelers were running side-to-side and so were the pilots with they're black boxes on their pushcarts. Sooner than I had realized the hour wait was over and the 45min flight was in the air. I think I only looked in the mirror to refill, and retrace the little eyeliner and eye shadow I wore, by that time the flight had landed and it was time for us to exit the plane. The Airport was so little compared to MIA. I walked down the one flight of stairs, looking around to catch Dale's appearance but I didn't see him so I walked on the outside of the airport, all I could see was different color cars with `Taxi' signs hung in the windows or marked on the frame.

Through all of the so-called `Taxi' cars; there in the middle of nowhere, parked a black 1974 stingray corvette. The car was beautiful; you couldn't help but notice the difference. Catching my attention, the door opened and outside stood Dale. I can assure you my Pussy was beaten out countless beeps, let alone I was ready right here and now. He came around the car with his hand behind his back as I walked towards him with my purse hanging on my forearm and the other hand hanging free.

"My baby is here with me!" He was happy, you could tell from the expression on his face, and the grip around my waist. Pulling my face in an upright position, without a thought my lips convened up with his and we kissed as if we haven't seen each other in years. I liked this man, god damn I really like this man I thought to myself.

"How was your flight?" He asked.

"Before I could realize it, we were here. So I guess that was a good flight." I mention, as he held me around my waist crossing the street to get to the car. He slowly moved one hand into his pocket, and pulled out a long jewelry box. I stood at the passenger door, trying not to look surprise. He leaned the opened box in my direction, and there laid a diamond Bvlgari watch. I couldn't help but to grab his neck swinging both of my legs around his waist. He didn't seem to be surprise about my happiness; he just held me, and swung me around. Landing back on the side of the car, his eyes caught up with mine and my tongue just went into his mouth and we kissed. I just couldn't seem to get enough of him physically or mentally. I could already feel this is going to be my best weekend ever!

He opened the door for me and I sat in. Observing the car in the little time I had before he made it to the driver side. The back window was divided into too slabs which gave it its sleek appearance, detailed was charcoal grey leather seats, and a gearbox with colorful buttons like a race car. Dale took a seat and opened the sunroof of the car, and revved the loud motor, as we pulled out of the airport.

I must tell you the sky was just as blue as I ever saw, the sun was so hot, and the trees moved with the wind as if they were performing a dance. Dale drove along the water, and parked the car underneath a shade of trees. I was puzzled and wondering what was he about to do. I looked around and docked in the water was a wooden rowboat; one which was propelled by oars. I took a deep breath as soon as he stepped foot out the car, but became slightly nerves when he came on the passenger side. He kneeled down on his knees pulling one of my feet out as I turned my body to the side. He didn't say one word but started rolling the bottoms of my Frankie B's to my calves and unstrapped my sexy Bebe heels I wore. He took off his throwback Jordan's and rolled his Roca wear jeans up the same as he rolled mines. He then put his arms beneath my legs shutting the door with his foot still not making a sound none other than the birds chirping and the waters whispering all in this exact order. Dale carried me over to the rowboat that was docked in with a huge rope. I was not afraid; I felt loved more than anything. I pulled his head down to me and kissed him soft, not a long time just a real romantic soft peck on the lips. Then I kissed him again and again, close capturing the vision that was registering in my thoughts. When our tongues release a smile increased so lovely and admiring over both faces.

"I liked that." Dale said I stared into heavens which was the clouds above us because right here and now I was approaching a feeling I never once met.

"Hold this baby." Dale said, as I held his phone and he stepped in grabbing the huge rope pulling the boat closer to shore.

"Get in baby." He said as he held it as steady as possible. I attempted to get in, as the water came back and forth above my ankles. He then untied the ropes and jumped on as well, immediately pulling two of the oars while the boat slightly moved. I grabbed the other two and we both rotated the oars until the boat was freely floating.

"It's going!" I mention as the boat rocked side to side moving slowly about.

"Harder!" He said, with a smile as I challenged the motion in his strong arms.

"Harder!" I added moving with the same pace he had as the water whistled beneath our strength?

"You like it?" He asked, as he continued to row.

"I love it." I carefully said with a huge smile.

"Chocolate I'm glad you could come." He said as I thought of how glad I was too, just that I didn't know how to explain it. I mean how could I??? It was too much zeal to represent, and he might would think I'm fucking crazy. First of all he meet me at the airport in this beautiful antique, bring along this beautiful Bvlgari watch, and now a rowboat ride just the two of us. Come on really who does shit like this?? How could I not be happy, now Becky would really say I fit the *Heather* description for real?

"I'm happy to be here with you." I replied.

"Come sit here." Dale said, as he placed his feet against the oars making a tiny space in between his legs for me.

"Come on." He repeated, as I carefully moved across and landed in between his legs. I laid peacefully as the sun was setting, while the wind blew which made it even more comfortable, and finally the movement of the water was full of relaxation. My mind was so peaceful, as I listened to his very heart beat. He was so tough, his arms were so very muscular as he rubbed me in every direction he possibly could. I was so very turned on by the friction of his hands that I nearly had to cross my legs tight.

I turned to look at him, noticing his nice full sexy thick lips, bushy eyebrows, and deep dimples that dented his jaws whenever he smiled. I couldn't stand another second right now without putting my lips over him, so I kissed him softly on his neck and then on his chest. I must admit, I was hot and boiling ever since that day I sat in his lap in Houston's but just didn't want to give it up so fast. However right long and now I'm on fire and there isn't much a water hose can do for me. I started sucking on his breast as he squeezed my butt for one of those auh-huu hugs, while tracing his tongue down my neck and all around my ear. My pussy was about to pop out, as my nipples stood as hard as he did. I somehow sat like I was on a horse, just before grabbing his jaws and kissing like I never wanted to let go. I released my lips from his, but the eye contact was so strong it lured my lips back to him before I could pull away. I was enjoying this, and I could tell so was he. Dale started sucking my face, and rubbing my thighs. I never knew how good it felt to get my face sucked... I used to think that's some gross shit when I saw it on porns but this being my first time I LOVED IT! He kissed me again and again from my forehead, to the very top of my feet. I was grinding my body as if we were already in bed, unfortunately I was fully clothed. The more he kissed on me I became hornier until I went to flinging my braids back and rippling my tongue across his upper body. I tell ya this man was such a tease, but my golly I needed this! Meantime the bulge in his pants felt like a stiff bark of a tree. Which added more to my desire... I began to rub his dick looking him straight in the eyes. I could see that temptation was now driving him and I crazy. I started breathing for air like I was some mad beast, but my tongue dispensed through the center of his chest as my nails traced down his side for ecstasy. He freely hung his head over the edge of the boat, and swung his hands overboard. Once I heard his toes pop and saw his hands curl, I really took matters in my own hands, and became freaky all at once. I began striping his pants and boxers off of him, as he wiggled his body and help get out of the clothes. I started licking in his navel, and blowing in it at the same time as I traced my hands up and down his body feeling nothing but chill bumps and slight movement of jumping, wiggling and shaking. He made noises which let me further know he was enjoying my affectionate side. I got bold and nasty with it as I ran my tongue along the sides of his dick. Which was standing stiff hard in the air, as if it waited for something to land on it just when the boat floated to the sand, a little further down than it originally embarked. He stood up naked, not even looking around and tied the boat back. I felt as if this island had belonged to us, as he boldly walked off board while his dick dangled like an elephant's trunk.

"Let's go over here!" He pointed to a wooded area and I followed him without force. I squeezed out of my tight Frankie B jeans, pulled off my shirt while my breast stood firm in the air and my nipples had gotten as hard as coins. Dale didn't waist anytime, it felt like a scene where I had returned from a trip or we were making up by the way he kissed and licked every part of my body. He licked me so good, for a minute I thought I was his dessert or maybe he had stumbled over love because lord knows it wasn't no ordinary licking.

"Chocolate, I want you." Dale said in a desperate voice. Panting for breath and seductively rubbing my body.

Laying me down in a thick grassy semi wooded area. Surrounded by trees I was so nerves but yet hot and horny as hell. He stood trying to put on his condom, while I kissed him and kissed him. He finally slid into the condom, and me being how hot I was I just about raped the damn man which made it even better. I climbed on his dick as if I was leading a race. I saddled up and took it from the top sliding it all the way in me. His dick pierced through my tight vagina which gave a pleasant seductive feel. A feeling that indicated I needed more, I wanted more and I was going to do my best. He had a dick that I truly loved from the first time he slid it in me, I could tell by the wetness of my body. He took one slow stroke and nearly pulled it out and then went back in like he was long dicking me nice and slow repeatedly. The dick had gotten so good rather he went fast, slow, in, out, or circles. He did it with every motion in his body and it must was his best cause I tell you the truth he was after this pussy like a bull would be in front of a red garment. The harder he fucked me, the more I shoved this pussy in his direction. Believe me I was determined to fuck him like no other, and that's just what I did. Through all the breathing, and love making dark had neatly spread throughout the sky.

Finally we got dressed and got back in the super-fast car racing down the sandy roads into another dark alley. He drove to a marina where several other boats were docked. It was too dark to see the shape and looks, but the seats were leather and the driving wheel was oaked which revealed this was a newer boat.

"Dale baby you don't think it's too dark to be riding out here?" I asked.

"Are you afraid Chocolate?"

"Not really but, um afraid of accidents." I said, as he flicked a switch that lit the whole boat up, and this was certainly a beautiful one. Dale grabbed and through me two life jackets as he looked around, checking and making sure everything was safe. I had become so afraid and not a bit excited at all as the waves kept hitting the sides of the boat so aggressively.

"Don't worry it will be ok." He said, while buckling my vest on first and then his.

"Dale what's out here this time of night?" I asked. As he had that smirk on his face.

"You'll see, baby just relax." He said, as the loud engine began and the speed started tramping over waves by its high speeds. This was one idea nor surprise I really didn't like. Shortly ahead I couldn't make it out entirely, but something was lighting up in the middle of the water. As we became closer it appeared to be a beach house on stilts. He drove the boat beneath the house and wrapped a rope around the strong poles that held the house above water.

"Chocolate we are here, this is my beach house." Dale said, as I became a little relieved that we would soon be out of the water and away from that speedboat. Not like this was better but it was cute and quite different, maybe I wouldn't be too afraid.

"Climb up baby." He pointed to the stair that I was supposed to climb up and he came behind me with my purse strapped around his wrist. Right above was a screened deck with patio furniture, and fake decorated trees. It was beautiful from the moonlight shinning down on the waters which was as black as night. He walked ahead of me and reached for the keys in his pocket. Pushing the door open wide, waving his hand for me to enter first. I walked in as he walked behind me, placing his hands around the small of my back, with my purse still dangling from his wrist. In the kitchen was a mini metal and blue wine cellar. He had sky blue furniture, which gave you the art deco look somewhat like a room that I saw in his house. There was an area rug that laid in the center of the floor, which each color from the pillows that lined the chair had claimed it. He poured two drinks while I was observing something I've never had seen before. There was a 42' flat plasma TV that covered up a pretty decent area on the wall. According to this deco style, it was obvious the same designer decorated both places of his. I loved the matching candles that traced the end tables, and a beautiful painting of a naked black woman photographed playing the cello.

"Here's to my wonderful Baby, someday who will be my wife." Dale said as he handed me a glass of dark wine.

"Wow. What a toast." I replied.

"Chocolate I really enjoy you. Ever since I met you, so much has changed for me." He said, looking into my eyes as I licked my lips. He came and sat next to me at the bar, placing my leg on his. We talked and talked. It seemed like there were strings he was pulling tighter, and tighter. It seemed the more he pulled, the more love my heart pumped just for him.

"Are you ready to shower?" Dale asked, as I remembered through all of this fun I suppose to have stopped somewhere and buy some clothes. Being I left my bag in New Orleans and didn't bother to go home to repack.

"Yes, would you care to join me?" As I slid off the barstool, pulling my shirt over my head. Dale sat on the stool observing as I bent down to pull my jeans off. I stood before him with only my pink and white jersey G-string panties on that read `boys lie.' He gently pulled me against him, this time putting me up on the bar, and sliding our drinks to the side.

"Baby its cold." I said, as my bare ass was resting on the bar.

"I'll keep you warm." Dale said slowly pulling my legs apart and so surprised I was when he began to use his powerful tongue... He licked it, licked, licked and licked. Without hesitation he spread my pussy lips and put his hard tongue down my hole, which felt, like a penis.

"Wow, um um um." I moaned as he rubbed my stomach, and sucked on me as If I had turned into a meal that was forbidden to use his teeth. He didn't stop or slow down he stayed at a steady pace. No matter how much I buckled, twist, turned, or shake he caught everything and sucked me in every hole.

After cumin three times just by him sucking on me I was helpless, I laid weak as ever in the same position we started in. I was honestly thinking did this brother go to school for this shit cause it was no way he missed one pussy-eating lesson. It just didn't make since to me to tell anyone this either, because I'm more than sure this was a feeling I couldn't explain. He then lifted me by my hand pulling me in an upright position. Picked me up and took me to the bathroom. There also he had a Jacuzzi and a toilet for his and hers. He turned the Jacuzzi on, while I sat on the toilet and watched it fill.

As soon as it was ready Dale put his hand out leading me to the Jacuzzi. I placed one foot in after another while Dale started coming out of his clothes as I watched.

"Dale how come if you haven't had a lady in a while. Why do you have to have a his and hers toilet and sink in both of your houses?" I asked, such a crazy question.

"Because I always knew what I wanted, it just was a matter of time I'd find her. From a little boy I always wanted a lady, whom I can treat like a princess, and respect her like my Mama. That's what she would be in my eyes. She will always be happy and thought of in every little thing I do." Dale said as he clicked the remote for the installed speakers in the corners of the bathroom *'Can I come came over'* by Aliyah was playing so clearly. Dale stepped in and sat in between my legs. ALMOST immediately I locked my legs around his waist, while I slowly began kissing him down his back, and up his side. It felt so good to him that he lifted out of the water and rested on the base. I got up on my knees, grabbing the hard stick that appeared to be calling for me. Once again Dale wanted it so bad, that I could see he was begging thru his eyes. I satisfied his craving when I placed it in my mouth and sexually sucked on him in every angle or rotation. He squealed, moaned and hustled for breath. I didn't attempt to stop, I moved in his direction. Yet twirling the opposite way, and pulling to the end very slow, nasty and romantic. I licked his right ball while teasing the left one with my gentle hands. I had become so freaky, that nothing even matter at that fleeting moment. He went to making noises so loud, I thought I was making a movie. He became louder and louder by every stroke I took. He continued yelling until I put my hand over his mouth and started back sucking his dick as if I was entitled to some type of ownership. His penis stood strong while it was taking a tour of my mouth, as every inch deposited itself by his every movement in and out. It didn't bend nor did it go soft. In routine I repeatedly traced my tongue, up and around his balls, then to the top of its head until he began shouting.

"Cho..Choco..Chocolate baby um um um.." Dale called as I calmly blew him up his ass. It must have felt so good that he bucked up like a woman and wined like a cat.

"Oh baby umm umm ummm ummm!" It seemed the more he screamed the freakier I became. He suddenly pulled me up and kissed me. Kissed me in a sense that he didn't want to stop. He rubbed his fingers around my pussy so nasty and romantic, then he slid his hands all between my ass cheeks, while kissing everything from my ear to sucking on my fingers. We got up from the Jacuzzi and I followed him out the bathroom dripping wet. He then led me into a room with big bedroom furniture. The wicker canopy was huge, the armoire was tall with a decorated wicker wheel to open it. In front of the bed was a wicker circle chest and a wicker straw chair that was placed in the corner. The curtains matched the comforter on the bed, and the fabric that lined the inner of the chair for comfort. He laid me across the bed and finish what I THOUGHT I had started using every piece of furniture for support or comfort in this sex trial we were rehearsing.

Morning had arrived and Dale had left me in bed alone. There was no smell of food in the air, nor were there any noises besides the pleasantly ocean waves. I got up realizing I actually had no clothes to put on. I slid his robe around me and went out to the screened patio and the boat was gone and still there wasn't a human insight. I went back inside washed my face and pulled my tangled braids back into a ponytail.

Realizing black as I am, I had a purple circle on my neck and a couple of burgundy ones on my breast too. Which let you know I enjoyed myself last night. All of a sudden I could hear something coming from outside. I hurried back to the patio, and splashing waters from the boat was the only thing that came visible. As the boat became closer I stood watching.

"Good morning baby!" From down below he yelled, wearing a muscle shirt and green cargo shorts.

"Hey why did you leave me?" I asked.

"Cause you were looking so pretty asleep, I didn't want to bother you." He replied, coming up with a bag in his hand.

"I got this for you baby. See if you can fit it, maybe we can check the shops out." As he handed me the bag, he playfully grabbed my arm and the two of us fell into the couch. I gave him a kiss. A kiss as if my husband just had arrived from a much longer journey, just before I pulled a white sundress from the bag that tied at the shoulders with red flowers all over it. There was a hair barrette decorated just like one of the flowers in the dress along with a very small sack to carry lipstick or coins in it. He also had a pair of flat tongue sandals that had red flowers covering the top of my feet.

"Oh Dale, thank you this is cute." I responded, as he pulled me in the living area and sat down.

"Go ahead and try it on." He said, getting comfortable in the chair. I walked over to the stereo and press play, and pulled the robe off slowly revealing nothing but my bare body that he left in bed. I bent down to put my legs in the dress so he could get a better view of my lips. I pulled it up slowly leaving my tits hanging out, and tying the shoulders up.

"I need a little help please." I said, as my breast dangled over the top of the dress. He gently put my tits in his mouth, pulling the dress with his index finger while letting them go easily into the dress. I turned around and bent all the way over retrieving the bag from the floor, feeling the wind that came between my legs, as I walked into the bathroom.

"Would you wash my back baby?" I asked.

"Sure." He said as he followed behind me.

I got into the shower and bathe; Dale stood on the other side of the bathroom watching as I lavender my body down.

"You are most definitely a woman." Dale said in a for sure manner. I wasn't sure what he meant by that. I just took it as a compliment.

"Turn around baby." Dale said, as he soaped the towel and scrubbed my back. After taking a shower, he waited with a big towel to dry me off. Dale sat on the toilet and patted the towel all over my body until there was no water visible. He put cocoa butter lotion all over me, he even put my deodorant on and offered to brush my teeth. I told him I think it would be best if he let me handle the rest. So I did the brushing. He still sat on the stool watching my every move as I slid the dress back on, emptied the bag searching for some panties. He smiled and went in that little sack for a purse and pulled out a pair of panties that was stuffed only he would have found them. They were yellow G-strings that read. *'If I had one wish?'* He really had picked these. I smiled and he smiled.

"Well, what will be that wish?" I asked.

"For you to be my wife." Dale responded. Answering so fast as if he was for sure just as I was so content by his thoughts.

"Well Mr. Dale, that's a wish." I replied.

"I really do like you. I don't mean to scare you with my inner emotions, however I can say it a million times I want to be with you. For sure a lifetime would be just enough to share with you. I think every day, time and date gets better. That's what's going to keep us going, believe in me baby. I got so much I want to do with you. Just trust in me. I'm definitely not asking for too much." He said as he took my hands in his "I can promise you. If you just give me a chance to show you, I'll be all you've been asking, looking and even praying for. You're all what I've been looking, and praying for." Dale said standing directly in my face, I was speechless didn't know what to say. I only had thoughts, and they were thoughts like *'maybe he had read my diary, or something'.* He had tendencies like a woman, when it came to romance. Time, space, or jealousy wasn't part of him, and he sure was not lacking trust, I consider him to be fair, and most of all he knew from the start what it took to mold a relationship. Unlike majority of the sorry men I have known, always scared to trust but quick to holler love. How could you begin to love if you don't trust?

"Just one chance." He repeated not moving an eye away from me as I felt the embarrassment drowning me and astonished by his conversation. I was so happy that it became noticeable. He placed his hands on my shoulders, and rubbed my brows.

"Don't worry about anything. Anything you think you're not too sure of, or about. Let me worry about it with you. I'm here for you. I want you to understand and believe in me, how I'm believing in you." I knew he didn't have a drink not like he was a wino, but the words that he was projecting I always thought they were fake soap opera words, or from some sort of romantic movie. He was so unrestricted, until he didn't know how those very words stuck to me like my script in this movie. I became numb from my knees on down. I couldn't move. I truly had instant belief and trust to just wrap itself around me. My feet unlocked and I moved back to put on my panties. He didn't pressure me for a promise, nor did he wait for an answer. He walked out as I got ready. I don't know what to do or say sometimes. He's too much like myself. Love life. Hate to waste time. Straight to the point kind of thing.

I twirled my braids unto a bun, wrapped the flower around to the side. Which gave me a Hawaiian look. I slid on the thong sandals that were very flat along with a sexy scrap that wrapped around my ankles. I washed and dried my face well, and traced my skinny freshly arched eyebrows with water. Although I didn't have my eyeliner or lip gloss, I looked very natural and looks of a true island girl. I walked out the bathroom quietly, while he sat at the bar looking out the window. I tipped behind him and gave him a hug around his neck. He rubbed my arms and continued to sip his orange juice. Shortly he turned around, observing the essence of my beauty. He gently rubbed his hand across the bun without moving a strand of hair. He touched the flower which was pinned behind my ear and said unique. He got up and put a hat over his head and a button down yellow shirt, which gave the comfortable at home outfit a casual afternoon wear also.

"Are you ready for breakfast?" He asked.

"Why sure." I responded spinning my dress around, flashing my ass to the air. We walked down the flight of stairs and got on the boat.

"It's your turn to drive us back to shore Chocolate." Dale said.

"You know I don't know how to drive this boat." I responded. Licking my lips.

"Don't you worry about a thing? It's just me and you out here, you think we can handle this?"

"Nah." I said, as I took a seat.

"There's no need to get comfy, you're going to take us on a ride." He said starting the boat up as I slid over in the driver seat. Before he could sit down I pulled down the lever, and Dale fell against the seat as the boat took off.

"Wow! Looks like you know how to use the gear." He sarcastically said, pulling his body over the seat, kissing me on the lobe of my ear. I continued to do the same, just got a little sassy with it. I was weaving side to side and speeding at the same time.

"Baby, I got this huh!" I yelled over the loud motor and crashing waves.

"I told you, we can conquer anything if we just put our minds together." He said, pulling the gear back up, until it slowed and started floating. He unlocked the seat with his feet, until the chair came into a spinning position. He spent me around and spread my legs open. Which he just seem to can't get enough of. I didn't feel up to it at that moment, but he didn't seem to care, and started to yam on my pussy. Of course smooth as this job was, I wasn't about to resist.

The day went great; we went shopping, and eating every sea food from conch fresh out of its shell, snapper freshly caught from the sea, and fried before our eyes. We shopped, visited other neighboring islands, played in waterfalls, made sand castles, even pushed each other on the swings. We did so much today until there is no way for me to begin telling you how much of a man he was. All I could say is Dale knew what it takes to make a women feel loved and spoiled rotten. By the time we made it home from the grocery store, Dale went upstairs while I promised to make dinner for us tonight. As I got everything seasoned and off into the oven, I phoned Jasi to see how she was doing.

"Hello." Jasi answered.

"Hello, you sound like you're feeling better." I asked.

"Yeah I feel a little better. How are you?" Jasi asked.

"Well I'm ok, over in the Bahamas with Dale."

"Ain't that's something. You must be a lucky girl, come from one trip to another." Jasi said.

"Please girl. So are you alright about that situation?" I asked, as she grunted.

"I don't even want to think about that right now. I'm home eating some crabs relaxing. Anyways where is Dale?" Jasi asked as she made her point pretty clear, so I ignored the fact that she was pregnant.

"He's in the bathroom, and I'm cooking us something to eat." I said, without a bit of romance in my voice.

"Oh are you the wife!"

"Please girl." I responded.

"Serious Chocolate, I haven't seen you this happy since Shanice came home from the hospital. You and Lionel was such a happy couple then."

"You mean miserable?"

"If that's what you called it, damn I would be afraid for you to show love." Jasi said laughing on the other end of the phone.

"Did Becky call you?" I asked.

"Yeah that jack ass called me. Asking was my organs and testicles alright. I told her she was right; I got a baby stuck in my ass. But you better believe not for long."

"Jasi don't talk like that." I said, pouring some diced potatoes in some flavored butter to steam, while the steak was baking.

"Girl that's life, I can't handle this right now. I'm trying to prepare for my career; Bruce is a married man regardless how good things appear. He's married! He's subject to leave anytime and I'm not bringing my child in this world in such a form. I'm sorry." Jasi said, as if she owed me that apology. However that was her body, I just didn't feel I needed to voice my opinion on something, which man has no control over.

"I'll call you back." I said, out of order not wanting Dale to hear our bickering. We ended the call, and seconds later Dale walked into the kitchen, wearing only a towel wrapped to his side.

"Baby it smells rather good in here." I smiled and stirred the potatoes. He rubbed me upwards from my hips to my tits landing a kiss dead center in my back.

"I'm really enjoying this." He said.

"So am I." I responded.

"I wish we can continue this, once we reach home." Dale implies. Of course I wouldn't mind living in that big house back in MIA. I thought to myself as he stood massaging my shoulders as I cooked. It became a little irritating so I just turned and faced him. He kissed me on the forehead and walked towards the freezer.

"Would you like a bite?" He asked, as he came towards me with a snicker ice cream bar.

"Of course." He placed the chocolate in my mouth, one that looks and shaped somewhat like his. I bit a tiny piece, he bit a bigger piece, and then he handed the bar back to me and I licked it and bit a great chunk from it.

"Wow!" He said, as I laughed and licked my lips as if I was tasting him.

*****

The time had come for me to return home, I woke up about 4:30am and could not get back to sleep. I tried not to twist and turn; because I didn't want to wake Dale, but yet realizing I'll be leaving soon and I needed his comfort. I didn't want to go home, I just really didn't feel I have to leave him. I most certainly thought he had supposed to come with me, I admit I really wanted him around more than I thought I did. I didn't know where that feeling came from, but it was a feeling of loneliness and I had the man here. Apparently it was the thought of leaving him after these great days we just shared. He made me smile for days, laugh out loud, and most of all I felt like I was with someone that I thought was RIGHT for me. Not really sure if I really knew what love is but I can tell you I felt a certain kind of happiness inside of me. Suddenly I could feel my eyes tear up, however I did my best to try and balance out my emotions but somehow the tears got the best of me for such a senseless matter that hadn't took place yet. I brushed the blanket and my hand over my face to wipe away any evidence. Dale suddenly moved his hand from under the cover to hug me tighter, as I sniffed.

"Are you alright baby?" In a scratchy tone he asked.

"Um Uh." I replied. As he squeezed my hands, he felt the wetness, and put the sniffing together. He quickly flicked on the lamp that hung next to him. Looked me in the face, and according to the redness of my eyes he was able to know I had been crying.

"What's wrong Chocolate?" He asked, as he sat up in the bed facing me. I was scared of what he would think so I played deaf. "Chocolate, baby if you won't tell me. I will not know."

"The thought of me leaving tomorrow." I said, as the tears no longer hid. He laid down and pulled me over resting my head on his chest. The water slid from the corner of my eyes, to the side of my nose, and unto his muscular chest. He rubbed my head, and wiped the tears as they came down.

"Baby don't worry about anything. I'll be home soon, and there's going to be no limits on how long you and I are together." He said with healing words. I hugged him tight as I possibly could, and said words worth passion. I poured myself unto him just the way he did earlier. I just couldn't resist, I had finally let go that guard that secured my love. He kissed and rocked me in his arms until I fell back asleep.

I woke up about 10:00am I could smell breakfast through the air. I slid on my night shorts, balled my hair into a ponytail. I opened the room door and followed '***I love you'*** notes on red cut shaped hearts all the way down to the kitchen, where I found cheese grits, bacon, sausage, and butter milk biscuits on the table. In the center of the table there were bright orange flowers and a strong handsome man standing at the end of the table. I walked in with a smile that couldn't be easily erased.

"Hey baby." He said and greeted me with a soft kiss.

"Hey honey, you got in here smelling good."

"All for you baby." He said, as I thought to myself how he was only making it more difficult for me to leave.

"Oh how sweet." I said grabbing his jaws, and locking my tongue with his. He was so sweet until no words pointed out a lie in any shape or form. He lifted me up on the counter; and I swung my legs around him to keep him in place.

"You just do something to me." Dale said as he looked me in the eyes, I shyly dug my face in his chest and begin to kiss him around his neck, as he arched up his shoulders and moaned. He gently ran his hand under the T-shirt I was wearing to only trace his index finger down the crack of my ass which felt so pleasantly good. I moved on kissing his shoulders as if I was a character in the stories making a love scene. Each kiss explained what he had written on those little hearts, and just as many as there were.

"Baby, I want to make you happy. I want to be that gate keeper to your heart." He said breathing hard.

"Baby I want you too." I said releasing the lock on his neck and kissing him excitedly even over his eyelids. He couldn't take the kissing game anymore. He snatched me up in position and to the room we went. He didn't seem to have wanted some head as he quickly put on his rubber and I immediately jumped on his hard dick just as fast for a ride.

I rode it like a smooth black sleek stallion, yet positioned like a pro jockey rider while sucking his finger like it was a sweet blow pop. He held onto my invisible scraps and whipped me with his imaginary whip as I rode on bouncing up and down. I turned to the back, as his dick grew longer and harder in me. I held his feet and bent all the way down, letting him poke every gut he could've possibly touched. He was pulling me, begging me, and calling me as I wined my body up to some serious reggae music which played in my mind. I swung my hair, and scooted this pussy back and forth all over his magic stick. Suddenly I turned this pussy towards his face and snatched his rubber off. He went right into sucking my clit, as we were now in the 69 position. I kept the hard flesh in my mouth while continuing to rotate it in every way I thought he liked. Just when he was about to slow down, I could feel his hands spread my ass cheeks apart. I became as nervous as I didn't know what to expect next and especially in this position. Getting a better grip over my cheeks as he spread them widely without warning I felt his warm tongue slither up and down my ass crack. My gosh I tell ya, I was stuck in a daze... His two lips hovered over my but hole and sucked me.... He paused for a second or two while blowing in me, and then he spit in my ass and ran his tongue up and down my crack once again, while fingering me at the same time.

"Oh wee!" It had felt so good that no other words could form. He licked my pussy just as good as I sucked his dick, until I couldn't even keep up the good work any longer. He turned me over and put on another rubber. He stuck his penis in as I squirmed up; but almighty when I was able to benefit. My pussy was wet as water and tighter than a cork in a fine bottle of wine. I thought about, *`forever'* and that's how I wanted him to be with me. Forever. I rolled my ass in his direction, I caught up with his speed, and fucked him left and I fucked him right. He became freakier with it, and rubbed his finger up and down my virgin asshole which got just as wet as my pussy. Not only was it the fuck of the century, but his sex game was insane.

"HE WAS INDEED A REAL MAN!"

Ms. Minnie and the kids were pulling out of the yard upon my arrival.

"Hello Ms. Minnie!" I said waving out the passenger window of my coworker Lisa's car.

"Hey suga, they in there knocked out. The door is unlocked go on in." Ms. Minnie said.

"Alright." I responded as she backed on out of the driveway.

"Thanks Lisa girl." I said, as I reached to give her ten dollars for gas.

"Girl please, keep that." She said, as she waved her hand back at me.

"No Lisa take it, gas is ridiculously high!"

"Child you think you gone need a ride in the morning?" Lisa asked, still not taking the money from my hand.

"No, I'm going to borrow Becky truck." I said.

"Alright then I'll see you tomorrow." Lisa said, as I threw the ten dollars in the seat and she tossed it back out the window and pulled off. I walked in the dark cold neat house, not a sound was going none other than the filter on the fish tank.

"Wake your ass up!" I yelled slapping her on the back of her thigh, watching her jump up with a bit of slob dried on the sides of her mouth and lines creased in her face.

"Chocolate come on now." She said, grabbing the cover pulling it over her head.

"Wake up, now your flight came back early enough for you to have had enough sleep." I said observing bags all over the room even new suitcases, lots of beads on top of the dresser, and a half of a joint the two of them must was smoking on.

"Becky!" I screamed again, as Nikki got up and walked towards the bathroom.

"Chocolate what do you want! Um tired."

"I want you to tell me about the trip."

"Girl that thing there should be good and sleepy, we missed our flight Monday morning so we left that night." Nikki replied.

"How did yall miss the flight?" I asked shaking Becky very hard.

"Nikki and I went to some concert Sunday night that lasted until Monday morning. Our intentions were to leave the party, but Nikki met some producer and before we knew it, we had missed our flight." Becky said, propping her head in her hand, blabbing away.

"Oh." I dryly said.

"Chocolate, when I tell you I had so much fun this weekend, I mean way more fun than we had in Daytona back in 95."

"For real." I said, as Becky sat up.

"Girl Saturday we went to the park, when I tell you they had a huge picnic, Jet Skis, and boats, I mean all that type of shit was going on. The ballers this year, was the kind that you knew for sure didn't mind spending that cash, and child they was just giving us those beads if we showed our ass or not."

"Tell her Becky about that boy." Nikki interrupted.

"Who." Becky asked.

"That tall ass boy."

"Oh girl I met some basketball player. That brother was so tall and handsome. He took us to the mall and we both went shopping on his ass. I had him to drop us off at Nikki room and I was going to meet him a little later. That man must have called my number a hundred times, I didn't pay him a bit of attention cause everybody was paying."

"Chocolate we didn't pay for one thing, not even dinner, or clothing. I guess it pays to be cute and fine." Nikki added.

"Well what happen with you?" Becky asked.

"Nothing much, just a little fun down in the Bahamas."

"That's it! Just a little fun. Well when you left all the niggas, shopping sprees, ballers, drinks, and maybe a man came through for you too." Becky added.

"Yeah that's it." I said, trying to throw the conversation off, cause Nikki was down my throat dissecting each word as they rolled from my tongue.

"I hear you I guess he must be the one that make you get a trim deep in your soul, that you can't ignore it." Becky singed *Monica's* song off her latest CD.

"Stop playing." I said, pushing Becky.

"Ok!" She said, but she knew there was a lot more I wanted to tell her, but like I said I will not put my business out in front of Nikki, I don't trust that hoe any further than I can throw her.

"How is Jasi?" Becky asked.

"She is doing well, I was over there yesterday. She the one told me you was coming back today."

"Oh, you didn't see her today? I'm surprised she didn't bring her nosey ass by here." Becky added.

"She say when she come from school, she was going to stop by here and pick me up." I claimed.

"Where is your car?" Becky asked.

"That shit ran hot just morning on my way to work, I called Jasi and she gave me a ride and I left the car right where it ran hot."

"Chocolate, face it you need a new car!"

"I know, but I ain't ready for those new payments."

"Well you have no choice, that lil '95 Honda keep putting you down. You damn near pay car notes. Every month you got to fix something and it doesn't be little shit, you should have got rid of it when the motor blew in thirty days."

"Yeah, you damn sight telling the truth on that. I might go and get me a used car next week."

"A used car!"

"Yeah a used car, I don't have money or credit like that to be walking off them folk's lot with their shit."

"Well you will have a little car note every two weeks and a broken down car here and there again."

"You should at least wait until Labor Day, when they be having them big car sales." Nikki said, as she pretend to be digging in her bag, while all in our conversation. This is why I didn't tell Becky about my time in the Bahamas, the bitch had ears like a dog.

"Yeah, they do be having those big sales." Becky said, trying to include Nikki in.

"Nah I'll just get a used one there's no since in me spending a dime when I am earning a nickel."

"Oh please, you always hollering broke Chocolate!"

"I am." I said, reaching for my purse, when my phone began to ring.

"Hello."

"Hey baby!" Dale said, as I got up from the bed, and walked outside the patio.

"How was work?"

"Well from morning it was not so good, my car ran hot, and put me down on the expressway. So I caught a ride to, and from work, but right now I am over Becky house waiting on Jasi to take me home. Then at work I had several memos to do and three meetings." I said, sounding as miserable and frustrated.

"Well it doesn't sound like you are having a good day. Where is Shanice?" He asked.

"My mama went to pick her up from school today." I said.

"Oh ok. Mona what's wrong with your car?" Dale asked.

"Everything! I'm just tired of fixing this and fixing that."

"What year is it?"

"A '95."

"Well if it's not the battery or tires, you minus well get a new car. I don't think it will be a good idea to be putting money into a car that's just aging." Dale said.

"That's true too, but right now I can't afford one. My credit is not even a little good, and I sure don't have all that money for a down payment."

"Is your credit very bad?"

"Yes Dale it is. I really don't want to talk about a car or credit right now, I'm just frustrated."

"Baby don't worry yourself up about a car, listen I'll call down to the rental car place and get you a rental for a week until I come back. Then I'll see my friend about your credit" Dale said as a little relief came over me. "Wait just a minute, let me call somewhere and I will call you back in about a half hour."

"Ok Dale." As I walked backed into the house, through the bay view window I seen Nikki car pulling out of the driveway.

"Chocolate come here look look!" Becky called screaming from the back of the house.

"What girl?"

"Look at these." Becky said pointing at the TV at some children on four wheelers going throw dirt roads.

"You think my girl too little for that?" She asked.

"Yes Brianna most definitely is, Julian and Corey might could ride one of those."

"Corey want to get those for them, for Christmas."

"That's cute, they will love that. You know they have the one seat go carts now with the cage over it and an emergency flag to pull if they want to stop."

"And how much them is?"

"I seen some for about eight hundred dollars. Now Brianna can ride on that, I might get Shanice one."

"I have to see that. So what happen over in the Bahamas?" Becky asked snapping back on a subject she was clear that I wasn't finish.

"I just really enjoyed myself so much to have to only come back home to this bullshit."

"Girl you make your damn self-stress, all your ass got to do is get a new car. Chocolate that old ass Honda is tired! Now tell me about this trip you left me down in New Orleans for, and damn that car."

"Becky don't start that shit, now you know Jasi was sick that was the only reason I left."

"I'm just tripping; you so uptight you might need to blow some smoke out of your nose." Becky said as she lit the joint.

"Whatever!"

"Well since you don't want to tell me about your trip. Can you tell me if you fucked him yet?"
"Becky you have a problem."

"Nah you beating all around the bush." She said snickering and reaching for her lighter, as the joint went out.

"To answer your question we didn't fuck, but he made love to me."

"Oh shit now it's making love." Becky said as she chocked on the joint.

"Actually I'll call it romance, and a dream come true."

"Yeah he was that good?" Becky asked, inhaling once again on the joint.

"Not only was he good, but he has that thug in him, mixed with a businessman, living comfortably, speed boats, vacation houses, good dick, no kids, and single. Now tell me that aint no dream."

"Yeah that sound like some good work already cut out."

"You better believe it is Becky, because this one here is mine." I said in definite, as I answered my blinking phone.

"Hello."

"Hey baby, you have a pen to write this down?" Dale asked as I reached over to the stationary that Becky kept by her phone.

"Yes."

"The confirmation for the rental car is R2575015J and that's at Rent Our Cars by the airport. All you need is your driver license, everything else has been taken care of."

"Thank you Dale." I said.

"OK, well you should be getting down there and ill call you tonight, if anything you call me." Dale said.

"Later baby."

"Later." He said.

"See here Becky this the shit I'm talking about. You need a little help you don't want to always ask, wait, or remind a motherfucker. You need someone to just volunteer, come thru and follow up when you need them from time to time. Now I just talked to him when Nikki was here, and was telling him about my car. He told me to give him a half hour he will call me back. Here is the confirmation for a rental car a whole week. That's a man never mind all those childish games and excuses."

"That's true, well baby you better hold on because it's rough out here on the yard! Even just being independent we fall weak too."

"Can you take me down by the airport to get this car?"

"Yeah." Becky said as she got up and slid on her jeans. "I guess you finally made them jaws pop and lock huh." Becky said laughing.

"Fuck you Becky, my Nookie just as sweet." I said as we walked outside.

We were in bumper-to-bumper traffic, Becky phone was ringing like crazy, and she ignored it as if it wasn't.

"Becky why don't you answer your phone?" I asked.

"It aint nobody but dried up Corey ass."

"Oh let me guess. You must have quit him for this week?" I asked.

"Nah, girl I aint got time for Corey shit no more and this time I'm dead ass serious."

"You was grave yard serious last time." I added.

"Nah I'm serious for real now."

"Hell just two weeks ago yall were so in love at your little barbeque I thought I missed the wedding."

"Yeah right!"

"Well what happened?" I asked.

"Remember when I called you that night and told you about that hoe Shawn?"

"Yeah."

"Girl I aint gone tell you, she came around late that night and poured sugar in my gas tank."

"Girl, you lying!"

"Yes she did that, but that bitch don't know she just struck a match against gasoline. Corey supposed to have been paying for it, but the engine is no better. So he say he's going to buy me a new truck, supposedly for Labor Day."

"That's messed up, girl." I said starting to go off, but what good is it if the person doesn't listen.

"Last night the asshole aint even come home." Becky said, as I sat quiet going through my phone ignoring the conversation, as we drove on.

Becky dropped me off in the front of the office, and pulled off to go home and cook for her kids.

"Good evening Mam, how may we help you?" The guy at the front desk asked.

"Yes I have a confirmation number for you." I said, reaching into my purse handing him the torn piece of paper.

"Your driver license please." He asked, picking up the phone and reading my confirmation number out. I handed him my license, and he went for a photocopy.

"Thank you Mam, your vehicle is unlimited mileage and we ask to avoid additional charges by returning the vehicle back with a full tank of gas on the return date. It should be pulling out front in just a minute." He explained reaching for a second pen and indicated where I should sign.

"Thank you Mam and enjoy your evening." He said, as I dropped the yellow copy down in my purse and walked out front to a red Monte Carlo.

*****

I just finished dressing, and walked over to the closet mirror observing my look, style, and walk before I left out to meet Dale at the airport. I wore a long jean skirt my Timberland boots, matching beige hat, belt and purse. I didn't think I was over dressed but I knew I was ready for any occasion. By the time I made it to the airport, I realized I was 20 minutes early before boarding time. I patiently sat in the concourse waiting on him to arrive as I could feel my heart beat beating twice as fast as it was a second ago. I squirted two sprays of romance behind my ears as my eyes sorted through the arriving passengers which was Dale's flight that had apparently arrived a bit early. I stood behind a column and watched for a second;

Dale came off board looking all around. I somehow tipped toed behind him and jumped aboard his back. He gripped me up by my waist and gave me a boost and spin me around.

"Hey baby." He said as I slid off his back.

"I miss you!" I replied, with a sudden kiss and not looking or worrying who seen me.

"I miss you too! Where is Shanice?"

"Today is Tuesday and its only 11:15am she better be in school."

"Oh that's right." He said as we walked to the car holding hands.

"How was your flight?" I asked.

"Not a problem." He responded, as we made our way through the darkened garage.

"Mona baby, I like it better when you with me." He said, out of order. "Baby those little nights I did get to hold you in my arms just spoiled me rather than living alone." He said as I tried to sort through that statement, maybe he was meaning he wanted me to stay.

"I enjoyed every minute of it too." I said, as he leaned me against the rental car and kissed me while sliding his huge hands up my thick thighs. Another touch took place as he swirled his tongue in my mouth. This time it was his delicate fingers that rubbed across my ticking pussy.

"I miss you."

"I miss you more." He responded, and went around to the driver side. "Mona did you ever find out what's wrong with your car?" He asked.

"Yeah, my Daddy said something about it needs a valve job and the pistons need to be replaced." I replied

"Oh no, because that will cost at least two to three thousand. You most definitely need to see about a new car."

"I know." I said, as the matter began to absorb my happy moment.

"What kind of car that you might have in mine?"

"Actually none, because I wasn't prepared for this." I said entering the highway.

"Are you in a hurry to go somewhere?" He asked.

"No not really."

"How about you exit off Hallandale, I have a friend at a car lot." He said, as I didn't want to tell him I was flat out broke and didn't have a savings with a penny in it.

"Dale..."

"No, you said you have nothing to do, so don't come telling me about no credit. As long as you have your license we can go see my friend." He said plain and simple cutting any excuse a loose. So I drove on. Arriving at an Infiniti car lot, where there were so many beautiful cars that I knew I couldn't afford.

"Um telling you now my credit aint gone move nothing out here."

"Women you don't know that, all you need to do is know somebody." Dale said as we walked into the huge sales center which smelled like new cars and had an echo as if we were in a hole.

"Hey buddy long time no see." A big husky man came walking up shaking and almost hugging the life out of Dale.

"I know man! It's been a long time but I am happy to see you too." Dale said.

"I am happy to see you to man!"

"Well Dale who is this beautiful lady you have with ya?" He asked.

"That's my woman Mona. Mona this is Phil, my old buddy from college." He said as I reached my hand out and he shook it easy.

"Are you back here in Florida?" Phil asked, as he spread his legs and jacked his pants up even more.

"Yeah. Doing work here and there, how about you."

"I had married about five years ago and me and my wife moved back here from Texas."

"Yeah, so yall pretty use to the sun huh?"

"You can say that again." Phill said, as he dug in his nose on the sly.

"I need a little help." Dale said, as Phill pulled his pants up one more time where you could see he practically lifted his balls.

"Well what is it?"

"My woman says her credit is shoot, and she needs a new car." Dale ranted on as if I was purchasing it today.

"Alright, well let's look around the show room." Phil said.

"I want a car for her that's going to almost look like her, sexy but classy you know." Dale said as Phil, took another look at me.

"Now this is a nice car a 4 door G35 automatic." He placed his hands on the hood of the car and looked at me.

"I like a two door car." I added.

"Ok now you talking, I just wanted to hear how sexy you want your car." He said walking through another door which lead us to a bigger show room.

"This is our newest coupe. A 2-door G35 coupe, with leather and oaked interior." He said, as I stood trying to catch my breath. The car was so beautiful, even though I knew I didn't have the money but the looks of it easily made me say yes I needed it.

"You like it huh?" Dale said, without another guess. I slid my hands over the car, as I made it to the driver side, I couldn't help but to take a seat. The car was a shiny black and the seats were a leather smoke gray, the oak shinned as if it was just polished, and man when it started up, you should hear it.

"I love it." I said, as I twisted the wheel back and forth.

"It's about 29 to 35 thousand." Phil said without erasing my interest.

"Let's give it a try." Dale responded, not brushing off, or looking for something cheaper.

"Dale!" I said.

"Mona we just going to give it a try, I'll co-sign and pay the down payment." Dale added as we walked back to the sales desk.

"Now I need you to fill out this information and Dale you fill this out." Phil said. "And before I run this, let me ask you what you planning on putting down for the down payment."

"10,000." Dale said without letting off the pen, as I thought unbelievable.

"This is going to take a couple of hours, so if you want to have lunch or do a little shopping you can." Phil said as he walked from office to office and copy paper after paper.

"Ok, we are going to pick my daughter up from school and have lunch." Dale said, really leaving me in shock when he said *'his daughter'*

"That sounds fine, if anything sooner I'll call you." Phil added as, Dale pulled out his platinum card and was willing to swipe it.

"No not yet, let me get approval and then we work with money." Phil said, smiling at what was about to be a part of his commission. Dale and I left to pick Shanice up from school. We ate lunch before we headed back to the dealer.

Phil had called Dale and informed him that he had to pull a couple of strings, so to just go along as he says. However the car is going home today, I felt so good inside. At least I will have a dependable car, and that big down payment means my monthly ones shouldn't be so much. Soon as we returned, before I could grab a seat, or tell Shanice to sit down Phil handed me over the keys to my new hot ride.

I shifted the gears so swiftly and drove as fast as I could to reach Becky's house while Shanice was in the back seat telling me how much she had liked my new ride, and so did I. I called Becky, while I sat in her yard totting the squeaky sounding horn, Becky peeked out not realizing this was me so I continued on blowing.

"It's me scary cat!" I yelled as I opened the door and the whole car lit up inside. Suddenly her front door opened and she came outside.

"Wow, that's pretty! Who car is this?" Becky asked.

"Dale bought it for me today."

"Damn this ride is tight! Talking about sexy, that it is." Becky said, as she walked all around the car admiring its style.

"Thanks girl."

"Jasi seen it."

"No I haven't been by there, but that's where I am headed."

"Let me get some shoes I want to ride too." Becky excitedly said sounding the same way she did when I got my first car at the age of 17. She ran into the house and Shanice did also.

Corey came walking behind Becky when she came back out, as if he was ready to start fussing because she was leaving the house.

"Chocolate this tight. I know you going to throw some 20's on it?" He asked.

"Nah, I think I like the factory style." I replied.

"It's tight though. Hurry up and bring that fat ass back." He said to Becky; as he slapped her on the butt, and turned to walk back in the house.

"Corey tell Shanice come on!"

"Go ahead on, she playing with Brianna." He said, as I backed out the yard.

"Chocolate this is very nice, who credit you used?"

"Mines he just was the cosigner." I replied.

"This relationship must be real stable?" She asked.

"It might just be. Today he asked me to live with him but you know he went around it but I know what he was trying to say."

"So what's the problem? Are you going to?"

"I don't know. He was telling me he just bought another house in the Bahamas, and he wants Shanice and me to go."

"You know those tickets for Disney was expired." Becky said, interrupting my conversation.

"Well, why don't we all just take this trip to Bahamas with Dale?" I asked.

"You know I am down for whatever."

"He's talking like in the next week or two." I quickly responded.

"Girl yeah, Corey and I need some time away from that crazy hoe Shawn." Becky said, as her cell phone lit up.

"Hey Marco." Becky answered. As I accelerated my speed and exited off the expressway. The car hugged curves like a motor bike, as the air-conditioned blew like the compressor sat in the passenger seat, while the music played as if a designated band was in the backseat. I reached for my phone when I came closer to Jasi house and called her to come out side.

"Oh my gosh!" Jasi said, as Becky and I stepped out of the car.

"Damn Mona this is bad! Who's car?" Jasi asked.

"Dale bought it for me today." I said.

"Now yall tell me good pussy aint a savings!" Becky said, as we all just laughed.

"Chocolate what is it?" Jasi asked as she walked to the back of the car.

"Infiniti G35."

"I love it. Its so sexy." Jasi responded.

"It is." Becky agreed again.

"Oh yeah Jasi. Since the cruise to Disney was canceled, Dale wanted to know could you and Bruce join us in the Bahamas in about a week or so." I asked quickly telling a lie.

"Corey, the kids and I is going." Becky said, adding on.

"Maybe so, I hope I stop bleeding by then." Jasi said, as I looked back and tried to register when did she get rid of the baby.

"Bleeding!" I said.

"Chocolate don't act like you didn't know, I took her to get an abortion yesterday." Becky said.

"You know damn well I didn't know that!" I responded in attitude.

"Well we did it." Becky said in a nonchalant manner.

"Becky when do I suppose to stop cramping like this?" Jasi asked.

"Did you take that Tylenol with codeine that helps the pain, but you should be stopped bleeding before next week, if not hoe you must be a hog." Becky added, as she just laughed as if this was a joking matter.

"Oh let me tell yall now. You know my birthday next month Marco is going to buy five roundtrip tickets to Jamaica and that's where we are going to end our year." Becky said winning her thick frame up to Sean Paul and Beyoncé that was playing on the radio.

"Oh so Marco did say yes?" Jasi asked, dancing along with Becky.

"What you dancing for?" I asked.

"Girl see you never been to Jamaica, if you did trust me. You would be ready just according to the reservations." Jasi said.

"Um gone be so high, yall may have to hold me down with a bag of rocks or I might just fly away." Becky said, as we laughed.

"I like the Caribbean boys' accent and the food." I added.

"I don't want none of yall to buy me nothing. When I say, I want yall to party with me, I mean party with me." Becky said, as she broke it down.

"Alright Becky lets go. You heard what Corey said don't stay long."

"Child please Corey wouldn't give a damn if I stayed all night, just as long as I come back and put his ass to sleep he alright."

"You so silly, we glad you got those tubes tied." Jasi said.

"Child please yall aint got to be glad I got my tubes tied. Cause you know a clinic and 380.00 the baby won't make it in this here world." Jasi said shouting those cruel words out.

"Becky, you don't have to say it like that. Damn just protect yourself."

"Oh Chocolate please, if Chuck would have left one there I would have took you to the clinic too." She said without caring I didn't find a thing funny.

"Later Jasi! Don't forget to ask Bruce about Bahamas." I said as we pulled off.

"Does Dale have a house in the Bahamas?" Becky asked.

"Yes, remember the house I told you about that it takes a boat to get there."

"Yeah you did tell me that, but I am talking about a house that's safe and secure for the kids, not something yall fucked all over." Becky said, as I laughed at her silly provocative comment.

"Nah girl he told me he bought a new house I haven't seen it yet though."

"For real, cause we aint no school of fishes, and that's too much damn water for us to try and drank." Becky said laughing.

"You crazy." I added.

"Where is the rental?" Becky asked.

"Dale is taking it back in the morning."

"Damn Chocolate you didn't even let me smoke my joint."

"Sorry baby, you don't need it anyway." I said and totted the horn for Shanice.

"Bye! Oh what are we going to do for thanksgiving?" Becky asked.

"First lets deal with your birthday and Halloween."

"I got that on lock, Marco is gone get those tickets."

"I don't know." I said as Becky strapped Shanice in the backseat.

"Alright later." She said, walking back into the house.

"Thank you lord." I just felt so blessed; my life has been going around happy circles since I met this man. I can't say how he makes me feel inside, besides love.

"YOUNG, STABLE AND IN LOVE"

Becky was going through her purse for lotion, to give Corey and the kids just when Jasi and Bruce came walking to the twelve-seated dinner table. Jasi had changed into a full turquoise bathing suit along with a cute beaded wrap skirt and sandals.

"Wow! You guys made it" Becky said squeezing the lotion into Corey hand.

"Oh yeah, there is so much to see and do." Jasi responded.

"Man they have a set of dealers over there that Vegas needs."

"Yeah Bruce, we had an idea you were over there." I said.

"Dang Chocolate you are so ashy." Jasi said, scratching my arm.

"I know right all of us are, our legs look to be a finish race track." Becky said as the waitress walked up with empty dinnerware for the buffet. Corey like always so loud and rude, walked over to the buffet table scratching his balls, with his pants pulled halfway over his ass while Becky was walking with this smile that I knew, replaced the embarrassment she gets at times. We all followed each other along the buffet line, Dale put a scoop on my plate of almost everything he put on his, as well as Shanice plate. He's just a gentleman, he makes sure whatever I want I get, and he does almost everything for Shanice and I. When I say everything I mean from fixing our plate to laying the dinner napkin in our laps for spills. He would even blow Shanice food until its cool enough to swallow, he would open her straw, and even butter her biscuit. Corey on the other end smacking ridiculously loud, that the two boys thought it was so funny. Jasi fed Brianna and herself as we all sat and ate until we were full. After eating everyone was ready for their cabin for the next three hours aboard except the children. Jasi agreed to give the children a tour of the ship, while who ever wanted to rest could. While Jasi and Bruce hurried off with the kids, we headed to our cabin. The ship was so huge and compatible all around we couldn't help but get lost trying to get to our cabin. Along the rails, there were couples, families, and lonely visitors watching through binoculars. Dale slid over, pulling my hand leading me to the first vacant spot. Before I could adjust it or look through it, he unexpectedly kissed me as if this was the reason we stopped.

"I love you." He said as his eyes to me seemed focus and mines was at still.

"You hear me. I'm serious." Dale said, as he gently rubbed his hands across my face, pulled my chin to his lips, and lowered a kiss dead on my lips so softly and slowly.

"I don't want to ever leave you."

"Neither do I." I said gazing at what all had seemed to be around, beautiful blue water.

"Look baby." He said, as he turned the binoculars towards me. I leaned over a little and I was able to see, Bahamas which was a couple of miles away. Unfortunately we couldn't do the Disney cruise because it was cancelled. But man am I happier than a pig in shit that we ALL are cruising to the Bahamas.

"Dale!" I shouted as he hoped on my back.

"Ok I am sorry baby." He said patting me on my butt laughing when I was pretending to be mad. Then when I went to look up at him, he tickled me so hard until I fell to the ground. Onlookers were smiling just like me. They too felt the love chemistry the both of us was getting to know. He pulled me up by my hands, and threw his arms around my neck while we continued to search for our cabin. Quite a few more doors down we came to a sudden stop where Dale twisted the Rubbermaid key into the tiny door. The room was so dark, I waited until he took about three steps into the room then flicked on the light. The floor was covered with yellow rose petals. On the dresser there was a vase full of yellow and pink roses. Next to that there was a card that laid open and Dale stood watching my happiness unfold at the door.

"Baby you are all I have, I am going to see that you are happy everyday." He said leading me further in the room and quietly shutting the door. There was a pale of ice and a bottle of Moet, tied around the bottles were two balloons that read *'just because'*

"This is beautiful." I said, trying to refrain from the I love you word, which I think I did started to love him.

"Anything for you baby." He said facing me toe for a toe and eye for an eye. He reached into his pocket as if he was going for something. Without a doubt, he pulled out a little blue box that read "*Tiffany's'* which was a fine branded jeweler.

"Mona baby you know how I feel about you. I have told you, you are someone I want to be with for a lifetime. I enjoy each moment we spend and remember each smile you have shown. Here in this box is a gift. A gift I want to hold me for what I am about to say." He said, while I blushed and was hoping he wasn't ready for what he sounded like.

"This is a promise ring." Dale said as he opened the box and the ring was sitting with three nice size diamonds on top of a platinum band. I was shocked and weak at my knees.

"These diamonds are supposed to resemble a promise." He said as he held my hands into his, I was kind of relieve because I sure wasn't ready for marriage only after 10 mos. Dale slid the ring unto my right ring finger.

"I know once before, you told me *a promise is only a comfort to a fool*, but I have three and all I ask is for you to believe.

"I will."

"This diamond is a promise that I'll never leave you." Dale said as I could feel my eyelashes beating my eyelids.

"I promise, I'll be there through it all. To even see us at the end, when it takes us there and I promise everyday will be like the first day."

By the time he was finish I just knew I'd wake up from the dream of promises, however gazing down at my finger the three diamonds glistened back at me. I threw my arms around his neck and wrapped my feet around his waist, as he palmed me up my ass just how I liked it. Dale leaned me against the wall for better support, placed his two hands on my face with full attention and kissed me, letting go with a look of trust that's lined with honesty. The love for him started to grow more and more by the second. I had not only become horny but happy, lucky, surprised, thankful and blessed all in one.

"I love you." I said, trying to hold back my tongue, but my emotions were all over the place.

"Baby I can tell." Dale said, sounding so sure which was only the truth. He leaned over the bed and picked up two tied garbage bags.

"What is it baby?" I asked as I stood standing. It was more pink petals he started from the foot of the bed and ended pouring at the head of the bed. Then there was the second bag which was yellow and he did the same. He twirled me over to the bed by my hands, like Mister did Netty on her way to school. But he laid me on fluffy petals accompanied with a smooth drink of Moet. While I sipped on my drink, he reached down and slid off my shoes, and unbutton my top.

"Turn over on your stomach baby, I'm going to give you a massage." He said as I placed my drink down and flipped over. All of a sudden he jumped up and opened the bathroom door; out came floating about twenty balloons reading 'I *Love you*.' I was so happy, I just didn't know how to take this man. He then rested a warm towel around my neck and squeezed baby oil up and down my back and believe me it wasn't cold neither. He had a grip on my body as if he could rip the bones from beneath my skin, but a touch that will rock a worried woman to sleep without question or worrying. He began to massage my back up and down, side-by-side and through each joint that ever did bend. Boy am I so glad Dale saved this Disney vacation by quickly adding Bahamas and inviting the entire crew.

*****

The super-sized Excursion pulled over to the curbside, where Jasi, Becky, her three kids and I stood patiently. Dale was driving, while Corey sat on the passenger side, and Bruce was in the back with Shanice.

"Come on baby its time to have fun!" Corey said as he stepped out and the others as well to load our bags in. The truck was beautiful and big, very roomy and comfy with little gadgets such as, three DVD's and TV's. The kids quickly climbed to the back, Corey and Becky sat together, so did Jasi and Bruce.

Dale drove us around as the kids begin with the *OH's* and *Ah's*, just like I did but to myself. Dale bought another house since the last time I was here, so therefore I was new to this ride as well. I sat looking through the window while the conversations sounded back and forth. I thought back a year ago how I was giving this man a hard time; about to pass up a good thing, by remembering and comparing my past. Hell what can I say I am a typical woman, a black one at that! Where it doesn't take a second time for MANY of us to learn.

"What's on your mind baby?" Dale asked, placing his hand on my thigh.

"Nothing just observing the scenery." I said with a generous smile.

"You like it?"

"It's gorgeous."

"Do you think you can live here?"

"No not really, but vacations I can deal with."

"Why? It is nice here Chocolate?"

"It is, but home is home you know."

"So if we were to ever get married start a family, and I was ready to pick up and find another home would you come?" He asked, as that particular statement slapped me in the face, not only was this already in plan but with him *MARRIAGE* and a *FAMILY* is definitely my American dream.

"Well Dale it actually depends. Now if it's in the U.S. yes, in another country I don't know baby." I said, smiling.

"Well guess what?"

"What?" I asked intentionally raising my right brow, and squinshing my face.

"I'll follow you all around the globe if it meant being with you." Dale said.

"That is so sweet." I replied as I could feel a smile increasing upon my face.

"I love you, I truly love you. Everything about you." He continued, as he tighten the grip on my thigh.

"Dale do you go fishing!" Corey interrupted from the back seat.

"Yes I go sometimes when I'm here, but I love to go lobster hunting and spearing." Dale replied looking through his rearview mirror.

"Spearing! What you be spearing dawg?" Corey asked sounding just like himself on the block.

"In these waters they have barracuda and groupers half long as you, I like to spear those octopus too."

"You don't get any sharks?"

"Nah Corey; I stay away from them." Dale replied as everyone started to laugh.

"How about Bass?" Bruce asked.

"Yeah I get those too. Maybe we can go out on my boat, and do a little fishing tonight." Dale suggested, as he looked over at me.

"Me myself I love to fish, but I aint no hellava fisher at all." Bruce admitted.

"Shit pops aint never took us fishing, all I can say is throw your rod out there and see what you get in return." Corey said stuffing his mouth with the chips they were passing around.

"That's basically how you fish Corey."

"So what kind of boat you got?" Corey asked.

"I have a house boat and a speed boat." Dale replied.

"Yeah! I got to get me a toy like that, maybe a speed boat." Corey said, knowing he didn't have a pot to piss in nor a window to throw it out. I guess he was wishfully thinking out loud.

Dale drove into a neighborhood that looked far from the Bahamas, according to to my imagination.

"Wow, these some big cribs around here!" Corey said, as everyone eyes stretched and mouthed opened. Just ahead was a huge wall imprinted *'Bloomington estates'* decorated in Caribbean colors and an iron gate that looked to have guarded castles. There were beautiful mailboxes, colorful flowers that outlined the windows, stones that looked to be valuable, placed alongside the walkways. Trees and lawn looked like each strain was nurtured daily, cut and neatly trimmed. Dale pulled into a driveway, there stood a tall and big house with very few windows that was painted olive green and burgundy. What a splendid house I thought.

"Damn, I know it cost at least a million to live out here!" Corey said.

"Yeah, this is a very nice area, and the architect of its beauty is why it's worth the money." Bruce added.

"There is a couple of houses around here about a million, but mines is a four bedroom five bathroom for about 350,000." Dale responded.

"That's a pretty good price." Bruce said as Dale opened the door to the house, while us women fidget getting the kids together and of course gossiping.

The house was so huge it not only had one stairwell but it had two that meet at the top. He opened the drapes along the back wall; there was nothing but water outside his screened patio. His houseboat was docked out back following the dock was poles of what looked to be lanterns. Dale showed us around his new home and asked that we all make ourselves at home by sleeping, drinking and eating whatever and wherever. The guys had quickly decided they were ready to go out on the boat for a ride, so they loaded the kids up as well and left us ladies behind. Jasi, Becky, and I stood at the end of Dale's private dock for a minute as the kids waved goodbye. It wasn't long before we grabbed up a seat on the patio and continued gossiping.

"Girl, you better keep this here sport!" Becky said, changing the tone of her voice.

"I know right; look like you got yourself something." Jasi added.

"Yeah, girl it must be something look what he gave me?" I said waving my finger into their direction.

"It's a promise ring girl!" Jasi shouted.

"And the motherfucker platinum too!" Becky added. "Well what did he promise you?"

"That he'd never leave me, everyday will be like the first time."

"You don't suppose to tell nobody." Jasi rudely interrupted.

"Girl shut your superstitious ass up!" Becky said, as I got up to fix a drink.

"What was the last one?" Becky insisted on knowing.

"That we will grow old together." I said with a big smile.

"Damn, looks like cupid just shot your ass all up." Becky said as Jasi laughed out loud.

"Well Chocolate, you aint got nothing to lose just take love one step at a time." Jasi said.

"I know right. I just hope this is what it is." I said standing at the pantry door.

"Girl stop doubting it, you have to believe in it to feel it." Becky said, as she walked over to the fridge taking out a meal to prepare.

"I guess none of us will be lonely this Christmas." Jasi said.

"You don't know its only September." Becky responded.

"Well Becky if I can help it, my heart stops here." I added.

"Mines can't stop here; but it's benefiting." Jasi said.

"Yall, know me I can love Corey today, and don't fuck with him tomorrow!"

"Child please! Becky you full of it; looks to me he on the trip. Yall must be in love for the 70th time." Jasi said laughing and so was Becky.

"Ok yall bullshitting you gone see. Wait till my birthday next month."

"So what your birthday got to do with anything?" I asked.

"Ok play dumb. All five of our tickets to Jamaica came back, and we just gone have a good time, I'm coming back with me a Sean Paul on yall ass."

"Child please, well I'm coming back with Bennie Man! Anyways why you got five tickets?" I asked.

"I told yall, I'm gone party with a few guest."

"Well who are the other two tickets for?"

"One for Nikki, and the other one for Lela." Becky responded.

"That girl from Dallas?" Jasi asked.

"Yeah don't yall remember her?" Becky questioned.

"Just as well as we forgot her." I said briefly and looking the other way. Lela was one of those smooth bright-skinned Indian Jamaican chicks. Who had her priorities set straight, a husband and two beautiful kids. She married an Indian guy from Barbados that had lots of money.

"Well yeah she going, so she can take us around."

"That's right, her parents do live in Spanish town." Jasi said.

"Isn't Marco going to be down there?" I asked.

"Yeah and!" Becky responded.

"Baby that's Miss bad Momma, Chocolate she run her shit!" Jasi said, as she popped a bottle of Hennessey and I gathered three tiny glasses from the cabinet. We all poured ourselves a drink on ice, and sat back on the patio in the loungers sipping while Becky was blowing clouds of smoke into the air.

"Girl yesterday on that cruise, Corey wanted some of this ass so bad. I aint give his whorish ass shit, and tonight I might just act like it's that time of the month." Becky said.

"Alright get it took, trying to play hard." Jasi said, already sounding as drowsy as a wino.

"I kind of like it when he take it though, especially when he be talking nasty with it." Becky said as she laughed stomping her feet up and down with excitement.

"Becky you so silly!" I added and couldn't help but laugh because I liked it too.

"Come on now Chocolate, be real you don't like when you get it took from you?" Becky asked.

"A little bit, but I like to throw it on them when they mad with me. That's when you really know your man know how to fuck, they be trying to beat it all up, and that somehow makes things better." I said taking another sip of my drink.

"Girl you said a mouth full just now! Don't forget when they on that liquor too." Jasi said, refilling each glass.

"Oh nah yall, it aint nothing like coming from the club. You done dance all night that pussy all wet and you feeling good... Just a kiss on the hand, you be about to tear your panties off." Becky said, making all of us laugh. We sat and talked for more than an hour, and there were no sign of the guys.

"I'll be back I got to pee." I said.

"Child please, she can't handle no dame liquor, talking about some she got to pee." Becky said.

"Whatever." I responded, as I continued up the stairs, knowing I wasn't about to come back tired as I was feeling.

"I guess I suppose to cook?" Becky questioned.

"You minus well." Jasi added.

"Hell nah I'm the company."

"Shit I am too." I said, as I twist the knob to the Master bedroom where I threw myself over the bed.

Something cold, brushed against my cheeks, I turned over and opened my eyes to the very dark room and florescent green numbers on the stereo which appeared to be 4:15am. I had slept the whole time without hearing a voice or eating a meal. I could feel Dale hands rubbing up and down my stomach and soft kisses above my back while humming sweet tunes in my ear of jagged edge *"walked out of heaven'*

"Good morning baby." He said.

"Good morning." I responded with a smirk before excusing myself to the bathroom. I looked horrible as I stood before the mirror. I turned the shower on and quickly undressed and stepped into the shower.

I could hear him at the door by the time I lathered my body with soap, he walked in and placed my bag on the mini table that sat in the corner. I finished bathing, brushed my teeth, and I dressed myself in a gown I bought here especially for him. It was sheer pink with tiny sheer pink G-string panties. I brushed my Chinese cut bangs that hung in an 18-inch wrap, that he thought made me look like a cute black doll. Sprayed myself with Dior and was ready for tonight, feeling a little freaky and slightly tipsy. I walked out, while he was standing in front of the stereo, it was obvious he was checking me out, but it was a sexy look as if he didn't know what to do.

"What's wrong?" I whispered as I rubbed my nails across his balls and slid my tongue down his chest. He then grabbed me from the back of my hair a bit aggressive, but very sexy to me. He rubbed his hands down the bottom of my gown, and slid it up slowly, squeezing my butt and tracing his fingers through my legs.

"Baby you look stunning." He said taking a step back while turning me in each direction. "I knew I had myself a winner. Any way I look at you; all I can see is a woman of your caliber making it anywhere, and deserving the finest that life could bring." He said as I begin running my nails through the hairs of his goatee. "You are the one." Dale said as he turned back to the stereo, and I walked over to the bed and slid under the covers snuggling up with the extra-large pillows. It wasn't long after he slid in and cuffed me into his arms. My heart was racing and so was my clit. The music sounded so clear yet low, there wasn't a sound besides us breathing. He kissed me upon my back and down my shoulders, he rubbed me in every which way, until my semi shivering body heated up to his friction. I totally took control of him and placed my legs across him and simply inserted what I was dreading for.

"Damn baby, that's how you want it?" He asked, licking his lips.

"That's right baby, panties to the side and ready to ride." I replied.

"Damn, I love it when you're so nasty." Dale passionately whispered.

"Do you really? Do you like it like this baby?" I asked as I scooted my body up and down.

"Oh yeah baby!" He confirmed.

"I like it too." I whispered and gently kissed him on the ear.

"Let me make love to ya?" He asked, just before placing my breast in his mouth. I slung my head back as he gripped me around my waist, gently placing me on the couch. Kissing me on my lips, and feeling every part of me with his large hands. Easily and before I knew it I was pinned in a way that was brand new to me, a way I couldn't ignore but a feeling that took me way back. Lord this man was really showing out on me. He grinned and swept through each corner of my pussy that was left untouched from time after time.

"Be with me forever, not just tonight." He said gripping my face and waiting for an answer. "I'm talking about every night, like a family." He asked as it just hit me we were sexing bare. I could feel his natural flesh go in and out of my warm body, which led him to become so overwhelmed. I dare couldn't ask him to stop and put on a condom which would have been the right thing to do. Without interruption I let him continue as he buried his face into my chest and pinned me even tighter, as he motioned his dick in and out my tight hole. The feeling was good I began to cry as he was loving me. We were making love so passionately, I am almost certain that you would agree this type of love making could make a big part to any hit movie. I continued to grin in every direction in which my body would allow me to within these positions, even if the dick was feeling like it was going to tear the bottom of my stomach out. Despite the sharp pains through my side that I was experiencing which felt like lightning bolts. Suddenly without warning he slid his very hard dick out of me, and started licking my click. Oh my I must say I was totally out of control by this point, as he continued to kiss all over me. I'm talking all down my legs, up my ass crack, around my toes, and back to my click his tongue went. My toes were curled so tightly, as he jolted his tongue in and out of me several times. I nearly went into convulsions when he placed his mouth around my pussy as he sucked me and sucked me. Again without warning he jabbed his hard dick back into me once again without protection. I was speechless from this moment because lord knows all though we were making love I CLEARLY and MENTALLY took note that this man is fucking the shit out of me.

Morning had come, and the kids were making noise from every part of the house. Shanice was rocking in the chair watching TV with Brianna, both dressed in their pajamas.

"Good morning Mommy." Shanice said as I walked down the stairwell wrapped in my robe and pajama shorts.

"Good morning." I responded.

"Good morning auntie." Brianna called.

"Good morning."

Dale came from around the corner with a pitcher of fresh squeezed orange juice and a tray of buttermilk pancakes for the girls.

"Thank you Dale." Shanice said.

"You welcome sweetie." He replies as he rubbed butter over the pancakes and poured syrup over them. I stood observing him, he didn't touch me nor did he make this relationship seem as if he was my man and I was his woman. It appears to me he's trying more to be Shanice friend than he was trying to be my man. I walked in the kitchen to see what was left and laying on the counter was some fish he had cleaned and seasoned, a pot of grits slowly cooking, more pancakes and eggs under the warming light. I got a plate and scooped some eggs and a layer of three pancakes. He walked in swinging the syrup, placing his hands above my waste and smacking me with a quick kiss; as if we were too young to do this.

"What are you drinking?" He asked.

"Milk, please." I responded snickering and thinking to myself how he acting as if he's a brother of mine when he done fucked me part of the morning. However I liked that, because that was just a reminder to let myself know I got a man and not a boy. He poured me a glass of milk and began fixing his breakfast.

"Is everything ok?" He asked as I stood to the counter pouring syrup.

"Yes." I said.

"Did you think about what I asked you last night?" He asked, as I tried to register what didn't he ask.

"Forever!" He said reminding me.

"That would be nice, but Dale you know I just bought my condo a little over a year ago, I can't just pick up and leave so soon." I said, as I looked at the kids switch from channel to channel.

"Mona it's not so much of you leaving your place so soon, is it maybe you don't want to try and give love a chance?" He asked.

"No. I mean we only have been together for 10mos there is a lot of room for us to grow." I replied.

"Your right but time doesn't have anything to do with love, its feelings that makes the decision. I told you I love you, I don't have time to play those jitterbug games. I'm ready for children and a wife." He said without blinking an eye, or stuffing his face.

"I don't know Dale."

"Chocolate, I don't want to go home without you and besides you don't have to sell your condo if you don't trust me. I'll pay your mortgage. You can leave it vacant, and I promise at any time you or Shanice don't feel like what's mines is yours... you can pick up and leave, and I'll still be in your footsteps." Dale said, as I thought of how bad I wanted what he was proposing, however I was scared as hell. My heart was ticking so rapidly, and my nerves were dancing away in my stomach.

"Yes Dale." I boldly said.

"When?" He asked, not trying to give up until it was definite.

"Give me a little time, to take care of some business."

"A month." He said impatiently.

"Dale I have to get my bills straight, and pack up my things." I said trying to drag on so much work.

"Ok, I'll wait for you." He said, as I mapped a plan out just as quickly as he replied.

"I might just let my little sister have my place until whenever."

"Like I said you can leave everything, I'll make sure all the bills are paid every month. I just want you and Shanice with me." He said, as the options came better and better. I really aint got nothing to lose Daddy always said first you try it and then you trust. Money most definitely aint a problem to him, neither our wants nor needs when he's making over a hundred thousand a year. I guess I'll give it a try. He's already that father figured man somewhat like daddy whom I always prayed for.

"Good Morning Folks!" Corey said as he came down the stairs.

"Good morning." The girls responded.

"What's cooking in the kitchen? I don't smell them fish and grits." Corey said.

"Oh the girls had me to cook pancakes just morning, but I seasoned the snapper up over there for you."

"Alright I'll fry that up and cook a pot of grits." Corey said, as he viewed the fish on the cut board.

"You put these grits on Dale?" Corey asked.

"Yeah." Dale responded.

"Ok. Ok." Corey said, as I excused myself from the kitchen.

"Where your pepper at Dale?" Corey asked as Dale made a u turn back into the kitchen.

"Look in the cupboard against the wall, if you need more seasonings." Dale suggested.

"Mommy, can we fish today?" Shanice asked.

"You liked it yesterday?"

"Yeah, I want you to come." Shanice asked.

"Yes Shanice maybe later." I responded.

"Dale catch a big ole fish Mommy, he was jumping everywhere." Shanice said laughing.

"My daddy catch a baby fish." Brianna said, as Dale and Corey started to laugh.

"But Bruce fooled us, talking about he don't know nothing about fishing. He caught about 6 big yellow tails." Corey added.

"He knew how to fish, he just pimped us out there." Dale said as the scent of fish grease quickly filled the air.

"I want to go back out there." Corey said.

"Yeah, all of us are going to go. I got three jet skis in the storage out back. Maybe tonight we can have a fish fry and drink a little liquor." Dale suggested.

"That's straight with me." Corey replied.

"Hey Hey Hey do I smell those big tail fish up in here!" Bruce said entering the room.

"What's up fisherman?" Dale spoke.

"That's me! That's me!" Bruce said, laughing and popping his collar on his button down polo shirt.

"Feel up to a little fish fry tonight?" Dale asked Bruce, while I slipped away from the room and up the stairs. I went to the room Jasi was sleeping in, and she still laid sleeping. Apparently she must have gone to bed late. Becky was coming out of the bathroom blowing her nose as her sinus got to her as usual.

"Good morning snotty nose." I said.

"Girl what time you woke up?" Becky asked.

"Since 4 this morning." I replied.

"You're tired ass can't even handle a drink. You said you were going to go use the bathroom and we never saw you again."

"So what did you all do?" I asked.

"Nothing really just got fucked up even more, then Jasi went to bed before they came back from fishing. So I was left up by myself and I put the girls in the tub and dressed them in their pajamas while Dale had cooked some Steamed fish, peas and rice. It was so good. Then he played games with the kids, and I fell asleep. Leaving everybody else down stairs." Becky said, as she sat on the toilet, with the door cracked open and I sat on the floor, just about forgetting where we was.

"I guess, I didn't miss anything." I said.

"Not really, but I must admit you got yourself a good one. His performance last night was very country, I mean like family type shit. If thug or hoe anywhere in him; baby when he do let it out, you may kill him. He's a very nice guy, I seen how he interact with Shanice. When the boat came in, he went into the bag and got her pajamas, tooth brush and brought it to me while I was bathing them."

"I was wondering who went into my bag, cause he didn't even bother to wake me." I mentioned.

"I see, he one of those mans that can do everything with or without a woman." Becky said.

"Yeap, you hit it right on the head."

"I know!" Becky agreed. "Jasi still sleep."

"Yes." I responded.

"Girl she pissed me off a little last night too." Becky said looking into the mirror squeezing her nose.

"What she did?" I asked.

"Girl she got on that liquor and tried to bring that baby shit back up." Becky explained, with a look that wasn't pretty or funny.

"Becky come on now, everybody handle things different." I said, trying to change Becky not giving a damn attitude.

"I know but god damn, take responsibilities for your own actions stop blaming other grown motherfuckers for your shit."

"What did she say?" I asked, and couldn't help but to laugh.

"She just went to doing all that crying, saying she shouldn't have never listen to me about getting rid of her baby. When all a while, she the one made it clear she wasn't going to put her career on hold in which she had already came so far for."

"Yeah, but you know that might have been the liquor talking." I said.

"I know, but that's what shake the truth out your ass."

"So you think she meant it?" I asked.

"Chocolate I don't give a fuck if she did, cause guess what? When I need another one I'm going to ask her silly ass to take me to the same place I took her." Becky said sorting through her bag.

"Becky you so evil at times."

"I sure am especially when a women tries to stand in a childs place, I'll act like the boggy man on your ass!" Becky said as we walked to their room.

"Anyway, what you want to do today?" I asked, changing the subject.

"I don't know."

"Dale them talking about fishing, jet skiing, and later a fish fry."

"Yeah, I want to go out on the boat or at least the jet skis."

"You bought a bathing suit?"

"Sure did, one for me and for Brianna."

"That's cool, anyway Corey down stairs cooking fish and grits. The kids already ate."

"You got up and cooked this morning?"

"No I did not, when I went down stairs Dale had already made pancakes and eggs.

"Chocolate, you better keep this here man, this shit seems like it only starts in Hollywood on a set." She said, sliding on some shorts and t-shirt.

"Becky, I think this here is for real. He wants me to move with him now."

"Florida I hope!" Becky questioned, looking at me with the real sister look, eyes wide and lips popping.

"Yeah, in that house I took yall to in Weston"

"Oh girl."

"I know right, I think I am going to move there."

"Shit you better know! This man already bought you the car you wanted, gives you whatever you think you need, this better be for real... If it aint, god damn it you better pretend it is!" Becky said, as Jasi came walking through the door.

"Good morning ladies."

"Good morning suga." Becky said, with a smile as if she were never mad earlier.

"Oh my I slept like a baby last night." Jasi explained, as she joined us on the bed.

"So did I, until the roaster came in." Becky said, looking at Jasi, as the both of them pointed at me and laughed.

"So what's on the agenda for today?" Jasi asked.

"Jet skiing baby!" Becky announced.

"I haven't done that in a long time." Jasi said.

"I hope you got a bathing suit." I added.

"Yes I do, the same green one I had on when we were on the cruise." Jasi said.

"I'm hungry yall I think I better go and grab me some of this fish before those dogs down there eat it all." Becky said.

"Who cooked?" Jasi asked.

"Chocolate say Corey cooked some fish and grits." Becky said

"Yeah he was cooking it when I came up here earlier." I said.

"I'm hungry too." Jasi added.

"I'm going to take a shower, I'll see yall in a little while." I said as I headed to the room and they went off to the kitchen.

Shanice, and Brianna laid on the loungers, with their little bikinis on and of course far away from the water as they were afraid of the waves. The day was so beautiful and I was enjoying every minute of it. Bruce, Jasi, Corey and I raced up and down the blue waters on the super-fast jet skis; while Dale, Lil Corey, and Julian barbequed chicken and shrimps. We were truly having the time of our lives; we all were set and settled at this particular moment in this thing called life. It was at a point that I really realized money wasn't everything but it sure makes things a hell of a lot easier. Then on top of that; being in love and someone loving you back is more than happiness. It's a feeling and situation you never want to end. It's the kind of love that each moment matters and each second grows bolder. By the very thoughts of my happiness I gripped the handles of the Jet Ski and tackled the waves as if I was so experienced. When I turned to the left I saw Jasi whom had fallen off her jet ski at least six times. I was so happy she didn't know how to ride good enough, as that didn't matter because she would come by and splash water all on me with her little stunts she thought she knew.

"Hey you want to ride with me?" I asked Shanice.

"No Mommy, the fish gone get me." She responded.

"I want to ride." Brianna said, as I strapped her down with a life jacket and drove her in circles very slow. Shanice still stood there watching but yet not changing her mind. So I went over where Dale and the boys had started a little basketball game, with music blaring the voice of '*Bob Marley*.' It was a reminder to me that I knew everything was gone be alright. Lord knows, I didn't have a thought or a glimpse at unhappiness for quite some time now, and it felt good.

"Baby you want to play?" Dale asked, as I tighten the towel around my dripping wet body.

"No baby, I'm going to watch you play." I said, with a sexy look and a slight swing in my walk.

"Come on Dale!" The boys called to him while me and the girls munched on some grapes. Bruce and Corey had come out of the water, but Jasi and Becky continued to ride.

"Boys I know yall putting a whipping on Dale?" Corey asked as he came up to the court.

"Daddy come help us Dale beating us!" Julian said, as Corey jumped into the game.

"Ok now its three against one, watch how I dog yall out." Dale said as he dribbled the ball up and down the court and then shot it from the far corner.

"Oh man! Now you want to get technical." Corey said as he dribbled the ball down the court, and slammed dunk on Dale.

"Now is that how you want to play!" Corey said, as the boys jumped up and down.

"That's my Daddy!" Lil Corey said, as the exciting evening went on.

THANKSGIVING TOGETHER

We decided to have Thanksgiving Dinner at the new house Dale and I were now living in. The stairwell, table and centerpiece were decorated with fresh point setters. The candles were lit in a sequence from small to big, the turkey that baked all night, the sweet potato pies, and the real pine Christmas tree had smelled all through the house as if it was shouting the holidays are here. Ms. Minnie, Mama and Ms. Cure was in the kitchen preparing the decorations and minor trays while the guys were in the cinema room enjoying Daddy favorite actor Richard Pryor in `Which way is up' instead of watching the second biggest NFL game of the year ever. Jasi and I were on the patio watching the kids play kick ball. Becky was on her way back from seeing Nikki. Who has been locked up from the day we came back from Jamaica, she never made it out the airport.

"Jasi how do you know when you got a urinary tract infection?" I asked.

"You usually have pain at the bottom of your stomach when you pee." Jasi replied.

"I don't have any pain at the bottom of my stomach, but I piss like three times an hour."

"Damn, when the last you seen your menstrual."

"You know mines never regulated right, I can't even tell you. Maybe August or September?"

"Well you should be coming on soon, if not your ass might be pregnant."

"I don't think so, you know sometimes I go without having my period for at least 6 mos., but much as Dale been fucking me who knows what he left in here."

"You want another child Mona?"

"Of course!" I replied in a much serious tone.

"Really, all jokes aside." Jasi said, with full attention. "I said of course. Why you don't believe me?" I repeated with my eyebrows in an upward position.

"I guess things have really, just changed for the best." She responded with an admirable smile.

"Yeah, I would say so too. I feel happy and secure here, and he wants a child so bad."

"I see Shanice and him get along so good." Jasi added.

"He act like she his, and she love him too girl." I said, just when the patio door swung open.

"Yo-Yo the queen is in! The queen is in!" Becky said wearing her von Dutch jeans, button down top, her long silky straight hair hung beneath the cap and a pair of cute pointed toe pumps.

"What's up chick?" Jasi said.

"Hey punk!" Becky said slapping me over my head.

"Stop playing bull-dagger." I said, as we started laughing.

"Oh girl let me tell yall about Corey bitch ass!" Becky said, pulling a lounger near and took a seat crossing her legs.

"What done happened now?" Jasi asked.

"I was at the gas station yesterday, after washing the truck I was getting a fill up. Corey and Shawn had pulled up in that green raggedly ass Hyundai she be driving. I went back for my change giving them the funkiest walk that my pelvic had allowed your girl, and just like I thought Corey had came in, and I was getting a soda before I asked for my change on the fill up. He walked back where I was talking about man you gone let me see my kids or what? When I tell yall I gave that nigga a look that just made him hot. He started grabbing me around my neck and shit while his hoe was out in the car. He went to asking me why I do him like that and the begging shit talking about how he gone do better if I gave him another chance."

"No he didn't!" Jasi said, as I ignored the story like all the others, but somehow I think she

through with Corey since her truck incident. He never did get it fix or buy her a new one, instead Marco bought the Range Rover for her birthday.

"No girl listen to this! He went to saying you know I love you and I'll always will. I looked him in his face and said you and I can never be together and I promise you that. Then Shawn came in the gas station, screaming about give me my damn money and catch a ride with that hoe."

"She of all the hoes called you a hoe." Jasi said in disbelief.

"You should have slapped the taste out her mouth!" I said.

"Trust me it took a lot for me to keep quiet so Corey snatched away from her and started yelling he was asking me about my kids."

"He must love that stripper hoe." Jasi added.

"Girl you tell me what man don't love garbage, I don't give a damn if they got a good wife at home they still manage to find some garbage bag to cheat with." I replied

Listen yall!" Becky interrupted and continued with her story. "I told her dumb ass; he wasn't asking about the kids, he was begging and pleading like a bitch. Then he threw the five dollars on the counter I guess that's what she gave him for gas and walked out the store. So you know I had to work her. Honey let me tell yall how I set her ass straight. When Corey stormed out the gas station, I came behind her in line to get my change and pay for the soda, she rudely asked the gas cashier to give her five dollars of unleaded gas on pump three. I finally paid for my shit and got my thirteen dollars in change. I got in my truck and drove around the next set of pumps while she was pumping her gas to only reply to Corey question he asked in the station. "*Yo Buddy you made it this way, now another motherfucker gone be eating your turkey, and decorating your kids Christmas tree! Oh and you, yeah the whore over there when you stop shaking your ass for a dollar or two, then you can call me a hoe.... and I don't mean your average or a broke hoe.... I mean the good hoe which is what you should thrive to be. Yeah bitch I said it the kind that markets her pussy and not sweating all night for sixty or seventy dollars on a pole. Ask your so called nigga, his kids and I live in MY house, riding in MY shit. I'm a homeowner Bitch and drive a collectible hoe!* Then I pulled off on her ass without giving her a chance to say a word, so you know she was like a thirty eight hot."

"Becky girl you crazy." I said.

"I just had to read that hoe, and I finally got my chance." Becky added.

"So what's up with Nikki?" Jasi asked.

"She goes to court in February; but she is doing fine."

"Damn I don't know what Nikki was thinking about, that little bitty ass weed couldn't have been that good." I added.

"It was good, but hell nah not that good that I would try to bring a piece back. Trust me she regret that shit now, she cried almost the whole time I was there too."

"Mona!" Mama called from the kitchen.

"Yes." I replied entering the house, they were laughing out.

"What's so funny?' I asked while mama lie across the counter holding her side and Ms. Minnie with her hands over her mouth.

"Listen here Chocolate; I was telling your mama I seen Ms. Margaret that lady who use to live behind us dressed in a lumber jacket, a trucker hat and some big boots. She was walking with this bright skinned woman, and you know when you see an ugly red woman she ugly." Ms. Cure said.

"She sure is." I agreed.

"Well any way, I asked her how the boys doing she said the two of them was doing fine, so I asked her how her husband was doing? She grabbed up the red woman as if I wanted her; and said `*this here my woman here*.' Child I could have fainted, instead when I walked off I took a good look at this woman. She looked worse than a gorilla drinking vinegar, who aint even had enough ass to make a sick man soup, and Margaret hollering her woman." Ms. Cure said, as I dropped to the floor and Mama hollered out loud once again in laughter just to think of how a gorilla would look drinking vinegar especially when it frowns from the bitterness.

The lights were dimmed and each candle was lit, every seat sat boy, girl, man or woman. Ms. Cure was at the head of the table and signaled everyone for prayer. We bowed our heads as her strong voice spoke out.

Our Father which art in heaven,
Hallowed be thy name.
Thy kingdom come.
Thy will be done in earth,
as it is in heaven.
Give us this day our daily bread.
And forgive us our trespasses,
as we forgive those
who trespass against us.
And lead us not into temptation,
but deliver us from evil:
For thine is the kingdom,
and the power, and the glory,

forever and ever.
Amen.

"Pass the bread." Becky said immediately after prayer.

"Ummm umm, these chitterlings taste so good." Jasi said.

"Yes they do. Baby we got to have one of these at our house." Bruce added as he munched down on a slice of homemade corn bread which taste a thousand times better than jiffy.

"Alright now, I don't need everyone... Wait let me rephrase that, I don't need anyone getting so full until they can't tell us what they are thankful for this year." Ms. Cure said, as always in a somber tone.

"All man." Becky mumbled.

"Baby you got something to be thankful for?" Dale turned and asked me.

"You will see." I said, placing the fork down in the roast.

"That's that smooth talker." Dale said smiling, sneaking his hand under the table pinching me on the side.

"Slice me a piece of the jelly cake." Bruce said to Jasi as she walked over to the desert table.

"Mona." Bruce called as I slid over a seat, being Dale was up getting desserts as well.

"Mona, that's a real good man there you have. He really loves you, and I know you love

him too. I like to see you when you happy like this, I've been watching and listening." Bruce said, as I smiled, just to know someone else knew what I was feeling and what all I really was missing.

"Thank you, he really is an incredible man." I said, laughing the sympathetic matter away and slid to my seat just before Dale arrived with all types of cakes.

"Umm Umm." I said as Dale rubbed Red Velvet cream across my mouth.

"Ok now it's time to tell us what we are thankful for." Ms. Cure announced.

"Who wants to be first?" She asked, as everyone started yelling you first.

"Ok I don't have a problem, I have a lot to be thankful for." Ms. Cure said, as she walked toward the Christmas tree. "I am thankful, for my lord Jesus Christ to have let me see another thanksgiving. I am thankful for my neighbors, my friends, my health, and my mind!" As she continued on, nobody no longer looked at her because we knew she always had a speech and maybe a little holly ghost too. Yet haven't went one Sunday to church. The kids started getting back up for more desserts making noise and interrupting what should have been a manuscript.

"Ok, Now next." She said as we all gave a clap for a dismissal of a grand president.

"Come on now don't be ashamed, this is a thankful time of the year." Ms. Cure said as no one raised his or her hand.

"I'll go." Dale said, out of nowhere.

"Go ahead." Ms. Cure said.

"Alright!" Becky yelled, as everyone welcomed Dale.

"I am thankful to see another year, I am thankful and fortunate to have this nice, joyful, and precious family around this time of year. Most of all I am thankful for my sunshine,

my life, and my love for showing me there is a new begging behind any sad road." He said, as the room sounded off as if there were a thousand kittens purring.

"Auh auh." I said as he sat down and kissed me on the cheek.

"I love you baby."

"I love you too sweet heart." I said.

"Ok can we have the next person up?" Ms. Cure asked, just when Becky stood from the table.

"I am thankful for my kids, my life, and my health of course. I am thankful for you Mama and I love you." Becky said, as she got up and gave her mom and her kids a kiss.

The night had came to an end Jasi and I had finished washing the last dishes and trays, while Bruce was trying to convince Dale into buying a certain stock on his lap top.

"I enjoyed tonight." Jasi said.

"Yes it was nice, I enjoyed it myself."

"Chocolate girl, I be thinking about when you use to say what you wanted out of a man. Remember that big house swimming pool, stairwell, and garden. Remember you use to wish for that?" Jasi asked while I just smiled from ear to ear, because it was a dream that was so clear.

"Yeah Jasi I remember that."

"Baby you got it, take vacations with the seasons, big beautiful half a million dollar home, a damn good man who loves you, your G35, your stairwell, your pool, your French doors, marble bathrooms, bitch you even got a bar with a pretty expensive collection. No more Kaluaha, or wine coolers from the corner store, you can afford to make your own drink." Jasi said as we both laughed. "Chocolate girl, I have something I want to tell you. I mean you and only you for now." Jasi said, as she stood against the refrigerator.

"What is it?"

"Chocolate, you know Bruce is divorcing his wife."

"What!"

"Yes, please don't say nothing to Becky about it. However the wife had signed a prenuptial agreement so he's secured there, it's just his two boys. He bought a home in Houston, to open up a new office and asked will I come and help him."

"To live, or just a weekend thing?" I asked trying to sort this matter between her career, and his propositions. "What about school Jasi?"

"Next month being it's the last semester of the year, then finals, so I'm going to stay back and finish this semester and then move to Houston in February for about a year." She said, wiping the stove down again and again.

"A year! What about school?" I asked again...

"Well I only have eighteen months and one more state board test before my BA."

"So why come this close and just stop."

"I'm not just stopping, I am doing something that's going to benefit me as well."

"I don't know, but I just figured you are this close to finishing and meeting your dream face to face there is no need to stop or procrastinate."

"These extra medical classes and books is costing a fortune right long and now." Jasi stated the poorest excuse ever.

"What's wrong with taking a loan?"

"I need the little assets I got now, there is no need of me gambling with all I got." Jasi said, making a little since but not much.

"Well, all I can say is that we will miss you."

"Girl please, you know I will be down here at least 3 times a month." Jasi said smiling. "I wonder what Becky got to say." I asked.

"Let me tell that nut, please." Jasi said, as Bruce and Dale entered the kitchen.

"Alright I'll call and let you know." Bruce said, as Dale walked over and stood near me.

"Are you ready baby?" Bruce asked placing his arms around Jasi.

"Yes dear." Jasi responded.

"I might just take you up on that, make sure you call me tomorrow." Dale said as Bruce headed for the front door.

"Wait baby! Let me fix myself a drink." Jasi said.

"Alright now you know what that drink bring on." I said as we both stood at the bar downing two tequila shoots and she took one to go.

"Trust me Chocolate, I don't mind we haven't did nothing in a couple of weeks. I ought to fix his ass one and drop a Viagra in it." Jasi said as we both laughed.

"Girl you really want him to beat that nookie in." I said, as she grabbed her six thousand dollar beaded Fendi bag and headed to the door.

"Later girl." I said, as I shut the door and let out a sigh of relief, as the hot feeling rushed over me from the two Tequilla shoots I swallowed.

"Are you tired baby?" Dale asked.

"Not really, just relived." I said.

"Come here." Dale asked. I walked over to him, as he grabbed me in his arms.

"You are my everything." He said, in sweet whispers. All of a sudden, my stomach went to boiling and what seemed to be heat became very visible with sweat popping from my forehead.

"Are you ok baby?" Dale asked as, I pulled away from him and ran to the bathroom. There

wasn't enough time for me to open the toilet, before I knew it I had threw up everything I ate from morning till now and not only in the toilet but all over the white beautiful carpet that laid in the guest bathroom.

"Baby what's wrong?" Dale said, as I leaned over the stool vomiting for the second time.

"What did you drink?" Dale asked in a panicky voice.

"Two Tequilla shoots." I said, straining back over in the stool for the remaining. Dale opened the closet, wet a small hand towel and started washing my face.

"Baby let me take you to the room."

"No, wait please!" I said, as I quickly thought about Jasi in LA. But I knew I couldn't be pregnant.

"What hurts?" He asked, as he kneeled down beside me.

"I don't know." I said as I began to cry, I had became nervous all at once. It couldn't be the liquor, because I always taken shoots.

"Don't cry baby, just let me take you to bed you don't have to walk."

"No, I might throw up everywhere again." I said feeling a bit embarrassed and wet in the seat of my pants from all the straining I pissed on myself.

After a couple of minutes, Dale had slipped off my shirt, places his arm under my legs and carried me up stairs to the room. He went into the bathroom and prepared water for me to bathe.

"Don't move." Dale said as I stood in the middle of the floor pulling down my skirt. He had a dry towel, which he used to wipe the vomit off me that my legs was resting in. He removed my skirt my panties, my jewelry and pulled my hair back into a ponytail. I walked over to the Jacuzzi and sat in, as he pulled my vanity chair up and sat on the side.

"You feel a little better baby?"

"Yes."

"Maybe you are just too full."

"I think, I might have had so many mixed up foods, and the drink didn't make it no better." I said as Dale sponged my body down with warm water, and peppermint soap which felt so cool.

"I enjoyed your family here tonight." He said running the towel between my toes.

"Yes, I enjoyed everyone tonight too baby." I said, felling a bit better.

"Your Daddy is a pretty cool man."

"Yeah, he's very cool, just love to cook and watch TV." I responded.

"He told me the story about you when you were 2yrs old." He said smiling and looking down at me, as I smiled back wondering what all Daddy didn't tell him.

"Now my baby feel a little better; cause her smiling." He said as he kneeled down and kissed me on my forehead.

"What story Dale?" I asked.

"When he had everyone in the neighborhood looking for you, because they thought you had got lost. After he called the police, he heard a pot rattled. When he opened the cabinet there you were fast asleep." He said, as I laughed. "Your Daddy said you were not bad but you were so busy. I wonder will our little one be busy like you or bad like my Mama said I was." Dale said as he pulled my face to his attention.

"I don't know Dale." I said.

"I want to start a family Mona." He said, staring into my eyes.

"Soon Dale."

"How soon?" He asked.

"Dale I really don't want to talk about this right now."

"What, is it marriage?" Dale asked as my eyes popped big, and that sickness was for sure forgot about.

"Dale, excuse me the water is getting cold." I said, as I leaped over to get out and he sat patiently waiting for an answer.

"Mona, is it that you want to be married before having another child?" He asked again, as I still pretend not to hear that.

"Mona, why are you ignoring me, just listen please have a child for me." He said as he stood in front of me as I tied the towel around my chest.

"Dale, we need a little more time."

"A little more time, come on Mona how much time you want me to have. I've dreamed and prepared for someone like you, since I was old enough to know love. You are what I want, right now and forever Mona."

"Dale lets just wait until next year and try for it." I said, trying to overcome his thought that I couldn't seem to prepare an instant answer for.

"Ok. Mona, just promise me you'll think about it." He said, as he reached for the lotion.

*****

Jasi, Becky and I stood in front of the mall doors, with the rest of the holiday door busters. Becky was munching on a sandwich, I was afraid to eat right now, to scared I might throw up like yesterday. The doors finally opened and we all went in as if we were running a marathon. I entered one toy store and got Shanice everything on her Christmas list, while Becky had to hunt from store to store. I was leaving them, like every fifteen minutes to pee and I had nothing to drink.

"Chocolate, stop by the food court and buy me a water on your way back. You want something Jasi?" Becky said.

"Yeah bring me a soda." She said sorting through the racks.

"Chocolate don't buy you shit to drink, you already pissing like a damn puppy, next you might be shitting like a duck." Becky said as I walked off and gave her the middle finger and motioned my lips at the same token. It was the truth; I was pissing like a puppy why I don't know.

"Hello." I answered.

"Hey baby, are you broke yet?" Dale asked.

"Not quite baby, why you missing me?" I asked.

"Everytime you walk out my sight." He said.

"What's up?" I asked.

"Nothing I just was calling to tell you that I am going to stop by your Mama house and pick Shanice up to go with me to the vet, so Baby could get groomed." He said.

"Oh Ok, well just call Mama so she can have her dressed for you by the time you get there."

"Ok, baby I'll see you a little later." He said before ending the call.

I entered the restroom; there was a lady who had her baby cocked up on the changing table cleaning her. The bathroom was so stink, but I really couldn't hold it. The smell had upset my nose, and tied my stomach into knots. By the time I was finish peeing, I was feeling so sick. I don't know was it from the fumes of the bathroom or some sort of virus, but it sent me gagging all over again.

"Mam, are you Ok?" A voice on the other side of the bathroom door asked, as I was vomiting and straining water to my eyes.

"Yes, just a little upset stomach." I answered back, when I caught my breath. I came out of the stall my eyes were full of tears, and my dark skinned was washed in sweat.

"You may want to flush your face with some cold water, to feel a little better." A scrawny lady said, as she washed her hands. Without a chance to run water into my hands, I strained over the sink and vomited again. It was as yellow as a yellow chalk that wrote on a black board. The lady walked over to me and was rubbing my back as if she had knew me.

"Would you like me to call someone?" She asked.

"No, I'll be ok. Just ate too much mixed up foods yesterday."

"Did you eat anything just morning?"

"No I didn't."

"That explains its yellowish coloration. Is it bitter?"

"Yes." I said, looking at this scrawny stranger wondering how she knows what I was feeling.

"You may want to go and have that checked out." She said, as she reached down in her purse and handed me a gynecologist/Obstetrician business card.

"Take this card, I am the midwife for Dr. Greenberg." She said to me like she had already knew my results. She stayed with me until, I was ready to leave the restroom, and I didn't even stop to buy what they had asked for. I was just praying that I could make it back to them without falling out or striking the crowds attention by vomiting over the mall. I was feeling like I was on a rough ride, and was weak as a fragile bird that had been just born.

"Where is my water?" Becky asked, as I sat on the showcase where the dummy poised.

"Girl, I need to go home." I said in a desperate tone.

"Home! What's wrong with you?" Becky asked.

"Becky, I don't know, but I feel terrible. I can't stop pissing or throwing up." I said, as they both stood a side and looked down at me.

"Chocolate are you pregnant?" Becky asked.

"No! I was feeling sick like this from yesterday."

"Well you need to be going to the hospital." Becky added.

"No, it might just be that Tequila we had yesterday."

"You think you have been liquor poisoned too huh? Becky asked, as the questions played out as DEJA VU.

"Nah, she aint been no poisoned, cause her and I took the same shot from the same bottle." Jasi said.

"Please yall, just stand to the front with me I'll call Dale to come get me." I said, impatiently.

"No we will take you home." Becky said.

Jasi pulled the wagon of our bags, while Becky walked along side me. Jasi stopped over to the food court and bought me some coffee, and drinks for the both of them.

"Here, sip on this you might just got a slight hangover." Jasi said.

"Well how much did yall drink when I left?" Becky asked.

"Just two shots and I took one for the road!" Jasi said.

"See yall play this shit with each other, but not with me. Chocolate your ass pregnant too and just blaming it on that liquor, like Jasi did." Becky said laughing.

"Whatever!" Jasi said, as I didn't even have the strength to entertain Becky foolishness. Jasi climbed into the little backseat, Becky drove and I sat near the window in case I had to vomit again.

"Oh Chocolate, I love the way your car ride." Becky said, as she took the highway on weaving in and out of traffic.

"Slow down ambulance!" Jasi said.

"Sit tight, and shut up!" Becky yelled and continued to drive, my head went from side to side, my mouth was as dry as any famous desert, and my stomach was turning in a thousand circles. I couldn't help it or seem to hold it. I held my head out the window, with Becky's speed it went all over the door and in the back seat.

"Damn Chocolate!" Jasi yelled.

"She can't help it." Becky said.

"Well slow your ass down or pull over one!" Jasi said in the back seat. The second time it came I didn't even care that I was in my new ride, it went all on the floor of the car.

"All Chocolate come on, you messing up your car." Becky said.

\"Girl I don't." I started and vomit again.

"You want us to call Dale?" Becky asked, upon arriving in my drive way was only Becky truck.

"No, I'm sure he'll be back shortly." I answered.

"Where is he?" Jasi asked.

"Shanice and him went to take Baby to the VET."

"Oh, are you sure you going to be alright by yourself?" Becky asked.

"Yeah, I am telling you it's something I ate yesterday that didn't agree with my stomach." I said.

"Whatever!" Becky added, and loaded their bags into her truck.

"Just leave my windows down, put my keys on the table, and lock the door please." I said, as I hurried in and landed on the Natuzzi leather couch.

"Alright then, just answer your phone when we call to check on you." Becky said, as the two of them walked out the front door.

I laid helpless... Eventually I had fallen asleep and waken up to a bouquet of flowers, sweet rich chocolates and an I love you card. The sun had gone down and my phone registered 26 missed calls.

I got up to use the restroom, and to get something to munch on now that I was officially hungry. On the refrigerator was scribbled, ***You looked so beautiful, I had to leave you sleeping!*** I smiled evidentially he had come and gone. I fixed myself a ham and cheese sandwich, a scoop of banana pudding, and a glass of cranberry juice. I went upstairs to my room and took a comfortable spot on my bed just before taking a bite out of my sandwich I reviewed my *missed call list.* Becky and Jasi had called the most, and Chuck had the nerve to call me after all this time. Without another glance at the remaining of the missed calls I threw the phone to the side of me and took a bite from my sandwich. Ugggh I couldn't believe Chuck was calling me, I wonder what the hell he wanted. I know one dam thing I wasn't dare going to call him back to find out and as a matter of fact when I finish eating my sandwich I'm going to find a way to block his ass. I became so agitated, it's a good thing I missed that phone call, because I knew I would've hurt his feelings today.

After eating I felt much better, I slid on me a pair of big shorts and a t-shirt so I can go out and clean this nasty vomit out the car. My windows were up, and the black was glistening with the stars in the air. When I opened the car I immediately noticed that Dale must been the one to clean the vomit out, sprayed something on the carpet and washed the car. I wonder where he had went to. I stood upon the porch and called him.

"Hey baby." He answered, just as quickly as I could dial his number.

"Hey honey." I said.

"You just got up."

"A little while ago." I responded.

"I guess you were tired of all that walking in the mall, I see all those bags you got. What's up with all the vomiting?" He asked.

"I couldn't help it baby, it must be some bad virus."

"You need to go and have that checked out, before you get Shanice and I sick."

"I know, I'm going to go on Monday after work." I said.

"Ok, well Shanice wanted to go back to your mom house, and I am on my way home now."

"Alright baby I will see you shortly." I said ending the call.

I got up and did a little cleaning. I started to pull boxes from the other room that I never had the chance to unpack. There was so many of Shanice old clothes packed down, but they were still in good condition. I guess I'll just give these to the young girl that live by Mama. She twenty-two and got four children, no husband, and four different baby daddies. I'm glad mama beat my ass like she did when the street lights caught me outside, I'm even glad she didn't let me talk to boys until I was seventeen. Of course you know we all snuck and did it anyway. Playing the lil hunchy hunch games, Mama and Daddy, boys chase the girls, spin the bottle, strip poker, yeah we played it as a game until we got old enough to value it like precious pearls. I finished hiding Shanice Christmas toys, and took a shower and laid across the bed.

My desk looked a mess, without me even touching a thing. There were loads of memos to be corrected, distributed, and emailed and mounds of paper to be filed before the end of the day. It's been Five days of throwing up this stuff that taste like chalk in my mouth, and it doesn't get any better. I made an appointment to see that nurse I met in the bathroom a couple of days ago. I dragged my chair around the desk categorizing the files, on a growling stomach. I was too afraid to eat, because I might just throw it back up and if I don't eat something, this chalky taste becomes bitter and bitter. Over these past days it never crossed my mind of being pregnant, but if I am? How would I deal with it? I thought to myself, I have more besides help; there is a father for it, a sweet sister, and a family we will be.

"Mona! Are you going with Karla and me to lunch?" Lisa asked, as she buzzed through the speakerphone. Snatching me away from my daydream.

"Where are yall going?" I asked.

"Maybe to the sandwich shops up the street. I feel like sipping on some soup." Lisa responded.

"Oh, ok yes I am going."

"Alright meet us in the lobby in five minutes."

"Ok." I responded, pulling my drawer open for a mirror and a little lip-gloss for these ever so dry lips. My eyes had looked so white and weak, my skin was three shades darker and ten times dry, no matter how much I dapped myself with Lubriderm. Just before leaving I was interrupted by the nagging pain indicator, which reminded me frequently to urine. I strongly believe it's just a serious urinary infection along with a minor virus, I'll just see about all this tomorrow? Apparently I was taking too long, Lisa and Karla was standing by the elevators for me.

"You take forever, and know we only got 1-hour." Lisa said.

"Because you know fat ass gone be waiting." Karla said, as we walked through the lobby.

"Hey Honey, looking a little demoralized there." Steve said at the security desk, when today wasn't one of the days I felt like joking.

"You don't hear, your man today?" Lisa asked.

"I don't feel like playing with him today."

"Oh so serious, got a problem at home?" Karla asked.

"No! I just get tired of him sometimes." I said in such a snobby tune.

"Could have fooled me, you been flirting and playing for the past 2 yrs." Lisa said, winking her eye at Karla.

"Please, whatever!" I said, brushing the joke away, without a grin.

My appointment was scheduled for 12:15 it was already 12:45 and I hadn't been seen yet. I sat patiently, watching the door as it swung open and shut. Every other woman either had a big stomach, baby carrier or stroller. The door flew back open, and a set of twins with curly red hair and blue eyes in a double stroller came strolling through. What looked to be the father, stood back holding the door open for the nurses who were returning from an outing if not lunch. The lady I met in the mall two weeks ago was amongst the women; she wore a white dress decorated with storks and a matching jacket. Without a second look, she walked right over to me.

"Good afternoon, I see you've made it here." She said. "I'm sorry we really haven't met

properly, but my name is Sarah." She explained.

"I'm sorry and my name is Mona." I responded.

"Is this your second visit?" She asked.

"No, actually I didn't come that day I seen you. However I didn't get any better either so here I am. "I said with a smile.

"Oh ok. So what time was your appointment?" She asked.

"I believe 12:30 I said, without an attitude, as she gazed down at her watch and I looked down at mine which now read 1:05.

"My. Well just come along with me, and I'll take care of you personally." Sarah said as I gathered my bag and placed the magazine back on the shelf.

Following Sarah through the doors, the walls looked to be a portfolio of newborn babies up and down the hall.

"Those are Dr. Greenberg babies he delivered; he's a great Gynecologist and a #1 Obstetrician." Sarah said, as if I were interested.

"Alright Ms. Mona, I'll need you to dress for me in this gown and let a little urine in above this line." Sarah instructed. "Also I will need a little blood work to start the exam."

"I'm sure I don't need an exam, I had a physical about 3 mos. ago." I said, trying to avoid this long process.

"I'm afraid, all of our new patients must have blood. I'm sorry it's just part of the protocol." Sarah explains as she handed me a gown and proceed to exit the room.

I slipped off my shirt and danced around the room, to keep from wetting all over myself. By the time I unscrewed the top of the cup and manage to get my panties half way down, just when my urine begin to flow just enough to fill the cup. "I wet some toilets, washed my leg and cleaned my shoe from the missed urine. Not only was I upset because I pissed on my suede pink pumps that were only for the club, but also because my body was changing and I didn't know why.

"Mona are you dressed?" Sarah asked.

"Yes I'll be out in just a second." I quickly replied. I looked in the mirror and took a swallow of water from the faucet to kill the horrible taste that lingered in my mouth.

When I walked out of the bathroom Sarah was sitting on the stool with a circle that indicates a woman cycle. There also was a couple of tubes and needles spreaded neatly on the countertop.

"Now don't get afraid, one stick will fill all six of those tubes up."

"Ouch." I whispered, just by observing when she hadn't even touch me yet.

"Let's start with your last menstrual." She said.

"It's never been on track, since my last child." I responded

"How many kids do you have?"

"I have one daughter she is six years old."

"Oh ok." She said, as she jotted on her notepad.

"When was the last you can remember your menstrual."

"About 3-4 months ago."

"Were you on any contraceptives, or any tubal ligation procedure?"

"Contraceptives." I said trying to locate a meaning.

"You know like birth controls."

"I use to about six months ago."

"You not having your menstrual can be part of you feeling nausea and blotted. It's not necessary that there is a virus or pregnancy." She said as I felt a little relief. "Sarah the main thing that troubles me is that I constantly use the bathroom."

"Is it just urine?" Sarah asked.

"Yes."

"Well let's do a little blood work, to detect your blood sugar and other possible symptoms which represents a diabetic, but first I am going to do a pregnancy test and ultrasound. Something we don't normally do for our first time patients." She said as I hopped on the bed to verify that a baby was not in here. She pulled my gown up midway and applied a glob of warm gel to the bottom of my stomach. She placed a handle over the gel area and immediately there looked to be a fetus balled tight. So visible that I didn't have to squint my eyes, or ask a question. It was there, in my face. Another life was living in me. Sounds of water waves from the machine and a feeling of joy and excitement in my heart. That I knew would not only make me happy, but also will answer a prayer and become not only a sister or brother but a friend indeed. She moved it to the right, the left, up and down while the fetus was still balled in the same spot. It wasn't a clog or a piece of tissue it was a baby with a heartbeat.

"Congratulations Ms. Mona. It looks to me you are about 10wks pregnant." Sarah said with a smile so sincere, until I leaped from the bed and threw my arms around her.

She sat back on the stool observing her circle again. The joy I had, took the place of embarrassment, I undressed right there, trying not to miss a word not even an expression she was about to give.

"Your due date will be July 24,2004." She said, which had seemed so long when today was only December 9, 2003. I sat patiently not being afraid of the needle, and let her fill all six

tubes while I asked question after question. Sarah had completed my examination and handed me some iron pills, vitamins and an appointment card, which was scheduled two months from now. She was not only nice but very concerned; she had walked me all the way to my car.

"Ok, I'll see you soon." Sarah said.

"Bye." I said as I drove away reaching for my cell phone that registered two missed calls. One was from Becky and the other was from Dale. Right now I am too happy to speak to Dale, I really want to see his face when I tell him the news. I had to tell somebody so I dialed up Becky because I just couldn't hold it any longer.

"Hey honey?" I said.

"What's up Chocolate?" She asked.

"Nothing much, where are you?" I asked.

"I'm finishing up my shopping for our Christmas dinner."

"Oh." I said sounding as calm as possible.

"Where are you?" She asked.

"I'm headed home."

"Home, at 3:20 don't you get off at 5:00?" Becky asked.

"Yes, but I had a Dr. appointment today remember?"

"For what, your weak ass still sick from that so called virus."

"Well Becky, you are right once again. Girl can you believe I am 10 weeks pregnant!"

"For real!" Becky shouted into the phone.

"Yes girl 10 weeks."

"Oh my god!" She continued on with disbelief.

"Yes, and I still can't believe it."

"So what did they do blood work or a piss test?" She asked.

"They did both and an ultrasound because of my symptoms. The nurse was real sweet. Soon as she put that handle thing on my stomach girl that little heart was just beating away."

"What Dale had to say?" Becky asked as I could hear her smile through the phone.

"Becky girl, I don't know how to tell him. Shall I call him or wait till I get home."

"Auh uhh girl, bad as he wants a baby, he's going to be the happiest man on God's green earth when he do find out." Becky said.

"Yes he will, so you think I should call him?"

"He knows you went to the Dr. today?" She asked.

"Yeah."

"Damn. Well here is what you should do, go home and act as normal as possible. Tell him you got a little virus that's going around. Wait the nurse did give you some medicine didn't she?" Becky asked.

"Yeah she gave me some iron and vitamin pills she say it will help me with the nausiness."

"Girl that shit don't work! But anyway tell him the Dr. gave you some medicine and about a week you should be fine. Then in the meantime you try to hold the secret until Christmas." Becky said.

"Christmas!" I yelled.

"Yeah and believe me that's going to be the best gift for him in this whole wide world." She said.

"That sounds cute, but I am so damn happy right now."

"I know I know." Becky interrupted. "But if it takes you to write it down a thousand times do it and hide the paper. ***DO NOT*** I repeat ***DO NOT*** leak the secret out."

"Should I tell Jasi?" I asked.

"First off who all you told?" Becky asked.

"Nobody, you the first person I called. I didn't even call my mama."

"Aw, I feel so special. My friend really does love me."

"Whatever Becky, so you think I should keep it a secret from everyone?"

"Yes, but you know we can not keep it from Jasi that bitch will blow up if she knew I knew about it."

"Girl I'm going to try. I don't know if I can hold a secret that long." I responded.

"I tell you what, just take the damn pills and keep your mouth shut the same way you did when your ass was pregnant with Shanice in school, and aint want your mama to find out." Becky said, as we both laughed at that thought.

"Congratulations." Becky said, making me teary eye.

"Thanks girl."

"Well let me call Jasi, I'll talk with you later." I said, immediately dialing Jasi number.

"Hey chick when you get this message give me a call at home." I said. She must had her phone off being she was in TX visiting Bruce for a couple of days. I clicked over to the other line as my phone beeped it was Becky again.

"Chocolate I know what I was calling you for. What colors should I do the table? Cream and red or cream and emerald?"

"I like cream and red."

"Ok then bye." Becky said.

I drove down 95 picturing any and every nursery, name, even colors for the wall. How could I hold all this in I thought? That sounds like something the rich folks do, cause the majority of us wedlock's spend the whole 9mos. separated or mad at the fact. I pulled over to the gas station and picked me up some doughnuts and cold milk. I took a vitamin, ate the doughnuts, and swallowed down the milk.

By the time I made it home, I called to check my voicemail and it was one message. Dale telling me he picked Shanice up from school, and that they had a little Christmas shopping to do. I checked our mailbox, picked the newspaper up from the yard and turned on the sprinkler system. Shanice coloring book had torn pages where she and Dale had been coloring. Crayons and books were all over the table and so were his lap top. Her shoes and socks were underneath the table and backpack was slung on the floor waiting for somebody to trip over it. The kitchen was spotless, and on the cutting board was a pan of seasoned chicken. I washed a pot to put on some rice before I ran upstairs to take a shower.

I kicked off my shoes and prepared myself for a warm thirty minute relaxation time. Reminded by the sticky film on my stomach as I eased my pants down that I was officially carrying a child. I stood in the front of the mirror and took a look at my nude body. The only thing that was a bit suspicious, was my breast. The nipples stayed hard, and so black. I pushed my stomach out as far as it could go, and I turned in the mirror from side to side. I tried practicing sitting on the toilet and breathing as if I were already 9mos. Being I was

a kid when Shanice was born, I didn't get to act out rather for pain or joy. I had to pretend that there wasn't a problem to keep the older ones from picking at me. Especially being under Mama roof pregnant with no husband, you were the topic at anytime or place.

I jumped in and out the shower, through on a big shirt and shorts and started cleaning.

The house phone had frighten me, it was an unexpected beat to my attention.

"Hello." I answered.

"Hello?" A sweet voice said, in error.

"Hello I asked again?"

"Is Dale there?" A woman asked as if she weren't sure if she was calling the right number.

"May I ask who is calling?" I asked remaining calm.

"Is this Dales home or not?" She asked rudely.

"Yes this is our home." I responded back in the same shity tone.

"Well would you let Dale know that Sheila called?" She said as she began to work my nerves.

"Actually I can do better than that Ms. Lady, would you like his cell number?" I asked, in anger and flushing disbelief.

"Oh that would be great." She said changing her tone from shit to sugar.

"Being you are not a threat or a friend of ours, the very next time you call our house you need to call with respect addressing the day and me. As a matter of fact you give Dale a call and you can let him know you have met Ms. Mona, the number is 305-726-7010." I said as she paused in silence, which is a for sure sign of guilt.

"Thank you!" She said. Without a goodbye I slung the phone back on the receiver. I had to take a minute and recap what just had happened, I almost had to sit on my hands to keep from calling and cursing Dale out about a situation I don't know anything about.

"It's just the point how she called as if she had previous dates or plans to fuck him. She sounded surprised that someone was not only in her way, but she better know this man heart had found a new home with chains and locks around it. If she was something to him, evidently it must be some unfinished love, lust, fuck or a getaway. Nobody aint fixing to give me a run, I'm not even sharing. I had my times now this one I am going to be selfish and greedy cause its mines." I said, talking to myself all through the house, which didn't ease my anger. I turned the music up and started dicing up my seasons for the curry, from the smell of the garlic on my hands sent me gagging. I went back into the kitchen and wiped down the place, putting the chicken back into the refrigerator and turning the isle off. I went to my room upset, once the thoughts came running through my head *'How did she get the number because I know it was unpublished?'* I became very nauseated, and obnoxious wasn't the word. I put a peppermint into my mouth to execute the chalk taste that had filled my mouth. Every second went by that Dale didn't call me, I became more angry because I know Sheila told him my slick comment, perhaps he might just be thinking of a good excuse to tell me when he get home.

I awakened to many little Barbie accessories on my bedroom floor, Shanice was lying at the bottom of the bed watching cartoons, and the smell of curry had fumed the air.

"Hey Mommy!" Shanice said.

"Hey honey." I responded, getting up to use the restroom, on the other side of the bed

there stood a dollhouse and a car with two dolls as if they were a family returning home in Shanice imagination.

"Shanice what is all this?" I asked.

"Dale buy me this today." She said with a smile and back down on the floor to play.

"You want to see how the doorbell ring Mommy?" She asked.

"Wait Shanice I have to use the bathroom first." I said, slipping behind the door. I sat on the stool still hearing every word and tone Sheila called with; I knew I was more than upset I slept on it and woke up feeling the same pissed off way.

"Shanice if Dale keep buying you stuff, Santa is not going to have nothing to give you."

"Um-huh, a big baby doll, computer, games," Shanice said as she went on I thought of what all I missed or what all she added.

"Dale buy you something too." Shanice said which couldn't keep a secret to save her life.

"What is it?" I asked.

"Hey hey hey! It's a secret remember?" Dale said, as he walked into the room, and I walked right around him as if he was a stranger. I walked down the stairs to find the kitchen in a true mess. There was at least six dishes on the counter when he hadn't even started eating yet. The refrigerator and cabinets were wide opened, the two corn can goods were empty and rested on the stove top, and broom lying in the middle of the floor.

"Well hello how are you today?" Dale asked, as he stood in the dining area. I remained quiet and poured me a glass of juice. He came walking towards me and removed the glass from the counter as I put the juice back in the refrigerator.

"What's your problem?" He asked, as I looked him in his eye with a disfigured mind.

"Nothing!" I said, grabbing a towel from the full sink of water and started cleaning down

the counters.

"Mona, now I know there is something wrong, you kiss me and tell me u love me a thousand times a day. But today you won't even put your eyes on me, and you tell me nothing's wrong." He said, as if he didn't have a clue. "Mona something is wrong?" He continued to ask sitting on the counter top, as I went around him.

"Mona!" He said, jumping from the counter and walking behind me just as much as I walked back and fourth cleaning. "Mona come on now don't act like this." He said making me mad as hell, when he received the same damn call I received today. "Ok now, come on I hate it when someone can't tell me if there is a problem!" He said, loud and bossy.

"Oh yeah, well I hate a slick ass man!" I responded, reaching for the dustpan.

"What are you talking about?" He asked.

"Yeah! What am I talking about huh?" I said feeling hot as ever and mad enough to choke him "Sheila that's who the hell I'm talking about." I said, as his forehead wrinkled just as much as an elderly man.

"Sheila! How do you know her?"

"The same fuckin way you gave her the number! That's how I know her." I said, raising my voice and gripping the broom tighter.

"Mona I didn't give her this number." He said, with a slight grin on his face.

"Don't come to me with that bullshit! So how did she get the number Dale? Information didn't give it to her, nor the phone book." I said, as he continued trying to interrupt, but I wanted to let out everything I was holding in first.

"Mona will you just listen to me! I never gave her my number, besides she was a friend in my division who helped me out a lot." He said, as if I were supposed to believe him.

"Oh friends can't fuck huh!" I yelled.

"Mona it isn't like that, you are all I need. She called my cell, which she been had my number. The house number she must had got it from my mom." Dale said as I still didn't buy that one, I tied the garbage and walked out the patio to throw it away as he followed me.

"Baby it's not what you think, I'll call my mom now!" He said.

"Yeah you might had coached her already."

"Mona trust me, I had no idea she had our number. She didn't even tell me she spoke with you."

"Well she did very rude too!" I said.

"Baby, its nothing like that. Sit here let me talk to you" He said trying to calm me. I took a seat on one of the loungers and he sat next to me in another one. He didn't like to see me mad, every minute I was quiet he repeated the same story. I continued to fuss and throw anything near when he attempted to touch me.

"Dale don't put your nasty hands on me, you are just the typical man! I don't know where my sense was to believe my feelings and become another victim of love!" I said in a very angry tone, while Dale just stared. The blood came dripping down from my nose without me realizing, I just thought it was the heat boiling in me.

"Baby! He yelled, getting up from his chair, pulling some tissues from the box that sat near. He stood in front of me, placing one hand behind my neck tilting my head and pinching my nose with the tissue. Which was the only time I kept quiet for a minute and listen to what he had to say.

"Baby, there is not another woman I think of, dream of, dread for, or wish I was with. I love you and only you." Dale said as I watched him look me in the eye and not blink once. "I told her, I have met a woman that I love far beyond belief." Dale said, as the words echoed in my mind, and all that I worked for in this lifetime was put on a table at once. Love, trust, and honesty something so good that can't be defined in everyone. I'm speechless what shall I do or what more can I say.

"THE HAPPIEST MOMENT OF MY LIFE"

It was two days before Christmas Eve, which was the day I started my vacation early. I took my time cleaned and dust out the vacant room and guest bathroom for Dale's parents while he and Bruce went for a pig to cook tomorrow. I dust and put back all the extra utensils and things we didn't use on a daily base since the dinner was going to be at Becky's house. I went through some of Dales old pictures he had up in the basement, his mom Ms. Becca was very beautiful and his father was just as handsome. He was their only child, but they are not really close. Ms. Becca calls every now and then; I have yet to meet her, I only spoke with her over the phone. I think they would like this comforter set, it looks more like Spring though, but oh well its new and nice. I spread the comforter over the bed, added a few extra pillows and the room looked marvelous, nice and cozy for a guest. I stood back gazing at the room, hugging my stomach which seems to always crease a smile over my face. I've been trying so hard, but I tell you the truth these have been the worst days to try and hold a secret. Between Dale being super nice cause of that Sheila incident and all the excitement I felt he could have used some good news. Now we are just a day from the big news and man I'm feeling like I'm going to hit the lotto tomorrow for all the money in the world. Jasi found a cute card that's expressing what ten things I'd rather have the most, but at the bottom it says *`but I got you a little one inside'* and it points to a woman stomach. Becky searched several stores to find a pair white booties, and had this lady to lace them with green, pink, and yellow congratulations shoe strings in them and two bells. Somewhat like the big white shoes EVERYBODY Mama put on them when they first learned how to walk back in the days. I wrapped the shoes in a mini gift box, and looked at the gift a thousand times, shaking the box as if I didn't know what was in it.

The doorbell sounded all through the house.

"Who is it?" I yelled peeking through the door, there stood a woman and a tall man with looks that resembled Dales.

"Its Ms. B, Dales parents." She announced. I was totally shocked and embarrassed of this first impression they were about to take on. Without time to pep myself up, I opened the door and just what I thought I got four eyeballs staring at me from my head to my toe as if I looked any more eccentric than they did.

"Hello, you must be Mona. Finally we meet." Mrs. B said as she quickly brushed right passed me and through the door. Mr. B stopped and gave me a hug and added he's pleased to meet me.

"Dale!" Ms. Becca called.

"Oh, Dale went out for a while he should be in shortly." I said, wondering how come she arrived so early without calling anyone.

"I love this place, other than the last one." Ms. Becca claimed.

"Oh your tree is very beautiful, and this wall picture I would die for." She said, holding her chest and inviting her way through our house. Mr. B took a sat near the Christmas tree and watched the train go around and around while the temptations played low.

"Would you like a drink?" I asked, as Ms. B came walking back down the stairs.

"I just really love this place, who was the decorator.

"Actually him and I with a little time."

"Well you know that's all you need for anything just a little time." Mr. B said.

"Would you two like anything to drink?" I asked again, just a bit louder. "Yes." He claimed, as Ms. B walked into the kitchen.

"Well Mr. B, I have soda, water, champagne, and whisky." I said, afraid to hear what they would say next.

"I'll have a little old moon shine if you got some back there." He said, as if this was a new drink.

"Oh no Mr. B I don't have moon shine, but I may have Brandy." I offered, as I laughed along with him.

"Oh that sounds fine, I can deal with that."

"Alright now Dexter, we didn't travel way out here for you to act a fool." Mrs. B said, as she went into the cabinets and grabbed a glass for her.

"You have created a nice deco look for your home Mona."

"Thank you."

"When are you two planning a vacation to come and see us out in Detroit?" She asked, as she sipped on the little water she filled the 4oz glass with.

"Dale was mentioning he's taking off a month in April, and we were going to take a trip up there."

"Yeah you got to see it, it's very nice out there, lots of gambling and food everywhere." She said, as she stood and watched me pour a drink for Mr. B.

"What yall ladies discussing in there?" Mr. B. questioned with a smile on his face, as he walked over to me and placed his arms around my shoulders.

"Nothing much honey, just getting to know our daughter in law a little better." She said.

"Dale said, she was just as sweet as a melon and cute as a button." Mr. B added. "Auh, she sure is." Mrs. B said, as Mr. B took his drink and went on to the living room.

"He loves to see his boy happy, in this type of area. I mean you know a family environment, although we hardly get to see him now at least we know for sure he's not alone." She said as I stood nodding my head and smiling with generosity at my side.

"Are you guys planning to have any kids?" She asked, as I just wanted to hug my stomach so tight. Instead I rather not spoil the secret. I paused and didn't know what to say.

"What is it, you've just went away there for a minute. You don't care to have any more kids than Shanice?" She asked calling my daughter by her name; surprised I was that she remembers from the little conversations we had previous times over the phone.

"Well, yes I plan on having another child but how soon? Who knows?" I answered leaving enough room for an answer on each end of my reply.

"It will come, don't rush it on cause you already know it sure aint no quick job. Those eighteen years sometimes pass you by, or eighteen years of frustration drags on." She said as she smiled and nibbled on some strawberries she had washed and put into a bowl.

"Excuse me." I said, as I reached to answer the phone.

"Hello."

"Hey girl, what's up?" Becky asked.

"Nothing much."

"Have you wrapped all your gifts?" Becky questioned.

"No why?" I asked.

"Cause, I got to wrap mines." She explained.

"So what you gone come over and wrap them or what?" I asked smiling as Mrs. B smiled back at me and walked back into the living room.

"Yeah, cause mama in here cutting up her seasonings and stuffing her turkey for tomorrow." Becky added.

"Alright then I'll be here, but look hooker don't come over here half dressed. My sophisticated ass mother in law is here." I said whispering in the phone.

"Fuck them! You better be lucky my booty shorts that read *'bite me'* aint clean, cause I might can make the Daddy leave her and invest in me." Becky said laughing out loud.

"You might would try some shit like that."

"Just kidding damn, so how the little one doing?" Becky asked.

"So far I haven't threw up in two days, but it's going alright."

"You still pissing like a puppy?"

"Shut up crazy ass."

"Alright I'll be there in about fifteen minutes."

"Bye." I said, as I placed the phone on the receiver and felt a sudden taste of that chalk again in my mouth. I poured me a glass of water, which was all I could hold down. Walking into the living room where the Christmas music was louder than usual, blaring 'A White Christmas' by non-other than Otis Redding's version. The lights were dimmed low, and by the drapes pulled tight there was just a bit of sunlight showing. Mr. B had Mrs. B into his arms as if it was a prom night, they weren't aware that I was watching but I stood back quite some time observing. He rubbed his hands across her face, the same way Dale rubbed mines, he snuggled her close by the shape of her waist, and her feet moved alongside his. She kissed him time after time as if this was their first dance. They carried on as if they were still young and in love. Mrs. B even blushed when he began spinning her around while practically lifting her off her feet. My I thought to myself, would our love be just as deep as theirs or boring like others?

"Come join us!" Mrs. B Shouted, as I blinked back into reality and a more fun song begin blaring.

"Come on!" Mr. B waved his hand. I walked over and we made a circle and dance together to G wiz its Christmas by Carla Thomas.

"Come on Mona, let's step to the right, step to the left." She said, as I danced on and off beat.

"I'm sorry you guys, I'm not in shape for all of this." I said, as I trotted back into the kitchen for another glass of water, just when the doorbell sounded off. I peeped through the kitchen window and there was Bruce truck in the driveway.

"Mrs. B, your son is out there!" I yelled, as I stood at the door. And the both came running.

"Hey honey." Dale said, as he kissed me on the jaw and attempt to walk through the door not asking whose car was that.

"Hey baby!" Mrs. B said when she jumped from behind the door. She jumped into Dales arm, and he lifted her off her feet. Mr. B stood with a smile, Dale grabbed him into his arms and kissed him too, with a hand shake that they must carried from when he was a little boy, he smacked his finger on every beat and shuck his wrist to each encounter.

"I miss you son!"

"I miss you too Daddy." Dale said, as Bruce and I stood in the door watching the surprised reunion.

"Wait a minute Mama, looks like you lost a little weight and it looks good off you too." Dale said.

"Yeah, she should have lost a little, got me going to brunch by myself." His dad said, as he grabbed her back in his arms and kissed her.

"Daddy we got a pig, and I know you haven't forgot how you use to make it look so juicy

with an apple in its mouth." Dale said.

"I hope I can still do it, I haven't barbequed a pig over ten years now."

"Oh I'm sorry, Daddy this is Bruce. Bruce this is my father Dexter and my mom Carolyn." He said as Bruce shuck Mr. B hand and pecked Mrs. B on her hand.

"Nice to meet you both."

"Come on Daddy take a look at the pig." Dale said, as he pulled my hand to come alone.

"Wow this a big one here." Mr. B said.

"Yes it is, where you get this one here from?" Mrs. B asked.

"This fellow I know bought a trailer of them down from Carolina." Bruce said.

"Yeah, we need to clean that bad boy up and get him together."

"Well let me pull the truck around the back, so we can unload him." Bruce said.

"Dale do you got everything, or would you need us to run out to the store?" Mrs. B asked.

"I think so we did grocery shopping yesterday, but you know I don't think we have any apples, lime juice, or sweet potatoes." He said, with this suspicious grin on his face that matched Mrs. B's.

"Oh you think I'm making you a pie huh?" She said, as his father and him both laughed.

"Please Mama, I still haven't forgot about them neither. After all Ma it is Christmas."

"Alright son." She said.

"Thank you mama. I love you." Dale said as he grabbed me up close and kissed me with all attention looking.

"Looks like my baby found love." Mrs. B said.

"I have Mama, she has all the qualities you have and an astonishing personality." Dale said describing me to his perspective and squeezing my hand as I was trailing him to the patio. "Hey yall back there?" Becky apparently let herself in as I could hear her voice echoing through my house.

"Yeah we back here." Dale yelled.

"Good afternoon everyone." Becky asked when she arrived on the back patio.

"Hello." We all responded.

"Girl I almost left you." I said.

"I know, you get stink sometimes like that." Becky responded, folding her arms across her chest.

"No I forgot you was coming."

"Well where are you going now?" Becky asked.

"To the grocery store and get some stuff for the pig with Mrs. B." I explained.

"Well yall aint leaving me." Becky added.

"Good, lets drive your truck, please." I asked, as I hugged my friend and kissed her on the jaw just to see her get a bit upset like usual.

"Come on now, you bull dagger!" She whispered as she threw her hands around my neck laughing as if we were thirteen or fourteen again.

"You so stupid, you gone drive." I asked.

"Chocolate, I need a little help with unloading these gifts out my truck first."

"Bruce, can you and Dale unload Becky's truck so we can go to the store."

"Well let me go back inside to get my purse. Mrs. B said as she walked back into the house with me in her footsteps while Bruce unloaded the truck.

*****

Wrapping paper, bows, and tape was stuck everywhere and to everything. We sat on the patio and wrapped every gift. Jasi joined us as well. Through the fun of this all I was beginning to feel tired and nauseous mainly because of the pine scent that scented through the air. I really didn't want to leave the patio like that but I just couldn't bare another minute. I went into the room, turned the music up and the shower on, I thought I would puke my heart out today.

I took a shower, and prayed that Dale wouldn't touch me nor put on that aftershave tonight. I couldn't even go and say good night, rude of me it was but the changes it takes to create a life.

Christmas Eve was here, the drapes all through the house was pulled back, the gifts were stacked under the tree, and Shanice had made it home from seeing Lionel.

"Mommy!" Shanice hollered, as she ran upstairs and greeted me with a hug.

"Hey baby." I said, as I pulled her chin to observe her face.

"Daddy say hi." Shanice said.

"Oh he did, tell him I say hello too. I bought you some Christmas cards to send him Shanice."

"Today Mommy?" Shanice asked, never leaving her Daddy out.

"Yeah, we can color them and send them today."

"Ok Mommy." Shanice said, as Mrs. B walked around and stood by the room door.

"Good Morning Mrs. B."

"Good morning sugar. How did you sleep?" She asked.

"I'm so sorry Mrs. B I was so tired last night." I said.

"That's alright, I know how it is when that rest sneak up on you."

"Come Mona, come and taste this mix?" She asked, as I thought to myself oh no.

"I'll be down in just a minute." I said.

"Shanice don't do that!" I said, as I popped Shanice harder than ever across her shoulder, from jumping off the bed unto my back. She hollered out as if I had cut her neck or something. I was so upset because she could have hurt me, and before I could grab her and tell her what I hit her for Ms. B was holding her in her arms.

"What's wrong?" She asked.

"I popped her from jumping off the bed unto my back when I'm laying down."

"Oh Mona, she was just playing." Mrs. B said.

"No Mrs. B She could have hurt me." I replied.

"She don't know any better." She said as, I just had to hold my tongue with my teeth. Shanice and her left and went down stairs. I went into the bathroom to put on some clothes, and stood in the mirror observing the tiny pug at the bottom of my stomach and the dark lined that looked like someone had drew it. I don't know why, but for all of a sudden I started to cry. I was feeling really bad not physically but mentally and I didn't know why. I went back into the bedroom and turned on the music, and began to cry. The room door came open and Dale walked into the room, assuming I was asleep and throws his self-alongside me rubbing my back, while my face was buried into the pillow and eyes were drowning in tears. I tried to act as if I was asleep though, but he dug his hands into the pillow and pulling my face from beneath. There I couldn't hide, all that I wiped away still left my eyes red and irritated.

"Baby are you crying?" He asked.

"No." I said, pulling my face the other way.

"Mona, what's wrong baby?"

"Nothing, I just was thinking about a lot of things."

"Like what?" He asked, when I couldn't even begin "what?"

"Just life." I said.

"What, our life?" He asked, turning this whole scenario in a different direction.

"Nothing Dale, its nothing I'm fine." I said, pulling my body on top of his kissing and blowing him in his ear like he liked it.

"I love you baby." I said.

"I love you more." He replied as he gave me an ah-huu-hug and we both forgot about my sadness.

"Where you went just morning baby?" I asked quickly changing the subject.

"To go get your Daddy." He said.

"Where did you guys go?"

"He's outside with my Daddy, they doing the pig together." Dale said, as I thought how much I really just loved this man and this man loved me.

"Mama told me to tell you to come here." He said as I got up to use the restroom again.

"Mona, I bought Shanice a go-cart." He said as if I was going to be thrilled.

"Dale I told you about those things, they are very dangerous!" I said shouting from the bathroom.

"You did but hers is a one seated go cart with a cage around it instead. However I bought you and I a four wheeler."

"Whatever, Dale." I added, not even excited at all, cause he knows what I feel about those bikes.

I went down stairs and Mrs. B had bowls filled with mixture, crackling bread, red velvet,

Chocolate, and apple cake mixes. The stovetop had a three-layer apple jelly cake, Carmel and carrot cake.

"Wow Mrs. B you baking up a storm in here."

"Yeah, Ms. Minnie said I'm in charge of the deserts, and you're Mama in charge of the vegetables." She said, rattling off. If I hadn't known any better I would have thought she was one of their friends long time ago.

"Here taste this." She said dapping a little spoon in some orange mixture.

"Umm umm." I said as the sweet potato mixture tasted as good uncooked than any cooked pie I ever ate.

"You know that's Dale's special. I remember one Christmas he was about three, Dexter and him baked some cookies because Dexter told him that Santa comes at night and eat the cookies and leave the gifts. Apparently Dexter and I over slept and forgot to eat the cookies ourselves. Dale woke up before us and later on at the dinner table he brought it up. Santa had told him he didn't like cookies anymore, he wanted sweet potato pie because he was the best boy in the whole wide world. I couldn't believe my three year old, had already knew how to lie. From that day forward I pretended as if he had truly convinced me that Santa said those very words. So therefore I just agreed to cook sweet potato pie only Christmas time for Santa.

"All how sweet." I said, as I laughed and found the story cute.

"Baby give me a spray bottle." Mr. B asked, popping through the side door.

"Good morning sweetie." Mr. B says to me.

"Good morning Mr. B." I replied.

"Baby call me Dexter not even Mr. Dexter." He said with a grin on his face, "you have a splendid father out here." Mrs. B gave him the bottle and he went to finish the work.

"That man is a trip." She said, looking through the French doors as he walked away. "Mona, I met Dexter in 1961 and this 2004 I can promise you our love hasn't weaken or faded a bit. You know it just feels good to be in love." Mrs. B said.

"Mrs. B, I feel the same way. I want to be in love for a lifetime not just a century."

"That's right baby, think big like that. Live up to that, it's good to be pleased by one than disappointed by many." She said, as I started to feel comfortable and smooth with her.

"Get the phone baby." She said.

"Hello."

"Mona, where Carolyn?" Mama asked.

"Hold on."

"Mrs. B its Mama."

"Put it to my ear." She said propping it up with her shoulder, as I left her in the kitchen talking.

Shanice was fast asleep by the Christmas tree; I turned the train off and went back up stairs. Dale was just getting out of the shower; he had his towel wrapped around his back while he was brushing his teeth. I walked behind him and kissed him on his neck, he looked into the mirror and smiled. I walked into the room and sat on the corner of the bed, he came out with his manhood swinging loosely and hard. I hadn't sexed him in about two weeks, he walked up to me and I slid my hands between his legs caressing his balls and rubbing the big boy. It wasn't necessary for me to make another move, he was brick hard and I was throbbing. I got up to undress as he laid on the bed. There was no need for the kissing games, his parents was down stairs, and we was just playing a sneaking game. He rubbed my breast, as I slid up on his penis. It was a bit difficult to go in but when it went in, it was like popping my cherry all over again. The juices flowed, as he penetrated deep me. We were like two cars on a race track, racing in silence for the finish line but yet not one time either of us went out of bounce. We hung and flew past each climax, the more he gave the more I wanted, and the heat of our body cheered us on. Before I knew it we was through! Lawd have mercy that lil quickie was all I needed to put me to bed.

It was Christmas morning, Shanice, Dale, Mrs. B, and Mr. B, was all outside. By the time I reached the bottom stair I could see wrapping paper was everywhere. I stood to the front door, and Mr. B was scrapping Shanice down with her equipment, Mrs. B had the video camera and Dale was standing on his phone. It wasn't long before he spotted me at the door, due to Shanice yelling.

"Merry Christmas Mommy!"

"Merry Christmas Baby!" I said, as I stayed near the door without shoes cause in Florida on Christmas Day it was 78 degrees.

"Merry Christmas Mrs. B and Dexter!" I said.

"Merry Christmas baby!" They responded as Dale came walking towards the house with his phone glued to his ear. Of course I was wondering who the hell he talking to Christmas morning.

"Merry Christmas Baby, I love you." He said kissing me on the nose, and briefly removing the phone from his ear.

"Yes ok Bruce. I'll just speak with you later." He said, as I was all in his mouth while he hugged me in his arms.

"What are you and Bruce talking about this early Christmas morning?" I asked.

"Stocks baby." He said.

"Come in and see what Santa bought you." He said pulling me by my robe and slapping me on my butt. We went over to the tree, and there was two gifts left under the tree unwrapped and the others that belonged to my Mom and Dad was in the chair awaiting to be delivered.

"You open yours first." Dale said.

"Why?" I asked.

"Cause, I want to see how you look when you open it." He said smiling pinching me on the nose.

"No I want to see how you gone look." I said.

"Ok well lets both just open them at the same time." He said as I started unwrapping mines, he slowed up and watched me.

"I see you looking at me." I said laughing.

"I'm not looking at you, I'm opening my gift." He said while blushing, within the next second he got the paper off and realized it was a portable DVD player.

"Thank you baby!" He excitedly said, as I opened mines, there was a shiny jewelry box. In it was a platinum heart, chain and earrings to match.

"I love it!" I said, as I smiled and thought ***you just wait until dinnertime.***

Dale and I started cleaning the house, and played touchy touch games each time we picked up something. Before noon we were all dressed and headed over Becky house where we had decided to have dinner. Mrs. B had all the cakes piled into the Yukon they had drove down from Detroit. There was no need to drive our cars, so we car pooled Shanice, Dale and I sat in the back seat like we were sisters and brothers on a trip with Mom and Dad.

By the time we arrived, everyone was there. The food lined the long counter top as If it was ready for a portrait or buffet line. The colors were different in each bowl and the smell mounted together that it drug you into the kitchen with the desire to taste everything. Mrs. B & Shanice headed to the dining room table, as Dale and Mr. B carried in the deserts from the truck. I was so god darn on hungry, and my those collards was making it easier as the scent teased my pallet. I rinsed off a fork and lifted the lid from the pot, just to taste a spoon full.

"No uhh uhh!" Beky walks over removing the lid from my hand. Which was practically too late as I was devouring those juicy country made collards.

"Whatcha do that for?" I asked as I could taste the smoked neck bone flavor that accompanied the collards.

"Just bring your greedy ass to the table and eat with everyone else!"

"I am!" I said as Beck stayed standing before me with her hand covering the lid of the collards pot...

"Your black ass be late to every dam thang! Why don't you and the baby go have a seat and wait to be served properly?" She added with a grin.

"Whatever!" I replied with laughter just before exiting the kitchen into the dining area.

Upon entrance everyone surely seemed to have been waiting on us; we all sat at our places and prayed over the dinner. Conversations and laughter sounded from corner to corner.

"Becky and Chocolate yall got to see my new House." Jasi said.

"A new house!" Becky repeated.

"Girl Bruce bought me a house; which makes my house look like a dog house."

"Where?" I asked.

"Out in Houston Texas!"

"Yeah."

"When yall coming up there?" Jasi asked.

"Girl please, we don't play with those cowboys, and we told you that before you went out there." Becky added.

"Girl you crazy they got ballers out there." Jasi added.

"Hey so when you gone do it?" Becky whispered, cutting the conversation short about TX.

"Shh shhh!" Jasi said.

"In a little while." I responded.

"Ummm Umm Can I have every ones attention!" Dale said as he stood at the head of the table, while the ladies were whispering.

"Girl what?" Becky said, cutting her voice by the silence. I sat wondering did the two of them play a game on me, or what Dale wanted to talk about.

"Excuse me... Excuse me may I have a minute please!" He asked in a much louder voice.

"Yes!" The room agreed.

"Mona I have a gift I want to give to you, I couldn't be able to see your face expression but I know there will be many here that can. I want you to know you are just as breathtaking to me as anything I could imagine." He said, as I tried to figure what sounded like a hint in disguise. He reached down into his pocket as I gazed at every move he made. He gave to me a tiny box that was wrapped in white paper, and running with beautiful glittery ribbon. It was a box like no other, it was beautiful and suede with a silver hook. I unhooked the tiny box, looking up at him and the others with smiles on their face. Once I opened the box and slammed it back shut, it was so beautiful I didn't want to believe my eyes. There it was a ring not only a ring but a gorgeous engagement ring. One that glistened with diamonds and asked for marriage upon its review to any lucky lady. There were diamonds holding in each platinum prong which created a boss look. The camera flashed as I turned the box side by side, afraid to remove what I thought for years was a long dream of mine. Dale bowed on one knee, and placed my hand in his as he removed the ring.

"Marry me!" He said, without a speech, thought or idea. He was blunt and solemn. My hands trembled as my mouth mumbled yes. They clapped and wiped away tears of happiness, before the joy went away I had built my nerve back up to tell him what I'd been hiding. I reached into my purse and pulled the little Santa wrapped box out.

"This one is for you!" I said, as he took it and everyone looked at each other with questioning eyes as if this was not part of the half known plan. He took his time and unwrapped the gift and the card fell out first.

"No not yet!" I said, gently pulling the card from his hands. He finally unwrapped the box, and started shaking it to his ear as the bells on the shoes, sounded like a little child running through the house.

"I can't guess what this could be." He said.

"Open it!" They were cheering. He slipped his finger in and opened the box. There the baby botties with dangling shoestrings that read "*Congratulations*".

"Baby, oh baby. " Dale fell back on his knees, but this time on two as the booties dropped from his hand and at his side. He placed his ear to my stomach and everyone clapped. Dale couldn't stop holding me nor crying tears of joy.

We all packed up and headed for home, Shanice was crying to stay with Mama, but I made her come home tonight. By the time we made it there she was fast asleep, Dale carried her inside while I opened the door. He went to lay Shanice down, while I was in the kitchen fixing me something to drink.

"Good night Mona." Mrs. B said, as she walked through the door.

"I'm going to call it a night too." Mr. B added.

"Good night you guys, I am going to bed after this too." I said.

"Mama and Daddy yall calling it in tonight?" Dale questioned as he came back down stairs.

"Yes son, we tired been up since morning." Mr. B said.

"Good night baby." Mrs. B announced.

"Sleep tight." He said, as he came to the kitchen and stood in the entrance.

"Hey you sexy thing over there." He called.

"How may I help you sir?" I asked, as if I was on a movie set.

"By bringing that sexy body and those luscious lips over here." Dale responded, licking his lips standing back on one leg, as if he was some type of jig-a-low.

"Really, well how about you bring those strong arms over here and give us an ah-huh-hug!" I said placing my hand on my hip, presenting each curve, and including our unborn child.

"Without a doubt!" He said with a smile, the same smile he had the night I met him in the club.

"I love you." I said.

"I love you too baby, I knew you were the one for me." He said looking me in my eyes on a serious note, you gave me a hard time two years ago, and now you are just as sweet as candy for real."

"You know there really aint a good man in no club. I guess I just got the one who carried luck in his pocket and at my side." I said.

"Yeah, well since I met you I haven't been back. Mona you are mines and I am yours, you'll see we are going to grow old together. I mean like dip snuff and go to the park to feed the birds with our grandchildren." He said sounding like me and the girls having a conversation.

"Yes baby." I said as I kissed him and thought how our daydreams relate.

"Do you want to take a bath with me?" He asked.

"Sure babe." I replied rinsing the glass out and placing it back where I got it from.

"Great!" He replied, as he switched off the kitchen light and the both of us headed up stairs to the room. Although I really felt like sleeping but I knew in deed I had to bath first. By the time we made it to the room, I didn't dare attempt to take a seat, as I knew it would have had me fast asleep.

He stood watching me, as I undress for a bath. He turned on the Jacuzzi and poured my raspberry bubble bath that fumed the room. He pulled off his clothes, and stepped into the Jacuzzi. He sat in before me, and held his hand out to support me to sit safely. I sat in between his legs; he hugged me and rubbed my belly instantly as if this was what he was waiting on.

"Baby you don't know how happy I am." He said.

"So am I." I responded leaning my head back on his chest.

"When did you find out?" He asked.

"That day I went to the doctor."

"You told me it was a stomach virus."

"I know, I wanted to surprise you." I said, clearing up a lie.

"Baby you sure did." he responded, as he bit me slightly around my neck.

"You surprise me too." I said, as I wiped the bubbles from the platinum diamond ring.

"Mona, Its love, a feeling I can't explain and one I definitely don't never want to end." He

said as he rubbed my stomach up and down.

"I can't wait Mona. A boy is fine but a girl would be great." He added.

"As long as it's healthy, I'll be happy." I said.

"That too. When is her birthday?" He asked.

"Dale we don't know if it is a girl yet."

"Well when is the big day?"

"July 24." I responded.

"Wow, that's alright baby. Daddy here waiting." He said as he circled his hands around and around my little bulge.

IT'S WORTHY TO BE PRAISED!

Becky, and I sat at Fridays in the falls, waiting on this wedding planner I was supposed to meet up with here. Apparently she was late and Becky and I had almost finished our lunch.

"Chocolate girl, I don't know where this lady at."

"Child don't worry, I'll just call her up again tomorrow, if not call a new one."

"Are you really ready for this?" Becky asked.

"Of course, you know this is all I really wanted Becky."

"Yeah and you finally getting ready to have a family, that don't mean fly past me now."

"I don't know, Dale says he want about five children."

"Good luck, just wait a couple of years."

"I know right."

"These taste just like the skins I had in New York at this Pizzeria place." Becky said, as she rudely smacked on the wedges.

"Did you really like it there?"

"Mona to be honest I wouldn't mine moving out there."

"Girl you crazy, it gets so cold."

"Cold and fun too. Oh, by the way Jasi sent me some pictures today you got some." Becky mentioned.

"No." I responded.

"Mines I think in the car, if not they home. It's a picture of her, Bruce and that ugly ass dog."

"You so silly Becky."

"She got a nice house."

"She say they doing good out there."

"That's good, hell I'm really ready to relocate too, maybe I can do a little better there, cause in MIA I aint doing shit."

"Whats up with Marco?" I asked.

"Girl Chocolate, I'm glad you asked me about him. How about since Christmas I broke out with these bumps all over my stuff."

"Your nookie." I interrupted with a yucky face.

"Yes girl, and I am so embarrassed to go to the doctor."

"Well what it look like."

"I don't know, but you can tell infection in it, they yellowish." Becky said, shrugging her shoulders.

"It don't itch."

"No but it burns every now and then."

"Damn Becky, you mean to tell me this was since Christmas."

"No that was the last time I sex him, I noticed it when I was in New York for New Year's."

"You fucked anybody in New York?"

"Well yeah, but I scrapped up."

"Come on Becky you know you got to take care yourself better than that."

"I know right, but I aint got no insurance, and I sure aint going to no clinic."

"Becky, shit if something's wrong and you know something wrong you better forget what somebody say when they see you in a clinic. Hell something must be wrong with them too

while they in there."

"You want me to go with you?" I asked.

"No, I'm going to the emergency room tonight." she said with a cough that dragged on as if she had a carton of cigarettes a day.

"Hello you must be Mona and Becky." This tall woman who looked to have worn 90lbs asked.

"Yes." I said standing away from the table greeting her with a handshake.

"I apologize the traffic is crazy coming from north. My name Is Shareka and I am your wedding planner."

"Yes it is busy, mainly because of lunch. I added.

"Wow." Becky said looking surprised. "I love your purse!" Becky said, as she was unlikely to give compliments.

It was beautiful a large juicy Contur'e bag. I observed and analyze her professionalism, sleekness, and exquisiteness by the tone of her voice, thoughts and by the stride of her movement.

"So in your wedding do you got your colors all decked out and the line up? That's like the most easiest thing the brides really pull together."

"Not really. I know I want to be married in canary yellow, I want two matron of honors, and about four flower girls."

"Yeah there you go ideas like that I was fishing for." Shareka added.

"Well I guess." I responded.

"Now the hall, or where the wedding is going to take place, is a big decision. Our company has three theatrical halls as in renaissance, that's if you choose to have the swords and

crowns you know. Then there is the traditional room; which you can wear the big bride dress with the trail and horse and carriage theme. Then there is the princes hall, it's actually for the fifteens sometimes we host also. I've been dying to coordinate a wedding in the princess hall, it is so beautiful. I feel as if you can wear a sleek silk gown with a tiara made of real flowers and doves set out to fly free. "She said becoming so enchanted, and laying out quite a few ideas on me.

"Yes now that sounds beautiful!" Becky said.

"When are you due?" She asked, observing what looked to be a ball.

"July." I replied...

"And your wedding is scheduled for September 25?" She asked as her eyebrows nearly touched her hair line. "Do you think you will be in good shape?" She asked.

"Of course, I am determined. I've been waiting on this far too long."

"Oh she's gone loose the weight, we will be around that track as soon as the baby reach 2wks." Becky added.

"Wow!" Shareka said.

"She's just kidding, actually I'm not really trying to put on to much weight." I said looking over her brochures.

"In that hall we even can have two swings from the ceiling wrapped in your choice of flowers and two little girls or boys slightly swinging to the music."

"Oh now that's some real Disney shit." Becky said.

"No actually they will not have on dresses, they will look better dressed in real flowers like a bikini top and cute skirt covered with petals."

"I like that." I said.

"Well you think I can be one of those girls?" Becky asked.

"No, you will be too heavy, but a kid about 50lbs or less." Shareka added.

"I'm going to think about that." I replied.

"Here is a couple of pictures and the materials are in the back. I also have shoes, I require some low heels because you are standing in one spot for about 45min- to an hour."

"Yeah because she got calluses as big as a half dollar." Becky said, as we all laughed at her silliness.

"Here also is several menus and prices additional styles, glasses, napkins, and dishes. It should give you some ideas. Like this one here, it's in a packet you get Micasa crystal glasses, dishes, hankies instead of paper napkins, stiletto silver wear and here is the price." She pointed and continued on.

"Those are nice, look at these!" Becky said.

"Yeah those are very elegant."

"Believe me you can spend all day looking at dishes, lets get to the fun part." She said as she reached back into her bag and grabbed a note tablet that read things to include.

"This is a pamphlet that I give each bride, it helps you organize, analyze and play with your money before you spend it." She said.

"Oh ok."

"Now here you have all sorts of things to be reminded of like music, flowers, centerpiece, and so fourth and the little lines is where you can put the estimate and add it at the end to see if it's in your budget."

"Yeah she need that, you can't tell her she aint rich." Becky mention.

"I know, all brides assume they are until they come back from their honeymoon." Shareka replied with laughter.

"Well Chocolate, where are you going on your honeymoon?"

"I've always wanted to go to Morocco the pink city."

"Yeah that's a really beautiful place." Shareka added.

"Why not Brazil or somewhere in Asia?" Becky asked, being she had been all around; I know she could tell me about some beautiful places.

"I don't know, I just like Morocco." I said.

"And what about the ring?" Shareka questioned.

"I have to go shopping." I said as she reached back into her bag bringing more books out.

"Shareka, one thing for sure I want to do in my wedding."

"What's that?"

"I want us to say our own vows." I responded.

"Oh this is going to be a dear wedding." She said as she threw her hands on her cheeks. "Are you sure?" She asked.

"Yes." I responded.

"It's going to take a lot of nerves." Shareka continued as if she wanted to change my mind.

"Not to tell him how much I love him in front of my friends." I said.

"It's not that easy. When I got married, I was so nervous just by standing next to him at the altar, and when they said kiss the bride my knees acted as if they forgot their job and I fell into his arms."

"Really!" Becky said laughing.

"Well at least you fell in his arms and not on the floor." I added.

"I would have ran out of that church." she said as she packed all the brochures in a bag she bought for me to carry home. "I want you to look these over, and call me if you have any ideas, because I'll be looking as well." She said as she excused herself from the table while Becky watched Shareka as she switched off.

"Her thin ass, she might could have got in the swing." Becky said.

"Girl you so silly."

"She sounds like she knows what she doing though." Becky said, as she crunched on some ice.

"Yeah she do. Ouch!" I said as I felt a sudden movement in my stomach.

"What!" Becky said frightened half way out her chair.

"I just felt the baby move."

"Let me feel." She said as she slid her chair next to me and placed her hand on my stomach.

"Right here." I said as I moved her hand towards the side.

"Umm huu, I felt it." She said dragging along with another cough.

"Girl you need to see about that cough, because it sounds pretty rough." I said.

"I am." Becky responded, as she put the money in the waiters hand and we headed for home.

Dale was outside washing his car, by the time I made it home. He dried his hands off and came over to the car, opening the door and giving me a kiss and a pat on my tummy.

"How my lady doing today?" He asked.

"Super!" I said, as he got the few bags from the car and followed me in the house.

"Guess what Dale?"

"What sugar? He asked.

"Your little princess or sailor made its first move today." I said as his face lit up.

"Oh boy, I wish I was there." He said.

"Don't worry you know it has five more months ahead." I said.

"Well let me go finish up the car." He said walking back outside, while I sat at the table only to begin looking at the brochures. I didn't want to wear a big gown no matter if I gain or lose weight. I need something that's somewhat graceful. I flipped through the magazines and catalogs, after a while I got bored and called up Jasi.

"Hello." Jasi answered.

"Hey honey what you doing out there?"

"Nothing just laying here in the bed."

"Where is Bruce?"

"He somewhere child."

"You sound pretty bored?" I asked.

"Not really just relaxing, and missing yall crazy busy tales." Jasi said.

"My baby moved today."

"For real! I bet Dale was about to go crazy."

"No he didn't feel it yet, Becky did we was at T.G.I.F today with the wedding planner."

"Her crazy tale, where she at?"

"She at home now." I responded.

"So did you like the wedding planner, did she give you any great ideas?" Jasi asked.

"Yeah she was telling me about these halls they had, but I fell in love with the Princess hall. Shareka was talking my kind of ideas; with the flowers and sleek gowns unlike the big white dresses, and piano music. I even decided that Dale and I are going to write our own Vows to each other."

"Girl you bad, I can't wait till that September Day."

"I know right! I can't even wait for the baby in July."

"Mona, I am really happy for you. Whatever happened with Chuck?"

"Don't you question me about that asshole!"

"Just kidding just kidding. Dayum I am really happy for you though on a serious tip though."

"When you coming down here?" I asked.

"Maybe next month." She said, as if she didn't care to come back.

"Alright then Jasi I'll talk with you later." I replied.

"Alright then, punch Becky in the jaw for me." She said laughing.

"Girl Bye."

A DREAM THAT WAS BARELY HOLDING ON!

Becky was just released from the hospital two days before the baby shower that Jasi and she had planned. I drove down to General hospital alone, Jasi was supposed to be flying in tomorrow and I've been basically getting the things that Becky asked me to.

"Hello." I answered as my phone rang to the annoying ring Becky sat for herself.

"Hey where are you?" She asked.

"Getting off the exit."

"Well hurry up I'm downstairs in the lobby." She explained. I didn't know what really was wrong with Becky, she had turned so secretive in the last few months. I was surprise she told me about the syphilis; I guess she had no choice. Then this is the second time she been back in the hospital for pneumonia and always dressing with her belly out and on a diet. I just pray that nothing seriously is wrong with my girl, because I don't know what I'll do without her. I pulled up under the garage and Becky came stepping right out of the door.

"About time!" She said smiling as if she just left an interview or a good event.

"Girl please. How are you feeling?" I asked.

"I'm straight, they just had to keep me overnight to treat my lungs I got a touch of pneumonia."

"Again!" I asked in shock.

"Yeah I guess it's that night air." She hung her head down.

"Do you still be smoking?" I asked, while I tried to catch her eye to see if she was going to tell me the truth.

"Watch out! She screamed as I almost hit another car so into this conversation.

"No I don't smoke, and watch the road."

"What's up with your nookie?" I asked smiling, trying to make her feel a little comfortable about her timidity situation.

"I don't know Chocolate; it keeps braking out bad, now I have herpes and that done started breaking me out between my legs and my inner thighs."

"Damn Becky what is going on?"

"Girl I really don't know how to say it, but I know I got to say it. Rather if now is a good time or not. This is why I couldn't be in your wedding!" She said waving her hand over her body. "Look at me! Just look at me!" She screamed in tears with big questionable eyes. "Chocolate, I'm dying I have full blown AIDS!" She said as she turned and looked out the window. I dissected each word a million times a millisecond in my head. My friend. My friend. My TRUE friend has Aids. I couldn't take my eyes off the road, or take my hands off the wheel. My eyes turned into clear pools of water as I looked at hers which was filled with sorrow. I couldn't bear to drive another mile, I turned on my hazard lights and pulled on the shoulder of the road.

We sat in silence for a minute or so, I didn't bother to ask what, why or who. I cried, I cried like one that mourned for her mother.

"Chocolate, please chocolate don't cry." She said, as I tried to discontinue the tears by biting my lip, and that didn't help. I had so many good memories and I know so many bad ones to come. I know she will never be like Becky again from here forward.

"Chocolate please be strong for me, I didn't tell anyone but you. Understand what I'm going through, if I can fight it and bear with this physically and mentally I know you can. I know you can bear with this mentally Chocolate. You've always been the strong one, don't get weak on me not now that I need you. Please Chocolate please." She said as the water continued to fill in her eyes, as her lips begged for mercy. "I'm going to be alright Chocolate, we always come out on top. Remember." She said as if this was some simple fight.

"Yes, we will." I said as I hugged her, but felt as if that wasn't enough. I wanted to put her in my lap, and just tell her what she meant to me, by being in my life and what great impact she has on it. I didn't want to believe this just as well as she didn't.

"I love you Becky, no matter what happens in life, I'll always be here for you and you will always be my friend beyond any dying day. Be yourself Becky, and anything I mean anything you think you going through I want you to know you won't be alone. I'm here." I said as I uttered the words beneath my tears.

I dropped Becky off to her house, where her mom sat on the porch, her two boys were playing basketball in the driveway and Brianna was swinging on her swing set.

"Girl watch they bad ass." She said as she got out of the car.

"Mommy! Mommy! Mommy!" They all called as they nearly knocked her back down in the car with hugs as if she had been gone for months. They had gotten use to the fact that she hadn't been traveling so much in the past few months.

"Hey Ms. Minnie!" I shouted from the car not wanting to get out because I knew my eyes were blood shot red from crying my feelings out.

"Hey baby." She replied.

"Chocolate where Shanice?" Brianna asked.

"She's at home." I responded.

"Can she come over my house?"

"How about later Brianna?" I asked.

"Ok." Brianna replied.

"Ok cool and Becky I'm out of here." I replied to the both of them before leaving.

"Hey!" Becky said walking back to the car. "Are you going to get Jasi tomorrow?"

"Yes I suppose to why? You want to go?" I asked.

"No, I'll see you all when you get back. Where is the things I had you to pick up for me?"

"I dropped them over here earlier."

"That's my girl, but hey remember we can do this. Think of you and I like a tree, we can bare anything." She said as my heart got a bit heavier, while my eyes refilled with water.

"Later Becky." I said, driving away with teary eyes. I felt so sorry. The kids just started really being with her. Which is why I wonder how long she knew she was sick before she told me and why did she tell me.

"Hello!" I answered as it register Jasi.

"Hey baby what you doing with that big belly?" She asked.

"Nothing much on my way home." I said not even sounding a bit excited.

"From where?"

"Becky house."

"What she was doing?" Jasi asked.

"Nothing, just the usual." I said lying, because I knew she would have a thousand questions if I said I just picked her up from the hospital.

"I called there yesterday because she didn't answer her cell, and Brianna told me her Mommy in the hospital." Jasi said as, I just let her mouth run. Jasi had took off with Bruce and popped in town maybe once a month since January, so she really didn't know what was really going on with her girls anymore. She just imagined that I was happy and

blowing up and that Becky was still getting money and just planning this fairy tale wedding which at this moment meant shit to me. Like I say, since she left we might hear from her once a month, or talk very brief through messages, if not she would get back with post cards in the mail. Where she had been to India, Asia, Baghdad, Civitavecchia, Dubai, and France. Don't get me wrong I was happy for Jasi, but she just don't know what was here for her to face. Besides our simple friendship. I never knew, but felt the yearning that we needed each other to survive, regardless if it was for Jasi big brain and loans, my lectures, and poems, or Becky's jokes and personality. It's something that worked for the three of us which kept us smiling and a steady head. Without one we would be a tripod with two legs which wouldn't be able to stand good, not even against a wall.

"So are you coming to get me tomorrow?" She asked.

"Yeah sure I'll be there." I said, with my mind still in that ghastly state.

"Bye Chocolate I'll see you tomorrow. Wear something nice so we can stop by Bal Harbor on the way home.

"Alright." I said ending the call.

By the time I made it home, Dale had left a note on the table that he had went fishing and will be back later tonight. I went into the kitchen and whipped up me something quick to eat, and swallowed down those big horse pills which I was getting very sick of. I laid in my room and grabbed a hold to myself. I told me to be strong, and that everything was going to be alright. At least I could've told myself that but believing it was another.

The next day came and I drove around the airport in circles looking for Jasi to be standing outside, all a while she was sitting at an unauthorized booth.

"Hey blind bat." She said as I pulled over to the curb.

"What's up baby?" I responded.

"Dang look like you swallowed a melon!" She said as she threw her luggage in the back and took a seat.

"I know right. The doctor say its all baby."

"You look pretty though." She added.

"Thank you but my man tell me that everyday girl." I mentioned, with a smile.

"That's so sweet." Jasi said.

"He is, he even bathe me and lotions my legs every day." I said, bragging.

"I know you love that, but you better slow up eating foods with salt that's why your legs swollen."

"This the second time they got swollen like this, you know them ole folks say if it swell the third time you gone have that baby soon."

"Why you just didn't find out what it is?" Jasi asked.

"I didn't want to, cause Dale wants a girl and I really don't care, so I just decided to let it be a surprise for the both of us."

"Alright Heather." Jasi said laughing, bringing that crazy name up again. "You think you gone loose that weight before the big day which is only three months away?"

"You'll see." I said.

"Oh girl I seen this really nice hall for a wedding, exit right here." Jasi said.

"Child I already found a hall."

"I know but look at this hall, it's really nice." She continued.

"Turn through here." She pointed.

"Now at the stop sign make a left."

"Here" I asked.

"Yeah." Jasi replied.

"Girl its only one car here, you think they open?"

"Yeah!" Jasi replied.

"Is this the back or front?" I asked.

"It's the front."

"Damn this shit looks deserted. I can tell you now I don't want no wedding here. They really need to pressure clean these damn walls." I said, as I parked the car but really wanting to drive off. This just seemed like it would be a waste of anyone's time.

"Girl just come on." She said as I waddled into this huge building from the outside it looked like a warehouse but the inside which appeared to look like a museum. There were two double kitchen like doors on the right side of the hall, when Jasi pushed them everyone stood up hollering.

"Surprise!!!!" I was not only frightened but thrilled at such a beautiful sight it was. The ceilings and walls had paintings of storks and babies everywhere. The decorations was a beautiful soft sage green and light yellow, just like the vacant room that awaited for the unborn child. The stage sat a beautiful chair especially for me. It was friends that I knew no one could have bought together but Becky. She was there as well running with her neck cut off, trying to make sure everything was right. On the stage was so many beautiful wrapped gifts, as well as big gifts such as a crib, bouncer, high tech swing, stroller and even a high chair was sitting up like there was a room available here on the stage.

"Oh my god! Thank you thank you." I said, as Dale came walking up to me, I hid a bit of my shyness in his arms.

"Hey baby!" Becky said as she pulled me away from Dale.

"Thank you!" I said as the three of us stood hugging and taking photos.

"Do you like it?" Jasi asked.

"I love it! I knew I was having a shower but I thought it was really going to be over Becky house next Sunday."

"Baby I can't let you know everything." Becky said with a grin just before heading off to start up the games.

Morning had come and I was up early in the morning, preparing breakfast for Becky and Jasi, being they were coming over to help fix up the nursery. I prepared Becky's favorite; corn beef hash, some smoke Georgia bacon and grits. I battered up some eggs and added them to the table, just when the two of them arrived. Dale opened the door and they came in with noise as if they were heading to a parade.

"What! You mean to tell me you rolled out of bed this morning?" Becky asked.

"I told yall I was going to be preparing breakfast before we start." I said.

"I sure can smell that bacon." Jasi said, as she went towards the kitchen.

"I'm hungry too." Becky mentioned.

"Guess what!" I asked, while they sat at the table, looking in my direction.

"What!" They responded.

"Yall better help yourself." I said, as I took a scoop of grits into my bowl.

"Some type of way to treat a guest." Becky replied.

"Child please whatever!" I said as I continue to scoop whatever I desired to have.

"Chocolate have you decided what color are you painting the room." Jasi asked.

"Girl you late, we did that last week." Becky replied.

"Yall already painted it?"

"What part don't you understand DING-DONG, we painted it last week like that sage green in the baby shower."

"Oh ok smart ass that is a unisex color huh?" Jasi asked.

"Dull?" Becky said teasing Jasi, on the other hand so happy to see her and just didn't know how to say it.

"What about the theme?" Jasi asked, as she talked with her mouth full.

"Now for a theme we have to wait on the baby, we can set up the furniture and hang the clothes." Becky mentioned.

"Well my my my! Chocolate is really fixing to have a baby and soon to be married." Jasi said, clapping her hand together.

"I know right." I said as Becky looked to have drifted off into a sad stage.

"Shareka came over to my house and brought along one of the dresses they are so cute, but I think its cut to low and show too much of my breast." Jasi said, as she finished up her drink.

"Shareka might just have the lady to add a little more up top or open it out one. Cause we can't have you showing those fake tittis." I said teasing Jasi.

"How your dress fit you Ms. Becky why you round her dieting like you the bride. Pretty soon you're going to need a bell around your neck, so we know you coming." Jasi said, as the

words insulted the situation Becky was going through and Jasi wasn't yet aware.

"No I haven't tried my dress on yet." Becky said without a joke to follow which was very unlike her.

"How does the shoes look?" I asked trying to get on another subject.

"They are really nice, and I love that tiara." She said as she went on. Becky got up and raked the food from her plate and trotted up the stairs.

"I know, I like the tiara too." I added, trying to act as if everything was normal and staying a distance from the terrible news.

"What's up with Becky?" Jasi asked, noticing immediately something must be wrong.

"Oh maybe she's going to start on the room." I said.

"Nah, Chocolate I know when something aint right. I can feel something's wrong." She insisted as she got up and raked her plate out as well.

"Becky!" Jasi called as she walked up the stairs, but there wasn't an answer back. I decided to sit at the table for a while, because I just somehow knew this would be the best time for Becky to tell her. I washed up the dishes, pots, swept and mopped the floor without any interruptions. I finished and went upstairs, where I could maybe even hear a pin drop, and there were the two of them sitting on the floor. They were not crying and they were not laughing but I knew Becky had already broke the news. If she didn't they might would have found something up here to discuss and debate about, but they wasn't. There wasn't a sound. They just sat folding the new clothes with faces as long as any interstate.

"Looks like yall can use a little help?" I mentioned as I sat in the chair.

"Yes." Becky said, with a mysterious smile on her face and Jasi continued picking up a small piece of tissue to wipe what she wouldn't let fall.

"Wow!" I said.

"What's wrong with you?" Becky quickly asked.

"I don't know I just felt a little pressure down here."

"Girl you only got three weeks, you might feel anything right long and now." Becky said, as Jasi continued to fold clothes as if I wasn't in here. Jasi was hurting and in a bad way, keeping a serious face and a still tongue wasn't good at all.

"Ouch!" I said as I breathed in.

"It hurts that bad?" Becky asked again.

"No, it's just pressure." I replied.

"You may just have a full bladder." Jasi said finally opening her mouth.

"Well let me see if I can use the bathroom." I said as I got up from the chair, almost immediately the water begin to run. Not just like any urine, but it was water coming that I had no control over.

"Look, I'm not doing this!" I said as I stood still and water was draining down my legs.

"Your water bag broke!" Jasi loudly yelled after dapping her finger in the liquid and smelt it.

"Dale! Dale!" Becky called running out the room. "I think Chocolate water broke!" She said as the two of them came running in the room.

"Baby are you ok? Are you hurting? Come on lets go to the hospital!" He said nervously stumbling over everything trying to wrap a towel around me. He lifted me in his arms, while Jasi hurried and packed a bag. We didn't waste no time, all of us jumped into Beckys Rover and headed to the hospital. I wasn't hurting but I was nervous because of Dale. He was acting as if I was having the baby alone and that there would be no doctor. He was

panting, breathing and doing the rubbing for me as Jasi took on the expressway like she was in an emergency vehicle. In my heart I was crying because I knew what Jasi was feeling, but in my mind I was screaming why did this have to happen to my friend. It was a thought that couldn't go away one that couldn't even be over powered by what brought me so much joy.

"Oww!" I hollered out as the pains started one after another as we pulled into the emergency area.

"PLEASE SOMEBODY, ANYBODY, MY WIFE IS IN LABOR!" Dale hollered through the opening doors. Men and Women came with a stretcher and immediately starting my IV. I had to sign and fill out so much paper work, the pains was coming so bad you would have thought I was writing left handed when I was right. The nurse came in and gave me a shot in my lower back, seconds later they put a mask of cool smoke over my nose which was anesthesia and as the seconds went by I was out.

"Good morning Ms. Lady?" Becky said as I wake.

"Where my baby?" I asked observing the room to find Dale in the corner rocking the baby away in his arms.

"Mona, are you ok?" Mama asked.

"I want to see my baby." I said, as Dale walked over to me and wrapped so tight was a little hat sticking out with pink and blue stripes which didn't make it easier for me to guest the gender.

"We had a girl, she weighs 8lbs and 3oz born at 11:36am." He said, as I turned my head to observe all the visitors that were here. I couldn't remember anything all I knew I was getting ready to have my baby.

"You are a new Mama now." Becky said as she rubbed my hands. I didn't have much

strength besides to ask a few questions and enough to keep my eyes open. I wanted to see her, but I couldn't hold her, I even was ready to name her but I just couldn't seem to think of anything right now.

"Chocolate are you hungry?" Jasi asked.

"No way Jasi! You remember she say the diet starts in the hospital as soon as she dropped her load." Becky said as I tried to laugh, and an awful pain was just pulling. I immediately stop and turned the smile upside down and grabbed my stomach which was packed with ice in a bag.

"I'm sorry baby, you had a C-section so it will be hard for you to laugh, cough, sneeze, fart or walk for a little while." Becky said as I felt the pain even more just knowing what had happened.

"Dale let me see her again?" I asked. This time laying my eyes upon her. She was beautiful. She had a head full of hair and peachy skin that look like it's going to turn dark according to the tip of her ears and the wrinkles in her little knuckles. I looked all over for her birth mark, there it was in her diaper on her left cheek. It was a heart which Id assume was a meaning of love.

"What are we going to name her baby?" Dale asked.

"I don't know." I said as I looked over her carefully, as she laid so precious in her dads' arms.

"I have a name for her." Dale said.

"What is it?" I questioned.

"Nayanza Camberly Becca." He responded.

"That's beautiful Dale." Jasi said.

"It means forever." Dale said, just like I thought. He had been doing some name searching for his Princess.

MY, DREAMS, HOPES, PRAYERS AND LIFE

Yesterday, Shareka and I had did the last minute shopping for my wedding. We drove downtown and bought plenty of MAC makeup and brushes for our faces which cost quite more than the idea make-up I had planned to purchase. However MAC gets the job done! The Bridal shower was lovely. Instead of having something so huge Jasi planned a day at the spa for the four of us. The fourth person was actually a personal photographer whom followed us throughout hotel Bentley on South beach constantly taking pictures of us while we laughed and joked about the good times. We caught up on so much girl talk without getting interrupted by none other than ourselves. We totally forgot about the photographer whom could have been listening to our business, and we certainly was not worrying about the masseuse as they were short Asians who I thought didn't know much English let alone ghetto slang. As our topics grew more and more I heard them laugh and I was certain they were laughing at Jasi story about Bruce and his first Viagra pill. Poor thing he ended up in the hospital, all because his penis didn't want to go down. Before I realized it, everyone was now conversing in the room, by either giving their opinion or offering their story. I will certainly tell you this was a time we all much needed.

Nayanza was now weighing 17lbs and she's going to be two months tomorrow, and I had lost 15lbs. I looked like I always wanted, Nayanza just seemed to have traced and defined my shape a little better than I had before. Starting all over with a baby hasn't been bad at all, but of course Dale was getting up more than I was in the middle of the night. I certainly believed that he could hear her before she even starts and never would he let her get angry first. This made things a lot easier. He was too in love with his child, the bonding time was incredible and so admiring. He would scrap her in the stroller for an afternoon walk everyday while I took the time to visit Becky at the hospital. Becky glands had swollen so huge until she was unable to talk. Jasi had finally moved back home from Texas, to support Becky by dropping and leaving everything behind. Ms. Minnie and all the grownups knew what was going on even the talk in the street when they see her. She really didn't like going out at all not even on the porch or a ride here or there. Becky would write every and anything she wanted to tell me. She hadn't eaten for two weeks, because of the sores that pierced through her milk white tongue. The hospital had become our hotel of agony, as we all waited for each new report or prognosis that we knew she weren't able to fight off without an immune system. The constant hum of the respirator accompanied us during the visiting hours and the blaring TV no one was for sure listening to. Becky went to therapy three times a week to learn how to walk all over again. The syphilis had ate off her pelvic bone and thrashed her skin with infected boils. I wanted to ask her where did this come from but I knew she couldn't tell me. I knew she was looking for Marco so hard, she had last seen him was during the Christmas holidays a year ago. She never knew Marco original first and last name not even a family member or a number she can call for emergencies. These past few weeks has been getting hard. More and more I stop focusing on my family, and wedding due to all the stress that was taking control of me. . Jasi would pick up where she knew I could barely carry on and pulled things through. Dale was very understanding, he knew what it was like to lose a love one or to be with them when they really can't be there for themselves. Things were happening so fast. It felt like I gave birth a month ago, it felt like that happy bridal shower was yesterday, but today... Today I thought.

"Lord Jesus have mercy." I called unto the lord as my tears begin to leak down my face.

"I need you lord...Heal her father, I ask that you heal her father in your name." I began to pray as this was the only way I knew how to make matters better. Grandma always said she gives her problems to god and he fixes them, just how he intends. SO I continued. "Lord I don't think I know much about praying, but lord I ask of you tonight for a little bit of understanding Lord. Teach me father, teach me how to be strong while your plan work on us. I'm not asking that you make everything better Father, but I ask that you heal her. Heal her father to watch her kids become adults. Lord Jesus I pray that you don't take her, and if it's in your plan lord, please strengthen us and prepare us to live with your plan. In your name lord I pray. Amen.

The final day had come; I was beautiful, glamorous, gorgeous, and undefined. The canary yellow silk gown perfectly outlined my curves. The baby left no out of bounce figure, looks to me she put things together and added to places right where they needed to be. The music blared all through the hall while Daddy and I stood behind the curtain up stairs watching everyone walked down the alternate stairs and to their respected places. We also watched my two little cousins Shania and Sharonnie slightly swung on wooden pallets hanging from the base of the ceiling twirled and decorated with the same beautiful canary flowers which aligned our hair and was decorated throughout the hall. Jasi stood waiting at the altar just as well as Bruce stood for the best man looking ever so daringly handsome and gorgeous. Lil Corey was dressed identical to Dale and boy was he clean. The ring barrel boy was carrying a hand held pillow which too was ruffled up with canary yellow silk material. In the center of the pillow was material sewn to be petals which comfortably held the big diamond that sat lonely waiting to accompany the engagement and promise ring which obvious was a matching set of ideas from day one. I was in taking the whole event in and the set up was going just as planned. I could see Shareka running from side to side, just before my walk. I then noticed her alongside Becky, although she changed her mind about three months before the wedding she still attended as my Jr. Bride clutching the sides of her wheel chair. I know she was too old to be my Jr. Bride, but the relationship we bare I had to make an exception. She sat in the audience just as frail as a young girl, her flowers were decorated into her hair and her dress hung in a manner she wouldn't even wear not even to sleep. Mr. And Mrs. B was in the audience sitting next to Mama.

Dale was stunning, his suit fitted perfect, and the color matched his dark chocolaty skin so nice. He had a look and stand that spelled out boss. The music started blaring as the four flower girls came down which was Shanice, Brianna, Britney, and Tamaya. They were so cute, they took the right steps and throughout just as many yellow rose petals on the floor. They weren't shy and they didn't pay attention to the owws and auhs. "Are you ready baby?" Daddy asked. As my heart seemed to be racing a hundred miles a second.

"I think so." I whispered.

"Just try not to miss a step, and everything will be alright once I hand you over. Congratulations my love!" He said with a kiss on my jaw just as my introduction began to play, and we glided down the steps. My gown had a trail that hung with hand sewn real flowers matching the ones that went around my tiara. I wore an elegant Bvlgari chain and dazzling earrings that was worth over $250,000 in which my Daddy rented upon his good credit. Everyone eyes were open wide. Dale stood in the Isle next to Bruce, with a smile a mile across his face, and deep as an ocean. As Daddy and I approached Dale he held his hand out as if he couldn't wait to touch his bride. Daddy slowly removed my veil from my face, and motioned my hand as a sign of giving me over to the man in my life. Daddy stood to the side as Dale and I stood before the preacher. The preacher started off with St. Mark 10:8.

Dale and I had made our own vows so after the preacher finish he stood to the side and let Dale started his vows. I stood just as nervous as a leaf looked against wind.

"Mona, when I met you, I met bonding, honesty, and trust. You are not only the blue in March skies, but you are the light in my life. I love you. I want you to know thy deed is great and thy heart is pure. You are someone I can tell my hopes, and fears with the deepest feeling of trust. You are a woman that brings me joy, which can never be told. You have even gave me a love that is more precious than gold. Mona the love we shared has made everything beautiful in my life. This is why I know you are the perfect wife." Dale said, as my nerves placed my eyes on every part of his face, from the trim of his beard, to the tape of his hairline.

"Dale, you are more than I can dream of and all that I can ever imagine. I like the way you think and I love the way you speak. Your love has not only up my taste buds but it has dressed me with love, and honesty, which has colored me with happiness, motivation and direction. Yet combed me with confidence, physical strength, and the best greatest change of a life time. This is why you and only you can be the gatekeeper for my heart." I said as I stood back and let the preacher do the preaching without moving an eye, or twinkling a toe.

"Do you Dale Orley Becca take Mona Michelle Anderson for your lawfully wedded wife?" He asked, as the grip became tighter on my hands.

"Yes I do."

"Do you Mona Michelle Anderson take Dale Orley Becca for your lawfully wedded husband?" He asked again, as I stared into Dales eyes remembering every good second I shared with him.

"Yes. I do."

"You may now kiss your Bride." He said, as Dale gripped my face and kissed me for the whole church to see. Not smuggling me in his coat or elbow hiding the view from my guest, but he kissed me gracefully. After the ceremony, but right before the first dance I looked in the crowd to find Becky, but what I saw was Corey pushing her in the chair with her mom and three kids heading out the door. I received so many gifts and congratulations but the one that really meant anything to me, rolled out in her chair without the benefit of saying later. I didn't want to make things look obvious while she was trying to get going being everyone was already looking at her, so Instead I called her phone and Ms. Minnie had answered on the first ring as if she was expecting a call.

"Ms. Minnie why are yall leaving so soon?" I asked with tears in my eyes.

"Mona, Becky isn't feeling well she was having problems again with her breathing so I'm fixin to take her to the hospital." Ms. Minnie said, as I just wanted to avoid my first dance and follow them. I promised I would never leave her alone. I thought to myself as I began to cry.

"Ok." I said with sorrow, as Jasi walked in and called my name. My makeup was smeared and my tiara was in my hand. I pressed against the wall starring at Jasi and wanted to know what was next. Out of all the days why this day...

*****

Spring was approaching and winter was practically gone. Although Becky had been diagnosed with HIV for about a year now her temper was quicker than a rattlesnake, and her feelings were as soft as a spoiled baby's. She asked Ms. Minnie her mom to stop all the visitors except Jasi and me. Corey her kids' father was still coming around, without a trace of the sickness perhaps he must be the carrier or who knows. Becky was about that cash and the sky was her limit. Jasi came and picked me up after work so we could go and sit with Becky, something we did daily. We would sit and look at recorded home videos from when we were kids. We had pictures we took on trips, proms, high school, New Orleans, Bahamas, Jamaica, baby shower, and a few when we were preparing for the wedding. This was just the beginning of memories that documented our friendship. Through it all Becky would sit with us as if there was nothing in the world a problem. When all a while the Dr. had discharged her on hospice care last week due to the syphilis, and pneumonia that they just couldn't seem to control. As the days went on, the matters got worse, it was almost every day we had to take her to General Hospital, either a blank call or some type of treatment or checkup.

Ms. Minnie was there on every beat, no matter what it was, she was there. AIDS to Ms. Minnie didn't mean ANYTHING; she cared for her only daughter as if she was a newborn just released from the Hospital. She would comb Becky's curly thin black hair, bathe her, brush her teeth, lotion her legs, and dress her. Something no one would have done, not even the man that got her in this horror, but a Mama is always willing. Even her Daddy Mr. Robert who hadn't been around for years, besides on the store porch. He had cleaned himself up and came along to help Ms. Minnie. Becky had suffered from a few strokes right after my wedding and Mr. Robert was her legs, he would lift her to and from anywhere and direction she wanted to go as she hated that wheelchair.

Tagged on the front door was a no smoking sign. Being she often was short of breath from time to time they would put her on the pump when needed. Jasi ringed the doorbell as I stood back with two videos from Cancun, a box full of pictures of her birthday bash in Jamaica, and the bridal shower at the spa.

"Who is it?" Lil Corey asked.

"Jasi." As he opened the door, Brianna and Julian came running down the dark hall. They too had changed for their mother; they knew when she didn't feel good. They would always whisper and keep their request to a minimum.

"Hey Chocolate and Jasi." Corey said standing in the doorway.

"What's up Corey? How are you?" I asked.

"Happy! I made the basketball team today."

"You did." Jasi said.

"That's good, now you better not have all them girls chasing behind you." I said, as we walked down the hall.

"Hey Chick." I said, leaning over Becky's bed as she laid staring at the walls, then smiled and looked towards the door.

"What's going on baby?" Jasi said smiling and rubbing her hand across Becky's hair.

"Where yall was?" Becky questioned as she did normally, stuttering the words out slow due to the stroke.

"Nowhere. Jasi came and got me from work, and we came here."

"Oh, you wore that to work?" Becky asked, pushing the button so her bed would recline up.

"Yes I did." I said doing a booty shake dance.

"Look what I bought!" Jasi added, placing a huge duffle bag at the foot of Becky bed,

"What's that?" I asked. Jasi quickly zipped the bag open and my was it full of photos and VHS video tapes,

"Wow what's all that?" Becky dryly asked, as I quickly recognized a group photo.

"Hell Nah I was so bald headed." I added, as Becky and Jasi too started to pull photos from the bag. I think this was a good decision to do at this time as I knew almost every day we came to visit Becky would just lie in bed like an old woman. Face lined with stress and sorrow, skin as pale as dull, tongue white as cotton and flesh look to have weigh more than the bones, by the way it sagged. Luckily today she seemed a bit more upbeat, moments later we began to look at the video a while, then back through the pictures. In almost every photo Becky was at her best. She was thick, shinning black skin, a shape that claimed unique a nice butt, hips and a small waist to match, with her exotic braids that hung down her back. Guys were in the backgrounds with their cameras, as if they were hungry pigeons in one photo.

"Dude back there like you a celebrity!" Jasi added, as I burst out in laughter. Shortly I noticed Becky was clutching another picture as she began to cry.

"Becky don't cry." I said, as she starred at the group picture of us in Jamaica dressed to kill and at the baby shower hugging in one big huddle.

"You know I really have messed my life up."

"Becky!" Jasi interrupted.

"No Jasi! It's easy for you all to tell me something, but understanding is something you all may never know. I'm tired! I really wish, I just didn't have to wake up in the morning."

"Come on Becky, don't talk like that." I said, as I placed her hands in mines which was literally cold.

"You all don't know what it's like, when you can't do nothing for yourself. You have to call on someone for everything. You have to not only hear what goes on in the streets; you have to watch how the street looks at you. Like you don't have eyes, nose, or lips. It hurts!"

Becky said in a trembling voice lead by tears. It was indeed her facts which pierced me and paralyzed my very soul. I mean I couldn't speak a word. I was so suddenly drawn back by her appearance and weak voice as if today was my first time visiting her. I listened to every word, and watch each desperate gesture she attempted at. It is now I would say she definitely had looked too age, way too older than a character she was far too young to be. Her eyes appeared to be fogyish with some sort of grey cloudiness tint to them. They no longer was brown, and I...

"Becky, we don't mind and never will mind if you call on us forever." Jasi said, as I snapped out of my daze.

"It's alright," Becky replied with another dragging awful cough.

After a while, I went into the kitchen and got Becky two yogurts and a ensure drink, which was all she could bare to swallow. We sat and watching an old episode of Saved by the bell. Skretch was one of the contestants competing poetry LIVE, and was making a fool of himself as always.

"Chocolate, Do that poem you did for me." Becky asked smiling while sipping on the drink with her eyes as big as marbles and as deep in her head.

"Which one?"

"The one you did when I was with Marco in London." She asked, as I just wanted to hold that thought inside, because reality was starring us in the face.

"Nah, I like the one about true love." Jasi mention.

"Oh yeah that was my poem." I said, hoping she would change her mind.

"Ok, but wait I like your other poem too. I read it in this article in the hospital Chocolate." Becky said, as I felt my heart flush. I knew they were going to put it in an article which was part of the winning process, but what I didn't know was that Becky read it.

"If I hadn't known better, I would have thought you were talking about me. I like it though," Becky said and paused for a second. "It's real. Well you can do the one you did in the eleventh grade. I guess I can understand, you don't want to make me feel no worst. It's something everyone needs to know, like you told me before sometimes experiences come too late and this one sure did." Becky said.

"It was called `Essence was no mistake!" I yelled and jumped out my seat while trying my best to hold back my tears that was building up once again.

"Yeah, do it Chocolate." Jasi chanted.

"Wait a minute let me see if I can remember that one." I said, taking another gigantic breath to hold in this pain that was nearly tearing me apart. The worst part about this type of pain, I had to contain it I couldn't let go, I had to understand, I have to be the strong, cause that is who she knew and see me as.... But lord knows I'm ALL sorrowed out.

"Hello!" Jasi yelled.

"Ok I was trying to make sure I got the words right." I added with a twisted lie.

"Yeah right, and hold that dress down we don't won't to see those funky panties." Jasi said, as Becky laughed loud as she could, not liked she always did, but loud enough where you would hear the wheezing and coughing.

"Wait wait!" Becky said. "Tie this around your head and move just like you did." She said, as I smiled and was for sure ready to perform that poem by twirling up my pin plats wrapping the towel around my head, kicked off my pumps and pranced around the room, as if there was a huge audience.

ESSENCE WAS NO MISTAKE!
ESSENCE IS A COLOR THAT IS OFTEN MISTAKENLY MENTION
IT IS THE COLOR OF BOLD, BEAUTIFUL, LOYAL, AND A
HERRITAGE THAT PAYS CLOSE ATTENTION.
ESSENCE WAS PUT TOGETHER WITH WIDE HIPS, BIG LIPS, AND KINKY HAIR.
BUT IT WAS A LOOK THAT SPELLED BOSS AND MADE EVERYONE STARE.
ESSENCE WAS DESCRIBED WITH GHETTO SLANG AND DISFIGURED FACES.
YES INDEED IT WAS THE STRONG MINDS, HARD TIMES,
AND OUR FAITH WHICH LEAD US PLACES.
ESSENCE WAS DESCRIBED AS UNEVEN ART.
IT WASN'T DESCRIBED FOR A SINGLE MOTHER WHOM DID MORE THAN JUST HER PART.
ESSENCE WAS SCIENTIFICALLY DESCRIBED, BY THE ARCH IN
OUR BO-LEGS WAS ESPECIALLY FOR MONKIES
AS YOU CAN SEE THEY DIDN'T DESCRIBE US ACCORDING
TO OUR BEAUTIFUL AFRICAN COUNTRY.
ESSENCE IS BLACK
ESSENCE IS COMFORTABLE
ESSENCE IS AT EASE
ESSENCE IS DETERMINE
ESSENCE IS ME.
FROM THE STRIDE OF A BLACK WOMANS WALK SPELLS STRONG.
TO THE TOP OF A BLACK MANS HEAD PRONOUNCES KING.
FROM THE BLINK OF OUR EYE EXPLAINS FAITH!
TO THE MOTION OF OUR LANGUAGE SPELLS UNDERSTANDING.

FOR EVERY TEAR CRIES 'THERE IS A GOD.'
TO EVERY MISTAKE THERE IS MOTIVATION
NOW WHERE WAS ESSENCE MISTAKENLY MENTIONED?

"Beautiful, yes it is beautiful." Becky said as she bowed her head.

"That was nice." Jasi added.

"I know when I die you may not want to talk at my funeral but I wanna ask you to do two favors for me and talking is one of them."

"Becky why you keep talking about dying?" I asked.

"I thought you were strong?" Jasi said.

"I am, but I am tired also. Just listen please yall." Becky insisted.

"I want yall to help Mama raise my babies please. I mean if they need anything, I mean anything, yall know just how I do. I'd turn all the way around if they needed a juice. I'm not asking yall to do nothing I never once did. Yall my girls, I love yall forever and always will. Help me finish living my life through my children." Becky said as the both of us wiped tears away from our faces. I rubbed her hands again which remained colder than usual.

"Come on yall don't cry, yall make me sad." Becky said, as she went on with her wishes. "Chocolate and #2 I want you to say a beautiful poem for me, I mean a good one. The same way you describe me then, I want you to describe me now, just like that poem in the article."

"Becky why you acting like this." I said.

"I just want to know that everything is going to be ok. I have no more use here, and you know that." Becky said, as she picked up her 6:00 meds from the dresser and dashed it down with her bottled water she kept near the bed.

"I just don't like when you talk like that. Don't tell me anything, it's already hard. I can only do so much, I just ask you to try. There is a lot here for you to live for." I said with such a demanding tone as if she really had a choice.

"Chocolate we all have to die someday. I know you are angry, I can tell it every time you come around, but all this was indeed my fault. I'm the one who played these games, turned those tricks, and not take care of me. So don't be mad, just understand what I'm going through. I am going to a better place I pray." Becky said as Jasi reached over in the bed and hugged her. "Maybe in a forest." Becky said with a smirk on her face, while I found nothing to be funny. "I want to be a tree; where they are somewhat like humans without mouths. They share leaves for shade and bare each other limbs for any reason possible, like the two of you. I know I'll never know two other girls just the same." Becky said as she began to cry, more than I ever seen her. She had asked us to leave; instead we sat in the living room till 3am.

It had been 3 days since I had seen or talked with Becky. Every time I called or came by Ms. Minnie says she sleep. Friday morning Mama had called me, and ask me to stop by her house on the way to work. Mama, Peggy and Trina car was parked in the driveway when I arrived which was a bit unusual. Before getting out my car, I think I better call and check on Becky. As I began to place the call I noticed my mom front door opened and closed. Perhaps they heard my motor and was checking to see who pulled up.

"Hello." Mrs. Minnie answered

"Hey Mrs., Minnie how is Becky this morning."

"Good morning Mona. She sleep… But Jasi stopped by this morning and got the kids to do a little shopping" Mrs. Minnie replied.

"Wow on a Friday?"

"Unfortunately yes." Mrs. Minnie replied. I didn't take any notice or asked any further questions, perhaps Jasi was trying to console the kids mind.

"Ok Mrs. Minnie I'll see yall later today, its already been about 4 days since I been around there.

"OK." Ms. Minnie replied and hung up the phone. Once our call ended I gave it a little more thought. Mrs. Minnie didn't seem a bit happy at all. I reached in the back seat to grab my purse and mistakenly dumped everything out.

"Oh crap!" I said, and dropped the now empty bag on top of the pile of mess that poured from it.

"Hey Chocolate." Mama said, as I walked in.

"Hey Mama, how are you?" I asked.

"Blessed, come have a seat over here." She said as she guided me to the sofa but I leaned against the stair instead.

"What's going on Mama?" I asked, looking at my mail that was laying on the end table, but for some odd reason I had a feeling inside me that something wasn't right.

"Chocolate I don't know how to tell you this." She said as Trina came walking down the stairs and wrapped her arms around me which was so very unusual.

"What's wrong?" I asked, with a terrible feeling inside.

"Becky died, the night before last." As the words came at me one after another, I couldn't cry, blink, or move. A speed of flashbacks toured through my head very quickly reflecting some of the good times we shared back in the days. Hide go seek, Double Dutch, hop scotch, the secrets, the fun, and soon the flashes came to a halt.......

"No!" I yelled, kicked and jumped up and down.

"We couldn't tell you, but Ms. Minnie said she died that very night you were in the living room. I didn't know how to tell you, neither did Ms. Minnie baby. Jasi had said it would be best if we just wait." Mama said, as she rubbed my back to calm me down.

"Oh no Mama, please tell me no Mama, I didn't get to tell her bye." As, I fell down to my knees; she sat on the floor beside me. The tears came down my face, as if it was a faucet on full force. I had no control, just pain of hurting memories.

"It's gone be ok." Mama said, as Dale came in and took a seat.

"I didn't even get to say good-bye, I told her I won't leave her Mama. I told her I wouldn't."

I manage to go to my old room in the house, and cry my heart out. For comfort I began to writing any and everything about her, but it all just seemed to long on paper. Yet it was a life that had been cut far too short. By noon visitors had poured to the house, I didn't want to see anyone not even Jasi. I stayed camped in the room sorting through old pictures and notes.

Today was Becky's funeral which was the day after Mama told me she had died. I didn't have much time to grief alone or gather with old friends before they put her into the ground. It all was happening so very quick which left me to wonder how someone could have held back such terrible news about a person that they knew had been so precious in my life. She wasn't that typical friend that you meet when you are that little girl then practically grow apart when you become older or relocate. She was that type of friend I actually cried for when she had to go home, when she was in trouble, or when she was scared. She was that type of friend that we hung on the phone till 3 and 4 am in the morning listening to slow jams on Hot 105 radio station reminiscing on good and bad relationships or even dropping to sleep on each other. She was that type of friend that I NEVER felt embarrassed or too little to tell her my DEEPEST secrets and never had to worry if she would recite them to someone else. She was the type of friend if whatever it was I didn't have and she had it... Trust and believe she made a point to ALWAYS make it equivalent with just her share... Man o' man this hurts like hell.... I could go on for hours of just telling you just how much she meant to me... The more I contemplated I became so sad and weak all over again, there was nothing much for me to do right now but pray which was all I knew how to do.... *"Lord Jesus, I come to you in this time of need... hear me oh lord. You said if I ask I shall receive... Lord you took someone so precious from me and I don't know if I can go on... I ask for your mercy Lord... I ask you to strengthen me Lord, make me whole again, make me understand, teach me oh Lord, teach me how to accept your plan. Lord I ask for your help, and lord father whatever it may be you need father I ask that you show me. Lord I can't handle this and I know you as my savior haven't bought me this far to forsake me. I can't, I can't do this alone my god and I know you can help me thru it.* Amen...I got up and instantly with the spirit of God I felt a little better, I slid on my stalking's and lastly slipped on my shoes. I walked over to my bathroom and my face was almost swollen past recognition. My eyes were so very puffy, my cheeks wore that permanent sad look upon them, and my lips appeared to be a bit bigger than normal. I pulled a face towel from the shelf and soaked it with hot steamy water, I squeezed the rag dry as I could and laid it upon my face. I stood for a second or two deeply breathing in and breathing out. Followed by a whisper I said these words to myself "No more crying Mona!" I surely wanted to agree but my heart was so mushy that a plain ole thought could easily ignite me ANYTIME. I pulled the towel from my face, which of course remained swollen. I added a bit of make-up perhaps this may make me look a little bit better. I gently pulled down my left eyelid with my ring finger and easily guided the pencil perfectly across my inner eye. I then pulled the right eye down and my hands begin to shake. I wanted to laugh about a memory I was having but instantly water filled my eyes. I quickly grabbed the tissue tabbed my eyes and completed the black eyeliner I chose to wear. Perhaps this will remind me if I cry long enough I'll look like a clown or maybe even the Joker. Before going downstairs I took one final look in the mirror and walked out of the room. Through the living room window I could see cars and people standing outside. Mrs. Minnie agreed to have the arrangements at my mom house VS Becky house which I thought my friend wouldn't mind. I paused for a second as I stood looking through the window, I saw groups of girls and guys from high school conversing and laughing amongst each other yet all of them were decked out in black. I wanted to get this day over, but my I was so nervous and scared to even open the door.

"Lord give me strength, give me strength please" I asked as the water leaked beneath my chin. I stood a second more and with the help of anger I let it push me right out the door.

"Please can I have all of you join hands for a prayer." The funeral director announced.

Dale was at my side and my father was at the other. I remember placing my hand in theirs and that was just about all I remembered. I didn't hear the Pastor nor did I see images of anyone's face. I saw pitch black until it was time to get into the cars to begin the homecoming celebration of Becky. Jasi, and I were ushered into the family car, which tailed the Hurst Becky was driven in. Upon entering the main highway there was a necessary U-turn that needed to be made and wow there were a lot of U-turns being made. Becky had so many friends that came out today just by the show of cars was quite impressive

"You ok Chocolate?" Jasi asked breaking the silence as we drove on.

"Not really."

"I know... I'm sorry I ..." She started apologizing about what I didn't know, I was so full of pain that nothing mattered, and I mean NOTHING AT ALL. Just at the top of the road I could see the church coming up, I also could feel my nerves going practically wild. I was so scared, if these are the correct words to describe this feeling. The driver opened my door, and Dale stepped out first. Jasi stepped out and so did Bruce. I sat waiting as I could see the door of the Hurst was now opened. My eyes was pinned to the back of the casket and my body was numb. The Pallbearer slid the casket from the car wearing their carnation pink gloves.

"Baby are you ready?" Dale voice echoed as I now caught full glimpse of the casket as her mom, dad, and kids were now following into the church doors.

"Mona" Jasi called.

"Mona come on we got to go." Jasi added, as I was now witnessing everyone walking into the church and I may have been the only one left behind sitting in the car.

"Mona baby be strong, you can get thru this." Daddy said as he reached his hands into the car and I followed.

By the time we walked into the church I could feel everyone eyes, on me. The church was full to the capacity, and my seat up front seem like it took forever for me to get to it. Upon the family row sat Mrs. Minnie first whom stared in one direction, Becky dad who continued to wipe his face with a handkerchief he carried, Corey was so sad as he sat clutching unto Brianna whom was too young to understand, lil Corey and Julian cried upon entering the church., then sat my mom, my dad, me, Dale, Jasi and Bruce. Sadly right across from me was her white and pink casket, which starred me in my face.

The Pastor began preaching and the church began shouting, and crying.

"I feel like we should have a lil church up in here yall!" Pastor Wayne announced dancing down the pull pit to the sounds of the guitar.

"Yall don't hear me though!" He said!

"Preach it pastor!" One of the ushers shouted back.

"My father said Let not your heart be troubled: ye believe in God, believe also in me." Pastor shouted as the Piano released one of its tunes....

"*I*n my Father's house are many mansions: if it were not so, I would have told you. Tell me you hear me though.... Auuuuuuuuhhhh auhhhhhhh the pastor began humming and waving his handkerchief back and forth...

"Preach on pastor preach on!" Members from the choir chanted as they stood up and clapped their hands and some was marching with the Holy Ghost.

"In my Father's house are many mansions: if it were not so...... "Pastor announced as he took a long pause and scratch the top of his head as if he was a bit worried. "Tell me you following me John chapter 14 verse 2!" Pastor instructed as he walked back and forth across the podium. *"In my Father's house are many mansions: if it were not so..." He paused again just before jumping up from the ground.*

"Go on pastor go on!" One of the tall deacons shouted as many members were now standing on their feet.

"He aint say his father got a box for you BUT he got MANY MANSIONS for you." Pastor recited with a step back then a sincere strong stand. *"If it were not, he said he wouldn't have told you so!* Come on now tell me you with me! He said it in this bible I'm holding its right here before your eyes..." Pastor shouted pointing to his bible. "God said: *If it aint so he wouldn't tell you so!"*

"Go head Pastor Wayne deliver that message" Another usher shouted!

"Pastor they don't hear you though, come back again!" A male voice from the choir shouted.

'Thomas saith unto him, Lord, we know not whither thou goest; and how can we know the way?

"Can you hear me? Pastor asked dancing in circles and talking in tongues.

"Jesus saith unto him, I am the way, the truth, and the life: no man cometh unto the Father, but by me..." Pastor shouted and begin jumping with the Holy Ghost. The ushers came around him and ensured he was safe by ushering him back to his seat behind the pulpit... The sprit was so heavy in the church today, I believe if pastor would have kept on he would've had me out my seat.

Suddenly a young pianist draped in a black gown with her face painted bone white began playing such heavenly tunes which became familiar as the song Silver and gold by Kirk Franklin. The choir was on tune, and then their came out a little girl draped in black scarfs with a painted bone white face also. It was such a beautiful performance and the tunes that came from the young woman's voice was impressive and believing. So many of our classmates and friends we meet over the years wanted to talk about how loving, caring and funny she was. Bianca was the first one to take the mic, she was a very pretty but nerdy girl who always was alone, and she never really had many friends. Her parents were rich but you couldn't tell by looking at her, as her personality didn't match the style of a rich young girl going to a regular school.

"Becky was the type of person that light up a room, whenever she came to class I knew I was going to have a good day. I loved her so much, she was the girl in high school that bought me out of my shell." She smiled at the audience and then continued. I remember she used to tell me I needed a boyfriend and hooked me up with the Quarterback of our football team which sat behind her in our 3rd period class. I use to tell Becky that Ricardo would never like me and today 8 years later he is my husband and father of our 3 kids," Bianca said as she wiped the tears from her eyes.

"I remember Becky said to me. You gotta talk to her she nice and I mean really nice."

"What you mean by really nice Becky? Does that mean she got a lot of money?" I asked and man Becky yelled at me and stopped talking to me for days. So I came to class with a muffin one day and she finally talked to me asking for a piece, so I told her the only way I'll give her some if she accepts my apology, She then said, NO the only way I accept your apology is if you go with Bianca to the homecoming dance, I was like Becky come on man." He continued on as the funeral goers laughed. Please be mindful at that time I was the star quarterback and Bianca didn't play any sports, SO I agreed with Becky due to her promise that she will accept my apology. Which rally mean she will start back talking to me and cracking jokes again. So I asked Bianca to homecoming the next day, hoping she would say no. He laughed and so did the funeral goers. That very homecoming night I found my soul mate which is Bianca. "Thanks so much Becky for introducing me to my wife!" Ricardo said and walked over to kiss the casket before walking off. There wasn't a dry eye in the audience, After Ricardo story I managed to smile and even laugh as I recall this story which was true love for many years. Soon it was my turn, I wasn't really scared at all anymore, and I felt as if I needed to show out for her just how she would have wanted me to do. Everyone starred as I stared back, my heart was racing but there was a message waiting to be told, not just the good times everyone knew we shared.

Lying in a bed, with silk white sheets.
Moonlight shinning towards our feet.
Kissing my lips, with a sexual taste,
Stroking my hips, and slowly rubbing my face.
As he caresses my body up and down,
Without a doubt I know this is true love what I found.
Departing ourselves slowly from one another,
Wishing I could be your 1st and only lover.
Lying in a bed with soft beige sheets.
Sunlight, Shinning towards my feet.
Scratching the bad rashes that got me here,
Wondering about test results with a great amount of fear.
Doctor walks in acknowledging it's too far gone.
Constantly crying and regretting the replacement of fun.
Day by day constant bawl movements take its place.
It was to my mom whom appeared with a worried face.
A*s I lay learning the definition of AIDS.*
I*gnorance of me now began to plays.*
D*evastation, it was to tell my special friends.*
S*lowly in black, as I watched the footsteps behind the box, I am carried in.*

LIFE WITHOUT HER?

It was every day I took off and went to the grave as if I was going to her house. I had cried each time I went. It has been eighteen months to be exact and it wasn't never a time I could just talk to her mentally without crying. I had to cry, it was just in me that I would never ever see my friend again. Which was something I couldn't seem to get used to. I lived every vivid memory, each time I went to the grave. I sat empty headed at times thinking about how much pain she went through. I had seen Becky undergo surgery, birth three kids into this world, endure emotional pain, survive financial plights and overcome all other struggles in her life. I just had never seen my friend as languid as she was in the last months here on earth. She use to stare at me with big questioning eyes. It was a look she always gave me when in doubt or needed advice, which she thought I could do anything but unfortunately this was a bit more than out of my lead. I was forced to take a year off from my job, I helped Ms. Minnie as much as possible with the kids and so did Jasi.

One day I fell asleep on the couch and my phone alarmed sounded off and the doorbell was ringing at the same time. I was afraid to look at the phone because it was the same ring that Becky set for herself and I hadn't heard it in quite some time. I jumped up; my heart was racing and eyes observing. I nervously looked down at my phone and realized it was an image of a sounding alarm clock displaying.

"Who is it?" I asked.

"Mrs. Minnie." She said, surprised I was cause she wouldn't drive only but to the store.

"Hey baby how you doing." She asked as she walked into the house and gave me a hug.

"Where is that fat baby?"

"Dale and Shanice took her out for a walk." I responded observing a colorful box.

"Here I found this in Becky closet when I was looking for some papers." She said as she handed me a colorful box that read: *If you were to find this it means I'm not in place, but I'll be happy if you pass it to my friend Chocolate who I know will keep it safe!'* The box fell to the floor, with a brush of pain and sorrow in my heart. In my mind I felt her presence here with me,

"Open it!" Ms. Minnie said. I sat at the table and untied each knot with my hand not wanting to cut the last of memories by one string or carve one scratch with a knife. In the box was pictures; pictures I had never seen. Some of the pictures were of me sleeping on trips with my mouth wide opened. Pictures from her slumber party when she was twelve, there were photos catching me off guard when I first learned how to drive, and even some when my hair wasn't combed properly, and of course many of them I was looking like aunt Jemima with my hair all wrapped in a scarf. There also was her half of the heart we once bought out of the candy store so many years ago in which she kept *Best* and I kept *Friend*. Enclosed were also letters we wrote to each other in our sixth grade civic class. Surprisingly I ran across a book of poems which was collected and written by Becky. Something I couldn't image she was interested in but it was a happy closure from a dear friend that I knew loved me just as much as I loved her. Upon opening the book the very first page was titled "Especially for you Chocolate:"

WHY ID RATHER BE A TREE!
DO YOU KNOW ABOUT NO WORRIES?
WELL LET ME TELL YOU, A TREE DOESN'T HAVE STORIES.
THINK ABOUT IT, CAN YOU RUN TO ANY OF YOUR SPECIAL FRIENDS.
CAUSE A TREE IS THERE FROM THE VERY ROOT TILL THE TIP OF ITS BEND.
WHAT ABOUT THE EVIL, THAT REWARDS THE GOOD OF OUR SOULS
WHICH IS UNLIKE A TREE WHO WAITS ON THE WIND TO BLOWS.
WHAT ABOUT OUR KIDS THAT'S TOO FAR GONE?
DON'T YOU WISH THEY COULD BE SOMEWHAT LIKE TREES THAT DANCES TO THE SUN!
I KNOW YOU KNOW, HOW DIFFICULT IT IS TO MAKE CHOICES!
UNLIKE A HUMAN, CAUSE A TREE GET ALONG WITHOUT VOICES.
WHAT ABOUT LOVE AND TO BE FORGOT ABOUT!
BUT ME AS A TREE, WAIT ON THE SUN AND WATER TO SPOUT.
THROUGH THIS ALL I KNOW THERE HAS BEEN TIMES YOU'VE DONE ALL YOU CAN DO,
MAYBE EVEN THOUGHT YOUVE BEEN ALL YOU CAN BE.
WELL I HAVE!
THAT'S WHEN I REALIZED, WHY ID RATHER BE A TREE.
Smile.

B/F 4-EVA

Printed in the United States
By Bookmasters